Suited

Marcel Legosz

To Izabella, Imogen, Maclean and Greyson

PROLOGUE

'You're a fat, ugly slut.'

He threw another empty bottle across the room, narrowly missing me as I cowered in the corner.

Nothing could be further from the truth. My mother was many things but she was not fat, certainly not ugly, and most definitely not a slut.

She had returned home from teaching English to migrant men who worked on the Snowy Mountains Scheme. We lived in Cooma – the Scheme's headquarters from 1949 – a small town in New South Wales, south of Canberra.

She taught four nights a week at the local school. Before marrying my father, she had taught at the primary school in Goulburn, a medium to large town north-east of Canberra. Construction on the 'Snowy' was winding down. Her services would not be required after the men moved on.

My father was a jealous man. He was convinced my mother was giving her students more than an education in the English tongue. Even at the tender age of nine I could tell that my mother wasn't interested in the opposite sex, my father included. She was happiest in the company of women who would often visit. Some would stay, and I would hear footsteps from my parents' bedroom to the visitors' room, which was next to mine. The walls were thin and the floorboards creaked. My father was a heavy sleeper when he drank, which was most days.

He arrived in Cooma with his parents from Victoria in 1952 as a seventeen-year-old. It was where they set up their upholstery business. He had finished his schooling, so he started work with his parents and took over the business when his father died in 1958. His mother died the next year. He was married in 1962 and I came along in 1965. I was christened Tomasz. Everyone, except the old man, called me Tommy. No matter how insistent he was he couldn't convince anyone to call me by my Polish name. His name was Zygmunt and he hated being called Ziggy. Everyone called him Ziggy.

I never remember him being a hundred per cent sober but he had an excellent reputation as an upholsterer with a constant stream of work – not only local but from as far away as Canberra and Goulburn. I recall a truck arriving one day during the school holidays with a load of timber-armed visitor chairs that needed new fabric seats. They were from government offices in Canberra and were needed by a certain date. He drank almost non-stop while on that project. My mother said she had never seen such fine work. How he had managed intricate hand stitching with so much alcohol in his body was short of a miracle. He slept even heavier during that period.

They divorced in 1982 and the next year I moved to Sydney. I had turned eighteen and a simple six-hour drive had freed me from the constraints of country living and a hostile home environment. Thankfully, golf had kept me out of the house most days after school. I had relished caddying for the A-graders, eager to learn everything about the game. The club professional, recognising my natural talent, encouraged me from the age of eleven. It coincided with the laying of the final grass green – before grass they were sand. The project had started before I was born and I can recall my father going crook about the slack-arse ground staff and their slowness in grassing them. He refused to volunteer around the club but was happy to complain. I realised when I got older that 'Mona' wasn't a first name exclusive to females. The transition from sand to grass was the catalyst enabling me to win many amateur titles over the next seven years.

It wasn't only my golfing talent that attracted attention. At sixteen, with manly good looks emerging, I caught the eye of a female bar attendant and after several attempts to lure me into the storeroom she succeeded, robbing me of my physical innocence and introducing me to a different world. For the next two years it was full-on golf, sex, and school – in that order. I found school easy and my parents were never subjected to adverse reports.

University life – compliments of a scholarship – and professional golf had beckoned and I had wheels. A rusty Ford bought from my earnings working in the old man's upholstery business during the school holidays along with finding, then selling, golf balls – hundreds of them over the years. I had always asked for money for Christmas and birthdays because I knew any presents my parents gave me would be rubbish. I was a low-maintenance child and flew under the radar. They paid little attention to my interests so slipping me money on those occasions was easy for them and great for me. I rarely spent any. I loved seeing my bank balance grow. I loved money. I knew money would let me escape – set me free.

*

In 1983, even with my lack of big-city nous I knew if I wanted to drive out of the city during rush hour, I had to allow more time.

Jumping ahead nearly twenty-five years – why the fuck can't I remember nothing's changed? In fact, it's gotten worse. Sydney traffic on a Friday afternoon in summer resembles a crazy anteater kicking the shit out of a termite's nest.

One thing I can remember is joking to my poker mates telling them I had a twin brother with half a brain and I had the other quarter …

My regular jaunts down the coast to Diamond Harbour Casino would be much more enjoyable if I used even a half of that quarter. Once out of the city it's easy driving and the coastal views are stunning. Lots of beaches, great camping sites and safe swimming. Great for families; we'd never been.

I rushed through the casino's revolving glass door. I was out of breath and grumpy.

'You need a bigger car park, Trevor.'

If I can blame someone else for my slackness, I will. More often than not I have to park on the main road and walk up the casino driveway.

The air-conditioning calmed me and I smoothed my thick hair into place.

'Afternoon, Tommy,' said Trevor, greeting me with a polite smile. He was all class. I didn't have to be a mind-reader to know that he knew I always ran late. He stood tall and proud, despite a slight limp, and had been the doorman at the Diamond Harbour Casino from the day it opened in the early seventies. I had been a regular for the last fifteen or so years. He had thick, jet-black hair similar to mine but with a tinge of grey on the sides, and searching blue eyes that didn't miss a trick. Funny thing was I didn't know much about him. It was usually small talk between us when I entered or left the place.

He'd watched me change from a slim, athletic professional golfer who travelled the globe, into a lard-arse couch potato who now, aged forty-one, still travelled the globe preferring to spend hours at casino tables, and more hours at restaurant tables. I hadn't grown any taller than my 190 cm but wider, to 110 kg. Sadly, I'd had to buy bigger cars. The restored MGB could no longer contain my body mass so I'd upsized to a Ford, then a Holden, and finally a silver Chrysler 300. I had to agree with the salesman, it was a flash set of wheels built for comfort.

I moved quickly – by my standards – through the reception area, giving Eldon a wave, then down the ramp to the main gaming room. Eldon, like Trevor, was part of the furniture, having been at the casino from day one. He was around fifty with light-brown hair, kind brown eyes, and a complexion that women would kill for. He was shoulder height to me and well rounded. I'd never tell him he could afford to drop a few kilos – pot, kettle, black. Eldon was unashamedly gay and I was convinced it was that trait that made him such a caring bloke. He always managed to find me a room if I was unable to drive home. He knew me so well.

The noisy poker machines had been pissing me off. I'd complained on many occasions that there shouldn't be pokies in the vicinity of gaming tables. It ruined the ambience. I headed for the table and, typically, only one seat was empty. The poker tables are set up in a particular sequence. The first four are close to the rear wall with the next four at right angles to the corridor. The final four are close to a small grandstand where the thirty-two finalists play during tournament poker. My table for this cash game was near the rear wall. It was the furthest from the pokies so lent itself to normal speech. Friendly sarcasm floated around the table upon my late arrival. I was immune to it now but was more than happy to give them a dose of their own medicine when the opportunity arose. The seven players were regulars at the tables and our paths often crossed. We looked forward to the no-limit Texas hold 'em poker tournaments and big cash games that were held at all the major casinos around the world.

As we settled in the waiter took our drink orders and positioned himself to be at our beck and call throughout his shift. A generous tip always kept him nearby.

I couldn't help but overhear an American guy behind me trying to explain to his wife how the game was played.

He started by telling her the two players to the left of the dealer button place a bet before any cards are dealt. The dealer button – a small plastic disc – moves around the table one place after each hand is finished. The two bets are called blinds. The small blind is usually half the amount of the big blind. The casino sets the blinds.

'Ya still with me, honey?' he asked.

'Uh huh,' she said.

He told her each player is dealt two cards, facedown. They can look at their own cards, but leave them facedown so other players can't see them. These are called the hole cards and if a player wants to keep playing, they can match the big blind, raise the big blind or fold.

'Now, foldin' means throwin' ya cards in 'cause they ain't any good.'

'Uh huh.'

'When the bettin' gets back to the small blind, and if they wanna keep on playin', they have to match the big blind if there ain't been no raisin'. If someone else has raised the bet the small blind has to match the raiser or raise more. This goes on till everyone's got the same money in the pot; that's the middle of the table. Ya still with me, pet?'

'Uh huh.'

I looked around to see if the dealer was heading to the table so the game could get underway and maybe shut this guy up. The player beside me rolled his eyes and quietly swore.

The Yank went on. 'The next three cards are dealt face up and are called the flop. The players still in the game can match the flop with their hole cards. There's more bettin', raisin', foldin' and also checkin'. Do ya know what checkin' is, petal?'

'Somethin' we have for Sunday dinner. It's good they feed the players though. I guess they get a mite hungry thinkin' 'bout all this stuff.'

'Why do I bother? Not checkin' like that. Checkin' like ya do with ya make-up an' stuff to make sure ya look gorgeous for me when we're out. It means if the first player to bet don't wanna bet he can check and other players can do the same.'

'Uh huh.'

'Where the fuck is the dealer?' I muttered. I'd downed my first drink and had ordered another.

'Now, the next card dealt is called the turn card. At home we call it Fourth Street but I won't complicate things for ya too much. That's dealt face up and there's more bettin' and stuff like before. The last card dealt is the river card ...'

'Is it turned over same as the turn card, honey?'

'Sure is, otherwise they couldn't see it.'

'Why isn't it also called a turn card?'

'I think ya gettin' a mite tired, pet. I was about to say it was dealt face up but you will insist on interruptin' me. It's called Fifth Street back home. Anyhow, the players select their best five cards and bet until they stop. They turn their hole cards over and whoever has the best cards wins. Have I made it simple enough for ya?'

'You're real good at explainin', honey. You're right. I am a mite tired. Perhaps you'd better stay here and I'll go look at them sophisticated types playin' chemin de fer. From here it looks mightier simpler than this Texas hold-all.'

I turned slightly as she was about to leave. She winked and smiled at me. It made me think she was the long-suffering wife of a know-all who loved the sound of his own voice.

'Jesus, Tommy. What the hell was that about?' the guy to my left mumbled. 'And what the fuck is chemin de fer?'

'It's a variation of baccarat, which is not played here. I recall watching it at a casino on the French Riviera back in the late eighties when I was playing the European Golf Tour. I reckon she was having a lend of him. He wouldn't have had a clue what she was talking about. I'd love to have him at our table. It would be like taking candy from a baby. Shame. I'll have to take yours instead.'

The guy chuckled. 'Do they always talk like that?'

'Some of them do. Mainly the tourists.'

The dealer arrived, apologised, shuffled the cards and dealt.

The first few hands went as expected with fairly low-level betting. In poker, players try to get a 'read' off each other before committing to heavy bets. A few players have excellent poker faces while many are a dead giveaway. They get a good hand and they fidget, breathe differently, rub their eyes, or scratch their balls – any number of telltale signs.

The blinds of $250 and $500 for this game were higher than several guys were used to and that was making them watch their stacks even though they could buy more chips if they ran low. This was the beauty of cash games. In tournament games once your chips were gone, so were you.

We'd been playing for a couple of hours when the K♠ and 10♠ hole cards caught my attention. I had the big blind so I checked after three guys called and the other four folded. We now had $2250 in the pot. The Q♥, Q♦ and J♠ at the flop made us pay attention. I checked but the guy on my left bet $1000. The other two called. I needed to stay in the game, so I called. The pot was now $6250. If the Q♠ and A♠ were still in the pack a royal flush was a chance. It would be a real talking point if I could pull it off.

The turn card was the A♠. It gave me an ace high straight, nothing to be sneezed at. I decided to bet the pot. The guy on my left raised $10,000 and the other two called. These guys were hard to read. Were they holding off for a bigger pot? There could be any number of high-card combinations at this stage. My straight could be the poorest hand if these guys were holding queens or aces. A pair of jacks in the hole with a flop like that can be a winning hand any time. I pondered the odds of me pulling the Q♠ on the river. I had four of the five highest spades, meaning nine were left either in the pack or with the other players. It was killing me. These guys were real pros and it was my turn to bet. I was undecided.

After getting a hurry-up call from the dealer I called the raise. We now had $71,250 in the pot. With four players left in the game, bluffing was a possibility but with these sorts of cards on the table the combinations for good hands were many.

It was now time for the river card. The dealer was about to flip the card when a muffled noise plunged the place into darkness. My first reaction was to cover my cards and chips. People were screaming and shouting but it was only moments before flashlights played around the room. I looked up and saw maybe ten men dressed in black from head to toe armed with pistols and sawn-off shotguns. The man who appeared to be the leader held a loudhailer and told the casino staff to move to the counting room and the rest of us to assemble in the showroom. We were told they were here to rob the casino, not the patrons, and no-one would be hurt unless they did something stupid.

We grabbed our cards and chips and walked nervously to the showroom. I'd noticed one guy had also scooped up the dealt cards and the rest of the deck. The doors were locked. We huddled under tables and chairs not knowing what to expect. A gunshot and screams from outside the showroom probably meant someone had done something stupid and had most likely paid the price. I heard more shouting closer to the showroom door and had the uneasy feeling we were not immune to the violence. I glanced at my phone. I had no reception.

I have never considered myself a brave man but I had a big stake in the game with an outside chance to win. I wanted to see the game finished. Adjoining the showroom was the coffee shop kitchen and a door with glass in the top part. I told my fellow gamblers to stay quiet and made my way over to the door. It wasn't guarded or locked. I assumed the low-life scum had taken over the casino, including the CCTV room.

Even though the building was in darkness enough light was coming in through the floor-to-ceiling windows for me to see that the kitchen staff had recently prepared supper for the high rollers. I couldn't resist the urge to slip through the kitchen door and grab as much food as I could carry. No-one knew how long it would be before our release. I eased my way to the kitchen benches and noticed a trolley had been loaded ready to be taken to the small coffee shop next to our poker tables. I stayed alert for any scumbags that might be about while I topped it up with more food. When I was happy the coast was clear I shoved a curried egg sandwich in my mouth and pushed the trolley through the door and over to my poker mates.

I spoke quietly. 'Well, what are we waiting for, let's finish this game.'

'Are you joking?' asked one guy.

'Why not?' I replied. 'There's nothing else to do while we're stuck in here.'

The food aromas brought other patrons to where we were hunkered down and after a brief discussion one of them offered to act as dealer. The guy who had grabbed the dealt cards and deck off the table set them up on a table in the corner. I suggested we have a feed before we continued the game. This was a selfish idea on my part because the food looked as if it had been prepared for me. Gourmet party pies and sausage rolls in a portable bain-marie, custard tarts, chocolate éclairs, house cakes and sandwiches. All that was missing was a bottle of bourbon. Shit happens.

Barney, the volunteer dealer, appeared a likeable chap and was impressed with the status of our game. He told us he knew a few of us by sight having also been a regular at the casino, albeit playing at much smaller-stakes tables. He made sure we had replicated the game in progress. We were keen to see the river card.

I held my breath as he slowly turned the card. Lights shining from mobile phones revealed the Q♠. I couldn't believe it. I nearly choked on another curried egg sandwich. Why did this have to happen in a dark room? This was hopefully going to be my five minutes of fame, apart, of course, from the name I'd made for myself in the late eighties when I eagled the last hole at the European Golf Championship to come from behind and win by a shot.

*

Perhaps it was sad the five million in prize money had meant more to me than the trophy. A few pros at the time had said I was playing golf for the wrong reasons. Bullshit. I was in it for the money and, if the truth be known, so were they. Trouble was many of them were hypocritical pricks who put on a fake façade when in the public eye. My winnings financed my gambling. I made no apology. Over time I had slipped down the golf rankings because of my love of poker, although my bank balance had gone up. I couldn't be bothered practising every day, going to the gym, eating healthy. Having meals provided at casinos around the world during big games seemed a better option. The fact I had more money than I could spend tilted the scales in favour of plush chairs at card tables.

*

With my game face on, I opened the betting, knowing I couldn't be beaten. Even though I liked these guys, I wanted to bleed them dry so I had to make sure I didn't scare them off. I bet the pot and waited for the play to move around the table. Barney was terrific, he kept everyone in order, relaying the bet amounts and making sure the game was played in accordance with the rules. The guy to my left raised $100,000. Thank the gods for high denomination chips. The player on his left folded. The guy on the button called, meaning I could call with $100,000 or re-raise. Even by my standards this was a high-stakes game. I was now pretty sure four queens and a full house (aces with queens) were with the two guys – otherwise, why would they keep betting? The food on the trolley was disappearing fast. I'd better wrap the game up, glory or no glory. I shoved the last piece of chocolate éclair into my mouth and counted my chips. I had $400,000. I went all-in.

Barney re-counted my chips and told the others they needed $300,000 to see my cards. After a few minutes of staring me down trying to get a read, they called. I couldn't believe it. Maybe they thought I had a straight and was trying to bluff them out. In the failing light of mobile phones, I turned my cards over to reveal my K♠ and 10♠ – a royal flush.

'Read 'em and weep, boys,' I said. Even in the poor light I could see the colour draining from their faces. At the urging of the onlookers the guys turned their cards.

It was as I suspected. The A♦ and Q♣ and the A♣ and A♥. Their hole cards gave them four queens and a full house – aces and queens. I guess I couldn't blame these guys for playing it out. I was surprised they hadn't raised more at the turn seeing as they had full houses at that stage. I can't remember too many games where a four-of-a-kind has been beaten.

'I guess you guys can write that one down as a bad beat.' Bloody hell, over the years I'd had my fair share of what should have been winning hands go down the gurgler.

The guy to my left, although looking shell-shocked, smiled at me. 'Don't leave town, Tommy. We want a chance to win it back.'

'Don't you worry,' I said with a grin. 'I want another chance to win more off you.'

We shook hands in the true spirit of the game.

I was flattered by the back slapping and congratulations from everyone. Barney pushed the chips towards me and the doors suddenly opened. The flashlights hurt our eyes as they lit up the room, finally resting on our table. The leader sauntered over to us as if he had all the time in the world. He told us the main casino safe was under a time lock. They couldn't access the millions secured so they would have to supplement their takings from the counting room with our cash and valuables. A slight oversight in an otherwise well-planned heist, he admitted. He told us the gunfire earlier had been to convince the casino staff they meant business and no-one had been hurt.

His men moved among us removing cash from wallets and purses, collecting watches, jewellery and anything else of value. That alone would be a tidy sum due to the well-heeled punters who I knew would be wearing Rolex, Tag Heuer and Cartier among the better-known brands. The leader gave me the impression he was a card player because when he saw my royal flush, he slapped me on the back while giving the others a sympathetic look, then casually slipped the Rolex I had received as part of my European Golf Championship win off my wrist. He joked to me that I would have to wait for the time lock on the safe to activate before I could collect my winnings. I told him I would be happy to sleep on the floor if it meant I could leave the casino with nearly a million and my life. He called his men together and they quickly left the room. My knowledge of the casino was enough to know they would have scored around ten million from the counting room; not a bad haul even for a botched job. I didn't back away from my earlier observations that they were low-life scum.

In a few minutes the lights came on and the jittery security staff brought us out to the main gambling area. If you had walked into the casino you would not have known a robbery had taken place. I noticed staff quickly throw a cover over a roulette table that was covered with ceiling plaster. The result of the gunshot. Drinks were still on tables, along with patrons' chips and cards. The fucking poker machines were flashing and making a racket. If I'd had a gun, I would have shot the Queen of the Nile.

My chips, totalling $1,485,000 (of which $996,000 was profit), were wrapped in a tea towel off the food trolley and held close to my chest. My heart was thumping. I wasn't sure whether it was euphoria or shock. Either way, the evening's events had had an effect on me. I headed over to the teller's cage and waited while my chips were counted. I was given a receipt and told I could see the boss in the morning to arrange the transfer of all or part of my winnings into my Swiss bank account. Although I have money in Australian banks for general use, I like the security and privacy of the Swiss system – high returns, low risk. In the meantime, Eldon, having seen my washed-out look, appeared at my side and told me my room was ready.

FEBRUARY – 2008

DAY 1 – SUNDAY

'Jack Bird, to what do I owe the honour?' I mumbled into the phone.

I blinked a couple of times; looked at my watch and realised I'd slept another nine-hour night.

*

Before the casino heist a year ago, I would have been lucky to sleep six hours a night. It had always seemed enough, but for the last year I felt the need for more. Helen Smith, my psychologist, had told me post-traumatic stress affected people in different ways. I kept telling myself I was okay and the casino heist hadn't worried me. After all I had won nearly a million bucks at the highly unconventional poker game and had been feted by all and sundry, from TV chat shows to glossy magazines. The Sydney newspapers ran the story for the best part of a week – photos, interviews, opinions. The Government Opposition queried the police investigation and asked why no-one had been caught. Predictably, the circus moved on to other issues and after a couple of months – apart from at Diamond Harbour Casino – the event was rarely mentioned.

The casino had insisted on paying for a group of us to have therapy and, even though I considered it a waste of time, I had the time so I was happy to front up. Helen was easy to talk to and appeared to show a genuine interest in my poker and golf. I didn't know how many more visits I would need but knowing how tight casinos are with their money, I didn't think they'd keep it going for any longer than was necessary. Apart from the change to my sleeping patterns I didn't think I had any overhanging problems. But what would I know? Maybe I did need more sessions. For all I knew I could be a whackjob and be none the wiser. I did know I was a bloody good poker player and nothing else mattered at the moment. I wasn't scared of casinos, sudden loud noises, food or bourbon.

The casino heist had been a hiccup in an otherwise fairly smooth, extremely enjoyable and profitable twenty-year career of golf and poker. A couple of promising relationships had failed to develop – I've no inkling why. How could golf, poker, drinking and regular world travel have any bearing on the longevity of a relationship?

*

'You must be joking, Jack,' I said, after listening to him for a few minutes. I swirled the mouthful of bourbon from last night's glass to clear my throat.

'I haven't lifted a golf club in anger for the best part of ten years and you're asking me to partner you in a Pro-Celebrity tournament in Vegas?'

'Fly over to LA, pronto,' he said, his New York accent reviving memories of days gone by. 'I can get you into shape in six months, no worries. We know you're a natural and I know you've done it before when you've gone off the rails. Once you set your mind to do something you simply get on with it.'

'What makes you think I want to?' I was starting to tire of our conversation. My mind was on the big poker game starting in a couple of hours. I had enough time to get cleaned up, have a feed and get myself to the Four Winds Casino.

'You must be out of circulation,' said Jack. 'Don't you know there's another million-dollar, winner-take-all hold 'em tournament at Vegas around the same time? The organisers are trying to build the whole thing up so they can pull the best golfers and the best poker players into the one place at the same time. With your natural talent at both disciplines you'd have to be in with a good chance to pull off the double. Never been done before, buddy. If Silver's Grand Casino is involved it will be well organised *and* exciting.'

*

Jack had been the player I'd beaten in the European Golf Championship and because of our close friendship and his great sportsmanship he hadn't held a grudge. He had gone on from there and won nearly every top tournament in South America. He gave the top Argentinian players a real golfing lesson when he won all three of their major tournaments the next year. I followed his progress even after I'd stopped playing because he deserved good results from the hard work he put into his game. Although not a natural he was a bloody talented golfer. He finished in the top five in North America the year after

13

South America, claiming the Canadian International and the Houston and Florida Classics against the top fifty players in the world.

Money was not an issue for Jack. His collection of Corvettes was testament to not only his wealth but his excellent taste in cars. Unlike me, he'd stayed true to golf and won his money playing at the top level. He played around a dozen tournaments a year and rarely finished out of the top ten. He had the same sponsors for clubs and clothing we had been fortunate enough to attract early in our careers. Our birthdays were on the same day but he was two years older – and possibly ten years smarter. For many years on the pro circuit we would try and celebrate our birthdays together on the eleventh of September. If we were in the States and not playing golf we'd meet up in LA and paint the town red. I considered myself a solid drinker but Jack could leave me for dead when he was in party mode. We were known in golfing circles as 'the terrible twins', based on our similar physical attributes and attitude to life. In September 2001 Jack, thankfully, was in Spain setting up a coaching academy and was removed from the tragedy in his home city. I recall him sending me an e-mail wishing me a happy birthday and telling me where he was and that he was okay. At the time, getting a phone call connected was extremely difficult.

*

'Give me a couple of days to think it over, Jack, and I'll get back to you.' I hung up and pulled open the curtains. The view from my penthouse apartment over the marina never failed to impress me. The luxury yachts and motor cruisers that rarely ventured to the open sea glistened in the brilliant sunlight. Sun-bronzed wankers paraded themselves along the boardwalk trying to impress. The funny thing was that by trying to be different they looked the same.

I wandered into the shower thinking about Jack's proposal. I wasn't overly interested in the golf. I could easily front up for the poker tournament and not raise a sweat. I knew Jack would persist, so for the time being I tried to put it out of my mind until after the poker game in the afternoon.

As I stepped out of the shower, I took a closer look at my physique in the mirror and realised I was in pretty bad shape for a guy who, at forty-two, should be taking more care of himself.

'Fuck you, Jack,' I grumbled to my reflection. 'If you hadn't rung me, I wouldn't be worrying about this shit.'

*

I poured myself a drink while I got dressed then headed down to Jacques, my favourite restaurant. It was right on the waterfront close to my apartment and had the right vibe. Good food, good service and good riddance to the posers who couldn't afford to eat at this type of establishment. The hands-on manager, Claude, once again welcomed me with open arms and a kiss on both cheeks. He'd been in Australia for years but maintained his French ways. His head chef, Erik, seldom left the kitchen but when he did, he treated me the same. I didn't mind. It gave me a sense of belonging.

Experience had taught me a big lunch would lead to drowsiness mid-afternoon and as I was keen to clean-up at the poker table, I settled for a Caesar salad with double bacon and a glass of house white.

My phone rang as I was finishing lunch. It was the PR guy from the casino letting me know I had twenty minutes before the game started. I asked him if he knew who else would be there. 'The usual suspects,' he told me. This could be fun.

I headed back to my car in the basement car park and drove to the casino. It was newer than Diamond Harbour although not as big and glitzy; but when seated at the poker tables, much the same. Gaming staff in crisp uniforms, gamblers in the minimum of dress requirements and fucking noisy poker machines. I parked at the entrance and saw the efficient Clive on car duty. His red hair stood out against the muted grey stucco planter boxes lining the entrance. Evergreen shrubbery softened the hard edges and the fragrance from the rows of freesias countered the exhaust fumes from the idling vehicles waiting to be valet-parked. Why patrons didn't turn their engines off I'll never know. A man can only park one vehicle at a time. A doorman was always available to hold keys until Clive returned. Anyway, I knew he would look after my wheels. The usual fifty dollar note certainly gave him incentive to take extra care.

It was a relief to get into the air-conditioned casino. The place was crowded. Eight tables were set up for the tournament. According to the noticeboard it was a knock-out format, meaning the winner from each table would play off for the main pot. A couple of hundred thousand wouldn't go astray. Thinking about Jack's Corvette collection made me wonder whether I should be investing part of my wealth for my retirement. But the reality of it was, while the bulk of my cash was held in Swiss bank accounts accruing a healthy return, why run the risk of investing in a venture that might go belly-up and cause me grief? I had more money than I could probably spend so I turned my thoughts back to the game that was about to start.

I saw familiar faces, although none were allocated to my table, and I was seated on the dealer's right and had drawn the dealer button. It gave me a chance to get a read on the other players. Well, what a weird bunch of players they were. Sunglasses, baseball caps and upturned collars were the order of the day; a common ploy to hide their emotions. They should have been in straitjackets because a player's hands are usually the big giveaway in a poker game.

At two o'clock the first cards were dealt and by three-thirty, two tables had finished with the winners relaxing at the bar waiting for the rest of us. I was surprised. There must have been loose betting for them to finish so soon. In many tournaments the play can go over a few days.

I had mixed fortunes up until this point and had worked out it was not only the cards giving me the shits but also the other players. They were amateurs; firstly, with no clue how to behave in grown-up company and secondly, how to play poker. Finally, I was dealt the A♦ and K♣ – the best hole cards I had received all game. I had the big blind and when the betting got back to me no-one had raised. If the flop was handy, I'd go in hard and sort out these bunnies. The dealer turned the A♠, 2♥ and 2♦. There could be anything out there. I was in two minds when the small blind folded and the dealer asked me what I wanted to do. I placed a bet I hoped would scare the others off, but they were like vultures around a rotting carcass. After spirited betting the turn card was shown and it was the A♥. Anxious arses squirmed on chairs. I laid my biggest bet so far. I could read these jerks like a comic book. Four of them folded and the other two called. I had a feeling one of them had the other ace giving them a full house, aces and twos like mine; however, I had a king, and if the river card was also a king, I had a good chance of getting the best full house.

The dealer laid the river card on the table. It was the A♣. To get a full house of community cards was one thing, but I'd never had four aces in all my years of poker. I was feeling cheery now. I went all-in, wondering whether they thought I was bluffing about having four aces or maybe a full house with a high pair of hole cards. Either of them could have thought the other had the fourth ace. To my amazement, they followed, and we now had an audience around the table. I turned my cards, watching for their reaction. One guy slid his cards to the dealer and stood while the other flipped his over to reveal quad twos. He swore, shoved his chair over and stormed out of the gaming area with his mate in tow. Before they got too far, a remaining player yelled out, 'Hey guys, it ain't over till the fat lady sings.' They replied with one finger salutes as they headed for the casino door. The railbirds clapped and cheered; not only for me but for the fact two wankers had been eliminated.

I had renewed vigour. It would be a hand I'd remember and it would remind me why I play poker. With six of us left and with me leading the chip count I felt I could unsettle them and wrap things up before dinner.

We were hanging in there with mixed fortunes and I now had the small blind and was dealt the K♣ and J♠. When the betting was back to me one guy had raised. I called, two folded and the other guy called. The flop was Q♥, K♦ and K♠. I now had three kings but was well aware that for the others to still be in the game there might be paired queens, which would give someone a full house. I pushed a large bet out and was matched. I was expecting a raise but perhaps my winning hand a while ago had unsettled them. Anyone holding pocket queens would have been pretty happy. The turn card was the 10♥, possibly giving someone a straight or another full house if they had pocket tens.

I decided to check simply to see what they would do and, as I suspected, they were all over the table. The guy to my left went all-in and the other player quickly followed. Even though I had a set of kings, a feeling in my gut made me throw my cards to the dealer. When I get these feelings, they are either hunger pangs or a sense of foreboding that much better hands are in play. I signalled the waiter who took my order and reappeared moments later with a double bourbon and a bag of chips. I settled back to watch the river card get dealt. The guys turned their cards over; the A♣ and J♠ and the Q♦ and Q♣, giving them a straight and a full house. Pretty flash hands without the river card. It was only a formality for the river card to be turned. It was the K♥. I couldn't believe it. Another four-of-a-kind in one session. The long odds on getting the king justified me mucking my hand but it still left me wondering what could have been.

With our numbers dwindling we played silly buggers for hours until I went all-in on a pair of eights hoping to suck them in. I did, but the flop was of no help. Another eight on the turn had me behind one guy and the river; well, it ran dry and I was out of the place.

It was dark when I got to my car and although I'd lost fifty grand in half a day, it wasn't at the forefront of my thoughts. When I was back on the freeway it was Jack's voice in my head. He's bloody persistent even in my brain. I gunned the Chrysler, keen to get back to my apartment. I poured a drink and turned my phone on. Five missed calls, all from Jack. Fuck me drunk. I'd told him to give me a couple of days before I'd give him my answer. I was about to hit the sack when it rang.

'Bloody hell, Jack. I told you I'd get back to you after I'd had a chance to think it over. More's the point, don't you sleep?'

'Time is of the essence, Tommy Dabrowski. We can sleep when we're dead,' he said, ignoring my annoyance. 'They're not going to hold up the tournaments waiting for you to get your fat arse over here.'

'You haven't convinced me that playing both tournaments will be the best thing I've done for a long time. Have you forgotten I still have celebrity status here after my big win last year?'

'Come on, Tommy, you haven't been overseas for ages. It would do you the world of good to have a change of scenery. Pardon me for saying this but I think your mental health could do with a recharge, too.'

'You're not going to let up, are you? Fax me the details and let me check 'em out. My e-mail is out of action at the moment.'

'You won't regret this,' said Jack. The relief in his voice was almost enough to make me say yes. 'You should have all the info by the time you're up and about in the morning. Sleep tight, my friend.'

DAY 2 – MONDAY

I had a fitful sleep and was glad to wake up. I opened the curtains, pleased to see the sun again.

I suddenly remembered I had an appointment with my shrink at eleven. I couldn't remember when I'd last been. I was still sleeping longer so maybe a lingering demon was lurking deep in my subconscious. She'd be the best person to sort it out. I showered and headed down to the small restaurant on the ground floor for breakfast.

*

The complex, Marina Bay Apartments, is different from others in the area. The first six floors are deluxe hotel suites and the remaining fifteen floors are luxury apartments with mine, the penthouse, especially luxurious. It has three large bedrooms, two with ensuites, and a guest bathroom. The ensuite off my bedroom contains a spa that can hold four people with ease. Because of my size it's not too big. The lounge room has a comfortable leather two-seater couch and seating for eight in plush individual recliners next to a billiard room. The service lift would have had a decent workout getting the components for the full-size slate-based table up twenty-one floors. Custom-made shelving units contain my golf trophies and memorabilia collected over the years.

A bookcase runs halfway along one wall filled with my favourite topics – poker, golf, history, several atlases and dictionaries. *Penthouse* collector's editions sit discreetly at one end. The articles are mostly bullshit but the photos are of exceptional quality. Behind a sliding panel is a wall safe that needs a key and combination to open. It's a great place for my stash of cash when I play at Aussie casinos where I don't have a line of credit – not many. I never carried the key on me. It sits in a cavity I carved out of an old dictionary.

The craftsman-built timber bar is decadently stocked with enough top-shelf spirits to keep me and visitors drunk for a year, and an internal wine room, off the billiard room, holds dozens of extremely good wines that are ever-increasing in value. The dining area and the kitchen, with enough accessories to embarrass a small restaurant, aren't given nearly enough use. I neither had, nor made, time to cook. Why cook for one when I could get the best restaurant food close by? Maybe one day I'd get to share my place with a special person, although they would have to be tolerant of my lifestyle. Even though the complex provides a laundry service I prefer to do my own personal washing and the utility room is set up with the latest appliances.

Access to the apartments is restricted and, coupled with efficient staff, provides a safe environment. The ground floor also contains a bar and lounge area for guests and their friends while the basement has the obligatory car park and storage facilities for the permanent residents.

*

I finished breakfast and made it to her office on time.

'Good morning, Tommy, come on in.'

Her voice was soothing, almost hypnotic. Probably not a bad thing for a shrink.

I smiled at her. 'Good morning, Helen.'

She stood to one side while I walked into her office. I immediately felt embarrassed and apologised.

'No need to apologise. You're my client and I invited you in.'

'Old habits die hard but I've got things on my mind and I guess my manners slipped.'

She laughed. 'Gosh. We could have a session evaluating the first minute of our meeting.'

I sat in an extremely comfortable leather chair. One of two.

Helen's receptionist walked in with two large mugs of coffee. She said hello and placed them on small tables beside our chairs. We thanked her and she closed the door behind her.

Helen raised her eyebrows and smiled. 'You'd better share with me what's on your mind. It seems serious, seeing as how you barged into my office.'

Once again, she had put me at ease. Another reason I didn't mind coming to see her. I'm a lousy judge of peoples' ages but if pushed I'd say she was about forty. She was level with my shoulder and her toned appearance made me assume she didn't spend all day indoors with the likes of me. Her pretty face and blue eyes distracted me. Up until now I hadn't thought of her as anything other than my therapist but, for whatever reason, today I was seeing her in a different light.

'Have I got two heads today, Tommy?'

'What? Oh sorry, I was miles away.' I could feel my face warming. 'Um, I got a phone call yesterday from a mate I haven't heard from for a while. He's asked me to go to Los Angeles then Las Vegas for a big golf and poker tournament. I'm not sure I could play golf at that level after years of being bone idle, but Jack – that's his name – reckons he could snap me back into shape within six months and give both events a big shake.'

'Do you think getting back into shape would do you any harm?'

'No, I guess at my age I should be making more of an effort to be healthy. I probably need motivation and reason.'

'Living beyond eighty in relatively good health with no money concerns should be enough motivation and reason. From what you've told me in previous sessions your golfing ability was second to none, and had you not traded your clubs for cards you might still be in the winners' circle. I think your mental health would benefit a great deal with a distraction such as Jack is offering, to say nothing of your physical wellbeing.'

I sipped my coffee, giving me a chance to absorb Helen's words of wisdom. 'You're making sense but I'll have to think hard about it.'

'Changing the subject, Tommy, are you in a relationship?'

'Not at the moment.' I wondered where this was going.

'When was the last time you were in a relationship?'

I reflected for a moment. 'Maybe five years ago. It was good while it lasted.'

'Why did it end?'

Once again, I had to take a moment. 'When I think about it, I guess if *I* had to hang around while my partner spent days on end at poker tables in tournaments around the world, maybe in cities not overly conducive to tourists, then I would consider I was playing second fiddle. Perhaps at times not even in the band.'

I paused while I took another sip of coffee. It was good. Maybe Moccona Espresso. 'Everyone needs and wants attention when they're in a relationship and if they're not getting it, what's the point of hanging around? I couldn't blame her for moving on.'

'Do you want to be in a relationship and, if so, what would you do to maintain it in such a way you were both happy?'

'I'd love to be with someone. I haven't been out of Australia for a couple of years, which doesn't worry me. I'm enjoying being at home. I'm still playing lots of poker though. Whether that would still be a turn-off depends on the type of person. Maybe another poker player,' I laughed. 'I can't see myself giving up poker at this stage. I guess if someone comes along and knows what to expect, so be it. In saying that, relationships have to be give and take. Whether I can compromise, I'm not sure.'

'Will it worry you if you never get into another relationship?'

'I don't know. I'm only human. It's not *worrying* me at the moment. Let's see what impact LA and Vegas have on me if I decide to go.'

'Do you have any friends, Tommy?'

'Depends what you mean by friends.'

'Simple enough question. Let's say people you're on good terms with.'

'Well. The people who work at Marina Bay Apartments would be my friends. We get on well. We have a laugh and stir each other but we respect each other as well.'

'Any close friends?'

'I'd consider my golfing mate Jack and four poker mates from Pommy land as close. Unfortunately, we don't catch up as often as we should.'

'How about friends from childhood?'

'When I was young, I didn't form childhood friendships. It was only when I hit the pro golf circuit and the poker scene that I made a few good friends. Until then the opportunity never arose.'

'Why didn't you have friendships growing up? Many children form lifelong friendships while they're at school and during adolescence.'

I shifted in my chair. 'Perhaps we could talk about it another day.'

'I'll look forward to it.' She made notes in my file.

She enjoyed talking about the heist and its ongoing effects. She was pleased I was getting more sleep but suggested seven to eight hours was sufficient. Getting into a sleep routine was good for body *and* brain.

She stood and walked me to the door. She shook my hand, wished me good luck and asked me to call her when I got back. She sounded as if I had already made the decision to go.

As I walked out of her office and into the bright sun I wondered where she had been heading with the relationship and friends questions. Perhaps I'd find out on my next visit. I shielded my eyes from the sun until shop awnings provided shade. I was looking forward to lunch.

*

I had a steak and a couple of glasses of wine at Jacques, then headed back to my apartment where, true to form, in a sealed envelope was Jack's paperwork. When I'd purchased my penthouse apartment, I had been made aware it came with a 24-hour reception service that included mail delivery, security, car detailing and room service. The monthly fee for these services was justified and it wasn't as though I couldn't afford it. In fact, I had paid a year in advance only a month ago so if I ventured abroad the complex's management would make a small profit in my absence. I wasn't too worried. It was reassuring to have that type of service.

I sat at the antique desk I'd inherited from my maternal grandfather and opened the envelope with the 18-carat gold letter opener my mother gave me after winning the European Golf Championship. I ran my fingers over the two small sapphires embedded in the handle. My mother must have known my birthstone. The stones were vivid blue and although sapphires come in every colour in the rainbow – the red ones are called rubies – the blue ones are the most sought after.

My grandfather was a clever yet sneaky old bastard. He had built the desk in sections so it could be easily dismantled. He'd used screws and timber dowels to great effect. It included hidden compartments only opened by pressing secret panels. Many of them housed my poker chip collection. I have made it a habit to get a few chips from each casino I play in and I've also got a nice selection of early American scrimshaw chips I'd bought online a couple of years ago.

*

It's amazing the shoulders you rub when you play poker and it doesn't take long for people to learn about your interests. I remember when I first went to America playing poker and I was seated at a table with an impeccably-dressed retired army major from England. His name reflected his class: Charles Pointon-Jones. I was a cheeky bugger back then and we were having a laugh so I asked him when was the last time he'd got his end in.

'Not that it's any of your business but if you need to know, it was 1950.'

We'd laughed and made crude remarks.

'I don't know why that's so funny,' he'd said, looking at his fob watch, 'it's only 2230 now.'

It was then I knew I'd made a friend for life. For the rest of my stay in Texas we played countless hours of poker and, despite his age, his mind was as sharp as a tack; and judging by the amount of money he won from me, I had much to learn. He had played at the finals tables at many World Series tournaments and took down many a celebrated player.

After one particular tournament a group of us was having a drink when he said, 'Did I tell you about the time I went on a tiger hunt in India?'

'No.'

'Well. I was stationed in Rajasthan, north-west India. Tiger country. Thousands of the blighters and they made excellent trophies. This particular day I was on the lead elephant; one of five. The others had senior army staff onboard. We were trekking through this high grass when suddenly a tiger jumped into our path.

'*Grrrowl.*' He paused. 'I shit myself.'

'When you saw the tiger?'

'No, just then when I said, *grrrowl.*'

We'd fallen about laughing. Fuck, he was a funny bloke.

Over the years we kept in touch and when our paths crossed he would often have a small package of chips, mainly antique, for my collection. It was a sad day when I heard he'd died. Charles was a true gentleman who never bragged when he won and, more importantly, never got angry or abusive when he lost. If I've learnt nothing else out of life it's his poker etiquette that I'll carry with me always.

*

I sorted out the paperwork from Jack, not convinced I could get myself ready for top level golf. I remembered back to my best golfing days when my fitness coach explained that if a good athlete stops competing, although the body loses its condition, it doesn't take too long to get back into shape because the foundations have been laid and they remain in place. It was something to do with the brain receptors remembering muscle training and aerobic management. Shame my brain couldn't remember how much bourbon I'd drunk.

I didn't have anything on for the afternoon so I decided I'd grab my clubs out of my storage room and head to the nearby golf club where I might be able to convince myself I could possibly do this.

'Lucky' Phil was polishing my car as I stepped into the basement. He was twenty-eight, a shade under 180 centimetres, slim but with broad shoulders. He looked like a swimmer. He loved surfing. His greatest assets were his charm and his teeth. He had the whitest, most even teeth I'd seen in a long while. Combined with his stylish hairdo and boyish good looks, it made him popular with the ladies.

I called him Lucky because he was always the guy on duty who got to clean my car. Although it never needed much more than an occasional wash, he made out to his boss he would be busy with my vehicle. The boss rarely ventured into the basement so Lucky had it easy, pretending to sweat it out while listening to the races on my car stereo. He always offered me race tips and he was rarely wrong but horse racing wasn't my thing. He took great pleasure though in telling me how much he'd won, particularly when he wagered my generous tips on the nags.

'Give me five minutes and she'll be ready,' he said, pretending to wipe the sweat from his brow. We smiled because he knew that I knew that his boss didn't know how good it was working in the basement.

'No worries, I've got to get my golf clubs out of my storage room.'

'You be careful lifting those things,' he said with a laugh. 'The heaviest thing you've lifted lately has been pocket aces.'

'Stick to cleaning cars, Lucky. I'll handle the humour.'

I opened the bag cover and inspected my clubs. They were nearly twenty years old. If I was going to be competitive again, I'd need to upgrade to the latest and best available. I'd have a talk to the club pro. I lifted the bag into the boot.

I arrived at the course and found the practise area empty. Good for me. No-one around to watch me make a fool of myself. I walked into the pro shop carrying my bag. It felt much heavier than the last time I lugged it around. I asked the young bloke behind the counter if I could speak to the club pro.

'That's me, I'm Maurice,' he said and extended his hand. He didn't look a day over seventeen; fresh-faced and friendly.

'Sorry, mate. They breed pros young these days.'

'No worries. I'm twenty-one and have been a pro golfer since I was eighteen. I was state amateur champion three years running from when I was fourteen and won my first pro event the week after my eighteenth birthday.'

I introduced myself and admittedly wasn't surprised he didn't know of my golfing exploits. He would have been a youngster when I was in my prime.

I showed him my clubs and looked around the pro shop. The latest clubs looked so different from my current set. Maurice knew his business. He selected a set that appeared as if they had been tailor-made for me. I warmed-up and spent half an hour hitting into the net with each club. They felt great and surprisingly I felt pretty good too. Club technology had come a long way. I was keen to hit the outdoor practise area.

I may have been acting rashly but I paid for the clubs and a couple of boxes of the latest model balls, then realised my bag was looking antiquated. I selected a new one that had more space for all the junk golfers carry around. I took my old clubs back to the car, then grabbed a bucket of practise balls from Maurice and headed to the practise area. I was still warmed-up so I grabbed my driver and hit the first ball. I couldn't believe it. It was as if I had it on a piece of string, dead straight a few metres short of the 250-metre marker. I teed up another and did the same thing. Out of fifty balls I hit five bad ones. What I call bad most golfers would jump and yell and high-five their playing partners. I had always been hard on myself when it came to golf and I suspect that is why I played so well. If my game wasn't right, I would practise my arse off until it was.

I moved down to the 'irons only' practise area and after twenty or so shots moved to the chipping and putting area. Every golfer knows that after a lay-off the short game is the hardest to remaster. Putting was always a highlight of my game, but based on what I was seeing I needed to spend much more time at it.

After I'd finished and had a chat to Maurice, I headed home. I didn't feel too bad and over dinner I decided to call Jack and tell him what I proposed to do.

Grilled fish and a fresh garden salad washed down with a sparkling mineral water at Jacques was a good beginning. I took the lift back to my apartment. I felt pleased. Part of me couldn't believe what I was about to do; but surely it couldn't be a bad thing. It would mean getting out of the apartment, getting fit, getting fresh air and hopefully getting a couple more trophies for the cabinet. Not to mention create more work for my Swiss bankers.

'Hi, Jack,' I said, not bothering with my usual bourbon in my recliner. I knew he'd answer the phone even in his sleep. He hated missing out on anything. I once contemplated nick-naming him *horse*. He could probably sleep standing up.

'Guess what? You can stop hassling me. If it'll make you happy, I'll come over to LA and see what happens. I've spoken to my shrink and what she said makes sense, so with both of you ganging up on me I'd better come. I have a few conditions, though. I want a stop-over in Hong Kong, and maybe Hawaii for a week or two, to acclimatise. The casinos in Honkers might allow me to pick up extra spending money for Vegas.'

'What do you mean *acclimatise*? You're not going to the fucking North Pole. Granted it won't be as warm as Sydney but you don't have to justify your reasons to me. Deep down I think it *is* the casinos you want to visit and that's fine. Do you realise they don't have casinos in Hawaii? Ah, I get it. You want to sit on the beach and watch the girls go by.'

'Damn. You know me too well.'

'Either way, Tommy, your decision to come over is probably the best one you've made in a while.'

He was happy now. We discussed a few more trip details and after an evening of TV I crawled into bed around midnight.

DAY 3 – TUESDAY

I woke at eight and couldn't move. My body was wracked with pain. I felt as though I'd been hit by a bus. The only part of me not hurting was my brain which was unusual based on my liking for bourbon.

I tried to get out of bed but couldn't roll over. I realised what the problem was. Hitting a hundred golf balls in an hour after not exercising for years was always going to take its toll. I rang the reception desk and, after explaining my predicament, asked if the kitchen could rustle up breakfast for me. I told them to bring their master key. I couldn't get to the door.

A short time later a timid knock on the door broke my concentration. I was visualising whether I would be able to get into shape in time for the big events.

I groaned. 'Come in.' I slowly edged myself into a position so I could eat.

'Good morning, Tommy,' said Sylvia, placing the tray on the bed. 'You not too good today? You party too much. You should be more careful.'

'Not too much cheek from you today, Sylvia.' I tried to get comfortable while telling her what I'd done. She was most sympathetic although I detected a slight smile as she turned to open the curtains.

Sylvia Nguyen was a shade less than 150 centimetres tall and slightly built. Her skin was the colour of a double-shot latte, her hair dark and her almond-shaped eyes brown and alert. Her small stature was well compensated for with a bubbly personality, good looks and a sense of humour.

'How's your mother?'

'She not so good, Tommy. Getting too old. Can't move around. Much like you.'

'You don't let up, do you?'

*

Sylvia was one of the nicest people I'd met. She'd started work at the Marina not long before I'd moved in and we took an instant liking to each other. Her English wasn't the best but she had a good brain and was a quick learner. As time went by, she told me about her past and how her mother and father had fled Vietnam as boat people after the war. Sylvia was born in 1985 in Sydney's West and was named after the nurse who had delivered her. Sylvia was a breech birth, and her mother was so grateful for the help she received it seemed like the right thing to do. Her parents were protective of her and, as they couldn't speak much English, her early years were spent learning Vietnamese. Despite this she excelled at school, although she wasn't able to complete her education because she needed to support her parents. Her father held down a cleaning job and her mother had part-time work at a local restaurant. Their income was low and Sylvia believed it was her duty to help. It was how families survived in poorer countries and it was ingrained in tradition.

Sylvia had told me way back she didn't want to be doing this type of work forever and I'd said I'd be more than happy to help out with her further education. She had a thirst for knowledge; particularly subjects like history, geography and art. She didn't mind mathematics but reckoned it was better for me when I played poker.

I also enjoyed history and geography, and as a youngster I'd found that using mnemonics was helpful in remembering particular facts. Sylvia was intrigued and during our many discussions I shared some I'd created. One that she liked related to the five largest countries in the world. Russia, Canada, USA, China and Brazil. The mnemonic was *Rusty Cans Under China Bowls*.

She treated it like a competition and created many, taking great pride in telling me her latest verse.

Many Early Monarchs Are Very Elegant had been her latest for remembering the female English queens (Mary I, Elizabeth I, Mary II, Anne, Victoria and Elizabeth II). I remember asking her about Lady Jane Grey and her nine days as Queen. She had given me a stern look and said, 'Don't get me started.' How unfair, she had told me. A pawn in an evil man's game, she had said.

Her ability to remember dates was incredible. She could recall the royal houses from the Normans to the Windsors, including the reign of each monarch. She would astound me with things such as the names of the four US Presidents carved into Mount Rushmore in South Dakota, along with the build dates and the designer's name. Her knowledge of Australian Prime Ministers was in itself impressive. Her school trips to the museum had always included time spent admiring the great nineteenth century artists whenever they were exhibited. As a result, her interest in the Impressionists brought a smile to my face when she reeled off the names of the pre- and post-Impressionists, as well as the leading four and their works. She knew the names of many authors, poets and musicians and could recall their works with amazing clarity. I quickly concluded she was extremely intelligent.

I'd suggested she enrol in English improvement classes, then apply for a place at university and undertake an Arts degree majoring in either history or geography. I had no doubt she would excel due to her determination to better herself. Her wish to eventually go to Vietnam as a teacher was a dream I was sure she would achieve. If I could play a small part in her dream I would. When I had told her I would pay for her university fees she'd almost fainted. I explained I was living a charmed life so I was in a pleasant position to help out.

*

'You want masseur to come up and get you fixed?' she asked, as I managed to make inroads into the breakfast.

'Yes, please. I have to get myself organised for this trip.'

'We miss you when you go. How long you away?'

'I don't know. I'll have an open air ticket because my friend who is organising the trip might throw in a few surprises along the way.'

Derrick, the masseur, turned up not long after Sylvia left. After he'd set up his table I managed to climb on and endure the worst half hour I can remember.

He had fingers of steel and at one stage I thought he was going to reach in and rip my heart out. He assured me it was in my best interest to work through the pain as I would benefit from it later. He scolded me like a parent scolds a naughty child when he told me I should have had more sense than to hit golf balls the way I did after such a long lay-off.

Duly chastened, I took his advice and after a hot spa I went for a walk along the promenade, had a large espresso, and then headed back to my apartment to read through the paperwork again. I dug my passport out of my desk and was relieved I didn't have to renew it for another year. I noticed my torturer had left his business card. Perhaps he knew his services would be required again.

I decided a swim in the salt water pool next to the gym mightn't do me any harm before I rang Jack. The warm water was therapeutic and Jack could tell from my voice I was committed to his plan. He apologised for laughing when I told him what I'd done at the golf course. I realised I'd been a dickhead; however, it was a good wake-up call as to how much work I had to do to get into competition shape.

'I'll get you booked on Qantas to Hong Kong Monday week and let you know where you'll be staying,' said Jack. 'Hopefully that'll give you enough time to get yourself organised.'

'I've done enough travelling to know what I need to do.'

Jack was a fusspot but I went along with him as I knew he would get the best plane seat and accommodation for me.

Feeling fired up, I rang the Four Winds to see if any hold' em cash games were happening in the evening. The reply was positive and, suddenly remembering I hadn't had lunch, I decided on an early dinner. Funny thing was I hadn't felt hungry. What a difference a day makes. I headed for Jacques.

The grilled ling with crispy skin paired with a garden salad again grabbed my tastebuds. I couldn't believe how quickly I was able to switch things around. I did weaken though with a glass of vintage white. Head chef Erik tried to convince me the peanut butter bombe with chocolate would be good for me, but I managed to resist.

After a leisurely meal I walked back to the apartment basement and noticed Lucky had taken my golf clubs from the boot and put them back into my storage room using his master key. He had left me a note to say he'd cleaned them before putting them away. I think my name should have been Lucky. I made a mental note to talk to him about my car while I would be away. It would need a regular run and a service and I knew I could trust him to look after it.

I drove out and headed to the casino. Clive was bewildered when I told him I would park my car and walk around. I slipped him a fifty out of habit.

I walked over to the bar and without thinking bought a double bourbon. I wasn't too fazed and convinced myself that abstaining from all that is bad is not good. I scanned the gaming area and noticed familiar faces I hadn't seen since I was in London at the Victoria Sporting Club playing the *Late Night Poker* TV series. Heaps of guys back then were slow to adapt to televised poker. The lipstick cameras on the sides of the tables filmed players' hole cards for the viewers at home. It was TV, after all, and viewers wanted to see all the action. It gave viewers an insight into how players played their hands. It was almost a teaching aid of sorts: bluffs, check-raises and so on.

Keith, Harry, Mick, and George stood as I approached and we laughed and shook hands in genuine friendship. Talk about four middle-aged peas in a pod. They looked lean and fit. Their typical English accents were complemented by the Aussie slang they'd picked up along the way. We spent the next hour reminiscing. George reckoned that since they had read about the casino heist in several London daily papers they should be in awe of my presence. Harry reckoned lightning wouldn't strike twice so we should head down the coast to

Diamond Harbour and I could show them firsthand how it went down. I brushed off their stirring and suggested we grab a seat at a cash game that was about to start.

As I got off my stool Mick gave me a funny look. 'You're not moving too well, old chap.'

When I explained what I had been doing and what I planned to do they couldn't help but crack up and I immediately realised I should have said nothing. I wouldn't hear the end of it. After they settled down Keith, who I'd played golf with years ago, reckoned I stood half a chance, knowing how good I was. He suggested we have a drink after the game and have a chat about the trip.

These guys hadn't lost their touch and even though Harry had hardly raised a bet he'd accumulated a tidy stack. He was a tight player and even though we could read him reasonably well he managed to bluff us beautifully every now and again. He reckoned mixing it up didn't mean doing different things with the same hand but doing the same thing with different hands. It worked for him.

I wasn't on my game and after a couple of hours I told them I'd wait at the bar.

As I walked past the roulette table, I glanced at the screen that showed the previous ten spin results. They were red. I looked at the table and everyone was backing black. One bloke had every black number covered with what looked like $50 chips. If black came up, he'd be a happy man.

Roulette is not a game I usually care for as the only skill required is to be able to get your chips on before the croupier waves his hands over the table and says, 'No more bets.'

Going against my better judgement, I put ten $100 chips on red and five $100 chips on the third 12-segment to the derision of some players. I stood back and watched the marble spin. It fell and bounced around the wheel and finally settled. Stunned silence for a split second, then an uproar. The ball had dropped into thirty-two red. The croupier raked every chip off the table except a stack of ten and a stack of five. They were mine. He matched my stack of ten with another and my stack of five with two more. Even-money payout for red and two-to-one for the third twelve. He pursed his lips in what might have been a tightly suppressed smile. Without missing a beat, he announced to the table, 'Place your bets.' It was the easiest two grand I'd made in a while.

I picked up my chips and looked across at the guys at the poker table and gave them the thumbs-up, then eased myself onto a bar stool. I'd had a couple of drinks when they turned up. They'd had mixed fortunes. Mick was out of sorts while Harry had cleaned up on the last all-in hand.

'You haven't told me why you're here,' I said. 'Perhaps it's the lure of the hot Aussie summer?'

'Spot on,' said Mick, flicking his greying hair off his forehead. It complemented his good looks. For as long as I'd known Mick, he'd always worn his hair long. It suited him apart from when he wore his jockey helmet. 'We've been in Oz for a while but if I keep playing like I have I won't be hanging around much longer.'

'Harden the fuck up, Mick,' I said, giving him a friendly thump on the arm. 'You know you always win more than you lose.'

'Harry's got a couple of gigs while he's in Oz,' said Keith. 'Don't know whether you remember, Tommy, but Harry was a studio drummer for several years and at one stage he was the standby drummer for the band Velox. Their resident drummer had heard Harry play and when word got out, he was in big demand at recording studios and live shows.'

I interrupted, 'Velox had a few records in the charts in the late seventies if I recall. Admittedly I was young, but it's pretty timeless stuff. Were you the drummer on any of them?'

'I played on their final album *Live at Ely Common*. It was recorded in front of around twenty thousand fans. Heaps of uni students from Cambridge turned up. They loved our music. It made it to number three on the album charts and stayed in the top ten for five months. One track was used for the opening music on the TV drama *Ravine*, which ran for seven seasons. It's still shown on UK TV and we get pretty tidy royalties from it.'

'Right place, right time,' I said.

Keith continued, 'Anyway, after Harry's parents died, he inherited a great property in Mayfair as well as three working farms that provide him with a filthy income.'

'Why are you sitting around here when you should be up to your knees in cow shit?' I asked with a smile.

Harry laughed. 'Good question. Considering the bullshit flying around here I'd probably be better off. Fortunately, I'm not the sort of bloke who likes getting his hands dirty, albeit much to my old man's disgust. Because of my sickness when I was a kid, I never developed the sort of physique a man on the land needs. I took a liking to indoor activities and the day in Year Five when I picked up a pair of drumsticks, I knew my future would be in music. Poker is like music. A great poker hand and a great tune; they get played over and over in your brain. Anyway, as I was their only kid, they had bugger-all choice but to bequeath me the fuckin' lot.' He laughed again as he combed his fingers through his thick, brown hair. Like Mick, he was good looking without knowing it. These guys certainly didn't have egos.

'Not that I objected, mind you,' he said. 'Professional people run the farms on long leases and I get a tidy income, not only from them but the Mayfair property as well. I'm doing these drumming gigs as a favour for the Velox studio boss. He's finally decided to set up a studio in Oz and as he has signed on some bands, he's running a few concerts to get things rolling.'

'Hope that doesn't clash with what I've got organised,' I said. 'I wouldn't mind turning up for a look.'

'Down to business, boys,' said George. 'Give us more details on what you're up to, Tommy. We were having a chat during our poker game and as we aren't in a hurry to get back to London, we wondered whether you'd mind us tagging along. None of us have been to Hong Kong for ages and you look like you might need chaperoning.'

'We'd been planning to go back to London via LA anyway, eventually,' said Harry, shouting us another round.

'I'd be more than happy to have you guys tag along. Maybe you and I can have a few rounds of golf in Honkers, Keith.'

Keith wasn't blessed with good looks but what he lacked he made up for in bucket loads with cheekiness and charm. He had no trouble attracting the attention of the opposite sex.

George chimed in. 'Sounds like a plan. We're staying at the Condor Towers while we're here. It's a stroke of luck we're at this casino because there's one attached to the Condor, but we enjoy spreading ourselves around. Perhaps we can get together tomorrow and fine-tune the travel arrangements. Why don't you come over for lunch? Harry's treat, seeing as he's loaded after tonight's big win.'

Harry smiled in agreement as we headed out of the casino, but not before they gave me another ribbing about my awkward gait caused by my foolishness on the driving range. I thumped Mick on the arm again for good measure and said good night.

I found myself humming as I walked to my car. I felt pretty good mentally; however, I had a feeling I would be getting the masseur up again in the morning. Things were moving at a rapid pace and I had a gut feeling I should not try and be Superman too soon. Baby steps. I had a long way to go.

I parked my car and took the lift to the fifteenth floor and got out. I opened the fire escape door and climbed the remaining six floors to my apartment. The lactic acid was ripping through my legs when I opened my door. Geez, I do stupid things. It had been three days since Jack had first rung, and now here I was thinking I was twenty years old again and invincible.

I had a shower and after an hour or so on *PokerStars* online, I hit the sack.

DAY 4 – WEDNESDAY

I woke at sparrow fart and when I rolled over it didn't take Einstein to work out I would be calling Derrick and his hands of steel soon. I couldn't face breakfast. I knew Derrick wouldn't be at work until nine, so I dragged myself to my desk and updated my diary for the coming week. I noted a few things I had to make sure I did before I flew out. I would travel light because, if Jack was true to his word, I would need a new wardrobe.

I knocked over yesterday's cryptic crossword before ringing Derrick. He happened to be in the building and could be at my place in half an hour. Although I felt he hated me I must admit he knew what he was doing. When he'd finished with me and after I'd stopped howling, he wrote down a series of exercises I should do as part of my new regime. Lots of wrist curls and hip rotations among them. I was grateful, thinking I would get a head start on Jack's upcoming treatment.

I had another hot spa that melted the pain from Derrick's fingers, and after a cool shower decided I'd walk to the Condor. I had a spare couple of hours so I called into the nearby TAFE and managed to speak to Yvonne, the Course Coordinator, about English improvement classes for Sylvia. Yvonne reminded me of an old-fashioned librarian: tall, hair tight in a bun, wire-rimmed glasses, and a loose-fitting pleated skirt. Her blouse and bra, however, were perhaps a size too small. Her breasts looked as if they wanted to escape their confines and smack me in the face. I couldn't guess her age.

She was professional in her manner and appeared blissfully unaware of her distractions. She listened intently and advised me that, based on what I had told her, Sylvia had a good chance of mastering the arrangement of words to the extent that she would not only become fluent in English grammar and expression, but also be able to cope with university studies.

Yvonne agreed with me that an Arts degree would be the best for Sylvia seeing as she displayed the technique of being able to remember dates, names, places and events without any difficulty. Even so, she told me to make Sylvia aware that uni wouldn't be a cake walk.

*

I could relate to what she was saying. I dropped out of uni after a year when the lure of professional golf grabbed me by the balls. After thirteen years of institutionalised education I had considered the relative freedom of uni would be easy to cope with, but the distractions of sport and the temptations that came with it proved me wrong. My love of mathematics, particularly probability, didn't wane, however, and I was able to put that skill to good use at the poker tables. When I had told my tutor I was quitting uni to play golf and poker he said I would be wasting my life. Little did he know that in the next ten years I would earn more money than he would earn in a lifetime of teaching. He would have argued that it's not all about money but turning one's talents into achievements. I had the talent for golf and poker and considered I could achieve more doing that than becoming a mathematician.

*

Yvonne said it was obvious Sylvia was keen to get started, so the best thing she could do was to enrol at TAFE for the next term, starting in three weeks.

She also advised me to let Sylvia know she would be in a class of predominantly recent arrivals to Australia and, although she has been in Australia all her life, it wouldn't hurt her to get back to basics. In hindsight, it was a shame Sylvia's mother had not pursued the English language on her arrival all those years ago.

'You've been a great help, Yvonne,' I said, shaking her hand. 'Thanks for your advice. I'm sure Sylvia will do her best.'

'With you as her mentor, I've no doubt she will.'

I checked her blouse, then my watch, as I walked out the door, and realised I'd spent over an hour with her. Time well spent. I hotfooted it to the Condor. I was looking forward to catching up with the guys and making the final arrangements for the first leg of our trip. Whether they would stop off at Vegas on their way home was a matter for discussion.

The polite doorman at the Condor directed me to the private bar where I found the four guys relaxing over drinks before lunch. I ordered a sparkling mineral water, much to George's disgust. He reckoned I was as weak as piss. I told him I could drink him under the table anytime but now wasn't the time.

36

George enjoyed life to the fullest. He, too, had good looks to match his black hair and blue eyes. He wore a five o'clock shadow all day. I wasn't sure whether it was genetics or a dull razor. His tattoos gave him a tough look but he was an easygoing bloke.

'You'd remember that Mick did track work for Benny Chan at the Hong Kong Turf Club years ago,' said George. 'Well, he's kept in touch, so he rang him last night after we got back here and he says he can get us into one of the best hotels on Hong Kong Island.'

Mick butted in, 'The Colonial Oriental. It's not too far from the Hong Kong Golf Club, which should suit you.'

'More importantly, where is the nearest casino? We'll need to hit the poker tables,' I said.

'Benny covered all the bases,' said Mick. 'The Golden Dragon Casino is on the island as well so you'll have nothing to complain about except your golf game and bad beats.'

'Cheeky sod,' I said. 'Come on, let's eat and we can talk more over a nice steak.'

Mick hadn't finished. 'Poker's not real big in Honkers yet but Benny knows where the best games are played. They use US dollars at their poker games as many of players are from the US but they do a good exchange rate for Aussie dollars so we won't be too hard done by.'

We tucked into a lunch that would have fed eight. My steak was so tender I could have used a plastic knife. I weakened and had a glass of red. The lads ate as if it was their last meal.

'How come you lot can eats like pigs and stay as skinny as greyhounds?' I asked.

'I don't know about the rest of us but Mick's certainly a greyhound,' said Harry. 'All prick and ribs.'

We laughed.

'You're only jealous,' said Mick, grabbing his crotch and pouring more wine. 'We'll work this off in the gym tomorrow.'

'You know how your mate Benny has picked out some great spots for us in Honkers,' I said, 'well, the guy who's getting me to LA – Jack Bird, who you wouldn't know – was going to sort all that out. I'm happy with what you guys have organised so I'd better call Jack and let him know that all he needs to do is get air tickets. Are you guys happy to fly Qantas?'

'As long as it stays in the air we don't care how we get there,' said Harry. 'My only requirement is business class even though it's only about a ten-hour flight. Why have all this money if we don't spend it on life's little luxuries, eh?'

'I couldn't agree more,' I said, as my phone started ringing.

The number on the display wasn't in my phone memory but I answered it anyway. It was Eldon from the Diamond Harbour Casino down the coast. He told me that Trevor the doorman was finally hanging up his coat after thirty-four years. Management had decided he deserved a fitting send-off and Eldon was tasked with sending out invitations. He was hoping I could attend at short notice at the end of the week. When I asked why me, he told me I was not only a regular but management and staff held me in high regard.

'Did the events of last year have anything to do with it?'

'Maybe,' he said meekly.

'I'd love to come down and see the old bugger off.'

I went on to tell him I had four mates with me from London who I hadn't seen for a while and ask, as they were keen to check out the casino, if it would be a problem if I brought them with me.

'I can't see why not,' he said. 'Any friend of yours is a friend of ours. The farewell starts at seven and it might be a long night. Do you reckon the lads might want to stay? If they're anything like you they probably won't be too steady on their feet by the end of the night.'

Now wasn't the time to tell him of my plans and current health regime, so I said I would ring back and confirm once I'd spoken to the guys. I rang off and filled them in on the conversation. They were extra keen now to check out the place so I called Eldon, booked five deluxe rooms, and told him we would see him late afternoon. I suggested we might have a gamble before things got underway.

I could see the boys were getting restless after the long lunch so I suggested we play blackjack for a while. Harry turned up his nose while George couldn't get out of his chair quick enough. George was a card counter. It wasn't his fault he had a photographic memory. Mick reckoned it was a pornographic memory. This was the sort of banter I had missed so much when I had left the Europe scene and come back to Australia.

George wasn't known at the Aussie casinos so I told him he should play it cool and not win too much. He didn't need to draw attention to himself. Knowing George, it would only be a matter of time before he would have a big pile of chips in front of him.

After we played for a few hours I told the guys I was heading home to get some rest. I proposed we meet up after breakfast and I'd take them on a tour of the northern suburbs and shout them lunch at Sydney Tower. I suggested they bring their swimming gear.

I had a leisurely walk home and after reading through my mail relaxed and watched a couple of taped episodes of *Little House on the Prairie*, one of my all-time favourite TV shows.

With my brain becoming more settled, sleep came easy.

<h1 style="text-align:center">DAY 5 – THURSDAY</h1>

My phone woke me and even though it was only seven-thirty I realised I'd had another huge sleep. It was overactive Mick.

'Where the bloody hell are ya, Tommy? We're down here in reception and they won't let us come up. Talk about security.'

I laughed. 'They were right to not let you come up anytime, let alone this early hour. You'd run riot. Put Lionel on if he's behind the desk.'

I spoke to Lionel and told him it was okay to let them come up. Lionel could program the lift so it came straight up to my penthouse.

I jumped out of bed and threw on my tracksuit and had a quick wash. I was ready for the knock on the door. In came the boys with George sporting a black eye.

'What the hell happened to you?' I asked, as they looked approvingly around the place.

Keith explained. 'George is a sucker for the less fortunate. After you left last night we went out for Chinese and, as we were walking along the main road, George saw who he thought was a homeless bloke sitting against a shop front. He went over to him and offered him a few dollars. For whatever reason, the bloke took offence and not only did he give George an earful, he also gave him a black eye. George reckoned the bloke was either pissed, stoned or both so he back-pedalled out of any further trouble.'

Mick reckoned it wouldn't stop George from doing what he does.

'Have you guys had breakfast? I can get room service if you like.'

'We're good, thanks,' said Keith, smiling. 'Some of us get up at a reasonable hour and get organised before the sun is halfway up in the fucking sky.'

'Slight exaggeration, Keith. Anyway, you guys make yourselves comfortable and I'll get brekky sent up for me.'

Keith and Harry headed into the billiard room and it wasn't long before the sound of snooker balls slamming into leather-bound pockets resonated into the lounge room. Keith was interested in my collection of early ivory and Bakelite balls that I stored in another custom-made display cabinet.

'Do you mind if I knock over this hard neuf-neuf, Tommy?' asked George as he settled himself into a recliner.

'What the hell are you talking about?'

'The sudoku in today's paper.'

'What did you call it?'

'A neuf-neuf. It means nine-nine. Nine numbers across and nine numbers down. It's easier to say neuf-neuf than sudoku.'

'Bloody sight harder to explain it, though,' I said, glancing at Mick looking out the window through my telescope.

'Can't see a bloody thing, Tommy,' he complained, trying to adjust the focus.

'It's not for looking at people, you perv. It's for star gazing. When it's clear you get fantastic views of the night sky. It's surprising considering the bright city lights. Sometimes I head up to Barrenjoey Lighthouse with it if I'm keen for an uninterrupted view. It's amazing what you can see. We can go there one night if I can drag you away from the tables.'

'Yeah, I'd like that, Tommy. Perhaps you can show me the Southern Cross and the two pointers.'

I gave him a dig in the ribs and laughed. 'You are talking astronomy aren't you, mate? You don't mean Kings Cross. Knowing you, I can never be sure.'

'You're not wrong there,' said George, without lifting his head out of the paper.

I finished breakfast and had a shower. We piled into the car and drove over the bridge, and shortly after turned onto Mona Vale Road. I told the guys we would come back via the coast road. I turned left when we hit the coast road and stopped at Bilgola. I showed them where I went to summer camp when I was at boarding school.

'Reckon you got up to mischief here, knowing you Catholic school boys,' said Mick, with a sly grin.

'Yeah, plenty of smokes, sweet sherry, green-ginger wine and wishful thinking. You weren't much better, according to Harry.'

'He's only jealous because he missed out on all our fun.'

The friendly banter continued as we got changed into our swim gear and spent an hour in the saltwater pool. The guys loved it.

Mick was at the other end when he shouted at us, 'We won't be shark bait in here!'

'They have been known to leap over the concrete edge when the waves are right,' I said, winking to the others who were ready to get out.

'Look out, Mick! There's one coming over now,' shouted Keith, trying hard not to laugh. His voice was so loud a couple of other swimmers stopped to check.

'Fuckin' hell,' said Mick, 'I'm outta here.'

As he got out, he could see us cracking up with laughter.

'You pack of bastards,' he roared. He grabbed our towels and threw them into the pool.

'Always remember, boys, I get the last laugh.'

He sauntered off towards the change rooms leaving us to wring out our towels and work out how we were going to dry ourselves after our showers.

George laughed. 'If that's our biggest problem today I don't think we've got too much to worry about.' He flicked me on the arse with his wet towel.

We finally got ourselves organised and headed back. We had a quick stop at Manly then to the city for lunch. I told them they could get fantastic photos from the Tower. Keith and Harry had new digital cameras. Harry was getting into photography. He told us he was keen to learn more about the technical side whereas Keith was more of a click-and-move-on-to-the-next-shot kind of guy.

'Are you guys set for tomorrow's trip down the coast for Trevor's farewell?' I asked, as we drove into the Condor's car park after a great lunch.

'It should be fun,' said Keith. 'Fancy a cash game tonight, Tommy?'

'You don't have to ask me once,' I said, laughing.

'Don't you mean twice?'

'Do you remember the TV series in the eighties called *Perfect Strangers*?'

'Before my time, old boy.'

'Piss off. Maybe it wasn't on Pommy TV. There was a Greek guy called Balki who had trouble with English phrases and he'd say once instead of twice.'

'Hilarious, Tommy. Guess you had to be there. Anyway, if you don't need to go back to your place you may as well hang around here, have dinner and we'll get into it,' said Keith.

Before dinner the boys went to the hotel's gym and pool while I sent Jack a text to update him on the arrangements. I also rang Sylvia and asked her if she would be free for lunch tomorrow so I could give her the good news about her further education. She was excited and couldn't stop thanking me. I told her not to get too excited until she heard the whole story.

Over dinner with the guys I told them about Sylvia. George was interested in what I was proposing. He had always had a philanthropic vein running through him. Back in London his involvement with homeless people was well known. He was instrumental in getting many hundreds of London's homeless off the streets, with community shelters set up in a way they could become more self-sufficient. Many supermarkets gave food that was a smidgen past its 'best-before' date. Otherwise it would have been dumped. Food halls had been set up throughout London. They provided one hot meal a day for those who couldn't fend for themselves. Several major clothing retailers made available the previous season's stock they couldn't sell. He lobbied many a politician who frequented the Vic club and, as a result, the government provided bigger subsidies to the homeless. George was aware they had only scratched the surface, but at least it was a good start.

Keith had told me quietly that George had given heaps of money to local charities, most of it anonymously. He had interests in a few lucrative financial services businesses ensuring he was never worried about his cash flow. It's all about the staff you employ, he'd told Keith.

We played cards for hours. When we decided to call it quits, George had probably won enough to set up another food hall back in London. He had attracted the interest of the casino pit-boss, who eyed him suspiciously when he saw his huge stack of chips. I'd taken a break from my poker game and casually gone over to George and whispered in his ear that the eyes of the casino were on him.

'I can't help it if I'm brilliant,' said George, with a cheeky grin. 'Okay, I'll back off if it helps keep the peace.'

'It will help you stay in one piece, if nothing else.'

He stacked his chips in the plastic trays and we headed off to find the others.

'We need to sort out tomorrow's arrangements before I head back to my place,' I said to George, pausing at the roulette table and glancing at the screen.

'Bugger me,' he said. 'The last three spins were zeros; I've never seen that before.'

I glanced around the table and noticed a Chinese bloke with so many chips he had the bottom end of the table covered. Other players had to hold theirs.

'Look at 'em, George; all $50 chips. Do you reckon he was playing zero?'

'I reckon he was, Einstein.'

The others were propping up the bar and, as I'd had a pretty profitable night, I told them I'd shout us a late supper. We headed to a trendy restaurant a couple of blocks away. It was called the Hollow Tree. The main feature was a magnificent sculpture crafted out of a Tasmanian oak tree salvaged from a hydro-electric dam site before the waters had begun rising. Inside the tree were beautifully sculptured native Tasmanian animals. They were made from Huon pine timber also salvaged from the dam. The workmanship was amazing.

The restaurant was popular with tourists and the comments in the visitors' book indicated this particular eatery wouldn't be closing down anytime soon.

Pancakes were our preference, topped off with great coffee and brandy.

I told the guys I was having lunch with Sylvia tomorrow and would pick them up from the Condor around three. They were happy to fill in the morning without me. Mick and Keith had an interest in antiques and collectables.

*

Mick had given up riding horses after some serious falls and had acquired an interest in antiques when he became involved with Benny's sister, an antiques dealer, in Hong Kong. She had been intrigued with his stories of his great race wins, and also his injuries – particularly the hoof-mark scar on his lower back, a testament to the risky business of horse racing.

In his prime, Mick rode and won races at several top courses in England. Ascot had been his favourite hunting ground. In one particular season he had ridden in all nine Group One races and had finished in the top three six times. His skills didn't go unnoticed. He was asked to ride the favourite in the Grand National at Aintree but at a race meeting the prior week he had been thrown from his horse. Another jockey had nudged Mick's horse into the rails. The horse had stumbled, and Mick had fallen awkwardly and broken his leg in two places. Complications caused him to miss a complete race season and, although his sister had taken leave from her job to nurse him, it was then he decided it was time to retire. He was able to pay her the wages she would have lost but she wouldn't have a bar of it. 'We're family,' she'd told him.

With his riding days behind him Mick concentrated his efforts on antique collecting. He was always on the lookout for items he could have shipped back to London. He had a magnificent Georgian house in North London that he reckoned could never be filled even if he lived to be a hundred. He was a shrewd investor and loved the stock market. He derived an income more than enough to supplement his antique collecting, travel and poker forays. His involvement with Benny's sister didn't last. Their travel arrangements often clashed and she wasn't into long-distance relationships.

*

Keith's interests were more left field. As a child, he had followed his father around old building renovation sites and while growing up had acquired hundreds of old keys, many with locks. They were valuable, particularly the old castle locks and keys, but he mainly enjoyed the history of them.

Keith's father, before going into the building business, had been a navy salvage diver and had passed on his knowledge to his son. They spent any spare time diving on ship wrecks off the English coast.

While studying Spanish history at school he had the brainwave to dive for sunken treasure. He mentioned this to his father who, after some convincing, was able to access archival maps that showed sunken galleons. Armed with the details, Keith and his father travelled to Portugal and, from no-questions-asked Portuguese and Spanish ship hire businesses, put their scheme into action.

After eighteen months of hard work they were able to buy their own boat, and at the end of their fifth year Keith's share was enough for him to never have to work again. George was able to invest a large portion of Keith's money in ventures that ensured him a steady income. Keith's father was exhausted and wanted to retire as well. Keith's mother was overjoyed the day they came home and told her they'd sold their boat and were hanging up their wetsuits.

His love of golf started a while after his initiation into the world of poker. It was due to his chance meeting with a top-ten ranked golfer he played against in a European poker tournament. They hit it off right from the start and, although Keith had won the tournament, the golfer was so impressed with Keith's attitude he suggested he try his hand on the course. Keith's perseverance and natural ability paid off and he played in many pro-am events alongside his mentor. Over time the poker tables lured him more and more and he played less and less golf. He didn't mind because that was where he'd met me and George's mates, Mick and Harry.

*

I gave them the address of several antique shops in the eastern suburbs. As we finished our supper, Keith mentioned that he would keep an eye out for any old poker chips in his travels.

I drove back to my apartment after happening upon a late-night supermarket. I went crazy and had a full trolley when I got to the checkout. My parking spot at the Marina was fairly close to the lifts. I pressed the stop button on one of them so it would stay open while I made two trips to my car to unload my shopping. I had to work fast. It didn't like being told what to do. Once up at my apartment I unpacked, got myself a coffee and, before I went to bed, got my paperwork together ready for my lunch with Sylvia the next day.

DAY 6 – FRIDAY

It was another beautiful day in paradise as I opened the curtains. It was nice to wake early without a sore body or the bloody phone ringing. It had only been a few days since I'd started my health improvement regime but I was feeling much better. So much so, my walk-in pantry was looking more like a health store than a spare cupboard. I enjoyed a leisurely breakfast of cereal, eggs on toast and coffee while killing the cryptic crossword.

I checked my watch and worked out I had enough time for a round of golf before I was due to meet Sylvia. I rang the course and was told it was Veterans' Day but I would be more than welcome to join them. This had been a regular club feature for many years but as the number of veterans was dwindling, they were happy for non-vets to join in. It was a Stableford competition and was considered a social event, and no-one took the game too seriously. The scoring was based on a player's handicap. A player off scratch (zero) scored one point for a bogey, two points for a par, three points for a birdie and four points for an eagle. A player with a handicap of five, for example, would score an additional point on the five hardest holes as indicated on the score card. A bogey would be worth two, a par three and so on. If a player had no chance of scoring any points on a hole, they could pick up their ball. It saved time and made for a quicker game. A score above thirty-six points was considered a good round.

I showered and dressed in lightweight trousers and a polo shirt. I had given most of my golf clothing to charity when I'd stopped playing regularly. I'd treat myself to the latest golf gear when I got to Hong Kong.

I made my way to the basement where Lucky was buffing the bonnet of my car.

'You should consider trading this monster in on something flashier now you're working on that Hulk Hogan body of yours,' said Lucky.

I suppressed a yawn. 'What would you suggest?' I was happy with my car and had never been overly worried about keeping up with the latest motoring trends. With everything that was going on, thinking about a new car was further from my mind than the prostate examination I had to endure on Monday.

'Well,' he said, not aware of my disinterest, 'you could upgrade to the Chrysler 6.1 litre V8. It does 0-100 in four-point-nine seconds. Or you could look at the Corvette C6 auto. It pumps out 321 kW and does 0-100 in four seconds. The Z06 will do it in three-point-six.'

'What rock have you been living under, Lucky? Perhaps you've forgotten what the maximum speed limit is these days. Why waste my money on a car I probably couldn't get out of first gear without breaking the law?'

'It's not about road rules,' said Lucky with a big grin. 'It's about the *look*, man. Think about the chicks you could pull with wheels like that.'

'The only pulling that's happening is you with your dick.' I gave him a friendly clip around the ear as I grabbed my golf clubs and hauled them to the car.

'Food for thought, Tommy,' he said, opening the boot. 'Now remember what happened the last time you hit the course? Take it easy. You don't want Derrick ripping your heart out again.' He was still laughing as I edged the car onto the ramp.

I arrived at the course to see about thirty guys waiting around to find out which hole they would be starting from. It was a shotgun start, meaning everyone started together and finished at roughly the same time. This gave everyone the chance to have a drink together after the game and reminisce about the old days.

I looked like the youngest bloke there and was slotted into a foursome and told we would be teeing off on the eighth hole. 'It's a par-3 with an elevated tee,' one guy said. I was pleased, as I felt a soft opening shot would suit me.

We headed over to the putting green for the obligatory practise then walked out to the eighth. They were funny guys and we did 'rock-paper-scissors' to decide the tee off order. I ended up hitting third and, surprisingly, landed on the green inside the circle. The circle was painted on some par-3 greens during this type of event so anyone landing their ball inside the circle would get a prize. I wasn't concerned about a prize but I was happy with my tee shot.

Because of my past professional status, I had a zero handicap but finished the day with thirty-nine points, which would augur well for the soon-to-be hectic time for me. I gave my prize for closest-to-the-pin on both par-3s back to the prize pool, thanked the guys for letting me play and apologised for having to leave early. I headed home to have a quick shower before meeting Sylvia for lunch.

I got to Jacques about five minutes before her. When she walked in, I'd never seen her so excited or nervous.

'I feel out of place here, Tommy,' she whispered, as the waiter brought a carafe of chilled water and two glasses.

'Don't worry. I couldn't be more pleased to have you as my lunch guest.'

'I hope the menu is not hard. I only eat out at cafés.'

'You'll be fine,' I said. The waiter placed two menus in front of us. One for the food the other the wine.

After we had perused the menu Sylvia selected grilled fish with garden salad.

'You must be a mind-reader,' I said. 'Fish is my dish of choice now I'm on the fitness trail.'

Sylvia smiled and appeared to relax but I could see the excitement in her eyes. She was like a kid waiting to open Christmas presents.

I ordered our meals, including a glass of white for me. Sylvia had to work later in the day so she stayed with the water.

The fish arrived and it was first class, as usual. Sylvia claimed it was the best meal she had had in a long time and couldn't wait to tell her workmates.

We declined dessert and, over coffee, I showed her my paperwork and spent time relaying what Yvonne from TAFE had told me. Sylvia realised it was not going to be easy achieving her goals but was determined to try hard.

I told her to go and see Yvonne and get enrolled in the English language improvement classes as her first step, then see how things work out. Yvonne would put her in contact with the university enrolment staff who would guide her through the registration process and subsequent course procedures. The three-year Arts degree covering twenty-four subjects would be a real challenge. Sylvia had the right mindset, though, so I was in no doubt she would give it her best effort.

As we got up to leave, she gave me the biggest hug she could manage based on my size in relation to hers. I had to bend over so she could get her arms around my neck. We laughed awkwardly and headed back to the Marina, where she ran into the staffroom like a child who had won their first blue ribbon in the school athletics carnival. I knew she would be impatient to finish her shift so she could get home and pore over the paperwork. I had a feeling she wouldn't sleep much. She would be as keen as mustard to be down at the TAFE office when it opened at nine.

My phone rang as the lift opened on the fifteenth floor. I climbed the six flights to my apartment. It was Mick, wondering if I had finished lunch. Apparently, they were keen to head down the coast as soon as I was ready. Pushy buggers. I opened my apartment door with lactic acid pumping through my legs. Bloody hell, I had a long way to go before I could say I was fit. I lay on the bed for ten minutes. I could have easily nodded off. I packed an overnight bag and headed down to my car. Lucky had taken my clubs out, cleaned them, and put them back in my storage room. Despite his funny ways he was great to have around.

I pulled up at the Condor a few minutes before two-thirty. The doorman came over and introduced himself as Barry.

'Mick warned me you'd be turning up. He said to be on the lookout for a big guy in a big car.'

'Cheeky bastard,' I replied, smiling.

'Leave your wheels here. The boys aren't far away. George told me you're heading down the coast for Trevor's farewell. Give him my best wishes, would you?'

They had known each other for years – ex-army mates – and it had been a competition of sorts to see who would retire last. I told him he could retire tomorrow and he would win. He laughed and told me to tell Trevor that's what he was going to do, if only to stir him up.

I walked into the bar and saw the guys perched on stools, knocking down cold Aussie beers. I declined their offer of a beer pointing out a sober driver was in everyone's best interest. With a laugh and a gulp, they finished their drinks and we headed out to the car. Mick had a friendly spar with Barry. The guys had befriended Barry as they appreciated having a friendly face greet them when they arrived or left the hotel and keeping an eye out for them.

Within minutes we were on the freeway heading south. It would take us a couple of hours to get to the Diamond Harbour Casino. Before long the guys in the back were asleep; comfortable in the soft leather seats. I drove, feeling relaxed and happy with the outcomes of the day. It was therapeutic listening to Vivaldi over the snores of George and Harry. I smiled as I glanced at them in the mirror. Mick was in the front seat. How he scored it I don't know. Being the smallest, I thought the others would have fought over it. I had a feeling Mick held sway with these guys but not in a nasty way. They got on well so they probably couldn't care less. Keith was out of my vision but he wasn't a snorer. I think his diving days promoted good breathing habits.

Mick stirred and asked how long he'd been asleep. I said about half an hour. He reckoned more like two hours as the car travelled well on the highway with next to no road noise.

'How long have you had this motor?' he asked, as I overtook a Mack B-double milk tanker with ease.

'Mid-2005.'

'What did you have before this?'

'An Aussie Holden Monaro V8, before that another Aussie icon, a Ford Falcon V8, and before that a beautifully-restored MGB that I bought off this old guy who had kept it in his garage for about ten years. His wife kept nagging him to get rid of it after he handed in his licence. He'd painstakingly rebuilt it over three years but had a mild stroke and couldn't drive anymore. I met him through a mutual acquaintance and I paid what he asked.'

'I can see why you moved up in size,' said Mick. 'But I'm impressed with the way you're tackling your fitness regime. Talking about MGBs, did I tell you the story about the penguin that went out for a drive one hot day?'

'You haven't but I reckon I'm about to hear it.'

'Well, it was a typical hot summer day and the penguin reckoned a drive in the country in his MGB with the top down would be a good way to cool off.'

'It wasn't an MGB, it was an Austin Healy Sprite,' interrupted George from the back seat.

'I'm sure it was an MGB. Anyway, he was tearing along a country road when suddenly the engine cut out. He rolled to a stop on the road shoulder and lifted the bonnet. Being a penguin, he didn't know much about cars, so he decided to call Roadside Assist. When the guy turned up, he winched the car onto the tow-truck and with the penguin up in the cab with him drove back to town where the local mechanic said he could have a look at it right away. The penguin went into the waiting room and noticed a vending machine in the corner. The weather was still hot so he bought an ice-cream. It started melting and was all over his face. At that moment the mechanic came in, "You've blown a seal," he said, to which the penguin spluttered, "No, it's only ice-cream".'

I laughed so hard I nearly ran off the road. George was cackling in the back. He told me he'd heard the story before but reckoned it was one of Mick's better ones.

Our laughter woke Keith and Harry. They were keen to know what was so funny.

'Mick's story about the penguin,' I said.

'Ah yeah, it's a ripper,' said Keith. 'Never get sick of good yarns like that.'

At four-thirty we pulled up outside the casino. Sure enough, Trevor, on his last shift, was standing at his post as proud as ever. He smiled broadly when he saw me and shook my hand for the first time in all the years I'd known him. I introduced him to the others, and after loading our bags onto a trolley he showed us through the foyer to reception.

I smiled at him. 'I haven't been away that long, Trevor. I think I can find my way around.'

'All part of the service, Tommy.'

I told him I would catch up with him later. In the meantime, we checked into our suites and arranged to meet in the bar within half an hour. It would give us time to get ourselves neat and tidy for the evening.

The guys were treating Trevor's farewell with respect. They looked a million dollars in coats and ties. I was impressed and I told them so.

'Anyone who can stand at a door for over thirty years greeting guests with a smile certainly deserves respect,' said George.

'Couldn't have said it better,' said Harry. 'My hips and knees would have packed it in years ago.'

'Have they taken up a collection for a present?' asked George, beckoning the barman.

I went over and spoke to Eldon who told me that one of Trevor's retirement wishes was to take his invalid wife on a world cruise. A cruise ship would be ideal for her due to her confinement to a wheelchair. She would be able to enjoy most onboard activities. I mentioned that my friends would like to contribute to his farewell gift. Eldon said he would be more than happy to add any donations we made to those coming from management and staff.

I told the guys what Eldon had said and they didn't hesitate in pulling wads of cash from their coat pockets, peeling off notes and stuffing them into my hands. I couldn't believe their generosity. When I questioned them, they were quick to remind me of our lucky lives and that we should never forget the guy who spends his working life in an often-thankless job, but maintains impeccable manners and loyalty.

I took the cash over to Eldon, who nearly fell over in shock. He couldn't believe four strangers would be so generous. I agreed with him and quietly told him they would probably win it back ten-fold before they left tomorrow. He smiled, gave me a wink, and placed the money in the safe. The casino had made all the arrangements for the cruise and any leftover money would be put on a credit card for Trevor to use at his leisure.

We had about an hour before the function started so I suggested we play blackjack. Getting full of booze beforehand and making fools of ourselves during the evening wouldn't be a good look. They agreed and, sure enough, before the hour was up the boys had recouped their donations. Not ten-fold – yet. It had been a long time since I'd seen a dealer deal so many blackjacks and top pairs to players and lousy threes, fours and sixes to herself. I think she was relieved when we left the table and headed to the function room where my big game had happened.

We were shown to our table. 'So, this is where it went down,' said Mick.

I received smiles and acknowledgements on the way and, even though they were insistent on me retelling the story, I said it would be better to wait until after the farewell. Mick sulked for a second until I flicked his cabbage ear and laughed. He was self-conscious about his misshapen ear. It was the result of another jockey's misguided whip in his early days on the track.

I guessed about a hundred people were seated at tables tucking into hot finger food, fine cakes and pastries. Bottles of Bollinger champagne were being popped and everyone was getting in the mood.

Senior management accompanied Trevor onto the stage. They were happy, making a fuss of their much loved 'first contact'. If visitors to the casino were greeted warmly their stay was off to a good start. Whoever replaced him certainly had big shoes to fill.

Several speeches were made and the CEO presented Trevor with his farewell gift. His wife was on the stage beside him and when he showed her what he'd been given they hugged and cried openly. It was a few minutes before Trevor could speak but when he did, he gave a most eloquent thank you speech. It didn't sound rehearsed. It came straight from his heart. I believed he had loved his job and was sad to be retiring. He finished by having a dig at me for increasing his workload over the last year, due to curious visitors who wanted to see for themselves the site of Australia's first casino robbery coupled with an amazing poker game. Management would have been pleased with the increased patronage.

Harry gave me an elbow to the ribs and said, 'Trust you to be in the limelight again.'

'I can't help being famous,' I said with a grin, pouring more champagne into the guys' glasses.

Over the next hour many guests left and Trevor made it over to our table. He shook hands with us and said he was humbled by our contributions. Apparently, Eldon had told him that management decided to match the donations given by staff and friends. They had been surprised when they saw how much had been given. It meant Trevor and his wife could enjoy a first-class cabin with all the perks. We had a good laugh, agreeing the casino could afford it and Trevor surely deserved it. I mentioned Barry was retiring tomorrow and had outlasted him but I couldn't keep a straight face.

'That bastard,' said Trevor. 'I'll fix him when I'm next in Sydney. I might put on a disguise and make a real fuss as I walk through the door. In fact, I might even exaggerate my limp to make him feel bad.'

'Why's that?' I asked.

'Well, when we were in the army together, he knocked me down with a truck. He was skylarking about and was pretending to run me down but he was useless behind the wheel and misjudged the distance between me and the front mud-guard. I was out of action for three months while my leg healed but it hadn't been set right so I was lumbered with a limp. It meant I was useless to the army so I was discharged. Barry felt so bad he quit as well. I didn't hold it against him because good mates don't let a ten-tonne truck come between them.'

Mick laughed. 'If the truth be known, it did.'

George chortled, 'Good one. I'd like to see Barry's face when you walk through the door. Tell me something, Trevor. Did the cops catch the blokes who robbed the place last year?'

'I'm good mates with a senior investigator and he told me they haven't got much to go on. Even their snitches are light on for information. They questioned all the staff and one guy appeared nervous when asked about the time lock data sheet for the main safe. They have a suspicion, and it's only a suspicion mind you, he might have given the thieves wrong times for when the safe could be opened, but that's not strong enough evidence to charge him with anything. He shut up like a clam and left the job not long after the first investigation and hasn't been seen since.'

'Do you think he might have been paid for his silence?' asked George.

'It wouldn't surprise me if it was more sinister than that.'

I looked at Trevor. 'The ringleader seemed like a reasonable bloke. Not the type to bump someone off to keep them quiet. Pay them off, maybe.'

'Like my cop mate said, these gangs are well organised and can't afford any loose ends. If something does go belly-up someone is held accountable.'

'Well, they certainly missed out on a much bigger haul because they couldn't access the safe,' I said. 'Enough to make even the most in-control bad guy get pissed off.'

'Even so,' said Trevor, 'ten million isn't bad for a night's work.'

'You're not wrong,' said George.

'Anyway, Trevor, we've held you up long enough. Your wife will think we've kidnapped you,' I said.

We wished him the best for his retirement and left him with his family and close friends and headed out to the poker room. As we walked through the reception area, Keith suggested we stay a couple of extra nights. It was a great place with a great atmosphere and they were in no real hurry to get back to Sydney. We looked at each other, agreed, and walked over to the counter where our request was quickly processed.

'I love doing things on the spur of the moment,' said Keith. 'Particularly because we get on so well and this place is a gold mine with the digging already done.'

'Eloquently put, old boy,' said Mick, pulling a wad of notes from his pocket as we approached the cashier's cage.

We were still playing at two-thirty when I decided to quit. Mick was on fire. He couldn't lose. He was making straight draws look common. He'd hole a pair of threes and make a full house. The only time he'd lose was with aces, kings or queens as hole cards. When you're having a night like that, you savour it, because there will be hundreds more where you go home early.

I remembered my prostate exam was on Monday afternoon but decided not to tell the guys. I'd make up an excuse to get back before three o'clock. I hit the sack and slept solidly until my phone alarm woke me from a dreamless sleep.

DAY 7 – SATURDAY

I hadn't felt this good first-up for ages. I showered and phoned the lads. We agreed to meet downstairs in the restaurant in half an hour.

Over breakfast Mick regaled us with his winning exploits and George apologised for getting the pit-boss agitated with his blackjack antics. I growled at him but it made no difference. He had made more in four hours than many casino workers would make in a year. He was, as usual, generous with his tips and was told he was welcome back anytime.

I suggested we drive down the coast. Sightseeing, swimming and lunch, before heading back to the casino.

'I reckon it will be a late lunch based on what you've got in mind, Tommy,' said Keith, as we walked back to our rooms.

'Well, we can leave the swim until after lunch if you like.'

'Fuck that,' said Mick. 'I'm not gettin' cramp for no bastard.'

He made me laugh. 'You and your old wives' tales. Let's play it by ear and see what happens. With this great weather it will still be hot later in the day.'

'Do you think we'll see any white pointers?' asked Mick, smiling.

'It's easy to tell you've been in Oz for a while. Where did you pick up that saying?'

'Barry at the Condor brought us up to speed on some Aussie lingo. We needed most of it explained to us though.'

'A few nudist beaches are dotted along the coast, so I've been told. Not that I've frequented any.'

George laughed. 'No doubt Barry would know the best spots.'

'With our lily-white bodies we'll be the odd ones out, so I would imagine keeping our togs on would be the best course of action,' said Harry.

I explained, 'In Australia, we call togs budgie-smugglers but we'll make an exception for Mick and call them eagle-smugglers.'

With roars of laughter and Mick once again grabbing his crotch, we went into our respective rooms and got ready for the drive.

'Don't forget your sunscreen,' I shouted, closing my door. Probably a waste of breath. They would most likely never have used it before.

The day progressed as I suspected it would; lunch was great and the guys were easy to look after. Keith tried his hand at surfing but gave up after repeated dunkings. The instructor said he had talent although it was well hidden.

'A back-handed compliment if ever I heard one,' said Keith.

We packed up our beach gear and arrived back at the casino around seven. I told the guys the Sydney Comedy Club was appearing in the showroom at ten and wondered if they would be interested. They said they loved Aussie humour; the ruder the better. We decided to have a meal at the new Chinese restaurant then head over to the show.

We were seated near the stage, which may have been a mistake. As the show progressed the guys were getting cheeky with the comedians. Audience participation was part of some professionals' routines and after another of Keith's comments, the compere, Stan, asked Keith his name.

Stan asked him to come up on stage which Keith was more than happy to do. He threw a few questions at Keith, asking him what he did for a living and so on, then turned to the audience with one arm around Keith's shoulder.

'I've got a mate called Keith. Like you, he's also a smart arse.'

The crowd roared and Keith lapped up the attention.

'A little birdie tells me you like computers, Keith. Would I be right?'

Keith nodded.

'Well, folks, the same little birdie told me a story about Keith. When he was learning about computers, he went to a few training classes. In one particular class the tutor was showing them how to format a Word document, something we're all familiar with. She said, "Go to File; Open; Go to Page Format." She paused while she spoke to her assistant, then said, "Keith, go to reception." Keith looked baffled as he searched the screen, then asked her, "Where's that?" She replied, "Downstairs near the main entrance. There's a phone call for you".'

The crowd erupted. Even Keith cracked up. He shook hands with Stan, gesturing to the audience, indicating that these comedians know how to handle hecklers.

The laughs continued as other comedians took to the stage and it was well after midnight when we left the showroom. We were pretty jiggered after a big day, so we said goodnight and agreed to meet for breakfast around nine.

DAY 8 – SUNDAY

We spent the morning relaxing by the pool. George sneaked away for a while to the blackjack tables and after lunch I had nine holes of golf with Keith. It was a par-35 course and we hired clubs, which made for interesting golf. I managed a four-over-par thirty-nine that included an eagle two on a short par-4. Keith was a tad out of practise but I could see his talent. He was pleased with his forty-one. My lucky eagle might have rattled him.

When we caught up with Harry later in the day, he told us he'd spoken to the resident band drummer and asked if he could practise for his upcoming gigs. After Wayne had listened to him play, he asked him if he wanted to do a few shows at the casino after his gigs. Wayne was heading over to New Zealand where the casino's parent company had opened a new casino and needed him to set up the band. Harry was flattered but told Wayne of his plans with the rest of us. Wayne reckoned he'd do exactly the same thing if he were in Harry's shoes.

We didn't see Mick during the day and missed him at dinner. I turned in early, telling the guys I wouldn't mind heading back to Sydney fairly early as I had a few things to do.

George laughed. 'I ain't walkin' back, so I guess we don't have much choice.'

DAY 9 – MONDAY

The guys were happy to be chauffeured home, although Mick wasn't his usual chirpy self. He told us he'd met a casino waitress who was flattered by his charm and attention. Her name was Angela Kingston but she went by Angie. She told Mick only her mother had called her Angela and only when she was mad at her. They had got talking while she was on her break and, from what she had told him, it appeared the seven-year relationship she was in was not a happy one.

Her partner, Danny, drank often and became violent when he didn't get his own way. Mick had told her that sort of behaviour was unacceptable and she was a fool to stay in a relationship that obviously had no future. She told him Danny was a fly-in fly-out miner over in Western Australia. He worked three weeks straight, then had a week off. The company paid his air fares to and from the mine. He would be arriving home on Monday. Angie was dreading his return. He would be all lovey-dovey, then hit the grog. The rough treatment would start.

Mick had told her he wanted to get to know her better and she had agreed to pick him up on Sunday morning so they could spend the day together.

'We had a great day,' said Mick. 'We drove down the coast and had lunch and chatted like old friends. She loved my Pommy accent. I explained what we were doing and she asked if she could hide in my suitcase.'

'We had lots of laughs,' he continued. 'I asked her if she had any friends in Sydney and she told me she had a girlfriend who worked for a big casino. I suggested she see if she could get her a job. She could be rid of this bastard and make a fresh start.'

'You certainly know how to pick 'em, Mick,' said George. We loaded up the car, paid our bill, and said our goodbyes.

'We swapped phone numbers and she promised to let me know what she decided to do. I told her I'd pay for a month's accommodation at the Condor if she needed somewhere to stay while she got organised.'

I nosed the car towards the highway. 'You've obviously got strong feelings for this lady,' I said.

Without another word Mick selected a Rolling Stones CD, pushed the play button, and sank into his seat. We realised he didn't want to talk for a while. He'd met a nice lady and was hoping for a good outcome.

It was interesting none of these guys had been married. Sure, there had been some long and short relationships but now I had the feeling they might be considering life further down the track. In fact, my own situation was playing on my mind more often than not lately.

Before I dropped the guys off at the Condor, I reminded them that next Monday we'd be flying to Hong Kong. George decided he would visit some homeless shelters during the week and see if he could help out, even if it was only with advice based on his success in London. Harry said he had a busy week with his gigs, and Mick and Keith were hiring a car and heading inland to some country towns where they hoped to score some colonial antiques. I mentioned Beechworth, which was not far over the border in Victoria, if they had time. I knew Keith was a sweet tooth. The Beechworth Sweet Co would satisfy his cravings. They thanked me for looking after them so well and I told them I'd be in touch at the end of the week, when we'd get together and fine-tune our trip. Harry reminded me he was playing at the Star Club on Wednesday night and he'd save a spot for George and me in the VIP area.

George's face lit up. 'Like they say, it's not what you know but who you know.'

I headed back to the Marina. When I saw Lucky, I told him not to clean my car until the next day as I had to head out again. I felt tired, so I took the lift all the way to my apartment. I opened the door just as Sylvia was about to open it from the inside. I scared the daylights out of her. She wasn't expecting me to be there. She had finished cleaning the apartment and was about to push her trolley into the lift area.

'You nearly give me heart attack,' she said.

'I'm not that scary, am I?'

'No, Tommy, I had my mind on other things. I wasn't concentrating.'

'That'll change soon when you start your studies. Your brain will be working overtime.'

'I can't wait.'

She threw her arms around my ample waist and gave me a big hug. I felt warmth in her hug, confirming the plans I'd proposed for her were well founded.

'I don't know how to thank you, Tommy, for all things you doing for me.'

'Don't thank me yet. Wait until you are studying late into the night and think what I've got you into. I can imagine you cursing me, wishing you were only doing your day job.'

'That will never happen. This my only chance to get my dream.'

Sylvia activated the service lift and waved as the doors closed.

I had an hour to kill before my appointment. I unpacked my bag and made a start on the cryptic crossword. I was starving but had to fast before my cholesterol test.

My doctor appeared concerned after he examined me. My prostate was slightly enlarged and, as a precaution, he recommended a blood test. The pathology nurse took additional samples to check my cholesterol, blood sugar, vitamin D, and liver and kidney function. She got me to pee in a jar. I asked whether she had anything bigger. She told me to be thankful I wasn't a woman. Fair comment. The doctor was concerned about my weight but when I told him what I was about to embark on, he was pleased.

'That's come at a good time, Tommy,' he said. 'I was worried about your sedate lifestyle. The blood tests will take two days, so give me a call and I'll discuss the results with you.'

'Thanks, Doctor.' I walked out of his surgery feeling apprehensive about the results.

I drove home. Strangely enough I didn't have much of an appetite. I hadn't eaten since last night. I should have been starving. I made a couple of egg and bacon sandwiches and a coffee for dinner, then plonked myself down in a recliner and, after a couple of hours of online poker and the early movie, called it a day.

DAY 10 – TUESDAY

I'd left a note for Lucky on the windscreen for him to let me know when he would be cleaning my car. I needed to talk to him about looking after it while I was away.

I was finishing breakfast when my phone rang.

'Good morning, Tommy,' said Lucky cheerily.

It never ceased to amaze me how someone could always be on a high. I must remember to ask him what his secret is.

'G'day, Lucky. I'll be down in ten minutes to have a chat about my car.'

'No worries, boss. I'll be waiting.'

I washed up my breakfast things and grabbed the note I'd made the previous night so I wouldn't forget anything I needed him to do.

When I arrived in the basement, he had my car in the wash bay.

'I've never seen it this dirty,' he said.

'Well. Over the past four days I took it off the beaten track, so it might pay to check underneath for any residue dirt as well. There might also be the odd snake curled up if you look carefully.'

'Fuck that, Tommy, you'd better be joking. I hate the bastards. If I get bitten, it'll be on your head.'

'No, it'll be on your arm, I reckon. I'm only jokin', mate. I hate 'em too. There's more chance of me picking the winners of today's races than you finding a snake under my car. He's probably curled up in your rag collection in the corner by now.'

'Cut it out, Tommy, I haven't got time for your fooling around.'

'Okay. I know I can rely on you to look after the car while I'm away. I've spoken to your boss and he's happy for you to give it a run once a week and arrange for a service which is due next month. Apart from that, everything should be okay. There's only one restriction, Lucky. No going to the races with your endless supply of chicks.'

'You know I wouldn't do that, I'm Mr Reliable,' he said, with a smile that showed off his perfect set of teeth. He uncurled his hose and started to wash off the layer of dirt.

I knew the next time I saw the car it would look as if it had been driven from the showroom. Lucky had a small workshop/office attached to the wash bay where he kept, among other things, a supply of touch-up paint so any stone chips could be fixed before they got any worse. He catered for the permanent residents in the complex. He had a job for life. He was damn good at it and everyone appreciated him.

I walked out into the bright sunlight, pulled my sunglasses down off my cap, and headed to the café for an espresso. I sat in an aluminium chair that barely contained my ample butt, rang the casino, and found out a cash game was happening in the afternoon. That would suit me fine as I could get a long power walk in before lunch and be ready for a session at the table. Only a handful of customers were sitting at the outdoor tables, giving me a good view of people walking by. Most of them were tourists who wandered along the waterfront admiring the yachts and throwing miserly tips into the buskers' hats. My chair was in the shade and the café was the sort of place I could spend hours people-watching.

I finished my coffee and as I got up to leave, I noticed a lady – she would have been in her early sixties, I guess – starting to slowly cross the road against the walk sign. I yelled out to her but she couldn't hear me over the traffic noise. I looked to my right and realised she wouldn't make it across the one-way street before the cars were onto her. I ran, shouting, and managed to grab her around the waist and drag her to the footpath. She screamed in fright as we fell to the ground, the passing cars missing us by centimetres. I looked down and noticed she had hit her head. She looked stunned but was conscious. A young woman rushed over and said she was a nurse. After asking if I was okay, she tended to the lady. She told me to phone for an ambulance. I sat with my back against a pole and, with my hands shaking, managed to give the dispatch officer our location.

It was only minutes before an ambulance arrived, together with two police cars. I stood, lost my balance, and fell into a shrub bordering the footpath. A police officer came over and asked if I was alright.

'If I hadn't gotten up, I would have been okay. I guess the fall to the pavement shocked me.'

'We'll get the paramedics to have a look at you after the lady is treated.'

The lady was talking to them and the police but she needed stitches to her head. They told her they would take her to emergency and get her checked over thoroughly. Once she was on the stretcher and being wheeled to the ambulance, she beckoned me over, but I wasn't too sure I'd make it. The police officer told her I was stunned so she mouthed a thank you and disappeared into the ambulance. I found out she was being taken to the Mercy General. I'd call in and see her later in the day. Her name, according to the police officer, was Rhonda Leibenstein. She was a widow with a daughter.

A police officer had interviewed witnesses for his report and after the paramedics gave me the all-clear, he came over to me to get my version of events. He told me she would have been heading to the mortuary if I hadn't intervened. He told me he would be recommending me for a bravery award in his report. I told him it was no big deal. I was happy she was okay and more than happy I would be okay for my poker game.

'That's the spirit, son.' He smiled as he got back into his patrol car and drove off.

I walked back over to the café where the barista was waiting with a complimentary coffee. I didn't say no. I was the subject of much back slapping and praise from those who had watched the incident. They were in awe that my big frame was able to move so fast. I told them that was why I wasn't injured to any great extent. I had too much padding.

I decided my power walk would have to wait for another day, although I was running out of days before we headed off on our trip. I wanted to continue my get-fit regime but I needed to be careful. I had much at stake over the next six months.

I walked back to my apartment and had a cool shower. I now had time for a rest before the game. I put my alarm on and lay down on the bed. I felt myself dozing off and when I woke after two hours I didn't feel as bad as I had expected. Maybe my body hadn't reacted to the shock … yet.

My well-stocked fridge yielded freshly cut ham-off-the-bone and tasty cheese. I knocked up a toasted sandwich and washed it down with a protein shake. As I grabbed a fistful of cash from my safe, I looked at the grog behind the bar. Hopefully with my get-fit program it wouldn't go to waste. Part of me didn't believe my health kick would be permanent, so I gave myself a mental slap around the head and decided I would go and visit Rhonda before my poker game.

Lucky had finished my car. He was a class act. Showroom result.

When I arrived at the hospital Rhonda was sitting up in bed reading a fashion magazine. They had checked for any brain injuries and put twelve stitches in her forehead, then moved her to a recovery area on the third floor. Her expensive-looking hair style was slightly askew as the nurses had pinned the front away from the bandage. Her blonde hair complemented the dark eyes that lit up her attractive face as I came towards her. I think she was pleased to get a visitor. She had phoned her daughter who would be coming to collect her in about an hour. I asked her if she wanted me to run her home to save her daughter the trip, but she said she had been enough trouble for one day. She told me she had been distracted thinking about her daughter's upcoming trip and had simply stepped off the kerb without thinking about the traffic. I didn't think it was appropriate to pry into the family goings-on, so we had a good laugh and didn't reflect too much on what might have been. Assured she was okay, I gave her a hug and she thanked me again. I walked to the elevator and pressed the ground-floor button. I would probably never see her again but laughed to myself, thinking about her retelling the story to her friends; telling them how a fat bastard rammed her into the footpath as she was crossing the bloody road.

*

I arrived at the casino and asked Clive to park my car this time. I didn't give him a reason. I walked to the poker tables and found an eight-seater with seven guys getting ready to play. I recognised most of them but sat next to a neatly dressed bloke I hadn't seen before. I introduced myself and he told me his name was Brian Watkins. He looked older than me, possibly closer to fifty than forty-five. How the fuck would I know? How can anyone know how old someone is? It's not like we're trees and you can count the rings. He was solidly built with thick, greying hair and weather-beaten good looks, coupled with sky-blue eyes. None of these attributes went unnoticed by the female patrons. He was oblivious to the attention as he appeared focused on the game.

The blinds were $100 and $200. A few guys were aggressive early but I was able to read them well, so I knew when a bluff was coming.

After about two hours of winning and losing I was starting to get a slight headache, which I put down to the fall. I didn't think I would be playing much longer. I knew from experience any distractions would have a negative impact on my game.

I was dealt the Q♥ and Q♣ hole cards in the small blind. Three guys to the left of the big blind folded. The other three called. I decided to raise pre-flop and Brian and one other called. With three of us left in the game and $4000 in the pot the flop appeared: Q♦, 4♠ and 10♣. They gave me a set of queens. It was my bet and I pushed $8000 over the line – double the pot. The other two called. This made me think they weren't holding a set or they would have raised my bet. Perhaps they were flat calling – calling a bet when a raise was expected. The turn card was the 7♥ which didn't improve my hand. I felt I had the strongest hand so I bet $30,000, which Brian called. The other guy folded. The pot was now $88,000. The river card was the 4♦ which gave me a full house. It was my bet. I looked at Brian and he was rock solid. I wondered what he had because he hadn't raised. Had he been waiting for the river card?

I decided to place a big bet – double the pot – and watch his reaction. I was about to move my chips across the line when he moved his head close to mine.

'Don't bet. Trust me. I've got you beat. I don't want to take any more of your money.'

I was dumbstruck. I had never experienced that sort of behaviour at a poker table. I eyeballed him. I couldn't get a read. I spent a couple of minutes thinking. The dealer warned me he would put me on the clock. The other players had no idea what Brian had said and were becoming restless. I looked back at him and checked. He also checked. I turned over my full house and looked at his upturned quad fours.

'What the hell was that about?' the guy next to Brian said.

The dealer collected the cards and pushed the pot towards Brian. He signalled for a chip tray and indicated he was finished playing. He asked me if I was done and, if so, would I mind meeting him at the bar for a drink. I picked up my remaining chips, excused myself from the table and followed him over.

'I'm intrigued,' I said, as he ordered a couple of beers.

'Well, let me explain myself,' he said. 'I was having a coffee this morning at a café down at the marina when I saw a bloke save a lady's life by dragging her out of harm's way. That guy was you. I'd know you anywhere. You tend to stand out in a crowd.'

'Well, yes, it was me; but that doesn't explain your behaviour at the table.'

'Let me finish. What you did this morning was heroic. For someone to put their own life at risk to save another is, well … I'm lost for words. I had quad fours and I knew you couldn't have had anything more than a full house, so I couldn't bring myself to take, at a minimum, another eighty-eight thousand off you. In fact, I want to give you your turn-bet back as my way of saying thank you for what you did today. This money is pocket money for me. I gamble for the mindfulness and half of what I win, less my travelling expenses, I usually give to charity.'

'I don't think I'm the hero here,' I said. 'What you're doing is amazing. I've been playing poker for years and you're the first person to tell me something like that.'

'I haven't told many people my story. I'm a fairly private person and enjoy my anonymity.'

I bought us another drink. 'Are you a local?' I asked.

He seemed to relax.

'No, I'm from Tasmania. It's where I can live quietly in the country and travel around without anyone taking much notice of me. I farm trees, alpacas and angora goats. I employ a farm manager who looks after the place and knows more about all three than I could possibly learn. He treats the animals as if they were pets and they respond accordingly. We've got shelters for them that homeless people would think palatial. When they're shorn, they become susceptible to temperature change, so we keep them snug in what my mate calls the Alpaca Apartments. Alpacas and goats get on well so they are happy sharing the accommodation. Alpaca wool and angora mohair is prized worldwide and as Tasmania has a great reputation for everything clean and green, my wool brings a premium price. It's ridiculous. As for the trees, there's about a hundred and fifty hectares of fast-growing plantation timber that gets harvested through a rotation method and saves the old-growth forests. You know the mantra, "trees are the lungs of the planet". Tassie has untouched forests up there with the best in the world, and the Greens put pressure on the Government to make sure they remain that way. Having plantation timber provides a good source of building materials, as well as woodchips for export.'

He was beaming with pride as he was talking; however, his mood changed to sadness when he told me about his wife.

'Liz died five years ago after a torrid battle with cancer and as we never had kids, I've got no ties. I miss her terribly, which is why I play poker. It takes my mind off the dark times. Before the farm we had a share in a small gold mine on private land on the west coast. When she died, I lost interest and sold my share. Between you and me, I'd never seen so much money. We'd made a huge fortune on the gold we'd dug out and although I knew a brilliant ore vein was waiting to be worked, my heart wasn't in it. It's extremely hard work and I'm not getting any younger.'

'Wow. What a story. I'm sorry about your wife. I wish I had more time to talk but I'm not feeling a hundred per cent right now. I think I'd better be getting home and get some sleep. I'm heading to Hong Kong on Monday, then onto Vegas for a golfing and poker tournament, and I'll be away for about six months. Would you mind giving me your number and I'll call you when I get back? It would be great to catch up with you again. I haven't been to Tassie for years.'

'I'd like that,' said Brian. He handed me a beer coaster with his name and number written with a gold-plated pen. I wondered whether the gold had come from his mine. I put the coaster in my pocket and got up to leave. I told him I didn't want my money back.

'I'd be more than happy for you to give it to charity if you're so inclined. I'm like you, Brian; I've got more money than I can spend so if someone else can benefit from it, that suits me.'

'It's been a real pleasure to meet you, Tommy. I hope our paths cross again sometime.'

We shook hands and I noted how strong his grip was. I could feel his callouses; the result of hard work on picks and shovels. Slightly taller than me and with his build, he'd be the bloke you'd want watching your back.

*

I made a mental note to tell Brian about my great-great-great grandfather Wojciech Dabrowski, who'd migrated from Poland in 1854 to seek his fortune on the Victorian goldfields. The lure of gold brought people from around the world, particularly China and Poland. They were hardworking risk-takers.

It wasn't until I'd moved to Sydney and started uni that a girl I was dating, who was Polish, happened to mention my name to her parents. They were local Polish Club members and were friends with a fellow member who had the same surname as mine. It didn't surprise me as Dabrowski is not an uncommon Polish name. He was cluey when it came to family history and, together, we tracked my paternal family to Wojciech's arrival in Australia.

*

I headed out to where Clive was waiting to bring my car around. I drove back to the Marina and took the lift all the way. I threw my clothes onto the chair and crawled into bed. I was stuffed.

DAY 11 – WEDNESDAY

I woke later than usual and felt as if the bloody bus had hit me again. I felt like crap. I got out of bed and noticed my right side from under my arm to my hip was a lovely shade of purple. I needed a spa. While it was filling, I had toast and coffee. An hour later I got out, looking like a 110 kg prune. I could move better so I considered an easy walk around the marina might loosen me up.

I remembered my blood test results would be available today. I'd call my doctor after lunch.

My phone rang as I was getting dressed.

'Have you seen today's paper, Tommy?' asked George.

'Not yet. It should be outside my door. I was going to read it over coffee down at the marina.'

'Spoiler alert, old chap. Your ugly mug is all over the front page. The headline is one word in about five-hundred font: HERO. Page three is covered in photos taken by witnesses to your big day out.'

'Ah geez, I didn't think it would amount to this. I'm not in the mood for any publicity. Are you doing anything at the moment?'

'No. What do you have in mind?'

'I'll come and pick you up and we'll go for a drive and get a coffee. I've got a hell of a lot of things to tell you.'

'I'll tell Barry you're on your way and you can pull up outside. I'll wait in the lobby.'

I picked up my paper on the way out and took the lift to the basement. Lucky wasn't there, for which I was thankful. I wouldn't have been able to get rid of him. I started the car and took a quick look at the paper. They were making me out to be something of a superman. One witness reported that I flew through the air and scooped the old lady up and landed her on her feet.

Fancy a reputable newspaper printing shit like that. I supposed it sold papers. I had to prepare myself for a heap of stirring from the guys. It was a good thing I was heading to Hong Kong in a few days. I could only hope the story remained local.

I arrived at the Condor and Barry saluted me through the window.

'Enough of that, you stirrer,' I mouthed.

George appeared through the revolving door. He hopped in and we drove off towards the northern beaches. I knew of good cafés along the way where I would be inconspicuous. With my sunnies and baseball cap I should get away with it.

George wouldn't shut up. He read the whole article out loud and kept calling me all sorts of complimentary names.

'Calm down, George. Anyone would have done the same thing. I happened to be in the right place at the right time. Anyway, I've got a better story to tell you over coffee.'

I drove for about half an hour against the traffic heading into the city. I had no idea what these people went through each day. I had never had to clock-on in an office or factory by a certain time. From my late teens it was all about golf; practise, play, travel and study. I fitted in poker when it suited me. I marvelled at my charmed life.

We arrived at Avalon and I pulled into a shopping plaza. It was a relief to get out of the car. George hadn't stopped bumping his gums the whole time. He couldn't wait for me to tell him my other news.

George ordered a hot breakfast and I settled for a coffee and double choc muffin; I needed pampering. We sat outside in the beautiful morning sun. I could keep my sunnies and cap on. Nobody gave us a second look.

'Come on, Tommy, out with it.' He acted like a kid sometimes, not a fifty-year-old philanthropist and brilliant blackjack player.

He didn't take his eyes off me while he ate his breakfast. He took in every word I uttered but couldn't help himself.

'Are you sure you're not bullshitting me, Tommy?'

'Why would I lie about something like that?'

'Because it sounds so fanciful.'

'Well, I've told you exactly what happened. Whether you believe it or not is up to you. All I know is I'm heading to Tassie as soon as I get back from Vegas.'

'Bloody hell, if you need company I'd be more than happy to come with you. I've never been there although I've heard their seafood is the best in

Australia. You know how much I love oysters. Give me a dozen and a couple of pints of Guinness and I'm set for the night.'

'Old wives' tale, George.'

He laughed. 'Well, I ain't fussy.'

'Let's see how you're situated when we're done in Vegas. You might be hankering to get home. It would be quicker to fly to London than back to Sydney.'

'I can run my businesses with my phone and computer,' said George, 'so I'd be more than happy to keep travelling around. It's been a while since I've had a good break. Technology is starting to take over so my job gets easier by the year.'

'Before I forget,' I said, 'Harry's got VIP tickets for us tonight at the Star Club if you're interested.'

'Well, I've got a meeting after lunch with a politician who's the chairman of the Sydney Homeless Improvement Taskforce. It should be over before five, so if you are able to come over to the Condor we could have dinner and head over to the club.'

'Do you realise the acronym for the taskforce is SHIT?' I said with a chuckle.

'It's not something to make fun of, Tommy. Homelessness is a serious issue, not only here but around the world. If we can make a dent in the number of homeless people with our programs then we're doing something right.'

'I'm sorry, mate. I know it's a serious issue but Aussie humour is what it is, and it's what makes this a great place to live. Surely the person who came up with the name must have known the acronym and had a laugh.'

'Yeah, you're probably right. It is funny when you think about it. I'll mention it at the meeting and see what sort of reaction I get.'

'Would you mind dropping me off before the bridge?' he asked.

'Why, are you thinking of jumping off?'

'No, I want to walk across and collect my thoughts before the meeting. I also need to send some e-mails to my staff in London. They'll be asleep when I send them but they'll see them in the morning.'

'Let's have another coffee, then we'll head back,' I said. 'I think I need a rest for a few hours. I was going to the golf course for some practise but yesterday's fall has made rotating difficult. I might have a spa then come over to the Condor.'

We enjoyed another hour at the café and drove back. George got out near the bridge and waved as I manoeuvred the car back into heavy traffic.

I parked in my spot. Thankfully, Lucky wasn't about again. I rushed to the lift. As soon as I got inside my apartment, I decided to ring the doctor. I was nervous but the sooner I knew the results the sooner I could do something about them if they were suspect.

The receptionist asked me if I could possibly come to the surgery. Dr Palmer wanted to discuss my results in person.

I headed down to my car and scored a hat-trick; no Lucky. It took me half an hour to get to the surgery. When I arrived, Dr Palmer was waiting for me.

'Right,' he said, without any small talk. 'I'm concerned about your prostate. Your PSA is four-point-eight, which is slightly above the recommended level of four-point-oh. Because we don't have any prior readings it's difficult to know whether your levels have been creeping up slowly over the years or if there is some other reason. In a healthy man of your age I would expect to see a reading below one.

'I would suggest you come back when you return from the States and we'll repeat the tests. We may have more of an idea of what's going on. With regard to your other tests, your cholesterol is seven-point-three with your LDL at five-point-seven. This is way too high but with the anticipated change to your lifestyle it should fall quickly. Once again, we'll do more tests when you return. Your glucose is six-point-five, and your vitamin D level is thirty-nine. You need to lower your sugar intake and get more sun. I want to see those readings around five-point-oh and eighty, respectively. Your liver and kidney function tests showed readings slightly above the acceptable range but not worryingly so. More golf, less poker, and a better diet should make all the difference.'

'Things could be better, I guess,' I replied, stating the bloody obvious.

'The sooner you get serious about your fitness the better,' he said. 'Do you have any questions?'

I showed him my bruises, and after telling him what I'd done he gave me a thorough check over. He admitted my padding did protect me in the fall but told me not to use that as an excuse not to shed at least twenty kilos. He told me my target weight should be 90 kg, based on my height of 190 cm.

He made me sit still for about five minutes. He took my blood pressure and with a reading of 123/74 I left his surgery on a fairly positive note.

I hoped to be feeling much better the next day. Maybe my power walk would happen.

With four days to go, I needed to get in touch with Jack and check for any changes to our plans. I looked at my watch. It would be around ten at night in LA.

'Tommy, old mate, what's happening?'

He sounded upbeat. He was more excited about the upcoming events than me. He was a glass-half-full kind of guy.

'Any last-minute details we needed to discuss?'

'I've e-mailed you the tickets so you can print them. Show them to check-in when you get to the airport,' he said. 'When you get to Hong Kong, please thank Benny for me, he made my life easy by arranging the accommodation. Your plane leaves at ten o'clock Monday morning so you should be in Hong Kong around six, barring any delays. Once you've settled into your hotel, you'll be ready for a big night I reckon, based on what you've told me about the other guys.'

'Yeah, they're pretty excited. You'd think it was their first time away from home. Anyway, if everything goes to plan, we'll arrive in Honkers safely and I'll give you a call when we've settled in.'

'No worries, Tommy. Have a good trip and take care. Oh, one more thing; I've knocked up a fitness program that I'll e-mail to you. Print it out. It'll give you some light reading on the plane.'

'Thanks for nothing, Jack.' As I hung up, I could hear him chuckling.

I selected some good clothes from my walk-in wardrobe and looked around me. What a shame to have to replace all this clothing with smaller sizes when I came back. I supposed it would be a small price to pay if I ended up a healthier specimen.

I had a shower, got dressed and drove to the Condor. Barry got a valet to park my car and, after a quick chat to him, I went inside where George was enjoying a beer watching a soccer match on cable TV. He stood and gave me a mock bow.

'Hail, almighty saviour of human life,' he said. I perched myself on a bar stool and elbowed him in the ribs.

'You're a funny guy. Yes, I'll have a double bourbon since you're buying. In fact, I might forgo my health kick and let you shout all night, including dinner.'

'Oops,' said George. 'I might have overdone it on the compliments.'

'I know sarcasm when I hear it.'

We had a good laugh and I asked him how he got on with the Minister for SHIT. He thumped me on the arm and filled me in on his meeting. Apparently, he was well received and they were impressed with his London programs. They asked him to put together a proposal that the taskforce would consider before presenting a case to the government.

'I'm impressed, George. There's no doubt about you. When you set your mind to something, you don't muck about.'

'Well, the homeless can't get off the streets with people talking about it. As I've said before, we need action, and if I can help out, I will.'

'You're a good man, George. How about another bourbon?'

We took our drinks into the dining room where we were treated to an excellent meal. I looked at my watch. As we weren't due to catch Harry's performance for a couple of hours, I suggested we hit the casino.

I sat to George's left at the blackjack table. I knew he would be counting the cards which gave me a better chance of winning a few bucks. The strategy worked and after an hour and a half I suggested to George we head off. He looked at me and realised what I meant. His fifteen-grand haul for such a short time was most impressive. We were able to fly under the radar this time.

We walked out into another beautiful summer night. 'You can't help yourself with that bloody card counting, can you?' I said.

George gave me a boyish grin and fanned his wad of $100 notes in my face.

We parked the car a block away from the Star Club. When we got to the door the security guys waved us through. Apparently, Harry had given them our descriptions: one cricket wicket and one beach ball. We were shown through to the VIP area where we were privy to an uninterrupted view of the stage and an endless supply of drinks and nibbles.

The band name on the bass drum was 'Crystal Curtain'. The guys walked onto the stage to a lively reception from the huge crowd. Harry was wearing a black fedora, probably to hide his receding hairline and help him blend in with the younger band members. What it didn't do was hide the permanent furrow in his brow. It gave him the look of constant worry even when he laughed, which was often. Nevertheless, he looked the part and when the music started, he proved he was a bloody good drummer. I don't have a musical bone in my body but I know good drumming when I hear it.

They played for the best part of an hour then took a break. Harry came up to our vantage point and knocked back three beers as if they were water.

'That's bloody hard work,' he said. 'I didn't realise I was so out of condition.'

'Well, it didn't show, mate,' I said. 'You were fantastic. You certainly haven't lost your knack.'

'Hey, Harry,' said George, 'have you been reading the papers?'

'No, why?'

I kicked George under the table. 'Ouch. What'd you do that for?'

'Time and place, mate.'

'What's going on?' asked Harry.

'Never mind, I'll fill you in later. Nothing to worry about,' I said.

'Okay. I'd better be getting back. Can I meet you guys at the Hollow Tree after the gig? We should be done in an hour. Two bands are on after us which means I finish early. Good for an old bloke like me.'

'No worries, Harry,' I said. 'We'll see you there.'

George and I stayed for about half an hour, then decided to take a leisurely stroll to the restaurant. When Harry turned up, and after George filled him in on my exploits, we enjoyed a great supper. I described my poker game with Brian and the offer to visit Tasmania when I returned from Vegas.

'Sounds like an interesting chap,' said Harry, finishing off a second piece of chocolate Jaffa cake.

He was full of compliments for the food and did a drum roll on the table with two knives, finishing with a 'tadaaaa'. After another coffee I drove them back to the Condor. When I got back to my apartment I was stuffed. It had been another big day. After I got into bed, I lay there wondering what the last week would have been like if I hadn't run into these four guys and Brian.

DAY 12 – THURSDAY

I woke around seven. I'd had a good sleep. I ran my hand over my side and could feel only a slight tenderness. I hoped the bruising had subsided in equal proportions.

I decided if I could rotate my body without too much hurt, I'd go for a long walk to loosen up, then head to the golf course and play as many holes as I could manage.

I had a shower and checked myself out in the mirror while doing some practise golf swings. Everything looked okay, apart from the bruising which was a nasty plum colour.

I had cereal and toast and took my coffee into the lounge room. After doing the cryptic crossword, I made a start on the neuf-neuf, as George called it. When I thought about it, it made sense. I spent about half an hour on it. Suitably bored, I looked out the window at a beautiful morning and decided fresh air was calling me. I'd wear shorts and short sleeves to soak up some vitamin D, as per the doctor's orders.

I wasn't sure what George and Harry were doing for the day but I knew they would be able to amuse themselves without me around. I had a feeling Harry would be taking his camera, hoping for some good photo opportunities. I'd sent a message to Mick to see how they were getting on. They were having a great time and had found several colonial antique writing boxes that would be sent back to London by the dealer. Keith had found the lolly shop at Beechworth and was cursing me because he had chipped a tooth on the irresistible boiled lollies.

I walked down the stairs and entered the lobby where I saw Sylvia polishing the brass railings that ran from the lobby to the bar area. She looked at me with a wide smile. 'You the most famous man I know, Tommy.'

'Thanks, Sylvia, but don't make too much fuss. I want a quiet day today without any attention.'

'Okay, Tommy. Take care and I see you later.'

I stepped out onto the footpath and headed for the walking path that meandered around the marina and malls and would give me a good hour of exercise. It felt good out in the sun. When I got back to my apartment, I was confident I could handle eighteen holes.

Lucky wasn't about so I loaded my clubs into the boot and drove to the golf club. The pro shop was empty when I walked in but I could hear noises coming from the ride-on cart shed out the back. I shouted out Maurice's name and he came in, looking dishevelled. I was about to ask him what was happening when a young lady walked out behind him. She was adjusting her hair in a ponytail and looked flushed.

I knew exactly what they'd been up to. To avoid embarrassing them I quickly asked if I could get a practise round in. Maurice's face reflected his appreciation of my discretion and said the course was fairly quiet so I'd have no trouble. I paid for my game and a bucket of practise balls, thanked him, and without another word walked out to the practise area. I would have loved to have been a fly on the wall after I left the shop.

I felt tight around my middle so my rotation wasn't the best but I still managed to hit the practise balls satisfactorily down the fairway. If anything, I was more controlled in my swing. Hopefully not too many wayward shots on the narrower fairways.

It was eleven-thirty when I teed off on the first hole, and by one o'clock I was back at the clubhouse, having played nine holes. I could have been two-under par if I hadn't hit my drive into the water on the dog-leg third hole. I'd gotten too smart, thinking I could drive over the row of trees. Instead, my shot ricocheted off a branch and into the bay. I ended up with a double bogey spoiling an otherwise good round.

I decided nine holes was enough, packed my gear into the car and drove home. Feeling pretty good, I decided to make lunch and try to solve the neuf-neuf I'd made a start on in the morning. It was a tough one. I had a habit of only writing the number in after I was certain it was right. I was using the logic method as against the trial-and-error method.

Trial-and-error solvers need pencils and erasers, whereas logic solvers work with pens.

This particular puzzle was rated as *extreme*, and they weren't wrong. I managed to get another half a dozen or so numbers out when my intercom chimed. It was Lionel from reception telling me he had a lady at the desk who wished to see me.

'Her name is Sarah Leibenstein,' he said. 'She's the daughter of the lady whose life you saved the other day.'

'I can come down or she's more than welcome to come up.'

I heard muffled voices, then Lionel said she would be happy to come up. I told him to show her to the lift. Then, wondering what she wanted, I quickly threw on some decent clothes.

My doorbell rang. When I opened the door, I was looking at the most attractive woman I'd seen. She was lightly tanned, slim but with a physique that told me she was serious about exercise. She was taller than average; the top of her head came up to my nose. Her thick, shoulder-length dark hair complemented dark eyes that sparkled when she smiled. Her generous mouth revealed perfect teeth. She confidently pushed out her hand and introduced herself. A moment passed before I shook it and invited her in. Her voice sent a shiver up my spine. This was one sexy lady.

I offered her a chair near the window and asked if she would like a drink. She settled for a sparkling mineral water. I placed two glasses on the table between us. The dress she was wearing rode up a little, revealing strong, shapely legs.

'I suppose you're wondering why I'm here.'

I smiled. 'It has crossed my mind.'

She relaxed and told me what her mother had relayed to her regarding the accident.

'I felt I needed to come and thank you in person. My mother is my only family as my dad, Reuben, died ten years ago.'

'You're not married?' I asked, possibly sounding overly optimistic.

'No. I've been too busy with my work to consider marriage. My job requires a lot of travel so it would be unfair to expect a family to be without a wife and mother for extended periods.'

'Your mother mentioned you were preparing for a trip. What sort of work do you do, if you don't mind me asking?'

'I'm a professional escort. I accompany high profile businessmen on overseas trips and act as their partner. A lot of these guys attend lavish functions and, in some countries, it's expected the man has someone with him. It doesn't necessarily have to be a wife. I earn $1000 a day and if there's a requirement to offer additional services, it's an extra $2000 a night. Because I work for myself, I can pick and choose my clients. I do have regulars who are terrific guys and treat me with respect. I was forty-one in January and realised

I'm coming to the end of my career, as younger women are more in demand. But while I can still make heaps of money doing minimal work, I'm happy.'

'I realise you didn't come here to tell me your business, but I'm intrigued. Have you been doing this all your adult life?'

'I have a degree in psychology that I got in my early twenties but I quickly became disillusioned with the academic world, and when this opportunity came up through a friend, I thought, what the hell? Sounds like fun. My knowledge of human behaviour puts me in a good position.'

'Would you like a coffee?' I asked, using the offer to break the conversation. I felt I shouldn't ask any more questions for the moment for fear of turning the conversation into an interrogation.

'Mmm, black, no sugar thanks.'

When I returned, I told her she hadn't needed to go out of her way to thank me but I was glad she did. It was nice to have a visitor like her instead of the four rogues. When I told her about them, she said it was good to have mates. In her line of work, when she went home it was usually alone. That was why she enjoyed the company and travel experiences with her clients.

'If you hadn't seen Mum crossing the road when you did, she probably wouldn't be here now and that would have broken my heart. I love coming to see her when I get home from my trips, even though I call her when I can. She's always keen to hear where I've been but never judges what I do.'

'Like I said to one of my mates, I happened to be in the right place at the right time. I'm sure anyone else would have done the same thing.'

'I'm not so sure,' she said. 'My experiences with people show so many are non-observant; or, if they do see something they could help with, they don't want to get involved. When Mum told me about you and that you got along so well, I felt I had to come and see you. I hope I'm not being too forward, but I find courage, kindness and humility highly attractive qualities. Plus, even though you're a big guy, you're easy on the eye.' She smiled, a hint of colour appearing on her cheeks.

I was feeling a little awkward and avoided eye contact for a moment. It had been a long time since I had attracted this sort of attention from the fairer sex; particularly one so attractive.

It was a good time to tell her what I did and she was interested when I mentioned Sylvia and her ambitions that I wanted to help with. She interrupted me often when I told her about the casino heist last year, keen for more details. She confessed the psychologist side of her was assessing the way I dealt with the drama. I told her I was seeing a psychologist who was convinced I was still having a few problems. The trip I was about to undertake would be good for my mental health, she reckoned. Sarah agreed.

I was trying to think of more to say but her presence was scrambling my brain. I had a beautiful woman sitting in my lounge room drinking my coffee and telling me I was easy on the eye. What she did for a living should be none of my business, and if there was a chance of seeing her again maybe I shouldn't let it bother me.

'I'm sorry if I've embarrassed you with my forwardness,' she said, sensing my unease, 'but, as I said, I only came over to personally thank you for what you did for Mum. The conversation did get away from us, I must admit. So many guys aren't comfortable with what I do; but it is what it is. I'm providing a service and getting paid well to do it. I could retire tomorrow and live comfortably off my investments but I enjoy what I do, so why not keep doing it?'

I couldn't argue with her logic but, from the look on her face, I could tell she knew I wasn't comfortable with her lifestyle.

'Look, I guess I'd better go,' she said, finishing her coffee. 'Can I leave you my card, please? When you get back from Vegas, if you want to catch up, give me a call. It would be nice to hear about your trip over dinner, perhaps.'

'I'd like to. Do you reckon your mum would join us?'

She gave me a huge smile as we walked to the door, where she gave me a kiss that felt like more than one of gratitude. She thanked me again for my heroics and said goodbye. I waited with her while the lift arrived and waved as the doors closed.

I walked back inside, took the glasses and mugs to the kitchen, gazed out the window, and wondered what the future had in store. It had been an interesting couple of hours. I had a feeling it would be a while before I got her out of my mind. She was smart, funny, caring and attractive, but …

The day drifted away and it was well into the evening when I realised I hadn't had dinner. For some reason I didn't have much of an appetite, so I made a bacon sandwich and washed it down with a coffee. The rugby was on TV and when it finished, I decided to have an early night.

DAY 13 – FRIDAY

Three days left before we flew out. I went through my checklist, then got out of bed. I felt pretty good. My bruising was apparent but not uncomfortable. A good day to head to the gym and the pool.

My phone rang as I was sitting down to breakfast. It was Mick. He and Keith were heading back from their antiques shopping tour and wanted to catch up for lunch and get up to date with our arrangements. We agreed to meet at Jacques. I told Mick I would ring the others and see if they were free.

I was the first at the restaurant and it was nice to relax after a good workout. The lads arrived, making their usual racket. Keith handed me a small package after they sat.

'A token of our appreciation,' he said. I opened the box to reveal a collection of poker chips. 'I picked them up at a place called Wangaratta, not far over the border in Victoria. Hope you enjoy adding them to your display.'

'Wow. These must have cost a pretty penny. You guys didn't have to do this. I've had a ball hanging around with you and I'm sure there's more fun to come. Thanks heaps.'

'It's the least we can do for the city's resident superhero,' said Mick, jumping up and taking on the stance of Superman.

'Sit down, you silly bugger,' I said, pulling him back into his chair. 'I've had enough stirring from George to make up for all of you.'

'Changing the subject, how did your other gigs go, Harry?' I asked, hoping to deflect any further attention from me. I was tempted to tell them about Sarah but thought better of it at this stage.

'Not too bad,' he said, 'although I think I took another ten years off my eardrums. The music is so much louder these days.'

We ordered our lunch and I asked the guys if they were happy for me to hang onto the tickets I'd printed off my computer.

'The less we have to do, the better,' said George, filling our glasses with champagne. 'We know we're in good hands.'

'What time do we fly out on Monday?' asked Mick. 'Not too early, I hope.'

'Ten's not too early is it, old man?' I teased, smiling at the others. 'I'll have a maxi taxi pick you up at eight-thirty with me already collected. We need to be at the airport by nine-fifteen.'

'Suits me,' said Mick. 'I'm looking forward to this trip, although I could have handled Oz for a while longer.'

'You can always fly back from Vegas with me if you don't have anything better to do.'

'Food for thought,' he said. He looked at the others and could tell they were digesting our conversation.

I could see Mick was thinking about Angie. I had a feeling he might not even make it to LA.

'Never say never,' said Keith, tucking into the grilled flounder.

'I've never tasted fish this good before,' said Harry, drowning the poor thing with enough tartare sauce for all of us.

We had another great time together and, as we weren't in a hurry to be anywhere, we sipped the classy bubbly late into the afternoon.

As we left Jacques, I asked the guys if they were happy filling in the next couple of days without me. I felt I needed time on my own. Try as I might, I couldn't get Sarah out of my mind. She was the type of person I could see myself spending the rest of my life with. My current thoughts conflicted so much with those I had yesterday. I was confused and felt if I didn't do something about it before I went away it would bug me the whole time and possibly spoil the adventure.

'We're grown men, Tommy; we can amuse ourselves until Monday,' said Mick, as they waited for a taxi.

'You look preoccupied,' said George. 'Is there anything bothering you?'

'All good, fellas. I'll give you a call on Sunday night to make sure everything's okay for Monday.'

'No worries,' said Keith as they piled into the cab.

I waved and headed back to my apartment where I put the poker chips from the guys in my desk drawer. I would sort them out later.

I sat near the floor-to-ceiling windows with a coffee and spent the next hour mulling over the events of yesterday. It's only a job, I kept telling myself. If I was lucky enough to get into a relationship with this lady perhaps it would be the two of us travelling the world. Gee, I could teach her to play golf and poker; we could live the high life. Steady on, I told myself. She was probably being polite asking about getting in touch after my Vegas trip. But the kiss as she left was electrifying, come to think of it. Maybe I was out of practise. Fat guys like me don't normally get too much attention from the opposite sex.

I decided to sleep on it and, if I still felt the same way when I woke up, I would ring Sarah in the morning. Not sure how I would start the conversation, though. I didn't want to stuff things up and ruin any chance of something happening.

I wasn't hungry so I played *PokerStars* online for a while. I was getting ready for bed when my phone rang. The number wasn't in the phone memory and for a brief moment I contemplated not answering it.

'Hello.'

'Hi, Tommy, its Sarah. Sorry to ring you so late, and I hope I'm not being too forward, but would you like to have lunch tomorrow? I want to discuss a couple of things with you.'

I almost dropped the phone. I couldn't believe what I was hearing.

'Are you still there?'

'Yes. I wasn't expecting a call this late, let alone from you. Yeah, I'd like to have lunch. Do you know Jacques restaurant, near my apartment?'

'I'll find it. Is one o'clock okay?'

'Suits me fine. Nothing wrong with your mum, is there?'

'No, she's recovering well. It's us I want to talk about. See you tomorrow. Goodnight.'

I said goodnight and hung up. I flopped down on the bed in disbelief. I couldn't see myself getting much sleep.

DAY 14 – SATURDAY

I woke as confused as when I went to sleep. It had been a restless night so I felt an easy morning until lunch time would be the best course of action. I was glad I'd asked the guys to do their own thing until Monday. It would certainly mean I didn't have to explain anything to them for a while yet.

I phoned Jacques and made a reservation in case the place happened to be booked out. I decided to put a load of washing on. I wandered into the billiard room, removed the table cover, set up the snooker balls and played a frame with my imaginary friend. We've played many times over the years, using different cues to make it authentic. The bastard beat me without much trouble. I'd get my revenge next time.

I checked out my wardrobe and got out a nice shirt and jacket to go with my jeans. I could take my jacket off in the restaurant and still look presentable.

As the time drew near, I took the lift to reception and walked out into another great day. It wasn't too hot so I didn't look out of place with my jacket on. I arrived as Sarah was pulling up.

She got out of her black BMW convertible completely unaware she had parked across two spaces. Nevertheless, the sight of her took my breath away. She was wearing a floral dress short enough to be sexy but long enough to be classy and a pair of high heels she was obviously accustomed to wearing. A slender gold chain around her neck and a slim wallet in her hand completed her outfit. I noticed she wasn't carrying her mobile phone. She was the real deal. I was punching way above my weight, but I didn't care.

She smiled and kissed me on the cheek as we hugged. She smelt fantastic. We walked inside and were shown to my usual table.

I felt relaxed in her company and set about organising drinks before the menus arrived.

'You look nice, Tommy,' she said, sipping her champagne. 'You must tell me about your name. I'm intrigued.'

'And you look stunning. I hope you don't think I'm strange, staring at you; but I must honestly say I've never had the opportunity to sit across from someone as attractive as you.'

She blushed.

'I'm sure you get more than your fair share of compliments in your line of work. Is it too early to blame the champers?'

She laughed and eased back in her chair while I reluctantly told her about my Polish heritage. Once again, she was attentive and genuinely interested; another great quality. Where does it end, I thought, as the waiter brought us menus.

'Have you been to Poland?' she asked, looking at me over the top of her menu.

'No. One day I might visit. I might get a chance to trace more of my family history.' For what it's worth, I thought.

We decided to share a seafood basket with a Greek salad, agreeing it would go well with the Bollinger.

'Do you mind if I tell you now why I wanted to meet you today, or would you prefer to wait until we've finished our meal?'

'I'm intrigued. I must confess I had restless sleep thinking about your call and wondering what you wanted to talk about.'

'When I came over on Thursday, I was getting organised to go on a trip with the CEO of Aquarius Australia. You've probably heard of them. They've got huge bore-water purification plants throughout central Australia. The CSIRO has verified the water they produce as 99.9% pure. I've been told the reason they don't commit to 100% is so that if an impurity is found they can't be held liable for false certification. They are so successful that construction is starting on similar plants in North Africa, Saudi Arabia and parts of South America. The CEO considers the projects so important he is personally heading the delegation to those countries. He's a single guy but, as I told you before, some countries have funny customs about unaccompanied businessmen doing business.

'We were supposed to fly out on Tuesday to Egypt but the CEO had an accident while water skiing yesterday. He hit a submerged log and broke his leg. It could have been much worse. Anyway, he's not going now but his deputy and wife are going instead, so my services are not required.' She stopped to take a mouthful of fish.

'That's a shame,' I said. 'I guess you were looking forward to the trip.'

'Well I was, and yet I wasn't; which brings me to the main reason for catching up with you. To be honest, I've thought of nothing else since I left you on Thursday. I'm not sure what it is but I feel so comfortable being around you and I'm disappointed you're going away on Monday. I know you're going with your friends and this might be highly presumptuous on my part – but would you mind if I tagged along?'

I nearly swallowed my fork. I took a swig of my champagne and, after what felt like an eternity, I told her I was extremely flattered by her request.

'I've done a few spur-of-the-moment things in my life but never something like this,' I said. 'We've only known each other a couple of days, yet I feel the same way about you. Do you realise I expect to be away for about six months?'

'You did mention it before. If things don't work out, I'll fly home. No harm done. Do you think the guys would mind me coming along? I wouldn't want to cramp your style.'

I smiled at her. 'My style is borderline crud, so I don't think that will be a problem, and the guys are so easy to get on with.'

She had a sexy laugh. My mind was racing. What could go wrong? And if it did, we were mature adults; we could work it out.

I was sure she could see my brain ticking over.

'How about you sleep on it. I don't have to fly out with you on Monday. I could catch up with you once you're in Hong Kong or even LA.'

I was looking into her eyes and knew what I wanted to say but thought better of it. She was right. Sleep on it and see how things are in the morning.

We spent the next hour chatting easily and shared the famous peanut butter bombe with chocolate for dessert. She told me she lived in Bondi, not far from her family home. When her father died her mother refused to sell the big house they had lived in for many years. Her mother still played a big part in the Jewish community that was part of Bondi's culture, even though she wasn't Jewish. Her marriage to Reuben had brought her into the Jewish community and she'd embraced it. Sarah was emotional while sharing her parents' story with me. Reuben, she told me, had been a tailor since he'd left school – which explained her excellent taste in clothes. People who weren't satisfied with off-the-rack clothing sought out his clothing range right up until his death. His reputation in the eastern suburbs of Sydney was well known and he was very well regarded.

As we finished dessert, I took hold of her hand and held it gently while we toasted her family memories and the future.

She reluctantly said she'd better be going as she was spending time with her mother who, although putting on a brave face, was still feeling the effects of her accident.

'She couldn't be in better hands,' I said, pulling her chair out.

I paid the bill and we walked out into a balmy afternoon.

'You're a sweet man,' she whispered in my ear as I opened her car door. Her lips traced their way around to my mouth where she lingered with a tantalising kiss.

I waited as she drove off. The growl of the engine and noise from her tyres caused pedestrians to pause and stare. I heard the car long after it had disappeared around the corner. A young couple pushing a pram walked past me. The man turned to me. 'She's a bloody lead-foot, mate. You should tell her to slow down.' I shrugged.

'Nobody's perfect.'

I walked back to the Marina and caught Lionel as he was going off duty.

'Are you working tomorrow?'

'No, mate. I've got some leave due so I guess I won't see you for a while. I hope you have a great trip. We'll miss your smiling face around here but the way time flies, you'll be home in no time. I've left notes for the staff regarding the management of your apartment while you're away.'

'Thanks, Lionel. I appreciate the dedication from everyone. It makes everything so much easier when I know I can rely on you to look after my place. I'll certainly miss everyone too. I'll catch up with Sylvia and Lucky tomorrow. I have a few things I need to talk to them about.'

We shook hands and I took the lift all the way. I grabbed a mineral water and once again sat by the window and reflected on the day.

I couldn't believe what had happened. I was nervous but excited about what might happen from the next day on.

I was dying to ring Sarah but we'd agreed to wait until the next day. I dozed off in the chair knowing I had a big fat smile on my dial.

My door chime woke me. I'd been asleep for about an hour. It was Sylvia.

I offered her a coffee but she said she was starting her shift soon and had to get back downstairs. She had a sad look on her face and told me she was not looking forward to not seeing me around. She wasn't working tomorrow so she didn't want to miss saying goodbye today.

I went over to my desk and handed her a present I'd picked during the week.

'We'll be able to keep in touch with this,' I said, as she tore at the wrapping paper, opening the box in excitement.

'Tommy, this for me?'

'There's no-one else in the room.'

She looked at the laptop computer with wonderment and switched it on. It took a few moments for the desktop to appear. It showed the short cuts to the applications I'd thought she would need for her studies. With e-mail included she would be able to write to me and keep me up to date with her progress.

Sylvia rang her supervisor and told her she would be a little late starting her shift. When she told her where she was, her boss said to take as much time as she needed as things were quiet at the moment.

Sylvia and I spent the next half hour going through her e-mail set up. When she told me she had been getting computer training from Lionel, I was happy and satisfied she would have no trouble with her computer work.

'You'd better get to work,' I said, and placed the computer and attachments in the leather carry bag. Unbeknown to her I also slipped an envelope into the carry bag. Hopefully she wouldn't find it until I'd flown out. It contained $5000 and was addressed to her and her family. They would spend it wisely. If Sylvia wanted to go crook at me, she'd have to do it by e-mail. It could be interesting.

As I handed her the bag, I could see tears running down her face.

'I hope they're tears of happiness because life's too short for sad stuff. Like Lionel said to me earlier, I'll be home again in no time. Your studies will take your mind off me pretty quickly.'

'You always on my mind,' she said, giving me a huge hug.

'I reckon when I get back, you'll be saying, "You *are* always on my mind".'

'I am looking forward to my English classes,' she said, deliberately emphasising each word while digging me in the ribs after each one.

'When you send me e-mails, I'll be able to see your progress anyway.'

I walked her to the door and watched as she proudly hung the carry strap over her shoulder and gave me a huge smile as she got into the lift.

There's a success story about to happen, I thought, heading back into my apartment. I didn't think for a moment she would achieve anything less.

I picked up my phone and rang the basement garage. No answer. Perhaps Lucky was off for the weekend. I sat at my desk and wrote him a note. It was to confirm what we had spoken about earlier regarding the welfare of my car. In the last paragraph I told him if he needed to contact me, he could get Sylvia to send me an e-mail. I thanked him for how well he looked after the car and as I sealed the envelope, I slipped $200 in with the note with a postscript telling him to make sure he wagered it on winners.

I wrote his name on the envelope, took the lift to the basement, and slid it under his office door.

I had a thousand and one things going on in my brain so I considered a walk in the late afternoon sun would be a good tonic to settle me down. Despite all the thoughts spinning around in my head, I had never felt this happy. Could it be love? People talk about love blooming quickly but I thought it only happened in books and movies. Maybe not.

I'd lost track of how long I'd walked but when I got back to my apartment, I realised I'd been away for the best part of two hours. No wonder I felt buggered as I stripped off and hopped in the shower. My bruising was fading and I felt confident I might be able to give my clubs a workout tomorrow.

I rang Keith and asked if he wanted a game tomorrow. He was more than happy to suggest he would whip my arse. I suggested we play for $500 per hole. He couldn't agree quickly enough, so I arranged to pick him up from the Condor at eleven.

I knocked up a toasted ham and cheese sandwich and finished it off with a coffee and port. I watched TV for a couple of hours, then got ready for bed. I felt like a kid going to bed on Christmas Eve, excited about what the next day might have in store. I closed my eyes, hoping to dream sensible dreams; Sarah dreams.

I woke not long after sunrise. I got up, opened the curtains, grabbed the paper from outside my door and made a large coffee that I took back to bed. The warming sun shone directly onto the bed. I felt great. I hadn't dreamed but it didn't matter. It still felt like Christmas morning. I wondered what it would be like to have Sarah open her eyes beside me and give me a smile that would melt snow. Perhaps I was still asleep and dreaming? Nope. I was wide awake.

I wanted to ring her right away, but realised a phone call before seven o'clock would be unfair. I spent the next hour reading the paper and completing the cryptic crossword. I was surprised, considering my excited state of mind.

I had a shower and a healthy breakfast and after washing up stood at the window and dialled Sarah's number.

'Hi, handsome,' she said after the second ring.

Her voice was chirpy and smiling which was all it took to scramble the words I was going to say.

I regrouped. 'Are you always this chipper this early in the morning?'

'More so this morning now I'm talking to you.'

We spent ages chatting about anything and everything, except her driving. It didn't seem the right time to bring it up.

We discussed the pros and cons of her coming to Hong Kong. I could see no cons. Her only worry was the guys might be put out with her joining the group. I reiterated what I'd said the day before about how easygoing they were. To put her mind at rest, I told her I was playing golf with Keith later this morning and would tell him what had been happening, and then let her know how he felt. I was sure after he spoke with the others they would be more than happy for her to join us.

I told her I would ring her tonight and we'd take it from there.

She wished me a good game, and I in turn told her to take care and give her mother my best wishes. I nearly felt like phoning Keith and cancelling the golf then going and spending the day with Sarah. I almost couldn't bear not having her around.

This was madness. Surely it wasn't normal to feel this way about someone with whom, only a few days ago, I didn't think there was any future.

I got to the Condor on time and Keith was talking to Barry at the entrance. I got out and asked Barry if he'd heard from Trevor. He told me Trevor and his wife were sailing out tomorrow and couldn't be more excited.

'Great news. Is that something you'd like to do?'

'No, I'm a landlubber. Give me a fast car and a blonde half my age and, mate, I'm a happy man.'

'Something's gotta kill ya.'

We laughed, then I told him I'd see him in the morning when I picked the others up for the airport.

'Hopefully they'll be waiting for you – but knowing these laid-back guys, we'll probably have to wake them up.' He gave us a big grin as I drove off.

Keith and I indulged in small talk on the way to the golf course, which I was pleased about. Telling him about Sarah would be better left until we were walking along the fairways where I could concentrate on the conversation and not the traffic.

The course was quiet for a Sunday morning, which worked in our favour. We didn't have to rush. Maurice was reserved when we came into the pro shop, but after we chatted for a while he loosened up. He realised I couldn't have cared less about his back-room liaisons the previous Thursday. If he'd had a cheer squad in the back room it wouldn't have bothered me. Good luck to him.

We grabbed a couple of bottles of water from the fridge, a large bucket of practise balls, paid our fees and headed out to the practise area.

We performed our usual warm-up routines and hit off the first tee. It was a par-4 downhill, reachable with a good drive. I was a couple of metres short and Keith landed a metre from the pin. An eagle putt earned him an early $500. I reminded him we had seventeen holes to play.

We squared the second. After our drives on the long par-5 third, I thought it was a good time to tell him about Sarah. He listened in silence, stopping at one stage to take everything in.

'George was right on Friday when he noticed you were quiet at lunch,' he said.

'Yeah, you can understand why. I was still trying to get my head around it. You've no idea what effect this woman has had on me. I've never met anyone like her and the lunch we had on Saturday; if it had been my last meal I couldn't have cared less.'

'Wow, I've seen you in relationships over the years but nothing like this. And it's only been four bloody days,' he said, preparing for his second shot from off the fairway in the first cut of rough.

His shot landed in the green-side bunker. It gave me the advantage. I was in the middle of the fairway about twenty metres further on. Using my fairway wood, I came up short. I only needed a bump and run to get me close to the pin where one putt gave me a birdie and a win.

We had a spell on the fourth tee and I answered many of Keith's questions about my plans with Sarah. When I told him of her concerns regarding joining us on our travels, he couldn't have been more supportive.

'We've known each other for a long time, albeit through the poker scene; but also long enough to know something like this wouldn't have the slightest effect on our relationships. The more the bloody merrier, I reckon. It wouldn't do you any harm to think about settling down either, particularly if she's everything you say she is.'

'You're a good mate, Keith, I value your opinion.'

We played the next six holes in companionable silence, apart from the occasional ribbing when a fluky putt dropped or a bunker shot went in the hole. I was having a great day.

We grabbed a sandwich and coffee after the ninth hole and checked our cards. Keith had won four holes and I three, with two squared. I was only five hundred down.

'Okay, Keith, I'm going to start playing now. I've loosened up and now it's no more Mr Nice Guy.'

Keith laughed and offered me the honour on the tenth tee. I smacked a huge drive down the middle which he matched. We squared the hole with birdies. This was turning into a battle of the titans. Keith's game was amazing seeing as he'd been out of action longer than me. He was a natural.

We continued on our way. When we teed up on the sixteenth Keith was two up with three to play. A par-5, 4 and 3 to finish. If I was to get my game into shape for Vegas, I needed to try much harder. It was difficult with so much going on in my brain but it was good stuff and I didn't want to let it go.

I won the next two holes with birdies. That made us square with the last to play. It was a tough par-3; rated the second hardest on the course. The flag was at the back of a split-level green. Club selection was crucial and I could see Keith was having trouble selecting the right one. Being a draw player, he needed to account for the slight breeze coming from left to right, otherwise he could miss to the right.

I had the honour and landed on the lower level. I had an uphill putt of about ten metres. I'd be happy with two putts from there to give me a par.

Keith selected a six iron and, after a few practise swings, fired off a beautiful draw shot that took one bounce and slammed into the cup.

He looked at me with a stupid grin on his face. 'Too easy. Want another round? Call me Tiger if you like.'

I slapped him on the back. 'Tiger made his first hole-in-one when he was eight years old. But what the hell, today it couldn't have happened to a nicer bloke.'

We walked up the fairway. I picked my ball up and got Keith's out of the hole.

'You know what, Tommy? That's my first hole-in-one and I'm glad it was you who saw it.'

'I reckon you ought to have it mounted.'

'Like the six you've got in your billiard room,' he said.

'Well, I didn't want to mention it; but seeing as you have, I can give you the guy's name who made the timber settings. Blackwood, old boy; your winnings should almost cover the cost.'

We got back to the pro shop where Maurice told us he saw Keith's magic shot. He told Keith he would get his name written into the special hole-in-one leather-bound register the club had been maintaining for thirty-five years.

'We give each hole a separate page,' said Maurice. 'Naturally the par-5s don't get a mention and only one par-4 has been aced – the first. That page has thirteen entries, the last being the previous club professional, four years ago.'

'Now, as for the par-3s,' he continued, 'the eighteenth, which you aced today, has been aced twice. Your ace today makes it three and puts you in a small but special group. Pro golfers from the States who were playing in the Australian Open and used this course for practise during their stay scored the others. That was seven years ago. You certainly have bragging rights, Keith.'

I laughed. 'Well he does like to tell a story. You'll have to tell Maurice about sunken treasure.'

'Time and place, Tommy.'

Maurice neatly wrote the details of Keith's exploits on the third line of the page that carried an ornate *18th – Par Three* at the top.

Keith signed the register and held it open while Maurice took a photo. A framed copy would no doubt take pride of place on Keith's mantelpiece along with the mounted ball.

We went into the clubhouse where about a dozen guys were having a drink. They clapped and cheered as we walked in. Keith soaked up the attention and shouted drinks for the next hour.

I had to almost drag him out to the car, reminding him we would be on a plane in seventeen hours, and during that time we had a lot to do, including a good sleep.

Our conversation during the trip back to the Condor alternated between our golf game, Sarah and the trip.

Keith called ahead and found out the guys were there and suggested we have dinner together so I could tell them about Sarah firsthand. I told Keith I'd drop him off, head back to my place, have a quick shower then come back.

I didn't tell him I was also going to ring Sarah.

I drove into the basement and gave my clubs a quick clean before packing them into a travel bag. I left them at the front of my storage room so I could grab them easily in the morning.

I took the lift to my apartment and jumped into the shower. I noticed my bruising had faded even more. I felt good after the game, physically and mentally. Life was good.

I dried off, dressed quickly and rang Sarah's number. Once again it didn't ring long. The sound of her voice made my heart skip a beat. It was as smooth as a great grandfather port.

I told her what my plans were and she made me promise to ring her when I got back from dinner, no matter how late.

By the time I got back to the Condor, Keith had told the others about Sarah and they couldn't have been happier for me.

'Bloody hell, Tommy,' said Mick, 'things can't get much better for you, can they?'

'I don't think they can, mate. Like I told Keith, I had reservations about her but she quickly put them out of my mind. I can't wait for you guys to meet her. You won't mind if she catches up with us in Honkers? She's looking after her mother while she recovers, then she can join us.'

We made our way to the restaurant. 'Not at all,' said George. 'If she's half as good as you say she is, we'll be in pretty classy company. Mick will have to behave himself unless he smuggles Angie in his suitcase.'

'Don't worry, I have thought about it, chaps,' said Mick. 'Unfortunately, she hasn't got a passport, and she needs to sort out this prick she's living with. If I had my way, she'd be on the plane with us tomorrow.'

Mick took a few moments to describe Angie. She was about his height, with a slim build, but five years younger he reckoned. She was a natural blonde, pretty, with green eyes he could look into all day. She had a good sense of humour but because of her relationship with Danny it didn't often see the light of day.

'You're the right person to bring it out of the darkness,' said Keith thoughtfully.

Harry laughed. 'You might be the same size as her, Mick, but from what you tell us she's better looking.'

George looked at Keith and Harry. 'If we're not going to die grumpy old men, we'd better pull our fingers out and find ourselves three easygoing, fun-loving, card-playing ladies.'

We laughed. 'Shouldn't be a problem,' said Keith, using his reflection in the laminated menu to smooth his hair.

'You never know what you might come across in your travels,' said Mick as we ordered our meals.

George filled our glasses with expensive red wine. 'If it's meant to be, so be it,' he said.

'Dinner's on me, boys,' said Keith. 'I took a lazy five hundred off Tommy today and I reckon we can put a dent in it tonight.'

We enjoyed a great meal and great company. After confirming the pick-up arrangements for tomorrow morning, I headed back to my place. The others were going to hit the casino for a few hours and then get packed, ready for the morning.

I felt so good I took the lift to the seventh floor, then climbed the stairs to my apartment. The lactic acid was ripping through my legs but it wasn't as bad as previous efforts. Perhaps thinking of Sarah took my mind off it.

I got changed, grabbed a coffee and called her.

'What's up? I didn't expect to hear from you until much later.'

'I had a great dinner with the guys but they were hitting the casino, and I decided I'd come home and call you.'

'How considerate of you. Another quality I admire. Look, before we talk any further, would you mind if I came over for a while? It's not too late for me if it's not too late for you.'

'It could never be too late. It will, after all, be a while until I see you again.'

'Great. I'll see you in half an hour.'

Almost to the minute, my intercom buzzed. Sarah was at reception. I told them to send her up. A couple of minutes later I opened my door to a confident knock. The sight of her once again took my breath away. She was wearing what looked like the latest in sportswear; designer shorts, T-shirt and joggers. Her hair was in a ponytail and she was wearing minimal make-up. How can anyone look this great, I thought as I hugged her.

It was sublime to have her look up at me with her sparkling eyes and generous lips parted in a gorgeous smile.

We kissed on the threshold and walked in.

'What a great surprise,' I said as we sat on the two-seater lounge.

Sarah crossed her tanned legs, relaxed and immediately looked as if she belonged.

'Drink?'

'Not yet, I want to sit here with you. You make me feel safe and warm.'

She snuggled into my ampleness. 'I'm more than happy to dehydrate,' I said quietly.

We sat close for a few minutes. She turned and faced me.

'I don't want to be here alone when you jet off tomorrow. This might sound weird seeing as we've known each other less than a week, but I want to come with you. I've talked things over with Mum and she reckons life's too short to put things off. She's tough and can cope. She has friends she can call on if necessary. If you would like me to come with you, I have contacts at Qantas who can get me a seat on your flight at short notice if one's available.'

I took her face in my hands and kissed her.

'Ready for that drink? It's not too late for a champers, is it?'

I glanced at her from the kitchen and noticed she was wiping her eyes with a tissue.

'Is everything alright?'

'Couldn't be better, big guy. I'll make the call.'

Her contact at Qantas told her it wasn't going to be a full flight, so arranged for a business class seat. We enjoyed the champagne and talked for a couple of hours. I related what I'd told the guys and what their responses were.

'I can't wait to meet these blokes. You are so lucky to have supportive friends.'

'And they're clowns as well. I reckon we're going to get along fine. Like I said the other day,' I continued, 'if things don't work out, we won't die wondering. But if I've got any say in it, I won't be letting you out of my sight. I still have to pinch myself knowing I'm about to get involved with someone like you.'

'Relax, Tommy, I feel exactly the same.'

She put her glass down and swung her legs over the end of the lounge so her head was in my lap. I slipped my arms under her shoulders, lifted her level to my face and kissed her tenderly. She snuggled into me and for a moment it felt as if she'd gone to sleep.

'Don't get too comfortable with my size,' I said, after drawing breath. 'My doctor has ordered me to lose twenty kilos real quick so that my other problems like high cholesterol and blood sugar levels can come right. Plus, I have to get into shape for the golf tournament in Vegas. I've got about six months to do it.'

'I'd be more than happy to help out'.

'I'll take you up on your offer. I've got an exercise program to follow but I might need motivating.'

'Don't worry. I think I can get you motivated.'

She put her arms around my neck and kissed me. I didn't want the moment to end. She eventually pulled herself away and glanced at her watch.

'I'd better get going. I've got to pack. How exciting.'

She had more bubbles than the champers.

'I'll get a cab to the airport and meet you in the Qantas lounge, okay?' she said.

'Are you sure? I could have the maxi taxi pick you up.'

She laughed. 'No, you'll have your hands full with the others. Give me a call before you leave.'

'I can't believe we're doing this,' I said, hugging her. 'I don't think I'm going to get much sleep.'

'We can sleep on the plane but I reckon sleep will be the furthest thing from our minds.'

She gave me a cheeky grin, kissed me again as the lift opened, and was gone.

I locked my door and spent the next half hour packing my suitcase. I was travelling light as I intended to get my excess weight off as soon as possible. And besides, I needed new clothes. Hong Kong tailors were among the best and with Sarah alongside I knew I would be outfitted well.

I rang the guys and told them Sarah would be flying with us in the morning. They couldn't have been happier. I realised I didn't have time to contact the hotel in Hong Kong to let them know there would be an extra person. I'd sort it out when we got there.

I put my alarm on for six o'clock, then crawled into bed hoping to get a few hours of sleep. The following day was going to be the start of something special. I couldn't wait.

DAY 16 – MONDAY

I was awake well before the alarm went off. I looked at the empty pillow next to mine and pictured Sarah sleeping peacefully; one day, maybe.

I had a leisurely shower. I reckoned my bruising would be near enough to gone by mid-week. I certainly wasn't feeling any discomfort. I got stuck into a big breakfast. While I was eating, I wrote Sylvia a note that I left on the breakfast bar telling her to help herself to anything from the fridge. I asked her if she wouldn't mind cleaning anything else out and switching it off. No point leaving a fridge running for six months with nothing in it.

I had cancelled my paper but had Saturday's crossword to finish. With time on my hands there was a good chance I could knock it over before the maxi taxi arrived. I had made a concerted effort to stop rushing to be places. Trying to stay calm would help my blood pressure and no doubt a few other bad things going on inside me. I had started deep breathing exercises and found them soothing; plus, they would help with getting my lung capacity back to where it should be. I'd remembered from my pro golf days that shallow breathing caused the body to retain too much carbon dioxide, which didn't help the blood supply. Blood rich in oxygen was like fresh oil in a car. With all the parts properly lubricated, the performance is better.

I finished my coffee, washed up, packed the rest of my suitcase – including my laptop – and carried it to the door. I double-checked my coat pockets to make sure I had my passport, air tickets, phone and wallet.

It was ten to eight so I decided to head down to reception. I'd have time to get my golf clubs from the basement and be ready for the taxi by eight.

The taxi was right on time and we headed to the Condor. The driver pulled up outside and Barry came to my window.

'I haven't seen the guys yet,' he said, with a concerned look on his face. 'I expected them to be chomping at the bit to get on the plane.'

'So did I. I'll go into reception and rouse them up.'

The lady phoned George and, after a brief conversation, hung up and told me they would be down in ten minutes. I walked out to the taxi and relayed the message. The driver wasn't worried. The meter was running and he was chatting to Barry.

I considered ringing Sarah. As I pulled my phone out, I looked through the revolving door and saw the lift open and the guys walk towards me. Sheepish grins on four faces.

'Sorry, Tommy,' said George. 'We had a pretty big night and have only had a couple of hours' sleep. I'll tell you about it on the plane.'

'No harm done, fellas. If the traffic's not too heavy we should be okay. Sarah is going to meet us there. No doubt she'll be relaxing in the Qantas lounge with a coffee.'

'We can't wait to meet her,' said Mick.

They settled their accounts at reception while the driver and I loaded their cases into the taxi. We said goodbye to Barry and climbed into the cab. George had given Barry an envelope as he shook his hand. We knew what was in it.

Keith stuck his head out the window. 'I hope that young blonde comes along soon, Barry. You're not getting any younger.'

'Piss off, you lot,' he said with a big smile and a mock salute.

The traffic flow was pathetic. I gave the guys their tickets and nervously checked my watch several times, wondering what would happen if we missed our flight. I rang Sarah and told her what was happening. She sounded so happy to hear my voice.

'If I have to, I'll stand in front of the plane until you get here.'

I suggested she wait at the check-in since we wouldn't have time to relax in the lounge.

We arrived at the terminal with not much time to spare. A voice came over the public address system. 'Would Mr Michael Jamieson, Mr Harold Edwards, Mr George Thorne, Mr Keith Pinkard, and Mr Tomasz Dabrowski please proceed to the Qantas check-in. Your flight is now boarding.'

'Bloody hell, no wonder we call you Tommy,' said Keith. 'I'd lose my false teeth if I tried to say your whole name.'

'You're a mixed bag, Tommy,' said Mick. 'We're Poms born and bred. What's your background, with a name like that?'

'You're right, Mick. I'm like the frog that had a maternal English grandmother and Irish grandfather; a paternal French grandmother and a grandfather with the surname Dabrowski. So, I'm English, Irish, French and a tad Pole.'

George laughed. 'That's hilarious, Tommy. Have you been saving that up for us?'

'No, only for anyone silly enough to ask.'

We laughed as we got to where Sarah was waiting. I gave her a big kiss and hug and quickly introduced her to the guys as we placed our bags on the scales. She looked fantastic. For once the guys were almost lost for words.

'You weren't exaggerating when you described her to us,' Harry said quietly as we made our way to the departure area.

Mick leaned in to Sarah. 'If Tommy gives you any trouble let us know. We'll happily look after you.'

'Thanks, guys, but I don't think I'll be needing any help,' she said, quickly kissing me.

'No cheek from you lot,' I said, putting my arm around her waist and pulling her close. She felt terrific.

We showed our tickets to the flight attendant and walked down the tunnel to the plane. The conversation was a buzz of excitement. Anyone would have thought it was a bunch of kids going on holiday.

We were shown our seats and told that business class was light on so, once we were airborne, we could move about and relax. I could see five empty rows, so we would.

The plane thundered down the runway and it wasn't long before we were celebrating with champagne even though it was not much after ten. Sarah was keen to know about the guys and was amazed as they recounted the lives they'd lived.

'How come nice guys like you aren't married?'

Mick laughed. 'We would be if four of you had come along before now.'

Our glasses were topped up and we toasted the future.

We traded stories for the best part of an hour. Then the guys, after telling Sarah and me about their big night at the tables, eased back into their seats for some well-earned sleep.

We had cracked up when George told us he had been cautioned three times for card counting.

'That man will never learn,' I said to Sarah, explaining what card counting was.

She had never been into gambling but I was hoping to change that.

'I would be more than happy to show you the finer points of poker if you're interested. Hong Kong has great casinos.'

'You might be able to persuade me,' she said, resting her head on my shoulder and sliding her hand into mine.

'You wouldn't be interested in learning to play golf as well?'

She dug me in the ribs. 'I'll think about it.'

We sat in companionable silence and it wasn't long before Sarah was asleep. I slipped her hand out of mine and got up and walked around for a while. Apart from at poker tables, I was never one for sitting too long. With the others resting, I used the time to do my breathing exercises and felt good.

They woke for a great lunch and the champers flowed. We were given a snack mid-afternoon and told the plane was on schedule.

The half-hour ride to the Colonial Oriental hotel was a real eye-opener. I'd never seen so many high-rise buildings. The majority were apartments as land was at a premium, so the only way was up.

'Benny's done a great job with our accommodation,' I said to Mick as we were ushered through the vast foyer to reception. The area was decorated with classy wall papers complemented with dark timber and brass trimmings. Chandeliers sparkled and the carpet was plush and spotless. The staff were impeccably dressed and polite.

Our suites were on the thirtieth floor, all next to each other. It would be easy for us to keep in touch. The lift was ultra quiet and smooth. Mick used the mirrored walls to smooth his hair, knowing we couldn't help but notice.

'You can't help yourself,' I said. We laughed. We were going to have fun.

'I noticed the restaurant on the way in,' said Keith. 'It looks pretty flash. Should we give it a try tonight?'

We agreed to meet at eight-thirty.

I suddenly realised I hadn't made any arrangements for Sarah's accommodation. I felt embarrassed and was about to say something when she asked me what my room number was.

'3010.'

'How bizarre. That's my room number as well.'

We dropped our cases, and hugged and kissed in the corridor.

'Get a room,' said Harry, laughing, as they disappeared into theirs.

'The people at the desk were either diplomatic or used to this sort of thing,' I said, as we rolled our cases across the threshold.

The main living area was open plan with a comfortable-looking lounge suite and a writing desk. The small kitchenette held the obligatory appliances. It was apparent our main meals would be had either at the hotel restaurant or out and about. I didn't think it would worry us.

The master bedroom contained a king-size bed, a two-seater couch and dressing table. A sliding door led into the bathroom. It was huge; a double shower, spa and twin basins.

'I take it you're happy with the arrangements,' she said. She jumped onto the bed and let fly with the extra pillows they always toss in, thinking people sleep sitting up.

I fended off her attack and pinned her down, gently feeling her body submitting to my bulk.

'Oh, Tommy, I haven't felt this happy in a long while. It's crazy what we're doing but it feels so right.'

We lay on the bed and talked. We had so many questions to ask each other.

Sarah told me about her friend Dianne who had suggested she become an escort.

'Where did you two meet?'

'At a gym in Bondi. We were regulars. She stood out from the rest.'

'How so?'

'Well, she's taller than me, similar build but with bigger boobs. She's got an amazing figure and with a head of red hair to go with her green eyes and lightly-freckled face, she's drop-dead gorgeous. One day, after a couple of months, she came over, introduced herself and asked if I'd like to grab a coffee. We had a few coffee dates during which we got to know each other well and she told me what she did for a living. The rest you know.'

'When was the last time you saw her?'

'She moved to Tasmania about five years ago after she finished escorting. We call each other every couple of months to catch up on all the gossip. She met a guy who owned a vineyard and they got together for a while but things didn't work out. She moved to Hobart and got involved with a cancer support group, volunteering three days a week. She loves it. As her mother died from cancer some years ago, she thought she might be able to do counselling work. She received a lot of support during her mother's illness and, with training, felt she had enough confidence and knowledge to help others who were going through similar circumstances.'

'Wow. She sounds amazing and it's great you've kept in touch,' I said, thinking about Brian and *his* story and what if … perhaps I'd talk to Sarah about it later.

We showered and dressed but before we met up with the others, I sent Jack a text message instead of ringing him. I didn't want to spend time on the phone at this stage. Sarah sent her mother a message telling her we had arrived safely and were going well.

We headed to the restaurant. We settled for steak and salad with a couple of bottles of champagne and spent a couple of hours discussing our plans for the next week.

Mick was keen to catch up with Benny and hit the race tracks, Keith was eager to win more money off me on the golf course, and the other two wanted to be lazy; sightseeing, gambling and eating. Sarah was happy to be with us but was keen to start me on my fitness regime. Mick suggested she might have to get the whip out to keep me motivated. I reminded him of my pain threshold, hoping Sarah wouldn't take any notice of him.

We didn't make any hard and fast rules about getting together every day but agreed we enjoyed each other's company and would try to catch up for evening meals. We would have stories to tell. Sarah was keen to tag along with Keith and me on the golf course. Good walks most days, building up to jogging, combined with resistance training in the hotel gym would give me an edge when I got to Los Angeles where, no doubt, Jack would work me into the ground. I could tell he was determined to have me in top shape for the golf tournament in Vegas. I admitted to Sarah I hadn't looked at the fitness program Jack had sent me last week.

'What Jack doesn't know won't hurt him,' she said. 'I'm sure we're grown-up enough to know what to do. I bet he hasn't included yoga.'

'Yoga could be interesting. I'll try anything once.'

After coffee and port Sarah and I decided to head back to our room. The others were keen to check out the Golden Dragon Casino. I suggested to Keith we organise a game of golf for Wednesday at the Hong Kong Golf Club. He said he was happy to wait a day to take my money.

'Don't get too cocky. I might surprise you, particularly now I have my own cheer squad.' I leaned in to Sarah and gave her a peck on the cheek. She smiled and poked her tongue out playfully at Keith who raised his hands in defeat.

'Yeah, okay, I guess I'll have to tread on your ball when you're not looking,' he said with a laugh as we left the table.

I happily paid the bill and we said good night. Sarah and I headed for the lift and the others walked out into the Hong Kong night.

I closed the door behind us and for the first time with Sarah I felt awkward. I wasn't sure what was going to happen next. She sensed my awkwardness and took my hand and led me to the bed. She undid my shirt …

DAY 17 – TUESDAY

I woke with Sarah looking at me. She was smiling.

'You don't look so awkward now.' She planted a lingering kiss on my mouth.

I said nothing as I pulled her into my arms and lay there stroking her hair. If the world had to end now, I couldn't care less.

Diamond Harbour

The headline read: PLANE CRASHES – NO SURVIVORS. Angie looked closer at the newspaper lying on the table at reception in the hospital emergency department. She picked it up and carried it over to a chair. She was in pain but knew she would have to wait to see a doctor. She started to read the article, then realised the charter plane belonged to the company contracted to fly workers from Perth to the iron ore mines. The reporter wrote that, due to the crash circumstances, the victims' details would not be made public until next of kin had been notified and only then with their approval. Local police were on the scene and the coroner from Perth was being taken to the crash site.

Angie did some quick calculations. Although the pain in her head was getting worse, she deduced that Danny was possibly on the flight.

She pulled out her phone and dialled his number. Her call went straight to his message bank. Her next call was to the mines' administration office. She explained who she was but was told that, according to their records, she was not Danny's next of kin. Danny's wife lived in Adelaide, South Australia and she had been contacted. They were therefore unable to provide any further details.

Angie's protests fell on deaf ears and when the line went dead, she slumped in the chair.

'That fucking, low-down, slime-ball bastard,' she shouted, throwing the paper across the room.

A nurse came over and calmly asked what was wrong. It took Angie a few minutes to settle down. She told the nurse the story. The nurse looked at Angie's head and quickly took her to a cubicle but kept her sitting until a doctor was available.

The doctor did a preliminary examination and ordered an X-ray. He was concerned she might have a skull fracture. The nurse explained Angie's agitated state so he prescribed a tranquilliser. It worked quickly and Angie relaxed.

It was several hours until Angie was admitted to a ward where she would end up staying for a few days. The X-ray revealed a slight fracture but, fortunately, not in an area that would cause any long-term problems. In line with hospital procedures the police were notified. The doctor would submit his report and Angie would be interviewed.

Angie rang her friend Vicki in Sydney who was able to get time off work and drive down. She arrived later in the day and listened intently as Angie explained what had happened.

'Good fucking riddance,' said Vicki. The anger in her voice surprised Angie. 'How could the bastard treat you like that? He lives a double life, uses you and beats you up – serves him fucking right.'

Vicki was protective of Angie and, like Mick, had told her she shouldn't put up with an abusive partner.

'I don't suppose you know anything about his wife,' said Vicki, after she'd calmed down.

'Today's the first I've heard of her. To be honest, I don't want to know. If she doesn't know about me maybe she can grieve for Danny in her own way. He probably treated her the same, so perhaps there are two relieved women. His working three weeks on, one week off was obviously bullshit. He would have been going to Adelaide on a regular basis, I presume.'

'I guess you've got to try and put all this behind you and concentrate on getting well. He's not worth losing any sleep over. Dwelling on the past isn't going to help.'

'I'd like to get in touch with Mick. He's in Hong Kong but told me to text him anytime. He'll ring me back. That way it wouldn't cost me anything.'

'Sounds like a nice guy.'

'He sure is. Mick and Danny are, or were, like chalk and cheese. I wish I'd met Mick years ago. You'd like him, Vic; he's kind, funny and has a great Pommy accent. I could listen to him talk for hours.'

'You look beat. How about getting some sleep. I'll take your keys and go back to your place and keep an eye on things. If you don't mind, I'll sleep there and come back in the morning. I'll ring your work and tell them you'll be unavailable for a while. I won't tell them why. You can talk to them when you're up for it.'

Angie couldn't stifle her yawn. 'What would I do without you?'

Vicki bent down and gave her a hug.

She looked around as she closed the door. Angie was already asleep.

Hong Kong

Sarah had arranged breakfast in our room and we had not long finished showering when it arrived. We sat at the small table near the window in our plush dressing gowns. We were ravenous. I wasn't used to a cooked breakfast but changes to my circumstances necessitated additional fuel for my engine.

I looked at Sarah. She had damp hair and no make-up on and looked gorgeous. It was as if she could read my mind and she pretended not to notice, chewing slowly, looking out the window with the slightest smile on her face. She was *so* cute.

'How about we ease into your get-fit program,' she said, while munching on toast. 'We could spend today sightseeing and clothes shopping, then, tomorrow, golf with Keith.'

'Thursday start will be fine by me. I'm glad I've got you to help me shop. With your tailoring background and terrific fashion sense I can't go wrong. Whatever you do, don't ask my opinion on anything you try on because I know you could wear a sack and look a million dollars.'

Blushing slightly, she said, 'Keep up that sort of talk and we mightn't get out of this room today.'

Before we headed out, I sent Sylvia an e-mail letting her know we had arrived safely and that I hoped she was getting prepared for her English classes next Monday.

The day was a blur. I felt I was walking on air. Everywhere we went people couldn't help but look at Sarah. She was much taller than the average Asian and even though she had dark hair she stood out in the crowds. I could read envy on the face of every man we passed, even if it was written in Chinese.

The weather was considerably cooler than in Sydney so we bought warmer clothing and, with plans to visit Victoria Peak, agreed to buy coats.

We stopped at a quaint café selling tasty, healthy food. Most people we saw were slim due to a diet that mainly consisted of fish, rice and vegetables;

although Western-style food was making inroads and being embraced by the locals. I stood out in the crowds too; but for the wrong reasons. I made a mental note to ask the reception staff at our hotel the Chinese words for 'fat bastard'.

We headed back to the hotel late in the afternoon and ran into George as we got to our room.

'Are you guys free for dinner tonight?' he asked, following us in.

I looked at Sarah and her smile was enough for me to say, also with a smile, 'We have to eat, so it may as well be with you guys.'

'I'll talk to the others and let them know. We found a great restaurant at the Golden Dragon. Would you be interested? It may involve poker and blackjack afterwards though.'

'I can't see a problem. Sarah's been dying to check out our prowess on the baize.'

Sarah giggled, 'Well, I've checked out your prowess in other areas so it would only seem right.'

I couldn't argue with that so I put her into a fireman's lift, told George to piss off, then threw her onto the bed.

'Oh, I love to be rescued,' she said, her voice muffled by my lips on hers. As the door clicked shut, she responded with such passion it took my breath away.

We headed over to the Golden Dragon for dinner. Mick kept us entertained with details of their exploits last night. They had played poker and blackjack until three in the morning. Mick caught up with Benny during the day and the others spent a quiet one wandering around the crowded streets, soaking up the atmosphere and local beer.

Once again, George had made a killing at the blackjack table. He was adamant dinner was his treat.

The guys guided Sarah and me to the poker tables where Sarah perched herself at the rail and, while enjoying coffee and cake, watched us get into a poker game. George was happy to join us. Three others were at our table. They appeared to be locals and I was immediately able to give them made-up names based on their appearances: Chop Suey, Typhoon, and Noodle. Mixed-up and chatty; can't sit still; plain and thin with a serious disposition. Even though poker was in its infancy here, good players were emerging, keen to make a name.

After around an hour of play and not much action, and with Sarah a distraction in my line of sight, I was, luckily, still able to concentrate when I was dealt the K♠ and K♥; my best hole cards so far. The blinds were $100 and

$200. I was first to bet and decided to raise the big blind to $400. To my surprise, everyone called. The flop was the K♦, 10♣ and 6♠. George bet $500; Keith folded. I raised $500 and Chop Suey folded. The other four called. George threw his cards in. I think he was hoping to win a cheap pot but when five players called, he probably realised there could be sets of kings, tens or sixes. If he hadn't improved his hand with the flop, why bother continuing with others calling a raise? The turn card was the 3♣. It was up to me, so I decided to check; mainly to see what the rest would do. Typhoon and Mick checked and Noodle bet $500. Harry took his time checking this guy out. He was pretty solid. Harry called, then it was back to me. I considered Noodle might have a set of tens, sixes or threes at the most, so I raised $500, much to his disgust. He blabbered something in Cantonese – or it could have been Mandarin – but I did recognise the words 'bloody check-raiser'. Typhoon called and Mick could see what I was up to and folded. Noodle and Harry called and the river card appeared. It was the J♥.

It was my bet. I considered what could beat me. There could be two straights out there if someone had A-Q or Q-9 hole cards. I couldn't think why anyone would wait for the river card hoping for a straight. The odds are too great. I would have to trust my gut feeling. I was keen to keep the pot building so I made a conservative bet of $500. Typhoon called and Noodle raised $1000. Harry threw his cards in. It was up to me to decide whether I would call Noodle or re-raise. I glanced up at Sarah. She was engrossed in the game but smiled at me and made me wonder what the hell I was doing at the table with these guys. I studied Noodle until the dealer told me to make my play. Did he have a straight or a set? He had bet after the turn card which suggested he might have a set of threes. Who knew, he might have got lucky with a straight.

I decided to go for it. I called his $1000 and raised another $1000. Typhoon called and Noodle, muttering away, went all-in, pushing $7000 into the pot. It would cost me $6000 to call. Typhoon had called every bet. I wasn't sure what he was up to. Was he along for the ride or did he gamble on getting a straight? As for Noodle, he had been aggressive but I still thought he had a set of threes. I looked at the others around the table. They, like Sarah were engrossed in the game, but relaxed knowing they didn't have to make a tough decision. Harry had put over two grand into the pot but obviously didn't have the cards to continue.

I was in too deep by this point. I fiddled with my chips, sending Typhoon a message that maybe I was unsure of how strong my hand was. If he thought that and considered his hand stronger, he might call. That would boost the pot. I counted out $6000, fiddled with them some more, and looked at Mick and

Harry, who were smiling. At the dealer's insistence I slid the chips towards the pot. Typhoon swept up his chips and threw them into the pot. I couldn't work him out. Was it confidence or unsureness?

Mick chuckled. 'I guess he's calling.'

Laughter rippled around the table.

The pot was $38,200. Not the biggest pot I'd been involved with but an intriguing one, nonetheless.

Harry got up and walked over to Sarah and explained to her what was going on. She intimated to him she understood and showed me her hands with fingers crossed.

The dealer told Noodle to turn over his hole cards. He paused. A pair of aces appeared. Aces are the strongest hole cards but they're no good if someone is holding a pair of threes and flops another one. He had tried to out-bet us without considering what we might have. I knew I had this bloke beaten but Typhoon was a dark horse. Maybe he had the straight. It was my turn to show my cards. My kings brought cheers from the guys as Typhoon also turned his cards over to reveal a set of sixes. Normally a player doesn't show a losing hand but in this case it was a bad beat, I guess. Having a set of sixes from the flop must have bugged him, knowing there could be better hands at that point. I think he went along for the ride, perhaps hoping to pick up maybe another six, king or ten.

Noodle cursed then rushed from the table while I shook hands with Typhoon. He was gracious in defeat.

He laughed.

'Bloody Aussies,' he said in broken English.

The dealer pushed the pot in my direction. Sarah was clapping wildly as I gathered up the chips and told the guys the drinks were on me. They were keen to keep on playing but were happy to have a break to celebrate a good win.

I thanked Sarah for being so patient. I could never see myself sitting and watching others play poker for that long.

'I must admit I enjoyed watching you guys play,' she said, giving me a big hug. 'Your concentration at the table is amazing. I guess you have to stay focused when there's a lot at stake.'

'The time goes fast. Sometimes when I'm playing, I think it might be midnight when it's hitting three in the morning.'

We enjoyed a few drinks and then I told the guys we were heading back to the hotel. They were ready to hit the tables again so we said goodnight and left them to it. I told Keith I'd talk to him in the morning about our golf game.

He rubbed his hands together and said, 'Looking forward to relieving you of some of your winnings.'

'Fat chance,' I replied. Sarah linked her arm in mine and pulled me playfully towards the exit.

DAY 18 – WEDNESDAY

It was good weather for golf. I phoned Keith after we'd been down to the restaurant for breakfast. He was keen to get to the course. He had already spoken to the hotel staff. They had phoned the club and booked us in for eleven. We would be picked up out the front at ten-thirty. We had plenty of time to get back to our room, relax for a while and get changed; me into my golf gear and Sarah into, well, a sack maybe. I reckoned she could start a fashion trend and open a shop in Sydney called Saxon Silk. Yeah, sacks made from silk. She could pull it off – preferably in front of me. Bloody hell my mind wandered. It was her fault; too damn gorgeous.

'Have you heard from Jack?' she asked.

'Funny you should mention it. I was thinking at breakfast he hadn't replied to my text. It's not like him to be slow getting back to me. I assumed he would be hassling me to get the fitness program going.'

I looked at my watch. 'It should be afternoon in LA. I've got time before we go, so I think I'll give him a call.'

No answer. I got his message service. I left a brief message and hung up.

'Are you young'uns decent?' asked Keith, walking in the door.

Sarah laughed. 'Do you think we'd leave it unlocked if we weren't?'

'Reception rang me to say our ride is out front so we better get a move on.'

'I'll grab my clubs and we'll be on our way.'

The ride to the course in busy Hong Kong traffic was chaotic but when we got there, we were surprised at how peaceful it was. We could hear birdsong. Sarah did some stretching and deep breathing to clear out the cobwebs, encouraging Keith and me to do the same. We had a small bucket of practise balls each to loosen up before heading to the first tee.

We did rock-paper-scissors to see who went first, much to the delight of Sarah who reckoned we looked, and acted, like kids. We didn't care because we didn't have any cares.

Keith drove first. It was a par-4 dog-leg to the left. Keith's signature play, the draw shot, was spot on. Sarah was gobsmacked when she saw him hit the ball. It was the first time she had been on a golf course and she was loving it.

I hit my drive straight, cutting the corner, clearing the small tree and finishing a few metres ahead of Keith.

'You guys are amazing,' she said, as we walked off the tee onto the fairway.

'You ain't seen nothin' yet, baby,' said Keith. 'Wait 'till we get to the par-3s. I'll show you amazing.'

'Don't take any notice of him, he's full of it,' I said. Sarah giggled, put her arm through mine and walked contentedly along the freshly-mown grass.

'I presume we're having the same bets as last Sunday?' said Keith.

'I wouldn't have it any other way.'

We birdied the first then walked to the par-3 second. It was short. 110 metres, but we had to hit over water. Not much room for error.

Keith's gentle draw shot was short and rolled back into the water. Learning from his blunder, I played a longer iron and landed a metre from the pin. Keith conceded the hole that made me one up.

The next seven holes were squared and, as we were back at the clubhouse, we decided to have a quick bite to eat before tackling the next nine.

The tenth was a par-4 straight up a hill. We couldn't see the green, only the top of the flag. I hit one of my best drives that looked as if it bounced on the green. Keith followed suit but he may have gone too far.

We got to the green where, unbeknown to us, a grassy bank guarded the back of the green. Keith's ball was sitting proudly on top while mine was a couple of metres short of the hole.

I felt confident. 'Want to double the bet on this hole, Keith?'

'Why not. I don't mind taking a few more dollars off you.'

Sarah laughed. 'You guys are incorrigible.'

Keith's ball was sitting about three metres higher than the green and about ten metres from the hole. He was using hired clubs and didn't have a full selection, so he used his sand iron and hit the ball about fifteen metres into the air. It came down a metre from the hole and dribbled in.

Keith cheered, Sarah screamed, and I swore at the same time. Players on the adjoining fairway looked over at the commotion, waved, then played on, knowing someone had done something all golfers wanted to do.

We couldn't believe it; an eagle on a tricky par-4.

'You're a friggin' freak, Keith, a hole-in-one on Sunday, now this. Thank the gods you're not playing in Vegas.'

'Well, I might have to have a word with Jack. What's his number?'

'I think I've lost it.'

We had a good laugh. 'I didn't think golf could be this much fun,' said Sarah. She reminded me I owed Keith double.

'I haven't putted yet.'

'Double or nothing, old boy?'

'You're on.'

I spent considerable time over my putt but the ball stopped one turn short of the hole. Keith smiled and held out his hand rubbing imaginary money through his fingers.

'It ain't over yet, eagle-man. We've got eight to go. Anything could happen.'

'I suppose Sarah could play for you if you're feeling intimidated.' He was goading me now.

I looked at Sarah, who was brimming with happiness. Laughter filled the air as we headed off to the next tee. It wasn't until we'd finished the sixteenth that I had recouped my losses. We had two to play. Two par-4s. It was fitting we squared them. It was also fitting we finished the game all square.

Sarah gave us a celebratory hug, asking when she could begin golf lessons. I visualised her swinging the club with such grace I wanted to start right now.

A few drinks in the clubhouse and we were on our way back to the hotel. Keith was going to catch up with the guys and meet us for dinner.

I intended to make good use of the afternoon with Sarah.

*

Mick was sitting at the bar with George and Harry when his phone beeped. It was a text message.

Please call me, Mick. Love, Angie.

'I wasn't expecting that,' said Mick. He left the bar and walked to a quiet area.

He sat in a plush club chair, pushed his hair off his forehead and dialled Angie's number. It rang a few times and the voice that answered wasn't Angie's. It was Vicki. After she explained who she was and had a quick chat, she passed the phone to Angie.

Angie was sitting out of bed with a tube attached to her arm. The blood thinners would help reduce the swelling in her brain.

Angie spent the next half an hour relaying all that had happened. Mick could feel the anger building up inside him. Angie could sense it, so she told him everything would be okay, and he calmed down.

'I'm coming back to see you,' he said. 'I can't bear the thought of you being there alone.'

'Vicki's here with me and she's been a saviour but she has to go back to Sydney tomorrow. They're letting me go home on Friday if everything's good.'

'I can be back in Sydney and get down there on Friday.'

'Would you do that for me?' Her voice was breaking.

'Of course. I'm only here on holidays. It's not as if the guys can't manage without me. Although I do have to hold their hands now and then.'

She managed a weak laugh. 'I've missed you and I can't wait to see you. I keep thinking about our lovely day together. I hope there'll be more.'

'There will be if I've got anything to do with it,' he said.

They chatted for a while longer, until Mick heard the nurse say it was time to rest. They said their goodbyes. 'See you Friday,' he said, before he hung up.

Mick walked back to the bar.

Harry passed him his drink. 'What's happening, mate?'

'That was Angie. You know the prick she was living with, well, he's dead. Killed in a plane crash and Angie couldn't be more relieved.'

Mick filled them in on the whole story.

'What a fucking arsehole,' said George. He and the lads knew how to treat women well and they agreed that any bloke who didn't should be strung up.

Mick decided to act straight away. He went to reception and spoke with a lady who was most helpful. She rang Qantas and booked him a business class ticket for Thursday and arranged overnight accommodation at the Condor. He would have time to hire a car and get to Angie before lunch on Friday. He felt calm about his plans, but excited that he would be seeing her much earlier than anticipated. This could be the big change he'd spoken to the others about. They had ribbed him about being psychic but perhaps he would have the last laugh.

*

We showered together, dried off and got dressed for dinner. Sarah wore slacks and a short-sleeved knitted top that moulded to her shape. She had the knack of picking colours that complemented her complexion. I guessed in her profession she had to look good all the time. The thing is, she did it easily.

For a brief moment I reflected on her profession and wondered whether she would see this as the time to retire. I would pick the right time to ask;

perhaps when I proposed. I smiled to myself, once again thinking about the last week. How crazy was it?

'Penny for your thoughts?' she said, while styling her hair.

'I was thinking about the week we've had and how I've never been happier. I would have traded my Championship win all those years ago to have known you then. Who knows what might have happened? Anyway, that was then and this is now, and if your mother hadn't stepped off the kerb when she did our paths would have never crossed. Thanks, Rhonda.'

Sarah laughed and kissed me hard. 'Come on, don't get too sentimental. I've done my make-up and I don't want you making me cry.'

We swept out of the room and ran to the lift, knocking on the guys' doors as we went. They opened simultaneously, and heads popped out. It was hilarious, like the plastic ducks in sideshow alley, looking left and right, mouths open.

'Let's eat,' I said as the lift doors opened. I held them open while they made their way along the hall.

'Mick's got some news,' said George, while we rode the elevator to the ground floor.

'I'll tell you once we've got booze on the table,' said Mick.

'I'm intrigued,' I said. 'You don't usually need grog to get you talking.'

'This isn't the usual chit-chat, Tommy.'

The waiter poured champagne and told us he'd be back shortly to take our dinner orders. In the meantime, Mick told us about Angie and Danny. Sarah knew enough about the psychology of domestic violence to explain why some women stay in nasty relationships. It helped Mick understand the situation and made him more determined to make sure Angie was never put in that position again.

I patted Mick on the arm. 'You're serious about her, aren't you?'

'You bet, mate. When I spoke to her on the phone, she talked about the Sunday we spent together and I knew then it was more than a passing moment.'

'I know exactly what you mean,' I said, taking hold of Sarah's hand and kissing it.

None of us spoke for a moment or two. Love was in the air. The other three were looking at us with kind envy. I felt sorry for them but knew, when the time was right, they would find love too.

The waiter took our orders while we talked about Mick returning to Sydney. He was apologetic about leaving us but at no stage did we try to talk him out of it.

'I can't believe I'm sitting here with a bunch of gambling, drinking, fun-loving guys who have sensitivity and kindness oozing out their pores,' said Sarah.

'We're not just pretty faces,' said Harry.

She laughed. 'Now come on, don't get carried away.'

'We might have trouble getting through the door with these swollen heads,' said Keith, 'but thank you, Sarah, that's a nice thing to say.'

'Well, it's true,' she said.

Our meals arrived and we ate in relative silence, each seeming to know what the other was thinking. It was eerie but, at the same time, incredibly warm and companionable.

Mick asked me how the arrangements for Vegas were going. I told him I'd left messages for Jack but hadn't heard back.

'I'll send him another text when we get back to our room. It'll be early morning but he'll see it when he wakes up. If I don't hear from him, I think I might contact Silver's Grand Casino. Jack mentioned it was where everything was being organised. They might know where he is. He's pretty well known over there as he has a hand in many tournaments, not only in Vegas but along the West Coast.'

'Good idea,' said Keith. 'I'm looking forward to finding out more about the next stage of our journey. Mind you, I'm having a ball here and not in any rush to leave.'

'I'll let you know what I find out, hopefully in the morning. Will we see you before you fly out, Mick?'

'I'm leaving after breakfast. It would be nice to see you before I go.'

We spent an amazing couple of hours chatting, sipping, laughing, sipping, stirring, sipping, until a few of us started yawning.

Sarah put her mouth to my ear and slipped her hand on the inside of my thigh. 'It's time I got you home to bed, big boy.'

I swung my face around quickly and planted a kiss on her mouth.

'I think it's time we finished up here,' said Mick. 'We don't want you two getting arrested for upsetting the old folk.'

'I hope you don't mean us,' said Keith.

'No, George and Harry,' said Mick, jumping out of his chair to avoid a backhander from Harry.

'If I wasn't so tired, I could sit here with you guys all night,' said Sarah. 'There's never a dull moment.'

We hugged as we parted ways. We agreed to meet in the dining room for breakfast with Mick at six.

While Sarah made coffee, I sent Jack another text telling him to get his finger out and get back to me.

We took our coffee to bed.

My phone alarm woke us at sparrow fart. I leaned over to turn it off and noticed our coffee hadn't been touched.

Sarah stirred. 'Good morning, you amazing man.'

I leaned over, kissed her and lingered.

'Can you pinch me so I know this isn't a dream?'

'How will pinching you make you know whether it is or isn't?'

'It's far too early for all your psychology stuff,' I said, tickling her until she pleaded with me to stop.

She gasped for breath. 'You're a bully. Pick on someone your own size.'

'They're hard to find but as soon as I drop those twenty kilos I should be spoilt for choice. I've been reading up on weight loss and apparently the first few kilos are mainly fluid, but it doesn't matter. The scales in the gym tell me I've lost five.'

'You're great,' she said. 'Will you be up for a gentle jog around the park after breakfast?'

'As long as you don't bring your whip, I should be okay,' I laughed as we headed for the shower.

We got dressed and I checked my phone again as we were heading down to breakfast; nothing from Jack. I decided I'd ring him after breakfast. If I couldn't get hold of him, I would phone Silver's Grand Casino.

Mick was excited and chatty as we ate breakfast. He had been in touch with Angie several times since the original call. She was progressing well. Her headaches were now bearable and the blood thinners were doing the job. George suggested he bring Angie back to Hong Kong.

'First things first, my friend,' said Mick. 'She will need time to recover from her head injury before they'll let her fly, I reckon. Plus, she'll have to sort out Danny's shit. It'll be good for her to put it all behind her and start fresh.'

'With a great guy to help her,' I said. 'She couldn't be in better hands.'

We took the lift to our floor. George, Keith and Harry wanted to go with Mick to the airport to see him off. The taxi was coming in twenty minutes. Enough time for him to put his last-minute things in his bag and say his goodbyes to Sarah and me.

'Give Angie our love,' said Sarah, giving him a hug.

Mick and I shook hands.

'Have a safe trip, mate.'

'I hope you hear from Jack soon. Let me know what's happening. You never know; Angie and I might catch up with you lot in LA.'

'That would be great, I'll call you. See ya.'

We headed to our room, made coffee and enjoyed the views from thirty floors up.

'While you're calling Jack, I'll give Mum a ring,' said Sarah, heading for the bedroom.

No answer again. I rang Directory Assistance and got the number for Silver's.

I reached the switchboard and after hearing clicking and buzzing, I was put through to the Events Coordinator. I did a quick calculation and worked out it was early afternoon. I introduced myself and asked if she could put me in touch with Jack. I could hear her take a deep breath.

'My name is Rachael. I'm sorry to have to tell you, but Jack died last Friday. He had a heart attack during our meeting on Thursday morning. He was rushed to hospital but he never regained consciousness. The doctors had him on life support for over twenty-four hours but the damage to his heart was huge. They switched the machines off late Friday.' She paused for a moment, as if catching her voice. 'I'm so sorry you had to hear the news this way.'

I couldn't speak. I was gobsmacked.

'Are you still there?'

'Yes. I'm in shock at the moment. Can you give me your number? I'll ring back in a while.'

She gave me her direct number and said she would be back in her office in a couple of hours.

I thanked her and hung up.

I slumped into the lounge. I was gutted. I could feel the blood draining from my face.

'Mum said to ... what's up, Tommy?' asked Sarah, sitting beside me.

'Jack's dead. He had a heart attack. Died on Friday.'

'I'm so sorry, honey,' she said, putting her arms around my neck and nestling my face close. Tears were running down my face, melting into her T-shirt.

It took me a few minutes to regain my composure. I grabbed a tissue and wiped my eyes.

'Bugger the jog,' she said. 'I'll make us a coffee and we can sit and talk.'

I relayed what Rachael had told me. We spent the next hour talking, with me doing most of it. Sarah was an avid listener. I recapped Jack's and my early golf years together, telling her how competitive we were but how our mateship was always our number one priority. We looked out for each other; more than family, maybe. After I gave up golf, we went our own ways. Jack kept playing and winning golf at the top level while the lure of poker tables drew me in. No regrets.

'I spoke to him on Wednesday. He was pretty upbeat about everything. Shit, I can't believe it.'

'Did he have any family?'

'He had a sister, Anne, who married a German guy. Back in the eighties they lived in Hamburg and he would visit her whenever the golf tour included Germany, though I wouldn't say they were close. Jack's parents died when he was in his late teens. They were on a bus trip and a drunk truck driver hit them head-on. Jack had paid for their holiday out of his first win as a professional golfer. You can imagine how bad he felt. I think Anne blamed their deaths on him.'

'That's cruel,' said Sarah. 'The poor bugger's suffering from the loss of his parents and has to shoulder the blame for the accident. It's not fair.' She paused. 'Do you think she would have been notified of his death?'

'I'll try and find out when I ring Rachael. I don't know whether he'd written a will. It's sad to think of him lying in a cold hospital morgue waiting for someone to claim him.'

'How about we go for a walk, get some fresh air. When we get back you can ring Rachael. I guess we should tell the guys, but perhaps wait until you've got more information.'

'It's great having you around,' I said as we walked to the lift. 'You were about to tell me about your mum?'

'Yes, she said to say hello and was over the moon we're getting on so well. She said she's recovering quickly for an old bird and her stitches should be coming out next week.'

'It's nice to have good news,' I said.

'If you don't mind, I don't think I'll tell her about Jack yet. She's so happy her daughter has found a lovely man. Let's not spoil things.'

I smiled at her. 'I can't argue with logic.'

We walked for a long time. The park was quiet, the air still. The distant traffic was a steady hum. It was the right place to be. I decided to ring Rachael.

I put the phone on loudspeaker so Sarah could hear the conversation. Rachael answered promptly. I wasn't sure which questions to ask first. I guess it didn't matter as long as I got answers.

I explained in detail my relationship with Jack and how he had arranged for me to fly to LA, then Vegas, for the combined golf and poker tournament. She put the phone down while she looked through her paperwork, then confirmed I was entered in the tournament at Jack's request.

'Do you know if Jack's sister has been notified?' I asked.

'Yes, she was named as his next of kin on the certification papers he lodged with us a while back. She flew over on Saturday and met with a funeral home and made the necessary arrangements.'

'When is the funeral?' My voice was breaking.

'I'm sorry, Tommy, the funeral was on Tuesday. Jack has been cremated and Anne is taking his ashes back with her to Germany. If it's any consolation it was a big funeral service. Jack was well known in the golfing community here and in LA. The eulogy was a fitting tribute. Many of his friends spoke, recounting their experiences on and off the course.'

'I guess there's not much point me coming over if the funeral's already happened. I'm also not sure whether I'll come over for the tournaments.'

'I understand. There's no need for you to decide right now. You need time to take all this in. Why don't you give me a call when you've had a chance to sort things out and, once again, I'm sorry you had to hear about Jack in this way.'

'Don't feel bad, Rachael, you're only the messenger and I appreciate everything you've told me. Yes, I will ring you again if you don't mind.'

We ended the call. I felt sad and I put my head in my hands and cried.

Sarah put her arms around me and gently rocked me until I stopped.

'I guess I'm feeling sorry for myself, too.'

'No-one can blame you,' she said. 'It's a huge shock to lose someone you've had a long friendship with and even though you went different ways you didn't stop that friendship.'

'Jack was way too young to die. He should have had at least another forty years. He was fit and healthy. Shit, you never know, do you.'

'You know what, big guy? That's a huge part of why we're together. We don't know what tomorrow will bring and what we're doing is making sure we don't miss this wonderful opportunity to be with each other.'

We kissed, wiped our tears and walked, arm in arm, back to the hotel.

The guys were perched at the bar and waved us over. I told them the sad news.

'We're so sorry, Tommy,' said George, standing to give us a hug.

'I think we should have a toast to Jack,' I said, getting the barman's attention.

We raised our glasses and drank to Jack and each other, pledging not to let any opportunities for a happy life slip by.

'Let's have dinner tonight,' said Harry.

We agreed to meet at eight.

Sydney

Mick looked out the plane window as it started its descent into Sydney. It was dark but the city lights cast a welcoming glow.

The taxi dropped him at the Condor Towers. He checked in and as he approached the lift he heard a familiar voice.

'G'day, Mick, did you forget something?' It was Barry with his trademark smile.

'It's a long story, mate. What the hell are you still doing here? Don't you have a home to go to?'

'I knocked off late and was having a drink when I heard your unmistakeable accent.'

'I'm on Hong Kong time so I'm up for a beer. Fancy another one or two?'

'I've never been known to refuse free beer.'

'I never said anything about them being free,' laughed Mick. 'Why don't I dump my bags upstairs and meet you back here in fifteen minutes. I have to make a phone call.'

'I ain't going anywhere. See you soon.'

Mick sat on the bed and rang Angie. He knew it was late but she wouldn't mind.

'I can't wait to see you,' she said. 'The doctors are pretty sure I can go home tomorrow but I'll have to take things easy for a while.'

'Has Vicki come back to Sydney?'

'Yes, she left here this afternoon. She didn't want to go but she can't afford to lose too much time off work. She's got a good boss but fair's fair. The fact you were coming back eased her concerns.'

'I'm picking up a hire car at ten tomorrow so, hopefully, I'll miss Sydney's early morning traffic snarls and be down there in time to take you home. Not many people know it but I'm not bad in the kitchen, so if you like eggs I can knock us up a nice omelette.'

He noticed her laugh was getting stronger. 'Stop it, Mick, you're making me hungry. As nice as everyone's been here in hospital, the food is crap so I'll take you up on your offer. You might have to grab a few things from the shop on the way home though.'

Mick heard her yawn. 'You better get some rest. I'll ring you in the morning.'

'Thank you so much for doing this for me. Drive carefully.'

'I will and you're worth it. Bye.'

Barry was pulling on a long beer when Mick sidled up. There was one for Mick, begging to be sculled.

He ordered two more. 'Thirsty work this flying,' he laughed. They clinked glasses.

Mick observed that Barry and Trevor could have been cast from the same mould. Tall and slim, good heads of hair, kind faces and caring natures. They were the type of people you'd want to see first-up.

Over another beer Mick told Barry what had happened. It wasn't until he'd finished that Barry spoke.

'From what I know of you and the other guys from your time here, Angie is one lucky lady. I meet many people in my job. Some of them you wouldn't piss on if they were on fire; but you blokes are among the most decent I've met. It's been a real privilege to have made your acquaintances.'

'I'd prefer to call it a friendship. When four Poms can come to Australia and be treated the way you've treated us, it sets you apart from the rest. I tell you, Baz, I reckon I'd thump any rude pricks that walked through the door.'

Barry laughed. 'Restraint is one of the first things you learn in doorman school. Do you know you're the first person to call me Baz?'

'Don't those young blondes you're always going on about call you Baz?'

'No, they call me thumper.'

Mick laughed so hard he nearly fell off his stool.

'Geez, I'd better not have any more grog. It's gone to my head. Doesn't matter. I'll blame the jet-lag.'

'Yeah, right,' said Barry. He drained his beer and looked at his watch. 'I appreciate you telling me about Angie. Hopefully you'll bring her up to Sydney for some recuperation and call in.'

'If we do, we'll be staying here, so you'll have plenty of time to meet her. We might get a chance to have a drink.'

'I'd like that.' They shook hands and he headed for the exit.

Mick went into the restaurant for a late supper, and then took the lift to his room. He was ready for a good night's sleep – almost.

Hong Kong

Sarah and I spent the afternoon wandering the streets, enjoying the vibe. It was different each time we ventured out.

When we got back to the hotel, my head had cleared and I told Sarah I'd decided I didn't want to go to LA or Vegas. Although I'd had a good time in Hong Kong, I felt the need to get back to Sydney.

'I hope you don't mind,' I said, as we relaxed on the lounge with a coffee.

'Listen, I'd go to the South Pole if that's where you wanted to go.'

I laughed at her. 'Might be cold down there.'

'Wouldn't matter, you'd keep me warm.'

I pulled her into my arms and kissed her. She responded and once again took my breath away.

My laptop beeped. I dragged myself from Sarah's vice-like grip and looked at the screen. I had two e-mails; one from Sylvia and one from Jack's sister, Anne.

I opened Sylvia's first:

Hello Tommy.

Thank you for your message. You are bad man but kind. Mother and Father cry lots but happy tears. They pray for you. Glad you are okay. Everything is good here and looking forward to school. I let you know how I get on. Bye for now.

I explained to Sarah about the laptop I'd bought for Sylvia.

'What's the story about you being a bad man?'

When I told her, she looked at me and shook her head. 'You keep on amazing me. If I hadn't seen you with your shirt off, I'd swear you had a big "S" on your chest.'

'Ah yeah, S for stud.'

'Idiot,' she giggled.

I opened Anne's:

Hi Tommy,

I've been in touch with Rachael in Vegas about a few things and she told me about you and your connection with Jack. I'm sorry you found out about Jack the way you did. It wasn't until I got Jack's personal things that I saw all your messages to him on his phone and computer. I'm sorry you didn't find out sooner as Rachael indicated you would have wanted to come over for the funeral. If I had known I certainly would have held off until you got here. But as it was, I went ahead with the arrangements thinking I was doing the right thing. Please don't feel bad towards me. I didn't realise how popular Jack was in LA and Vegas until the funeral. The church was packed and so many people came up to me after the service to express their condolences. I do hope you'll accept mine on the loss of a good friend. Jack and I weren't close but he was still my brother. I hope you can understand.

Regards, Anne.

'Well, I suppose I can't do anything about it now. I'll have to accept what's happened and move on.'

'Yes. Holding a grudge won't achieve anything. Based on the circumstances, I don't think she could have done things any different.'

'You're right, as usual.' I gave her a hug and then replied to Anne.

I decided to hold off on Sylvia's reply until I was sure we were heading home.

'When do you think you'll ring Mick and tell him about Jack?'

'Perhaps I'll wait until tomorrow after we've talked to the guys over dinner tonight. I reckon Mick will be pretty excited to be seeing Angie, so it would be a shame to upset him.'

We got dressed for dinner, met up with the guys in the hallway, and grabbed the lift.

Over pre-dinner drinks I told them Sarah and I were heading back to Sydney, seeing as I wasn't going to Vegas.

'I'm sorry I've dragged you guys over here only to be heading home so soon.'

'Forget about it,' said Keith. 'It's not your fault. You didn't have to twist our arms to come here. We're free agents and extremely lucky we can come and go wherever we want, whenever we want. Not many people are as fortunate as us so don't be down on yourself. You've got your grief to deal with.'

'Thanks guys. I might hold off ringing Mick until tomorrow to tell him about Jack.'

'Well,' said Harry, 'Mick rang me when he landed in Sydney to let us know he'd arrived safe and sound. He asked whether you'd heard from Jack and I couldn't lie so I told him what had happened. I hope you don't mind.'

'You did nothing wrong, mate. In fact, you did me a favour. I probably would've broken down.'

'He was shocked like the rest of us and passed on his condolences,' said Harry. 'I guess if you talk to him tomorrow you can tell him your plans. He'll be down at Diamond Harbour for a while with Angie but you could still catch up with him. It might be nice for the four of you to keep each other company. You'd be good support for each other as well.'

George laughed, trying to lighten the mood. 'Bloody oath, Harry. Have you been talking to Sarah? You sound as if you know what you're talking about for a change.'

George certainly lifted our spirits. We had a good laugh, clinked our glasses, and toasted Jack again.

'You look buggered, Tommy,' said Keith. 'You could probably do with a good night's sleep, so don't feel as though you have to hang around here with us tonight. We're big enough and ugly enough to look after ourselves.'

George chortled. 'Speak for yourself. Harry and I are the epitome of good looks *and* charm.'

'You guys know how to cheer up a glum occasion,' said Sarah as we ordered our meals.

Sarah and I didn't eat much before deciding to leave. The others were going to finish off their food and then hit the tables, all feeling lucky.

'We'll catch up with you tomorrow sometime and I'll let you know when we're heading home. See ya.'

It was early but Keith was right. We were buggered. We got to our room, undressed and hit the sack. I couldn't remember switching off the light.

DAY 20 – FRIDAY

Sydney

Mick woke early and rang reception to make sure the hire car would be out the front at ten o'clock. He was assured it would be, so he headed for the gym where he worked out for an hour and swam for another half. He showered then went to the restaurant for breakfast. He was excited to be seeing Angie in a few hours.

He cleared his room, headed to reception and settled his account. He was surprised to see Barry at the door and, as he had a few minutes before his car arrived, they chatted in-between Barry greeting and farewelling guests. Barry had been asked to work an early shift. He didn't mind. He was used to an unpredictable work schedule.

'Your chariot has arrived,' said Barry as a near-new Holden Commodore pulled up at the entrance. 'You've got yourself a flash set of wheels. It pains me to say it but it puts my Ford to shame.'

'I've heard about the Holden-Ford rivalry,' said Mick. 'Only in bloody Australia are people so obsessed with one or the other.'

Barry laughed. 'It's part of our culture, mate. If your dad had a Ford and you bought a Holden you wouldn't be allowed in the house.'

Ever the professional, Barry put Mick's bag in the boot; but not before Mick grabbed his CD folder.

'Take care, Mick, and I hope to see you and Angie before too long. I hope she can get things sorted out real quick.'

'Thanks, mate. If I've got anything to do with it, she will. I've got a feeling this is all going to work out fine.'

Mick slipped a Bee Gees CD into the player, turned up the volume, waved to Barry and eased into the traffic. He wasn't going to Massachusetts. Where he was going was far better.

Hong Kong

Sarah's hand moving down my chest and over my stomach woke me.

'Don't you dare stop there,' I ordered.

'I've no intention.' I closed my eyes and let her continue her masterly manipulations. She slid on top of me, rising up, balancing on one point, finding what she came for, and then leaving us exhausted.

We lay back, silent. Words weren't necessary. I eventually prised myself from her arms, kissed her and walked to the shower. She came in as I was finishing.

'Coffee?' I asked.

'Mmm, I won't be too long.'

I boiled the kettle and was about to pour when my phone rang. It was Mick.

Sarah appeared from the bedroom. I mouthed his name so she went back in and closed the door. I heard the hair dryer. When she came out again, I'd finished talking to him.

'He's on his way down to Angie. I've never heard him so excited but I know how he feels. I told him we were coming home but not sure when, and said I'd let him know. He sounded pleased.'

I re-boiled the kettle. We sat on the lounge and, after reflecting on yesterday, talked about what we were going to do.

'I reckon we ought to fly home, check in with your mum, drive down to the Harbour Casino, book in for a couple of nights, then ring Mick and tell him we're already there.'

'You are a devious man, Tommy Dabrowski.'

'We've got until Monday to decide whether we'll book for another week, so why don't we spend the next few days relaxing? I'm sure I could convince Keith to have another round of golf. We could do more shopping and sightseeing and maybe poker. Would you fancy going to the movies tonight?'

'Great idea; I like it. How about we have breakfast and head out for a long walk.'

We wandered for hours before heading back to the hotel to catch up with the others for lunch. We spent an easy afternoon discussing our plans. The guys were going to stay on in Hong Kong for at least another week and then decide whether to return to Sydney or head to London. George was keen to check up on the progress of his homeless shelters, even though his project manager had advised him things were going well. He wasn't a micromanager but liked to get to the coalface and spend time with the real people, as he called them. He never tired of telling us how his various businesses wouldn't be successful without loyal, happy staff. Plus, it was bonus time and it wouldn't mean as much if he didn't present them to his staff in person.

I had a feeling Sarah and I wouldn't see the guys much once we left. It would be sad because in the two and a half weeks since I'd caught up with them, it was as if we'd never left off from the fun we had in London.

'What's up, Tommy?' asked Harry, noticing my distant look.

'I'm getting soft in my old age and was reminiscing over the past couple of weeks. Without a lie, it has been the best couple of weeks I can remember for a hell of a long time. You blokes would have to be the best mates a person could ask for. I don't think there's been a time when we've had a cross word. Not many blokes can lay claim to that. If you do go to London, I hope we keep in touch. You never know, I might be able to persuade this beautiful lady to join me for a visit.'

She smiled and kissed me on the cheek. 'You'll have a fight on your hands if you try to stop me.'

'What are you doing tonight?' asked George.

'We're going to an early movie, then see what happens.'

'Well, if you're at a loose end afterwards we'll be at the casino. Why don't you join us?'

'There's a cinema a few blocks from the casino. We could walk from there and catch up with you.'

New South Wales

Mick stopped for a coffee and doughnut at a small seaside town about halfway down the coast. He rang Tommy then Angie. She answered after half a ring.

'That was quick.'

'I've been holding onto it for the last hour. I didn't want to miss you if you called. The nurse put it in a ziplock bag while I had a shower.'

'I'm about an hour away so you should get some rest until I get there, okay? If I have to ring again, don't worry, I'll let it go through to your message bank.'

'Thanks, Mick. You don't know how much this means to me.'

'See you soon.'

'Bye.'

Hong Kong

'How about we go Chinese for dinner? It's not far from here. I noticed they have a banquet menu. We could get a banquet for two and try our luck with chopsticks.'

'I'm game if you are,' I said. 'I've never got the hang of them. Perhaps you can show me the finer points.'

'I'm pretty good. I can catch flies with chopsticks. Remember the *Karate Kid* movie?'

She squealed when I tickled her as the lift doors opened. The elderly couple exiting frowned as they passed. We giggled like a couple of kids as the doors closed, then kissed until they opened on our floor.

'Do you still want to go out for tea?'

'Time and place, Tommy,' she said sternly, as we walked to our room. 'By the way, big guy, what movie are we seeing?'

'*Ocean's Thirteen*. It's been out for a while and I've been meaning to catch it. If it's as good as the others it should be fun.'

'Might put a spring in your step at the casino later,' she laughed, disappearing into the bathroom.

A more Western-style Chinese restaurant would be hard to find. The staff were impeccably dressed and polite. The owners made a real fuss and the banquet was highly recommended. It was as if we were family. The menu looked appetising and after the prawn crackers, soup, won tons and spring rolls, I wondered whether I'd be able to do justice to the remaining dishes.

Even though I'd only been on my get-fit program for a couple of weeks I had noticed I couldn't eat as much as before. I'd cut out most in-between-meal snacks and was generally having smaller portions for my main meals. Combined with a gradual increase in physical exercise, I could feel a difference. If nothing else, I was determined to get my health back on track.

The chicken and beef with cashews, plum sauce chicken and pork, and barbecue pork fried rice was enough for four. It was delicious but we couldn't finish everything. As we walked out, Sarah presented me with a pair of chopsticks, gift wrapped in rice paper. Apparently, I'd graduated.

We caught a cab to the cinema and weren't disappointed. The movie, although not as good as the first two, was exciting and we chatted about it as we walked to the casino.

We were about two blocks away when I was suddenly grabbed from behind. Whoever it was must have been big because his arms wrapped around me with ease. I couldn't move but saw movement in front of me. As the figure got closer, I realised it was Noodle from the casino. Thinking it was a joke, I started laughing until I saw a knife pointing at my chest.

'You think you smart Aussies can come over here and take our money. Give me my ten thousand back you win off me and maybe I let you live.'

'I won that money fair and square. It's not my fault you're lousy at poker.'

I instantly regretted what I'd said, seeing the knife move closer towards me.

I suddenly heard a 'whoosh' as the guy behind me exhaled. His arms fell from around me and I felt him fall to the ground. I could feel other arms on me, slender but strong, and before I could take in what had happened, I saw a leg kick and the knife arc up. It flew into the air and, as it landed out of harm's way, I could see Sarah behind Noodle with her leg trapping his like a python, one hand around his chest and the fingers of the other digging into his scrawny neck. His eyes rolled in their sockets as she lowered him to the ground.

'He'll wake up in a while, most likely in a police cell with his friend.'

'Shit. What happened?'

'I'm more than a pretty face,' said Sarah matter-of-factly. 'You don't do what I used to do without knowing self-defence.'

'You said, "used to do". Does that mean—'

'Sure does, big guy. Someone has to look after you.'

I picked her up in my trembling arms and held her close, my mouth next to her ear.

'I love you.'

She pulled away, looked me in the eyes, and kissed me with such force I felt we might lose our balance and trip over the big lug lying on the ground behind me.

Someone in the ever-growing crowd must have called the police because within minutes a siren was blaring and getting louder.

The senior officer introduced himself as Senior Sergeant Kenneth Wong and asked what had happened. Witnesses would confirm Sarah had acted in self-defence. She assured him the two would not suffer any long-term consequences.

He bagged the knife and cuffed the two. They were still unconscious. He took our details, gave us his card, and asked if we could come to the station in the morning and make an official statement. We agreed, telling him we were intending to leave Hong Kong in a few days.

He told us our statement and the witness's statements would be sufficient to put the two behind bars for a long while. He and his partner manhandled

Noodle and his mate into the back of their vehicle. He turned and smiled. 'Please call me Ken, my other friends do.'

The locals were clapping and bowing as we continued our walk to the casino. After another block I stopped and faced Sarah.

'Remember when we first met and you told me what you did for a living and that you could pick and choose who you travelled with?'

'Yes.'

'And you said they were good guys who treated you with respect.'

'Yes.'

'Well, how come you need to know how to disable a small army?'

'They *were* good guys. Unfortunately, they sometimes had to associate with other business people who were sleaze bags, who would hit on me thinking I was a prostitute. Let me tell you now, there's a big difference between a professional escort and a prostitute. Some of these guys wouldn't take no for an answer. So when the going got tough a few bones would get broken. If we catch up with Dianne and you've got a spare hour or two, she can tell you stories that would make you cross your legs and bring a tear to your eye.'

I had to laugh. 'I'm so glad I need looking after.'

'I'm glad I'm the one doing the looking after,' she said, kissing me unashamedly, with people walking around us, smiling.

'By the way, that kick you did back there – if you feel you've strained your inner thigh, I should be able to ease the discomfort later tonight.'

'I'll certainly keep it in mind. In fact, I think I have a slight twinge there already.'

'Well, we'd better not keep you on your feet for too long. These things can cause ongoing problems and may take hours to remedy.'

'I hope so.'

'In saying that, are you still okay to spend time at the casino? I don't want you getting bored watching us guys playing poker.'

'I'm a people watcher. A casino is as good a place as any to watch a potpourri of human interaction. Anyway, if I get bored, I can always get a cab back to the hotel.'

'Not without me you won't.'

'Why? Do you think I need a body guard?'

'Touché.'

We walked into the gaming area and saw George at the blackjack table with huge piles of chips in front of him. As I patted him on the shoulder I leaned in and, while reminding him the eye in the sky would be watching him, told him

I had a great story for supper. He gave me an Aussie thumbs-up, a smile to Sarah, and turned back to the cards.

Being a Friday night, the casino was packed and the poker tables were full. Keith and Harry were ensconced in a game that looked pretty serious, so Sarah and I perched ourselves on the rail with a coffee and watched proceedings.

A new hand was dealt. Keith had the button and Harry had the small blind of $50. The guy under the gun – player three – raised the big blind, pushing $200 over the line. Player four called; players five and six folded; player seven called, as did Keith and Harry. The big blind folded. I could see $1100 in the pot. The flop appeared – A♦, 10♣ and 6♥. Harry opened with $1000 and everyone called. I was confused. No raises. Maybe slow-play was happening, whereby some players were hoping for a bigger pot for their strong hands. The best hands at this stage would be three aces, three tens or three sixes. If someone had two pairs, they could be knocking on the door of a full house. Long odds for flush but a straight was a chance. I was explaining this to Sarah when the turn card was dealt. It was the 6♦. If someone was holding two diamonds, they would be sweating on the river card to give them a flush. I'd want to be well in front before gambling on those odds. Still, that's what makes the game so intriguing. Harry checked, as did players three and four. Player seven, the guy before Keith, pushed out $2000. Keith called. Harry folded, along with player three. Player four raised $5000. He had checked the previous time around – interesting. Player seven called and Keith re-raised a soft $5000. The pot was $32,000 with player four to decide whether to continue. He was eyeballing Keith, who had turned into stone. I had a sneaking suspicion Keith had a set of aces which had turned into a full house and he was waiting for someone else to kick things along.

Player four glanced at his hole cards, usually an indication he hasn't got anything – unless he is trying to give the impression he's got nothing when in fact he's got a good hand. The dealer put him on the clock. After another half a minute of studying Keith, he went all-in. The dealer counted his chips and declared to the table a bet of $17,000 pre the river card. Player four was calling Keith's $5000 raise, then going all-in with $12,000.

Player seven fingered his chips, counted out $17,000 and pushed them over the line. Keith looked at Harry, then at me, and then to the ceiling, as if looking for divine intervention. Harry was non-committal and I shrugged. What more could I do? I thought he had aces and, if so, what did the others have to keep on betting? Another full house or four-of-a-kind?

'In for a penny, in for a pound,' said Keith, counting $12,000 in chips and pushing them out.

The pot was nearly $80,000. The three players stood and turned over their cards. Player four revealed the A♥ and A♣. He had a full house – aces with sixes. Player seven turned over the K♦ and Q♦ which gave him a flush draw – four to a flush. Keith flicked over the 10♦ and 6♣ giving him a full house – sixes with tens. He was coming second to a strong hand.

By this time George had joined us at the rail and was getting swept up in the excitement.

We cheered Keith on while the other two were pacing nervously. The dealer was determined to get his minute of fame before turning over the river card. The 6♠. Keith threw his hands up in the air and shouted, 'You fucking ripper! Quad sixes!' The dealer immediately castigated him.

'Sorry, boss,' he said. Duly chastised he rushed over to the rail and hugged us. 'I think supper's on me tonight.'

'I should bloody well think so,' said George. 'With a tad over fifty grand you could buy supper for everyone.'

'Not likely,' he said with a big grin across his face as he filled up the plastic trays with his winnings. Always the gentleman, he commiserated with the other players and then joined us as we headed towards the cashier.

'You took a big risk with your hand,' I said. 'The way you were playing I was sure you had aces. But that's poker for you. You could come back tomorrow night and lose twice as much. One card can make all the difference.'

'That's what I love about the game, even though you're stating the bleedin' obvious,' Keith laughed, passing his chips through the grill.

'Doesn't it worry you, carrying around this much money?' asked Sarah as we walked over to the café.

'We don't have to worry about anything while you're with us,' I said.

We ordered coffee and cakes.

'What aren't you telling us?' asked Harry.

'Yeah, what's this story you were going to tell us?' asked George.

'Okay, okay, calm down and I'll fill you in.'

I started with us leaving the cinema and when I'd finished the guys were mesmerised. They couldn't take their eyes off Sarah. Why would they?

'Bloody hell,' said Harry with a laugh. 'Heaven help Tommy if he steps out of line.'

'No need to worry guys, I know her weak spots.'

A slap on the arm from a blushing Sarah made us crack up.

Friday noon – Diamond Harbour

Mick arrived at Diamond Harbour, asked for directions to the hospital, and parked in a short-term parking bay near the main entrance. He walked into reception and, after finding out Angie's ward number, went into the kiosk and bought the biggest bunch of flowers he could see. A box of his favourite Cadbury chocolates caught his eye.

He took the lift to the third floor and walked along the corridor past the nurses' station, mentally ticking off the room numbers until he found room 317. He knocked gently on the door and, after a moment, opened it, spying Angie asleep in the chair. She was dressed and her bag was beside her. Her phone was tightly clasped in her hand. A wave of sadness came over him. How could anyone treat someone like her any other way than with love and kindness? He put the flowers and chocolates on the bed, moved her bag, knelt down beside her and kissed her on the cheek. She opened her eyes and her face broke into the broadest of smiles. She threw her arms around his neck and returned his kiss.

'Oh, Mick, I'm so happy you've come back. This last fortnight has been hell. Please tell me you'll stay.'

'I ain't goin' anywhere, sweetie. You're going to have to put up with me.'

'Mmm. That'll be easy.'

'First things first,' he said. 'Let's get you out of here and home.'

'I have to warn you, there's a heap of Danny's stuff you'll see.'

'Don't you worry about that. You concentrate on getting well. We can sort anything else out later.'

Mick remembered seeing a wheelchair outside the nurses' station. He wheeled it back to Angie's room. As she stood, she put her arms around his neck and kissed him. They hugged for a few moments and then, with Angie onboard nursing her bag, flowers and chocolates, he wheeled her to the nurses' station where she thanked them for looking after her. They wished her well and Mick pushed her to the lift. An orderly followed them to the car and retrieved the chair. Angie gave Mick directions and as traffic was light, they were at her place in less than ten minutes.

The house was at the end of a cul-de-sac and had uninterrupted ocean views. They were magnificent.

'You should see the Sydney to Hobart yachts as they pass by,' said Angie, while Mick put her bag near the dining table.

He opened the floor-to-ceiling, bi-fold glass doors and stood on the deck. The fresh air filled his lungs as he watched the sea birds ride the thermal currents. Their occasional squawks distracted him from looking into the distance. The ocean was blue, tipped with white caps.

'A bloke would be mad to go back to dreary Pommy land after seeing views this good.'

'You're not mad,' she smiled. She pulled him into a warm embrace.

Mick could feel her shaking so he held her gently, stroking her hair. After a few minutes she pulled away, kissing him as she went.

She found a vase in the kitchen cupboard and, after putting the flowers in water, she took her bag into the bedroom and was amazed to find the bedsheets had been changed and turned down, with a rose between the pillows.

'Come in here, Mick,' she shouted.

Mick walked quickly to the bedroom.

'Look what Vicki did while I was in hospital. How nice!'

'She's a great friend,' said Mick.

Angie walked through the house. The washing and ironing had been done, the floors vacuumed, furniture dusted, and fresh milk was in the fridge, along with two dinner dishes Vicki had prepared before heading back to Sydney. Two garbage bags of Danny's things were in the laundry near the back door.

'She doesn't finish her shift until six so I'll ring her then. In the meantime, we can have a coffee and talk. There's so much I want to tell you.'

'Do you want some lunch first?'

'I think I'll save myself for tea.'

Mick was happy to wait. He made the coffee.

Angie spent the next few hours talking about her relationship with Danny, the need to give the police a statement about her injuries, what to do with all his gear, and what she and Mick were going to do.

'There's plenty of time for us to plan things,' said Mick. 'After you've spoken to Vicki, I'll heat up a dinner dish. I noticed a bakery on the way here. I'll nick out and get some crusty bread. Would you be up for champers?'

'Sure would. I get the feeling I'm going to be spoilt.'

'You'd better believe it.'

Friday night – Hong Kong

Sarah and I left the guys at the casino and caught a cab back to the hotel. I spoke to the receptionist, telling her we might be checking out on Monday. She wasn't concerned and asked me to let her know sometime Sunday. She said she could contact the airline for us and arrange a flight on Monday afternoon if suitable.

I thanked her. 'These people are so polite and helpful,' I said to Sarah as we headed for the lift. 'How's your inner thigh, by the way?'

'That's for me to know and you to find out, big boy.'

She squeezed my bum as the doors closed. The lift had passengers, which was a good thing. God knows what we would have gotten up to.

'When we get back to Sydney do you reckon you could teach me some of those martial arts moves?'

'If you persist with your fitness training, including yoga, for at least six months I might think about it. To do those particular moves you have to be supple.'

'So, you're going to be around in six months' time?'

'If you behave yourself there's a good chance.'

'If I make you laugh every day, will that be enough inducement for you to hang around?'

'It will be a good start,' she laughed.

'What time do you think we should go to see the cops tomorrow?'

'Well, I'd like to get it sorted early so we've got the rest of the day to ourselves. I want to go up to Victoria Peak again before we head home. The weather is meant to be better than last time. We could have a nice lunch as well.'

'I think you're inheriting my planning skills,' I said, pulling her close.

Diamond Harbour

Mick put the dish in the oven and turned it on. He gave Angie a kiss, then headed out to the bakery and bottle shop.

He was away about twenty minutes. Angie had a good talk to Vicki.

She had set the table, removed the small water reservoir from the stalk, and put the rose in a slim vase in the middle. Mick noticed the plates were Villeroy and Boch.

'You've got great taste in crockery.'

'Thanks, I don't bring it out much. It usually gets smashed.'

'You know what? I reckon it's going to be out all the time from now on.'

'I hope so, Mick.'

'I haven't mentioned it but I collect antiques and bits and pieces. I've got some of my grandmother's old Villeroy and Boch back home. She was pretty keen on it and as I'd always admired her 1907 wall plate of Mettlach Castle she made sure I got it before she died. Maybe you'd like to visit my place one day.'

'It's my favourite brand and, yes, I'd love to. Wow. Things are moving pretty fast with us. I don't know about you but I'm feeling pretty comfortable being around you.'

'I'm pretty comfortable around me, too,' he laughed, gently caressing her face. 'It's strange, because my mate Tommy was telling me about the lady he met, not even a fortnight ago, and they feel the same way about each other. She came to Hong Kong with us. Talk about a couple of love-struck teenagers. They can't bear to be out of each other's sight.' He continued, 'I'll tell you something, Angie, I've met a few women over the years but the connection was never like this. It's hard to describe. It feels right.'

'Beautifully said, Mick. Now, where's my bloody dinner?'

Mick grabbed her and was about to tickle her when he realised she was still fragile from her ordeal and didn't need too much excitement too soon. Instead, he kissed her gently, walked to the oven, and used the oven mitts to remove the dish. It was chicken and smelled great. He sliced and buttered the breadstick, opened the champagne, guarding the cork with his hand, and poured two glasses.

'A toast,' said Mick. 'Firstly, to Vicki; she's amazing, and secondly, to us; we're amazing.'

Angie laughed as they clinked glasses and sipped.

'Mmm, that's good,' she said.

Angie's appetite wasn't back to normal; however, she managed enough to reassure Mick she was on the road to recovery.

After the meal Mick made her relax on the lounge while he cleared the table. He made plunger coffee and cheekily opened the chocolates.

Angie smiled and, with her legs tucked under her, snuggled into Mick while they sipped their drinks.

They spent a pleasant evening indulging in idle chit-chat, looking out onto the never-ending ocean, watching pleasure boats and the occasional cargo or cruise ship sail past.

Mick looked down at Angie and realised she had gone to sleep. He picked her up and carried her into the bedroom. He removed her slippers and pulled the covers over her. He kissed her on the forehead, quietly closed the curtains, and left the room.

He grabbed blankets from the hall cupboard and made up a bed on the lounge.

DAY 21 – SATURDAY

Saturday morning – Hong Kong

The police station was a short walk from the hotel and the polite duty sergeant showed us through to an interview room. It was similar to those I'd seen in police shows on television except this room had air-conditioning. It was bearable. I could imagine Noodle not getting the same considerations.

Ken walked in, apologised for keeping us waiting, and thanked us for coming. He placed a manila folder on the interview table, removed a classy-looking fountain pen from his shirt pocket and began the interview. He reviewed the details we'd given him last night and told us Noodle's real name was Lee Yang.

'He prefers to be called Mr Yang. He has a high opinion of himself. We like to think of him as a – what is it the Yanks say? – two-bit crim.'

He flashed his pen about as he spoke. I had a feeling it was maybe a gift or reward for service. He wrote copious notes as we answered his questions and after ten minutes or so was satisfied we had not incited the incident.

He looked at Sarah and told her Yang and his sidekick could not yet recall what had happened. They were subdued this morning and provided no resistance when interviewed. Apparently, Yang wasn't a nice guy and had a history of intimidating people and avoiding arrest. His profile, made up from various victims' descriptions over time, made him easily recognisable even in a crumpled state on the footpath.

Ken was grateful to Sarah and, when she jokingly suggested he might be in for a promotion if he was successful in the prosecution of Yang, he seemed to have a light-bulb moment and indicated he would drop a hint or two with his superiors.

He replaced the cap on his pen with a flourish and returned it to his pocket, closed the file and rose from his chair. As we walked from the room, he was profuse in his thanks and hoped the incident hadn't spoilt our holiday. We assured him we hadn't lost any sleep and wouldn't hesitate to return to Hong Kong at some stage in the future.

'Maybe on our honeymoon,' I said. I received a sharp dig in the ribs.

We shook hands and, with Sarah's arm linked firmly in mine to avoid further rib damage, walked out into the noisy Saturday morning traffic.

We crossed the road and headed to a coffee shop. 'You're a cheeky bugger,' she said.

I kissed her on the cheek. 'You bring out the best in me.'

We had coffee and took a ferry trip around the island. It stopped at various points to put down and pick up passengers – mainly tourists. Some locals took advantage of the upmarket service.

We arrived back in time for a late lunch, then headed back to our room. Sarah decided to call her mum and I thought it a good opportunity to send Sylvia an e-mail telling her what was going on.

I opened my laptop. One message from Anne:

Hi again Tommy.

With help from Rachael in Vegas I've managed to track down Jack's lawyer who's in LA. He's advised me that Jack had a will but because he didn't know Jack had died it hasn't been read. It's normal for relatives to be present where possible at the reading of wills, however, as I wasn't able to fly over again, I gave him the authority to open it. As you know, Jack had a collection of Corvette cars – fifteen of them – and he has bequeathed five to you. What you mightn't know is he also had another ten cars made up of Porsches, Ferraris and a Maserati. The lawyer and I have agreed you have first choice of any five. Jack would have been the first to tell you I've never had an interest in cars. I've discussed the issue of the remaining cars with the lawyer and he is in agreeance that their disposal, if you're willing, be left up to you. I realise this may be a big imposition on your time and I understand if you decline. There's no hurry to resolve this as the cars are kept in a secure compound along with cars belonging to other enthusiasts.

As the lawyer is the executor, he is happy to do an inventory of Jack's apartment's contents and send it to me. The apartment itself is on a long lease that can be ended at any time as there's a waiting list of people keen to take it over.

I will be most grateful if you will consider the situation and let me know your intentions. Regards. Anne.

'Hey, Sarah, come and check out this e-mail from Jack's sister.'

'… well I'd better get along, Mum. Look forward to seeing you next week. Yes, I'll make sure Tommy doesn't get into any more scrapes. Love you. Bye.'

'Whadd'ya mean you'll make sure Tommy doesn't get into any more scrapes?'

'Mum doesn't know I'm proficient in martial arts and she'd worry herself sick if she thought I might have to defend myself when travelling as an escort. I told her you got into a tussle but sorted it out.'

'Struth, she'll think I'm a superhero. One week saving her life, the next, disarming dangerous Hong Kong thugs single-handed.'

'Don't get ahead of yourself, big guy. You got one thing right though. You're my superhero.'

She sat beside me and pulled my head onto her lap. She spent a few minutes stroking my hair and caressing my face.

'I'll give you an hour to stop.'

She squeezed my ear. 'Show me this e-mail.'

'Bloody hell, Tommy. This is unexpected. What do you reckon?'

'I've no idea at this stage. The fact the cars are safe is something. I don't want to rush into anything.' I couldn't help but laugh. 'I reckon Lucky would come in his pants if I told him about this.'

'Who's Lucky?'

'He's the guy who looks after the garage at the Marina. He's a car nut and always has my car in showroom condition. It was only a fortnight ago he was trying to convince me to upgrade the Chrysler to a Corvette. Spooky, uh?'

'Perhaps he can go over to LA and sort them out.'

I laughed again. 'Shit, I'd never see him again. He'd spend the rest of his life driving them back and forth across the States with a different chick, or two, each time. He considers himself a ladies' man and he also loves the horses. He's always giving me tips that I ignore; then he tells me how well they've done.'

Sarah put the kettle on. 'I suppose it's not the worst problem you could have. What would you do with five classy cars? One for you and one each for the guys?'

'Gosh, that's not such a crazy idea.'

'I was kidding,' she said, pouring the coffee and bringing it over to the lounge. 'Why don't we head back to Sydney like we planned, catch up with Mick and Angie, and then over the next few weeks try and come up with a solution?'

'You're planning skills have hit top gear,' I said, sipping my coffee.

'There's no problem talking it over with the guys here before we head back either. You never know when another great idea might jump out and bite us.'

'Why don't we see if they want to have dinner tonight and we can discuss it? I must admit I like your suggestion about a car each, even though you were kidding.'

'There'd be a lot to sort out if you went down that track. But I suppose whatever way you choose there's bound to be *some* problems.'

I sent Anne a reply telling her I'd let her know within the fortnight. I also sent Sylvia an e-mail. I explained about Sarah, Jack, the guys and the fact we were flying home on Monday. I told her I might not see her before she goes to her first English class but I wished her good luck.

'You've got a lot of time for Sylvia, haven't you?'

'I admire people like her who are prepared to work hard for what they want and who appreciate a helping hand. I'm looking forward to you meeting her. I'm sure you'll hit it off.'

'She sounds typical of most Vietnamese people. They are hard workers and look after each other. The family bond is extremely strong.'

Dinner with the guys was most enjoyable. When I told them about the cars they were gobsmacked.

'The early model Corvettes in top condition are sought after worldwide. The first model in 1953 certainly looked better than it performed, but if you had one in mint or near-mint condition you could almost name your price.'

'How come you know so much about Corvettes, Harry?' asked Keith.

'Remember the band Velox I played in, back in the day? Well, the lead singer's old man had an early model Vauxhall Velox – that's how the band got its name. It was a big, family-size car and he would always be telling his kids that as soon as they were out of his hair, he'd trade the Velox in on a Corvette. He was obsessed and would tell anyone who showed the slightest interest all about them; including me.'

'Do you know what types Jack had in his collection, Tommy?' asked George.

'Only the makes and how many at this stage. I could probably get in touch with the storage company through Jack's lawyer.'

Sarah jumped in. 'Or you could send Lucky over.'

'Isn't Lucky your garage guy?' asked Harry.

'Yes, he is, and earlier I explained to Sarah who he was and whether I could trust him with twenty-five pricy cars. She's only stirring the pot. But don't worry, I'll deal with her later.'

'I'd be careful if I was you, Tommy,' said Keith. 'She might put the sleeper hold on you.'

'She usually does anyway; but I always remember what's happened when I wake up, unlike Noodle and his mate.'

Sarah laughed, raising her hands in defeat. A pink hue spread across her cheeks.

'Seriously though, if you guys come up with any workable ideas, I'd be glad to hear them.'

I asked Keith if he was up for golf tomorrow and, although he had agreed to go with the others on a harbour cruise, he was happy to have a quick nine holes early. We arranged to head out at eight.

The guys were going to a floor show before hitting the tables so Sarah and I said goodnight and headed up to our room.

'Will you come to golf tomorrow?' I asked.

'If you don't mind, I'll stay at the hotel and hit the gym. A good workout won't do me any harm, particularly if we're going to be sitting on a plane for ten hours on Monday.'

'Good idea. I might come back from golf and have a spa and a swim. Maybe we could grab lunch somewhere.'

'We're lucky people, Tommy.'

'We sure are.' I lay back and started thinking about the cars again.

Saturday morning – Diamond Harbour

'Knock, knock; time to wake up, sleepy head.'

Mick pushed the door open with his foot and placed the tray on the bedside table. Angie blinked and rubbed her eyes as he opened the curtains, letting the brilliant sunshine in.

'Good morning, Mick. What's all this?'

'You've got to get your strength back and eggs on toast is what you need. Freshly brewed coffee will kick-start your brain and looking at me will kick-start your heart.'

She laughed. 'How did I get into bed? The last thing I remember, we were on the lounge drinking coffee.'

'You nodded off so I carried you here and tucked you in.'

She looked across the bed. 'Where did you sleep?'

'I grabbed some blankets and crashed on the lounge.'

'You didn't have to, you could have slept here.'

'You needed a good sleep. We'll have plenty of together-time I hope.'

'You're a real gentleman, Mick. Come here.'

Mick leant down and Angie put her arms around his neck and kissed him.

'Sorry about the morning breath.'

He laughed and handed her a glass of freshly squeezed orange juice. 'This should fix it. And while you're having brekky, I'll have a shower.'

By mid-morning they had got themselves organised.

'Do you realise it's a fortnight since we had our day together?' she said.

'How could I forget? I was going to suggest we pack a picnic and head out somewhere further south, maybe, and find a secluded beach where we could relax. You might even feel up to having a chat about things.'

'What a lovely idea. There's bread in the freezer for sandwiches and the ham Vicki left in the fridge will be nice with pickles. There should be black pudding in there as well. We can always grab something else along the way if we need to.'

'Did you say black pudding?'

'Gotcha. Only kidding.'

He laughed and wagged a finger at her. 'Two can play at that game.'

He packed the hamper, including two glasses wrapped in a tea towel, and carried it out to the car along with a couple of picnic blankets. He'd pick up champagne before lunch.

Angie had dressed in a pair of shorts and T-shirt with strappy sandals. Mick was in his customary cargo shorts and short-sleeved shirt along with sandals. Their legs were tanned and Mick, more than once, caught sight of Angie glancing down at his. He had noticed hers earlier when she'd emerged from the bedroom.

Angie once again gave Mick directions until they got onto the highway. She relaxed, happy to listen to the CDs Mick had put in the stacker, which was discreetly positioned in the boot. It held ten CDs and was operated on the console between the front seats. Mick had selected the shuffle mode so each new song was a surprise.

They were ten minutes into the trip when Mick looked across and noticed Angie was asleep. He turned the volume down and breathed deeply – she was safe. He hadn't felt this good in ages.

Sunday morning – Hong Kong

I'd set the alarm for six. I liked a couple of hours to get myself organised before I set out. I'd arranged room service to arrive at seven which gave me enough time to have a leisurely shower and terrorise Sarah for half an hour. I had manhandled her into submission when the doorbell rang. I gave the trolley-boy a handsome tip, then wheeled the trolley into the room.

'Are you sure you want to play golf?' asked Sarah, between bites of toast. 'It's not fair to leave a girl in this condition.'

'So sorry. Maybe the gym workout will take your mind off me for a while.'

'Well, if it doesn't, you'd better watch out when you get home.'

'If that happens, I'll lie down and take it like a man.'

Sarah giggled. 'Finish your breakfast and get out of here.'

Keith was waiting in the hotel foyer chatting up the pretty Asian receptionist as I walked from the lift.

I looked at her and smiled. 'Hate to break up the party, but I need to take money off this man.'

'He was telling me he took money off other guys last night so don't feel bad if you take some off him.'

We laughed. 'Tell me all about it in the cab.'

The guys had had one of their best nights at the tables. George had cleaned up as usual at blackjack, and Keith and Harry, while playing at separate tables, won a few big poker pots.

'How's thirty-five thousand US dollars for quad twos sound to you, Tommy?'

'Sounds bloody great. What did you beat?'

'A full house and a flush. I was apprehensive to start with because the blinds were \$250 and \$500 and I hadn't played at a table like that for a long time. My hole cards were the A♥ and 2♥ and I was on the button. Everyone folded around to me. My money was holding up well, so I called the big blind and so did the small blind. The flop was three twos; can you believe it? The turn was the 10♠ and the river the 7♠. These guys were throwing money into the pot like it was poison. I knew I couldn't be beaten so I kept raising and they kept raising back. It was cruel of me for not calling, but what the fuck; they'd take my money given half a chance. What are the odds of getting two four-of-a-kind on consecutive nights? I love Hong Kong, Tommy.'

'Yeah, they're rare as a rule, but three weeks ago – the day Jack first rang me – I was playing in a tournament against idiot amateurs and got quad aces. In another hand a while later I folded my hole cards after the turn. The bloody river card was a king that would have given me another quad.'

'Shit happens, big guy. Why did you fold?'

'Long story. You didn't run into another Noodle last night by any chance?'

'No. These were good blokes. A few of them were Yanks on holidays. They were louder than their shirts but overall they played the game well.'

'Tell you what, mate. I know I've said it before but I'm going to miss you guys. Sarah is too. She's only known you for a week but she's a good judge of people and she reckons there are ladies out there missing out big-time.'

'Well,' said Keith, 'the lady on the hotel desk caught my eye but I'm not sure she's interested in a guy like me. I'm no oil painting.'

'Shit, Keith. I've seen plenty of fucking ugly oil paintings in my time so don't put yourself in that category. Look, I never thought someone like Sarah would give me a second glance and now we can't get enough of each other's company. You'll never know unless you put yourself out there. Why don't you ask her out? If she's attached, you'll soon know. If she says yes, take her someplace nice and regale her with your youthful adventures of sunken treasure. It's sure to get her interested.'

'You always know what to say at the right time. But what the fuck does *regale* mean? To be honest, Tommy, I think you've got a plum up your arse.'

We laughed and it wasn't long before we arrived at the course.

A bucket of balls each belted down the practise fairway and we were ready.

Keith won rock-paper-scissors and decided to tee off first. It was a straight par-5 on a narrow fairway and he smacked the cover off it. He could make the green in two.

'Do you know that rock-paper-scissors is called Roshambo?'

Keith was howling with laughter. 'Fuck me dead, Tommy. Did you eat a fuckin' dictionary for breakfast?'

I slapped him on the back and belted my drive past his, albeit into the first cut.

'Not in too much trouble there, Tommy.'

We walked to Keith's ball and, as he was about to launch his fairway wood, three men appeared from the light bush off the fairway and started towards us. They were carrying lightweight golf bags and as they drew near, they pulled out baseball bats.

I glanced at Keith, he looked ashen. I felt sick in my stomach.

The biggest thug looked at me. 'Is your name Tommy?'

'Yeah.'

No sooner than I'd spoken I saw the blur of his bat. As it made contact with the side of my head, I heard him say, 'This is a present from Mr Yang with best wishes, you fucking Aussie prick.'

The sky turned dark as I felt my knees crumble and, as if in slow motion, I fell to the ground. As my eyes were closing, I caught a glimpse of Keith swinging his fairway wood …

Saturday afternoon – Diamond Harbour

Angie woke as Mick was getting back into the car. He had put a cold bottle of champagne and a large container filled with fresh salad into a cooler bag in the boot.

'Hello, sleepy head,' he smiled, restarting the engine. 'You've done a lousy job of keeping me company for the last hour.'

'I'm so sorry, Mick. I can't believe how tired I am. I guess the knock on my head might have something to do with it.'

'I think you might be right, Dr Kingston.' He leaned over and kissed her tenderly. 'Take it easy. I reckon we're not far from a nice spot to have lunch. Are you up for it?'

'Do bears shit in the woods?'

'Even when you're crook, you make me laugh. I love it.'

'I'll keep on making you laugh if you keep on talking in your Pommy accent. I love it.'

'Copycat.'

They drove off the highway down an underused track onto a grassed area near the beach. It was deserted. Small waves were breaking and the sun brought colour to Angie's cheeks.

Mick spread the blankets and set out the food. He insisted Angie relax. He presented her with a plate of food and a glass of champagne. This time he let the cork fly unchecked.

'Are you sure alcohol is okay?'

'The doctor said everything in moderation and don't get too excited. He doesn't want my blood pressure getting too high.'

'Does that mean what I think it means?'

'Not exactly. He said I could have sex four times a day as long as I didn't have an orgasm.'

'Did he?'

'Gotcha again.'

'You cheeky bugger. Just you wait – every dog has his day.'

'Woof.'

They ate their lunch in relative silence. The sounds of the waves and sea birds were accompaniment enough. Angie cleaned her plate with the last piece of her sandwich, took a sip of her champers, and leaned over and gave Mick a kiss he wouldn't forget for a while.

'What was that for? A simple thankyou would have sufficed.'

Angie's face dropped.

'Gotcha.' Mick pulled her to him and held her close. She released herself into him and they lay together in the sun.

'I think I'm falling in love with you, Mick,' she said, with a slight quiver in her voice.

Mick stroked her hair, lifted her face to his and returned her kiss.

'I loved you from the day I met you.'

Sunday mid-morning – Hong Kong

Sarah finished her gym workout, had a quick shower, then dived into the pool. She swam for half an hour. As she was getting out, two men blocked her path to her towel.

'Excuse me,' she said, trying to skirt around them.

One of them grabbed her arm. He was similar in height to her but with a wiry build, greasy hair, and an ugly, pock-marked face.

'We have a message from Mr Yang. Your fat friend might be suffering a bad headache for a while.' He paused, ogling Sarah up and down. 'Perhaps we could go into the showers for some fun. The big man might not be up for it for a while.'

'How about some foreplay first,' she hissed as she elbowed the man standing to her left in the face, then kicked his legs out from under him. He was much bigger and slow to react. With his arms still folded across his chest he fell awkwardly, hitting his head on the edge of the pool. The other guy still had hold of her arm. She spread two fingers and jabbed them into his eyes. He let go, screaming, and fell face-first into the pool.

The pool attendant, watching the events unfold from the other end of the pool, came running with his walkie-talkie up to his mouth.

'Are you okay, lady?' he asked, looking down at the two guys.

'I'm fine but you'd better get that one out of the water. He won't last much longer without air.'

It was only moments before the doors to the pool area burst open and two burly security guards hoisted the guy out. He was breathing but gasping in pain. Blood was seeping from his eye sockets. The other guy was unconscious but Sarah felt his neck and found a strong pulse.

'I'm getting sick of this,' she said.

She bent down to the guy she'd blinded, scruffed his shirt and put her face close to his.

'What has happened to Tommy, you piece of shit?'

At first, he didn't speak; but with her fingers moving to his groin he was quick to start talking.

He cried out in pain. 'They were going to get him on the golf course.'

'How did Yang know our movements?'

Another pause but, as Sarah's fingers tightened around his sensitive area, he told her Mr Yang has many eyes in many places.

'Well, he's got two less now,' she said, tightening her grip while keeping her other hand over his mouth, until he lapsed into unconsciousness.

The pool attendant looked over Sarah's shoulder. 'He's going to be oh-so-sore when he wakes up.'

'I have to find Tommy. Get an ambulance for these two arseholes and tell the police I'm heading to the Lotus Creek Golf Course and I'll contact them as soon as I've found him.'

Sarah rushed back to her room and was getting changed when her phone rang. It was Tommy's number.

'Sarah, it's Keith. Three blokes attacked us on the golf course. Tommy's copped a bad hit to his head. We're in the emergency ward at Peacehaven Hospital. They've got him in an induced coma and are prepping him for surgery. They have to release pressure to his brain real quick.'

'Bloody hell, Keith. I'm on my way. Are you okay?'

'Yeah, I've put the bloke who hit Tommy in hospital. Fairway woods and knee caps don't go well together. When he went down his two gutless mates ran off. It could have been worse if they'd got another hit in. I'll see you when you get here.'

'Okay, Keith, and thanks. I owe you big-time.'

Sarah rang reception and told them to tell the police she was going to the hospital, not the golf course, and to have a cab waiting for her. It delivered her to the hospital's main entrance. Keith was waiting for her. She hugged him. He felt her shaking.

'It's okay, love. They're taking good care of him.'

'It's not only that. Two of Yang's goons confronted me while I was swimming.'

'Shit, what happened.'

'Well, we might see them as they come through to emergency.'

'Oh no. You haven't, have you?'

'I'm afraid so. They didn't leave me with many options.'

'What's with this Yang guy? Can't he accept Tommy beat him fair and square?'

'Apparently it's about saving face. It's embarrassing to be beaten, let alone by someone other than a fellow Asian.'

'Fuck me. If I took offence every time I got beaten at poker by anyone other than a white dude I'd be in for life. Plus, he had shit cards, if I recall.'

'That's the difference. Have they said when we can see Tommy?'

'The nurse said they'd come and get us when they've done the surgery.'

'Oh, poor Tommy, please be okay. We've got so much living to do.'

Keith put his around her and they walked to a waiting area.

Saturday late afternoon – Diamond Harbour

Angie gave a shiver. The sea breeze was getting up.

'You go and hop in the car and I'll pack things up. Fancy a coffee on the way back?'

'I'd love one.'

Within twenty minutes they were eating chocolate brownies and sipping coffee. They were relaxing in a corner booth.

'Do you mind if we chat about a few things?' she asked.

'If you're up for it. There's no hurry.'

'The sooner I get this business sorted out, the better I think I'll feel. I wouldn't mind going to the cops tomorrow and giving them a statement. I know it's not going to achieve much, now Danny's dead, but I guess they have to go through the motions.'

'Do you want me to come with you?'

'I'd love you to come with me but I'm not sure how in-depth the interview will be. There could be some nasty stuff come out.'

'I'm a big boy. I can handle it.'

'I also want to get rid of his crap from the house. There's fishing gear, scuba gear, a couple of surfboards, mountain-climbing ropes, and fuck-knows what else. The lease is in my name along with the phone and power, so I don't have to muck around with that.'

'I reckon the Salvos will be pretty happy to get it. If they can make a quid out of it, it will be a win-win for everyone.'

Angie leaned across and held his hands. 'I'm so glad I was working that Saturday at the casino. Otherwise we would never have met. I don't want to think what might have been.'

'Let's get all this shit sorted out, and then you can start fresh. No looking back, okay?'

'Okay. Let's go home.'

The music took her mind off things as they drove home. They picked up Chinese takeaway – Angie's favourite – and spent the evening watching Australia play India in the one-day cricket. When it was over, Australia had won by eighteen runs. Ricky Ponting had smashed 124 out of Australia's 317. It earned him Player of the Match.

'The only problem with that game, Angie, was the Poms weren't playing. But to be honest I don't reckon they could have beaten the Aussies tonight. Ricky played a blinder.'

'It was a great game anyway. Your guys will get their chance but don't expect me to be cheering for you. I must admit I prefer cricket to rugby or bloody Aussie Rules,' she said.

'Perhaps we can go to a game when England plays Australia.'

'I'd love to, Mick. In fact, I'd go with you to watch two turds roll down a hill.'

'You'd what?'

'Gotcha again.' She laughed and snuggled back into his arms.

When it was time for bed, Angie told Mick he wasn't sleeping on the couch. They got changed and slid under the covers. She moved into his arms and was asleep in minutes. Mick held her until he was sure she was in a deep sleep. He slid his arm out from under her neck. She stirred and rolled over to her side. He smiled and closed his eyes. He was a happy man.

Sunday afternoon – Hong Kong

They had been waiting about half an hour when Senior Sergeant Ken walked into the waiting room.

'Trouble seems to follow you guys around,' he said with a solemn grin. 'How's Tommy?'

'He's in surgery so we don't know anything yet, except he got a nasty hit on the head, compliments of Mr Yang.'

'Well, Mr Yang is now in solitary confinement and has been charged with being an accessory to attempted murder. His associates have been rounded up and, based on what the pool guy told me, I'm fairly certain no charges will be laid against you. I must say though, you did a job and a half on those guys. One is permanently blind and won't be playing with himself any time soon and the other is nursing a broken leg and fractured skull. They have been taken to a hospital in Macau along with Mr Kneecap and will be out of circulation for a hell of a long time. The two guys who ran away at the golf course are singing like canaries. They have given us enough information to see Yang put away for possibly twenty years. We didn't realise he was running such a big organisation – extortion, drugs, prostitution and money laundering. We're currently raiding his headquarters and rounding up at least another ten of his gang.'

'If he's king of the heap, why would he risk himself walking the streets when he's got a bunch of goons to do his dirty work?' asked Sarah.

'It's about showing his men *he* is the top dog and is prepared to put himself out there.'

'What about the canaries?' asked Keith.

'We promised them protection if they spilled their guts, which they did; but we lied.' He looked at them both. A proud smile crept over his face. 'They'll get their reward on the inside.'

'The promotion's looking good, Ken.' Sarah smiled for the first time, feeling relieved at last they would be left alone.

'I shouldn't have to bother you again but if I do, I'll call. I guess you won't be flying home tomorrow?'

'Call me anytime, Ken. Until we speak to the doctor we'll be staying put.'

Ken smiled at Keith. 'By the way, nice fairway shot.'

'Thanks, Ken. I reckon I would have reached the green if it had been a ball and not a kneecap.'

'Give Tommy my regards,' said Ken, getting up. He shook hands and walked away.

It was another hour before the doctor appeared. He sat next to Sarah and smiled. The tears flowed down her face.

'I hope they're happy tears,' the doctor said. 'I had to drill two small holes above his left ear which led to an immediate reduction in the swelling, due to the release of fluid. X-rays show no brain damage, but he'll need a week or two of rest. He is one lucky man. If the hit hadn't glanced off his head things could have been much worse.'

Sarah wiped her eyes. 'We had planned to fly back to Sydney tomorrow but that won't be happening.'

'I think it would be at least three weeks before I'd recommend that he fly. But who knows? I'll keep an eye on him over the next fortnight and then make an assessment.'

'So, what you're saying is Tommy will be in here for two weeks.'

'Correct. We'll move him to a private suite with twin beds. You're more than welcome to stay. I think it would be less stressful if you're together. Speak with the administration staff. They'll be able to work out the details.'

He looked at his watch. 'You may as well sort out your hotel accommodation now because Tommy won't be conscious for another three to four hours. You should have enough time to get set up in his room before we transfer him from the recovery ward. I must warn you, though. He'll be groggy for a while and may have temporary memory loss, but the brain has an amazing capacity to recover from this type of trauma.'

'Thank you so much, Doctor. You've put my mind at rest.'

'If you've no further questions, I'll be off.'

'No, we're fine. Thanks again.'

Sarah turned to Keith and hugged him. 'Would you mind giving me a hand with Tommy's and my luggage?'

'Goes without saying. Perhaps once we've got you settled in, we can grab a bite to eat and a coffee.'

'Food has been the furthest thing from my mind. It's a good idea, Keith.'

Within three hours Sarah had packed up the hotel room, settled the account, cancelled the plane tickets and, with Keith's help, moved the luggage to the hospital's top floor suite. The beds were two king singles. They could be pushed together.

Keith had noticed a café in the hospital foyer.

'Looks heaps better than the ones in Sydney,' said Sarah.

They had a light meal with good coffee before Keith said goodnight and Sarah headed back to the suite.

She pushed the two beds together and lay down. She moved her hand to the other bed and closed her eyes.

*

Keith got back to the hotel and caught up with the others.

'Where the hell have you been?' asked George, as they ordered beer. 'We were meant to be on a harbour cruise.'

'Well, you knew Tommy and I were playing golf today, right. Well …'

Sunday morning – Diamond Harbour

This time it was Angie up first. She had cooked up a mix of scrambled eggs, crispy bacon, fried tomatoes and sautéed mushrooms. The toast was nearly done when Mick walked out. She kissed him tenderly, pushed him playfully into a chair and handed him a juice.

'What. No black pudding?'

'You're having that with cold rice for lunch.'

'Yum, my favourite.'

They ate together, laughed together, washed up together, had a shower together, then went back to bed and made love for the first time.

They dragged themselves out of bed in the early afternoon. They didn't have Angie's promised lunch. Mick fired up the barbeque instead and they enjoyed a couple of steaks and salad. It gave Mick the energy to clean out under the house.

Angie wasn't wrong. He couldn't believe how much stuff Danny had stored there. He could only carry a few things each time up the steep slope to the front gate. Steps would have made it easier. It was a good hour before he walked back into the kitchen. Beads of sweat on his forehead and damp patches under his armpits and back gave Angie the opportunity to give him a stir.

'I thought you were fitter than that,' she laughed, handing him a glass of iced water.

'So did I.' He tried to pull her into a sweaty embrace. She cleverly side-stepped him and ran to the other side of the dining table, putting obstacle and distance between them.

'Have a shower and I might consider a cuddle.'

'Deal. I've thrown a big plastic sheet over everything until the morning. I'll load up the car and drop it off at the Salvos and it will be gone – forever.'

Mick had a shower and Angie was true to her word; but the cuddle turned into a late afternoon of lovemaking ending with champagne, cheese and crackers. It kept them going until dinner.

Mick got the other dish Vicki had prepared from the fridge and put it in the oven. It was beef and mushroom. While it was heating through, he prepared veggies.

Angie looked at the table Mick had set and smiled appreciatively. 'I didn't think I'd be hungry after the steak we had for lunch and the afternoon snacks. Must be the workout we had in-between.'

Mick laughed and pulled a chair out for Angie. He got a peck on the cheek for his efforts and in return she got a gentle tickle in the ribs. She let out a squeal, making them laugh. They enjoyed their meal and drank the leftover champagne.

Mick decided to use the dishwasher as they were keen to watch TV. The Sunday night movie was *Wild Hogs* with John Travolta.

'Did you see *Easy Rider* with Peter Fonda?' she asked.

'Didn't everyone?'

'Well, this is a take-off of that. I saw *Wild Hogs* when it first came out and I loved it, so it will be good to see it again. By the way, you haven't eaten all those chocolates you bought me, have you?'

Mick looked at her sheepishly. 'Sorry, I've got a sweet tooth.'

'Bugger, I was looking forward to them while we watched the movie.'

Mick grabbed the box off the TV table and opened it – it was nearly full. 'Gotcha.'

'You're such a naughty boy. You know what happens to naughty boys?'

'I have a feeling I'll find out later.'

He gave her a kiss and turned up the volume. They nestled comfortably on the lounge.

Sunday evening – Hong Kong

I was watching Keith and Sarah walking down the aisle. She looked radiant in a pure white dress. How could this be? She's supposed to be marrying me. My head was pounding. I had to stop this from happening. Someone had hold of my hand. I couldn't move. Shit I was thirsty.

I opened my eyes. The light was blinding. If I squinted, I could see Sarah looking down at me with tears in her eyes.

'What's a bloke got to do to get a drink around here?'

'Oh, Tommy. You're back.'

'What's wrong with it?'

She laughed. 'You're sick and you're still a clown.'

'Where the hell am I? I was watching you and Keith getting married.'

'You can't remember being on the golf course with Keith today?'

'What?'

Sarah kissed me and put the straw in my mouth. The water tasted good. I felt my eyes closing again.

From far away I heard her say, 'Rest and we'll talk in the morning.'

DAY 23 – MONDAY

Monday morning – Diamond Harbour

The phone was ringing. Keith's number appeared. Eight o'clock in Hong Kong. It was early for Keith to be making a social call.

'Hey Keith, what's up?'

'What isn't up is more the point.'

'To use an Aussie phrase, don't beat around the bush, mate.'

'It's a long story but don't stress out, Mick. Tommy's in hospital but he's going to be okay. It started when he took ten grand off this Asian guy at poker. It was all fair and square.'

Mick paced up and down, listening to Keith recount events.

'Bloody hell, Keith, Sarah's a dark horse.'

'Not one to be messed with. She's one classy lady, though, and a hell of a nice one, too.'

'You're not wrong. Tommy's on a real winner.'

'How are you and Angie getting on? Is she on the mend?'

Mick looked at Angie, who had appeared from the bedroom, and smiled. 'She sure is. Things are going great. We're off to see the cops today. It'll be good to put it all behind us.'

'I can't believe so much has happened in such a short time. We've been having a ball here in Honkers, apart from Tommy's troubles. The good thing is we'll be here while he's convalescing. Not sure what their plans will be once he's mended. No doubt he'll talk to you as soon as he's back in the land of the living.'

'Thanks for calling, mate. Give them our best wishes and we'll talk again soon.'

Mick told Angie what had happened. She looked genuinely concerned about Tommy's ordeal.

'Why are people getting whacked around the head?' she groaned. 'The world's gone mad.'

'Well, the two pricks responsible are no longer in circulation, so let's try and surround ourselves with normal people.'

Angie grabbed Mick's hands and walked backwards towards the bedroom, her dressing gown falling open. 'Lovers, not fighters, I say.'

Mick forced himself to hit the shower. It would have been easy to spend all of Monday in bed; however, putting off going to the cops was not the best option.

'I'm not overly hungry for lunch yet, Mick. Will we go to the police first and grab something after?'

'Why not. We can drop Danny's stuff off on the way.'

While Angie showered and got ready, Mick loaded the car. It was stacked. She grabbed a couple of apples on the way out. They ate them while she gave him directions, firstly to the tip to offload the two garbage bags, then to the Salvos store. She apologised to Mick for not helping him load or unload the car. She couldn't bring herself to touch any of Danny's stuff. Mick understood, and with the help of a Salvos' storeman unloaded it onto the delivery ramp. The guy was grateful. Mick declined to give him any details. He could see Angie was keen to get going. The police station was a couple of blocks away along the main street. It stood out from the other buildings but not in a good way. Although most of the shops and office buildings had been well maintained, the police station was drab and wanting.

They walked in the front door. The hinges cried out for oil. The enquiry counter didn't need a bell. The desk sergeant lifted his head from his pile of incident reports and, after listening to their request, directed them to a waiting area.

The detective looking after Angie's case took them to his office. He introduced himself as Reg Harper and Angie introduced Mick. He was as tall as Mick, broad shouldered, with neck muscles that made wearing a button-up shirt look unnatural. His hand enveloped Mick's — a lettuce leaf over a hard-boiled egg. Angie noticed Mick wince.

Harper directed them to two grubby visitors' chairs as he moved behind his desk. It was a mess of files. 'I hope you're recovering well, Angela.'

'Angie, please, and yes, I'm good thanks.'

'Okay. First of all, I'll bring you up to date with Danny's background. We contacted our counterparts in Adelaide and they provided us with a file of domestic violence complaints his wife made. Over the past ten or so years she has been admitted to hospital four times with various injuries; some similar to yours. He'd been charged and processed; however, he never appeared in court to answer any of the charges as his wife withdrew her complaint each time.

'The Adelaide police talked to his wife after his death and she told them he said he would kill her if she went to court. She lived in fear. She knew he was having an affair but was too frightened to ask him about it.'

'It wasn't a fucking affair,' Angie shouted. 'We were living as a de facto couple. He would fly out to his mining job, do his shift, and fly back. I had no reason to suspect anything different. What a devious, horrible bastard.'

Mick put his arm around her and she calmed down.

'Sorry.'

'It's okay. I don't blame you for being angry. How often did he hit you?'

'I can't remember but I know it happened when he drank. He'd apologise straight after and promise never to do it again. How fucking gullible can a person be?'

'That's the thing. We try to give people the benefit of the doubt but it doesn't always work. Have you had any contact with his wife?'

'I didn't know she existed until I talked to the admin people at the mines after the plane crash. I don't particularly want or need to have any contact with her. This shit is over as far as I'm concerned. I just want to move on with this terrific man beside me.'

Harper asked several more questions, wrote in his file, closed it, and smiled.

'The old saying is still relevant; today is the first day of the rest of your life. Get out there and live it.'

Angie gave him an awkward hug and Mick shook his hand. They walked out into a beautiful afternoon.

'This calls for a champers,' she said as they walked arm in arm to the car. 'Take me to the casino. I'll check in with Personnel and see how long I can take off work. We can have a drink there and I'll introduce you to my workmates.'

'I hope it wasn't too hard for you in there.'

'Well, it had to be done,' said Angie. 'Now it's over. If we never talk about it again, I won't be upset.'

'I love your positive attitude *and* your nipples brushing over the hairs on my chest.'

'You horny bastard. Wait 'til I get you home.'

She reached down between his legs, almost causing him to collide with a police car driving into the car park.

They stayed at the casino until well into the evening, chatting with the staff who, although shocked to hear her story, wished her a quick recovery. The people in the personnel department were most sympathetic and told her she should take whatever leave she had owing and have a good break.

The restaurant manager took them into the executive dining room and treated them to a four-course dinner and Bollinger champagne. It was well after eleven when they were driven home in a casino car. They could pick their car up tomorrow.

Minutes after walking in the door they were in bed. Sleep came quickly.

Monday morning – Hong Kong

As Keith ended his call to Mick, he heard a knock on his door. George and Harry strolled in and, after making sure he was okay after yesterday's dramas, took him down to breakfast.

Keith told them he would ring Sarah after breakfast to see how they were and find out the best time to visit.

*

I woke to see Sarah asleep beside me. She looked so peaceful. The room looked strange and as I lifted my hand to touch her, the door opened and a woman with a breakfast tray walked in. She smiled, placed it on the table and left.

Sarah opened her eyes, looking straight at me.

'You're awake, big guy.'

'Where the fuck are we?'

'You're in hospital. You got a nasty knock on your head yesterday while you were playing golf with Keith.'

'Couldn't have. We're playing today.'

'Trust me, darling,' she said, stroking my face, 'it's true. The doctor said your memory might be vague, so relax and I'll tell you the whole story. How about brekky first? You have to keep your strength up.'

I managed half a glass of juice and a couple of spoons of cereal.

I needed a piss, then realised I had a catheter. It felt weird but kind of nice letting it go. Sarah saw me smiling.

'What are you up to?'

'Doing what comes natural but with no hands.'

She caught on and checked the bag. 'I'm no doctor but I reckon you should be drinking more plain water.'

'Yes, Ma'am.'

I heard a phone ring. Sarah leaned over to the bedside table picked it up.

'Hi, Keith. Yes, he's awake but can't remember anything yet. We'll have to take things slowly. How about leaving it until after lunch to come in? Okay. Bye.'

She crawled over the bed and kissed me gently. 'Okay if the guys come for a visit after lunch?'

'So, I'm in hospital, eh?'

She took my face in her hands. 'Yes, you are. Do you remember us going to the movies and having a run in with Noodle – or should I say, Mr Yang?'

'Yes.'

'Well …'

I lay there listening to Sarah tell me what had happened. It sounded incredible. She showed me her bruised arm.

'So, you blinded one of the guys.'

'If the truth be known, I did him a favour.'

'What do you mean?'

'You should've seen the guy. Pardon my French, but fuck he was ugly. He was so ugly, I reckon that when God made him, he made him as ugly as he could, then hit him in the face with a shovel. I've saved him the horror of having to look at himself in the mirror for the rest of his miserable life.'

I had to hold my head while I laughed and felt the catheter at work again.

I felt my eyes closing. 'Shit I'm tired.'

Thursday – after midnight – Hong Kong

I opened my eyes. The room was dark but I could see Sarah's silhouette in the bed beside me. My head wasn't aching but I needed a drink. I fumbled around until I found the bedside light switch. I saw a jug and glass. I was about to take a sip when Sarah woke, rolled over and gave a gentle squeal.

'Yay, you've decided to wake up. Talk about giving a girl a hard time.'

'What do you mean?'

'Well, the last time we spoke was breakfast time on Monday morning. It's now twelve-thirty Thursday morning. You've been out of it for two and a half days. You slipped into a coma that the doctor said was your body's way of healing itself. They stuck a fluid line into you, though, to keep you hydrated. How are you feeling?'

'Apart from a dry throat I feel good. At least my head's stopped aching.'

'Can you remember anything?'

'I can remember a prick with a baseball bat taking a swipe at me and you telling me how you didn't want to have a pool party with two nice gentlemen and something about a shovel. Bloody hell, Sarah, I'll have to get you registered as a dangerous weapon.'

We laughed and I noticed tears running down her face.

'Come here. Someone needs a big cuddle.'

She snuggled up and after a few minutes I told her about what I now knew to be a delirious dream.

'Why would I dream that?'

'Where were you standing in the dream?'

'I was looking from the front of a church towards the back and you and Keith were walking arm in arm towards the altar.'

'Could it have been you and I were getting married and Keith was giving me away?'

'Of course. How dumb of me. Your years studying psychology have well and truly paid off.'

'It's great to have you back, big guy. If you don't start eating soon, I'll have to think of another name for you.'

'How about the one Harry gave Mick? He called him a greyhound.'

'Why a greyhound?'

'All prick and ribs.'

Sarah giggled and slid her hand under the sheet. 'Well, you're part way there. Hopefully they'll take your catheter out so you can hit the track.'

'How are the guys going?' I asked, after I'd settled down.

'Well, they came in Monday afternoon and we played poker while you ignored us. On paper I took a few thousand off them. I told them if they didn't let me win, I'd break bones. Not sure whether that had any impact on their decision making.'

'Can't imagine it. I reckon they were overawed with your beauty which scrambled their brains.'

'Yes, that's it.' She laughed and gave me a playful kiss.

'I must admit, although the guys showed me the basics, they weren't aware I was watching their every move, which helped me to take their money. I'm not sure how confident I'd be in a real game. Keith said he heard years ago that Texas hold 'em only takes five minutes to learn but a lifetime to master.'

'There's only one way to find out and hopefully that'll be soon,' I said.

'Keith said he'd spoken with Mick and he was shocked to hear what had happened. He and Angie send their love.'

'Did Keith say how they're getting on?'

'They were going to see the police Monday afternoon so Angie could get all the shit about Danny sorted out then move on with her life. Apparently, she and Mick are getting on well. Keith gets the impression they're getting serious about each other. Another whirlwind romance.'

'The best type,' I said.

'I rang Keith on Tuesday and told him you were still being unsociable so not to bother coming in. Even though I said I'd ring him when you were back with us, he rang Tuesday afternoon and twice yesterday to see how you were going. I'll call him this morning after breakfast. Do you reckon you'll go back to sleep?'

'I'm wide awake at the moment but don't let me stop you getting back to sleep.'

'I've had a good rest while I've been here so I'm happy lying here, chatting. We might doze on and off.'

I saw every hour on the clock until daylight came through the windows. I nodded off every now and then but never for too long. I felt I was recalling many things that had happened before the knock on my head. The business of Jack's cars was occupying my mind. I stroked Sarah's face and she woke.

'I don't think it's fair I'm awake and you're not,' I said.

'Oh, Tommy, it's great to have you back. I didn't tell you last night but the doctor thinks he might be able to take your bandages off and get these bloody wires off you this morning. He's keen to get you on your feet. He doesn't want you losing your strength.'

'You won't get any arguments out of me. The sooner the better. I'd like to use the toilet like a grown-up.'

'Yes, I was wondering when things would start moving again. Be warned though, it'll probably make your eyes water, not having gone for the best part of four days.'

'Thanks for giving me something to look forward to. Don't dare feed me bloody prunes. I tell you what though; I'd love to sit out on the balcony in the sun. Do you reckon they'll let me?'

'No harm in asking the doctor when he comes in.'

'I didn't realise what a flash room this is. Much like a hotel room. Speaking of which; what's happening with our room?'

'The doctor recommended I check out and move in here, which made sense.'

'So, today's Thursday?'

'Yes. Why?'

'I haven't sent Sylvia an e-mail. I was going to do it Sunday night but I was otherwise occupied, one might say.'

'One could say that. Do you want me to send her one now? You could dictate it.'

'Good idea.'

Sarah fired up the laptop and opened e-mail.

'There's a message from her. Do you want me to read it to you?'

'Yes, please. I'm keen to know what she has to say.'

Hello Tommy.

I am home from my first lesson. I am happy. Nice people in my class and nice teacher. So much to learn. Hope I learn quick. Hope you and Sarah are good.

YOU ARE ALWAYS ON MY MIND

Maybe I have learn something.

Mum and Dad still pray for you. Good man.

Everyone here miss you. Lucky taking good care of your car. Has different girlfriend every week. He is funny guy.

Hope we see you soon. Love from Sylvia.

Sarah turned the laptop around so I could see the screen. 'What's with the capital letters?'

'When I was saying goodbye before this trip, she said, "You always on my mind," and I said that with her English lessons it wouldn't be long before she would say, "You *are* always on my mind." She's certainly got a good memory.'

Sarah typed my reply but I didn't mention what had happened. She wrote that we'd changed our minds and wouldn't be coming home yet, but I'd let her know. I didn't think my argument with a baseball bat was something any of them back home needed to know. Not yet, anyway. It wasn't as if they could do anything about it.

Sarah had arranged for a coffee machine to be installed in our room. The aroma of fresh coffee after so long made me forget I was in a hospital. The fridge had been stocked with breakfast food and the bowl on the table was loaded with fruit. She had been the busy organiser while I had been in fairyland.

We had finished breakfast when the doctor arrived on his rounds. He was thrilled I was awake and eating. He was keen to get me on my feet. He undid the head dressing and told us he was happy with the healing process. I would need a patch over the wound for a while but the monitor wires could come off and the catheter could come out.

He told me he would check me out again tomorrow but couldn't foresee any issues. His main concern was that I didn't exert myself.

'I hope you heard that, Sarah. No exercise for a while.'

The doctor smiled. 'No, that's not what I said. I want you moving about but be careful.'

I saw him glance at Sarah and grin.

A nurse stayed behind after the doctor had left and disconnected the wires. Removing the catheter felt weird but I had my independence back.

The nurse swung my legs over the edge of the bed and slowly helped me up. My legs were unsteady but I wanted a shower, so I made a big effort to get moving.

'The dressing on your head is waterproof,' said the nurse.

'So I don't have to worry about water on the brain, even though I've had a tap on the head?'

'Ignore him,' said Sarah. 'I'm not sure it was wise me moving in here. I'll probably have to put up with his wisecracks until I can escape.'

The nurse laughed with us and, once she helped me onto the shower seat, left me to my own devices.

I'd never had a shower sitting down but I could come to enjoy it.

'Hey, Sarah. How about having a shower with me. You can sit on my lap.'

'Didn't you hear what the doctor said?'

'You're all spoilsports.'

I felt much better after the shower, and with familiar clothes on walked carefully to the balcony. The air was sweet and cool. The hospital, while close to the built-up areas, was far enough away from the traffic that it wasn't affected by exhaust fumes and noise.

We sat drinking coffee. It was good to be alive.

Sarah told me she had rung Keith while I was in the shower and he told her they would visit in the afternoon.

'Might be a good time to find out what their plans are. I can remember George saying he might head back to London but I'm not sure what the others are going to do.'

'I rang Mum earlier in the week and told her about your incident. I didn't say anything about my part because you know it would upset her. She was concerned about you but when I told her you were going to be okay, she calmed down.'

The door opened and in strolled three likely lads laden with fruit, chocolate, flowers and a fairway wood.

'A souvenir to remind us how things might have been different,' said Keith. 'It's like I told Ken, I would have reached the green if it had been the ball and not a kneecap, so I reckon I would have won the hole and been one up and well on the way to taking more of your money.'

I looked at the others, laughing. 'God, he's still full of shit, isn't he?'

Harry gave the flowers to Sarah and she got a bit emotional. 'I can't believe you guys. You are so kind and thoughtful. I'd kill to have girlfriends like you.'

George put his hands out in a defensive motion. 'Please don't say the word kill, Sarah. You're scaring me.'

The roars of laughter brought the nurse to the door.

'You lot aren't drinking, are you?'

'Yeah. We're drunk on happiness,' said Sarah.

She rolled her eyes as the nurse smiled and left the room.

'Fuck, how cringe-worthy was *that*?'

We sat around the table and while I scoffed chocolates George reaffirmed his plans to head back to London on Monday. Keith and Harry were happy to stay in Hong Kong for a couple of weeks then head back to London via Las Vegas.

'I don't suppose you'd care for a layover in Los Angeles?' I asked.

'If it's about the cars,' said Harry, 'Keith and I have been talking and we'd be more than happy to sort them out for you. Tell us how you want to deal with them and we'll act on your behalf. We reckon we're business savvy enough not to get conned by the Yanks.'

'You guys have made my day. I've given this some thought, believe it or not. I'm fairly certain classic car auctions are held regularly in LA and it would be a straightforward process to whack 'em all in the auction. The auction people can put reserves on the ones they reckon might be worth big money, then see what happens. If they consider they should be split up over several auctions that's not a problem either. They'll have the cars on their site and if we tell them cash offers outside the auction process are okay, they should be able to move them easily. I'll contact the storage place and get things arranged. Then all you'll have to do is maybe sign some transfer papers. I'll also contact Jack's lawyer and let him know what we're doing.'

'Shit, I think the knock on your head has been beneficial. You're talking sense for a change,' said George. His chuckling caused the others to nod in agreeance.

'You're lucky I'm not allowed to exert myself. Otherwise, I'd throw this chocolate wrapper at you.'

'You haven't forgotten five cars are yours?' said Keith.

'No, I haven't. If you can determine which five cars will bring the most money, mark them as mine.'

Sarah and the guys looked at each other. An awkward silence hovered. Sarah was about to speak. I held up my hand.

'If I may continue. The money from their sale will be given to a few charities I've been made aware of. I'll pay for you guys to stay in LA while you sort things out. The money from the other cars will be sent to Jack's sister in accordance with his will.'

I could have heard the ash fall off a cigarette. For the second time in less than a minute the four of them were speechless; but only for a moment.

'You are one clever bastard,' said George, shaking my hand.

'Devious as well,' said Harry. 'We'll do our homework before we go to LA. Don't you worry, old mate; we'll see you right. Oh, and by the way, you won't be footing our accommodation bill while we're over there. It's the least we can do for an Aussie chum.'

'Thanks, guys, you're great. Look, I'm sorry, but I'm feeling buggered. Otherwise Sarah and I would love to take a few more thousand off you like she did last Monday.

'How did you know about that?' asked Keith. 'You were out to it.'

'Sarah woke me up running up and down the corridor telling anyone who'd listen how she whipped three Pommy arses.'

'Only because she threatened us with physical harm,' said Harry.

Sarah blushed. 'Don't listen to him, he's delirious. Go and lie down, you big bullshit artist.'

I was slightly unsteady as I walked to the bed. I realised the healing process was going to take a while longer. No sooner than I'd put my head on the pillow my eyes closed and the voices from the four slowly became more distant.

Thursday morning – Diamond Harbour

Mick looked at Angie across the breakfast table.

'How'd you fancy a trip up to Sydney for a few days? We could catch up with Vicki, cruise the harbour and check out the Opera House, which I admit I've yet to visit.'

'Shame on you, Mick! That's the first place tourists are meant to visit. The second is to walk over the bridge.'

'Oops. Haven't done that either.'

'I suppose you haven't been to Taronga Zoo or Luna Park.'

'Guilty as charged, your honour.'

'Well, I'm not sure I'm up for doing all that at the moment, but who knows. The Sydney vibe has a way of getting people excited.'

'Your vibe gets me excited.'

'Cut it out. You know what the doctor said – moderation.'

Mick laughed at her. 'What if I ring the Condor and see if they've got a suite available. If so, we could head up today, unless you've got something else you want to do.'

'Make the call, Mr Jamieson, then report to me in the bedroom. Doctors don't always know best.'

Hong Kong

Sarah and the guys sat around for the next hour drinking coffee and recapping what had happened over the past week.

'I feel bad leaving you guys with Tommy,' said George. 'But I have a responsibility to my staff, as you know.'

'Don't feel bad, mate,' said Keith. 'Do you remember when we were back in London organising this trip and we agreed we wouldn't tie each other down? Well, this is a classic example. You've decided to head home and if I decide to kidnap Sarah and whisk her off to a deserted island, I wouldn't expect any of you to be upset.'

'Why would you want to kidnap me, Keith?' asked Sarah. 'Don't you think I'd come willingly, so we could spend our days lazing, naked, on pure white sand, where I would be listening, not only to the waves breaking gently on the beach but, also, to your dulcet tones regaling me with tales of sunken treasure?'

'You mean to say you haven't told Sarah of your treasure hunting days with your old man?' said Harry, barely containing his laughter.

George was laughing. 'More's the point; Keith lying naked on a beach.'

'All right you lot. I know when I'm beat. There's no doubt about you, Sarah, you're one in a million and you're one of us. I think these guys would agree with me when I say if Tommy had to choose between his golf and poker wins and you it would be an instant decision. He's a lucky man.'

'And I'm a lucky woman, I think you'd agree.'

'Keep the noise down over there, some of us are trying to sleep,' I said, pretending to be annoyed.

'Did you hear much of our conversation?' asked George.

'I heard something about Keith being naked and thought I was having another nightmare.'

'Is it pick-on-Keith day?' said Keith. He stood and walked over to the bed. 'We'd better be heading off, old mate. Glad you're on the mend. Remember; a few extra days recovering here might make all the difference later.'

'Thanks, doctor,' I laughed as the others came over. We shook hands and off they went. I told them to behave themselves as the door closed behind them.

Sarah lay down beside me and I slid my arm under her neck. Nothing felt more natural. She smelt great, she felt great and she was great.

'How would you feel about going down to the café for a light meal? It might do you the world of good to get out of here and have a walk.'

'Not a bad idea. The snooze has recharged my batteries.'

We got changed into reasonably respectable clothes and headed out. The menu was as good as any hotel restaurant and the smells emanating from the kitchen made me realise I hadn't had a decent meal in days.

'I should have weighed myself before coming down. I reckon I've lost a few kilos.'

'Well, with the amount of time you spent in the bathroom earlier I wouldn't be surprised.'

'Don't remind me. I'm still tender. I feel as if I've been …'

'Stop. I don't need to know,' said Sarah.

She laughed as she poured a couple of sparkling mineral waters. Champagne was off my menu for a while.

We enjoyed our favourite: grilled fish and salad. It was salmon and the sauce was a new taste. Oriental. Delicious.

'Will we have a coffee here or back in our room?' said Sarah.

'I can't believe how out of condition I am after only four days. I think coffee back in our room might be the go.'

'Well. You have had holes drilled into your head. That might account for something. Anaesthetic and trauma have a way of wearing a person down.'

We took the lift to our top floor suite. As the doors opened, I saw a police officer seated outside our room. He stood as we approached and bowed slightly.

'What's up, officer?' I asked.

'Senior Sergeant Wong has ordered me to guard your room. No-one is to enter room unless they are hospital staff who have necessary clearance. He has left card on table and wants you to call him. I don't know anything else.'

'Thanks, officer.'

I picked up Ken's card and eased myself back onto the bed. He had written a note:

Tommy, please call me when you get back. Sorry I missed you. Your phone must be off. Ken.

I grabbed my phone, switched it on and rang his number. He answered almost immediately. I didn't speak again until I said goodbye.

'Tommy, what's up? You've gone pale.'

It took me a few moments before I could speak.

'Ken's coming over shortly. He told me Yang has made contact with some of his cronies who haven't been rounded up yet and has put out a contract on me. Ten thousand US dollars to whoever puts a knife in my heart or a bullet in my brain. Fuck me dead. What the hell's happening? This is bullshit. What's wrong with this guy? It was only a game of poker, for fuck's sake.'

'Okay, okay, honey. Calm down. This is a big shock, and I agree; but let's wait until Ken gets here. Try and keep calm. You can't afford to have your blood pressure going up. There's a cop at the door, so we're safe.'

'If Yang is in solitary confinement, how the hell can he have any contact with his gang?'

'Hopefully Ken will tell us.'

We didn't have to wait long for a knock on the door. Sarah asked who it was and Ken replied.

He came in looking worried. He shook my hand and asked how I was going.

'Yang is proving to be a problem. Apparently, his web of evil spreads further than we expected. We have discovered, through our internal investigations, some guards are on his payroll so he's been able to issue orders to his men. In particular to place a contract on your life. Although this type of thing is rare in Hong Kong it seems to be occurring more often since the handover of Hong Kong to the Chinese.'

'Christ. That was over ten years ago.'

'That's what I mean. Crime gangs have set themselves up in Hong Kong and, unfortunately, you upset a main player. If Yang doesn't get revenge it will be seen as a loss of face and may weaken his hold on his empire.'

'I can't understand why he was playing poker at the casino in the first place. Based on what you've told me about this prick I'm surprised he's not playing poker in his own clubs.'

'I agree; but these guys want to be seen out and about, particularly by their opposition. Strutting like peacocks during mating season.'

'Too much fucking testosterone if you ask me. What happens now? I'm stuck in this room for a fortnight. I'll go crazy; we'll go crazy.'

'I've spoken to the Police Commissioner and your doctor and we have devised a plan … it hinges on your acceptance, of course. We know you can't fly for a while, but with the cooperation of the Australian Consulate-General, you and Sarah will be issued with new passports and taken to a cruise ship that will deliver you to Tokyo where you will recuperate before flying back to Sydney. Once you are onboard the ship, we will issue a press release stating that an Australian tourist injured in a brawl died from complications after brain surgery. It will appear several pages into the main newspaper but we'll make sure Yang sees it. He will no doubt have his henchmen check with the hospital.

The hospital will in fact mark your record as being deceased. The record will also state that, in accordance with your wishes, you have been cremated and your partner has flown back to Australia with your ashes.'

'How would the hospital know my wishes upon my death?'

He smiled. 'An amendment – dated before your admittance – to the hospital's Standing Orders will include a clause that non-Hong Kong residents have to provide details of how they wish to be treated in the event they die while they are in the hospital. In your case, you were brought in unconscious but Sarah was able to provide that information. I'm not sure of the actual wording but it will certainly satisfy this situation.'

Sarah smiled at Ken. 'Sneaky but clever.'

'Jesus, Ken. There's a lot to get my head around. How soon do you need an answer?'

'Tomorrow morning would be good as the cruise ship docks on Monday. That will give the Aussies enough time to sort out your passports and for us to organise tickets and transport to the ship. You'll be on the ship for about six days which will give you a good chance to get back on track. You'll be able to get exercise and fresh sea air. Your doctor here will contact the ship's doctor and a colleague in Tokyo asking them to monitor your progress. All he will tell them is you had a fall, injuring your head and necessitating surgery. The doctor has told me he's impressed with your recovery and it may well be you can fly home from Tokyo after a check-up. You could be back in Sydney within a fortnight.'

He continued. 'As you can appreciate, the fewer people who know what's happening the better. The cruise ship people, apart from the ship's captain, will assume you are wealthy tourists travelling from Hong Kong to Japan. It's common for visitors to Hong Kong to also visit Japan to experience the different cultures.'

'What about my mates? One of them is flying back to London on Monday but the other two were going to stay here a few weeks longer before heading to America.'

'I would strongly advise they leave as soon as possible. When Yang is told you are out of the picture, he might consider taking revenge on them. Look, Tommy, I realise you and Sarah have a lot to think about, but if it was my decision, I couldn't wait to get on the boat. I'll go now and come back in the morning. Try and rest. You're still weak, you know.'

Ken stood and shook our hands, said goodnight and walked to the door. He spoke to the guard and left.

Sarah busied herself with the coffee machine while I lay there contemplating what Ken had told us.

'If anything happened to you or the guys, I could never forgive myself. I don't think we've got a choice. We're in a strange country with even stranger people running around thinking they can do what they like. The sooner we're out of here the better. Same goes for Keith and Harry.'

The coffee calmed me down rather than giving me a buzz. I was feeling better with Sarah snuggled beside me.

We talked well into the night, agreeing Keith and Harry should fly out on Monday when George does; earlier if possible.

The only interruption was the night nurse who changed my dressing.

Thursday morning – Diamond Harbour

Mick had rung the Condor and, as luck would have it, a deluxe suite was available. He booked it for a fortnight.

They emerged from the bedroom around noon. Angie wanted to call in to the casino on the way to thank everyone again for their support.

'Why don't we have lunch there before we head off?' Mick suggested.

Angie rang Vicki after lunch and arranged to meet her at the Condor around four o'clock.

The trip up the coast was uneventful and when they arrived at the Condor, Barry happened to be on duty. He welcomed Mick like a long-lost friend and gave Angie a warm embrace.

'You're everything Mick said you were,' she said, smiling at him.

'I hope he hasn't given away too many secrets. You know what these Poms are like.'

'Settle down, Barry. Get the valet to park the car, and behave.'

Barry laughed. 'Perhaps we can catch up tomorrow after my shift.'

'We sure will. See you then.'

They had time to unpack and for Angie to have a lie down. It was getting close to four when her phone rang. It was Vicki. She was down in the bar, halfway through her first beer.

Vicki saw them walk into the bar, and rushed to Angie and hugged her. Angie introduced Mick and he got the same treatment.

Vicki was a typical outgoing Aussie woman; friendly without being overbearing. Someone you could rely on. She had proven that with how she had looked after Angie.

Angie brought her up to date with everything, including the visit to the police for her interview and the getting rid of Danny's stuff from the house.

'Time for a new start,' said Vicki.

'You bet. And what better way than with this bloke.'

She leaned over and unashamedly kissed Mick on the mouth.

'Get a room, you guys,' said Vicki. 'Ah, that's right, you've already got one.'

'Listen, Vicki. Mick hasn't visited the Opera House, walked across the bridge, been to Luna Park or the bloody zoo. What kind of tourist is this bloke, I ask you?'

'Well, we'd better do something about it. I've got a couple of rostered days off due, if you'd like me to tag along. I haven't been to the zoo for years. It might be a nice day out.'

'Sounds good to me,' said Mick, ordering another round. 'How about tomorrow? It'll keep me away from the poker tables.'

'There'll be plenty of time for poker, Mr Jamieson. Among other things,' said Angie. Vicki rolled her eyes and laughed.

DAY 27 – FRIDAY

Friday morning – Hong Kong

I woke to the smell of fresh coffee wafting from Sarah's cup as she sat close to me in bed.

'Where's mine?' I smiled, looking up at her perfect features. How she can look so good so early in the day – no make-up, hair unbrushed – is beyond me.

'Ah, the sleeping giant awakes. How are you feeling?'

'Well, my head feels much better. I slept well, all things considered. I don't think we have much choice about staying or leaving. My hope is that Ken's plan works and we can get out of here before Yang finds out anything different. He's lower than a snake. In all my travels I've never run into a meaner prick.'

Sarah smiled. 'You don't mix in the right circles. Remember, I've got to get my friend Dianne to regale you with stories from the escort game of bastards and bigger bastards. Why don't you grab a shower while I knock us up brekky? Then we'll be ready when Ken comes over. I'm not sure when we should talk to Keith and Harry.'

'Perhaps after we've spoken to Ken. He might have more to tell us today. The guys might be happy to head off to LA soon if it means they are safe.'

I was enjoying the shower seat too much. If I was going to get my strength back, I needed to make an effort. Tomorrow.

Ken rang from the hospital foyer as we were finishing breakfast. Sarah and I had decided to leave our phones switched on all the time and keep them with us. I told him to come up. Fresh coffee was on offer.

He identified himself at the door that we had locked after the nurse had left last night. Sarah let him in, and over coffee I told him we would comply with his plan. He told us if Keith and Harry wanted to leave early, he could pull strings at the airport if they had any problems securing a flight at short notice.

'Might I suggest you don't have any physical contact with them? If Yang's men are watching the hospital, the guys would stand out and Yang would probably work out you were still in here.'

'I'd be disappointed if we couldn't say goodbye to them in person,' I said.

'Well, I have a solution. If the guys are happy to go with you on the cruise ship to Tokyo, they could fly to America from there at their leisure.'

'Ken, you're a fucking genius.'

'Steady, big guy. You'll pop a rivet,' said Sarah. 'As you can see, Ken, he gets excited pretty quickly.'

Ken nodded. 'I did notice. I think we can get things moving as soon as you let me know what the guys want to do.'

'We won't hold you up any further,' I said. 'I'll give you a call after I ring the lads.'

'By the way,' he said, 'your hospital records have been closed and filed away as we discussed. A common Hong Kong name has been slipped into the nameplate on the door and only the doctor can authorise access. For all intents and purposes, a suspect wounded in an armed robbery is occupying this room. He's been put in here to keep him isolated from the general hospital population. The guard will remain outside the door. Your meals will be supplied by a nearby restaurant and brought to you by our staff, dressed as hospital orderlies.'

'You are amazing, Ken. Thanks,' I said.

He finished his coffee and walked to the door. As he was about to open the door Sarah handed him a fresh coffee.

'For the guard.'

Ken smiled, closing the door behind him.

'While you ring the guys, I'll give Mum a call. It's been a while and she'd be keen to know how you're getting on.'

I grabbed my phone and rang Keith. It was fifteen minutes before I hung up. He had gone to Harry and George's rooms and corralled them to his where he put his phone on loudspeaker.

I relayed their side of the conversation to Sarah and she looked relieved when I told her they were as keen as us to leave Hong Kong.

'Harry's excited at the prospect of going to Tokyo. Apparently, he spent time there at a sanatorium when he was in his early teens. His parents tried to get special treatment for his ailments and he'd be happy to retrace those steps, particularly because the only treatment that worked was losing his virginity to a nurse twice his age who happened to be double-jointed.'

Sarah couldn't help but laugh. 'Why would being double-jointed have anything to do with him losing his virginity?'

I considered her question for a moment. 'Sex is similar to real estate – position, position, position.'

She poked me in the ribs. 'You're a funny bugger. Does Harry think he's going to find this nurse after all these years and expect her to perform gymnastics on him again? She'd be nearly sixty and probably a grandmother.'

'Harry is a glass-half-full type of bloke.'

'A wishful thinker, more like it.'

'You'll be pleased to know George has decided to come with us. He'll contact his people in London and tell them he's got business in Tokyo and will fly home from there. Keith suggested we fine-tune their LA layover while we're sipping champagne on the upper deck.'

Sarah smiled. 'How romantic.'

I rang Ken. He was another relieved person when he heard what the guys were going to do. He told me to rest and he would take care of all the arrangements. He apologised for us having to be stuck in our room for the next three days. The ship was arriving in port early Monday morning but not leaving until the evening. We would be spirited onboard as early as possible, where we would be free to roam the ship like normal tourists without fear. All new passengers boarding in Hong Kong would be screened thoroughly before being allowed onboard.

'You're not taking any chances, Ken,' I said.

'Firstly, we don't want anyone getting killed; and secondly, a diplomatic incident between Australia and China would be nice to avoid. Considering the current goodwill between both countries the last thing I want is for a low-life rat like Yang to come between us.'

'Couldn't have put it better if I tried. We'll lie low until Monday morning.'

'I'll ring you if our plans change,' said Ken, hanging up.

*

Sarah and I spent the next three days and three nights talking, eating, watching movies and perfecting gentle yoga moves, including deliberate slow-breathing exercises. She recommended I do them as often as I could as they reduced high blood pressure and promoted general calmness.

The shower chair eventually underwent a weight test and passed with flying colours; several times.

I phoned Keith a couple of times each day. They had checked out of the hotel and were holed up in a non-descript place on the other side of the island.

Ken was pleased when I told him what the guys had done. He would arrange for them to be brought to the ship in a taxi on Monday morning.

I wanted to send Sylvia an e-mail but decided I would contact her once we were onboard and let her know when we were coming home. I'd ring Mick as well, and send an e-mail to Anne and Rachael. I could clear up a few things while relaxing.

'It'll be nice to catch up with Mick. It feels like ages since we've seen him even though it's only been a tad over a week. I'm looking forward to meeting Angie, too.'

'From what we've been told she sounds nice,' said Sarah. 'Well-suited to Mick.'

'I hope it works for them. She needs a new start and Mick needs a nice lady to keep him in check.'

Sarah smiled. 'Much like someone else I know.'

'Changing the subject for a moment, young lady … I've noticed your phone hasn't rung once since we left Sydney. I was expecting it to be ringing regularly with requests from rich and famous business people wanting your services.'

'There's a simple explanation. I have two phones: one for my business and one for general use. The business phone is back in Sydney in my apartment. It has a recorded message on it that goes something like, "Hi, you've called Sarah. I'm unable to take your call. I'm overseas and will not be returning for the foreseeable future." The phone I've got with me is only known to Mum, you, the guys and Dianne. It makes it easy when it rings because I know it's a call from someone I care about. Mum rarely calls me though. She knows I'll call her when I get the chance. She's one of those special mothers who doesn't need to know where I am or what I'm doing every hour of the day.'

'You are one smart lady and I love you more every day. I don't know what I'd do if we weren't together. I can't thank your mother enough for having a senior's moment.'

Sarah laughed and as she gave me a playful slap, kissed me and whispered in my ear. 'I love you, too, Tommy Dabrowski.'

With time on our hands it was a good opportunity to tell her about Brian – our poker game, his gold mine, his alpacas, his angora goats, his trees and his perceived loneliness. I clumsily brought Dianne's name into the conversation and my efforts to reassure Sarah I wasn't trying to be a matchmaker failed dismally.

'Wow. An interesting man. Who knows what might happen? I do know Dianne is looking for love; but maybe in all the wrong places.'

'Are you're going to break into song?'

'No way. You haven't heard me sing.'

'Well, I suppose I can live with someone with one fault. Did I happen to mention he'd run a close second to George Clooney in the looks department? More rugged, maybe.'

'No, but tell me more. I'm all ears and I've got plenty of time,' she said.

I decided to change the subject slightly. 'I know we made plans for when we got back to Sydney but do you think you'd consider a holiday to Tasmania? It couldn't be further from Hong Kong, apart from Antarctica. Brian gave me his phone number when we met and said he'd like to catch up again when I got back from Vegas. Originally that was going to be in six months but our circumstances have changed slightly, wouldn't you agree?'

'Can't argue with you. I've never been to Tassie and yes, I would love to go. In fact, my darling, if you said you were going to Dakar, I'd come with you.'

'Where the hell's Dakar and why would I want to go there?'

'Don't you know Dakar is the capital of Senegal? It's on the west coast of Africa.'

'Oh, silly me, of course it is.' I grabbed her and moved her to the bed where I tickled her until she made so much noise laughing and squealing that the guard at the door knocked to see if we were okay.

'Yes, we're fine thanks,' I shouted.

Sarah wiped her eyes, laughing. 'I've had my workout for today.'

My phone rang. It was Ken. I put him on loud speaker.

'I will personally escort you and Sarah to the ship at nine o'clock tomorrow morning. We need to move quickly so you will need to have had your breakfast and packed your bags.'

'There'll be no delays on our part, Ken,' I said. 'Do you see any dramas getting us out of here?'

'Not at this stage. We are going to use three laundry trolleys and smuggle you via the service elevator to the rear of the hospital. A laundry service van will transfer you to the ship. In transit, the temporary decals on the side that say *24 Hour Laundry Service* will be changed and it will appear as a normal tourist transporter. You guys will get out at the wharf and board the ship like normal passengers.'

'Why three trolleys, and where will you be?' I asked.

'One trolley for each of you and one for your luggage. I'll be dressed as an orderly pushing a trolley. When we change the decals, I'll change my jacket and look like a tour driver.'

'You sound as if you might be enjoying this.'

'Well, Tommy, I wouldn't say I'm enjoying it but I am happy I've been put in charge of the transfer. As it's my plan, I'm confident of it succeeding.'

Sarah reassured him. 'You're certainly going to a lot of trouble on our behalf.'

'Like I said on Friday, the last thing we want is someone getting injured or killed. Yang has eyes everywhere.'

'Two less since Sarah's pool party,' I joked, quickly realising Ken was taking things seriously and I was using humour to hide my nervousness.

'Sorry, Ken.'

'No worries, Tommy. Get some sleep and I'll see you in the morning.'

'Goodnight, Ken – and thanks again for what you're doing.'

DAY 30 – MONDAY

I was awake well before the six o'clock alarm. The next six days on the high seas would be a nice change from a hospital room. I looked at Sarah. She was sleeping peacefully so I crept to the shower and was finished and had coffee brewing when she woke.

I passed her a mug. She yawned and said, 'I'm meant to be looking after you, not the other way 'round.'

I sighed and laughed. 'I could have done with your help in the shower.'

'At least let me put a fresh dressing on your head. The doctor left some here. He didn't see the need for a nurse to do it. It's like a big Band-Aid.'

She finished her coffee and carefully removed the dressing which had held up well over the past few days.

'Wow. Things are healing well. We'll take the spare ones with us. The less others have to do with us on the ship, the better.'

We had a good breakfast and while Sarah showered, I finished packing my case. I moved it near the door, along with my golf clubs. I'd put Keith's present in the bag as well. I'd make sure it took pride of place in my billiard room.

We dressed in comfortable clothes – suitable for folding ourselves into laundry trolleys but fashionable enough that we would blend in with the other cruisers. Once we were onboard we could smarten ourselves up.

I heard a knock on the door. I looked at my watch; it was right on nine. I asked who was there and, on hearing Ken's voice, opened the door. If I hadn't known better, I would have sworn he was an everyday laundry delivery driver.

'Great disguise, Ken,' I told him, moving aside to allow him into the room. As I closed the door, I noticed three laundry trolleys in the hallway.

He smiled but I could tell he was preoccupied. He didn't engage in much small talk. He handed us our passports and ship boarding passes.

We opened the passports, keen to know what our temporary names were. Mine was Neil David Connolly and Sarah's was Jennifer Mary Stokes.

'How original,' said Sarah, placing them in her bag. 'A mix of someone's parents' names at the Consulate, I'd bet.'

Ken interrupted our laughter.

'Please remember to use them until you get to Tokyo. The van is down in the loading bay so, if you are ready, we'll bring the trolleys into the room, get you and your luggage loaded and head down.'

'There're a couple of things before we go,' I said. 'There's food in the fridge we're happy for the staff to have; and also, the matter of my account.'

'I'll see that the staff sort out the food. There's no need to worry about the account. The Commissioner had authorised the department to settle your account. He considers what you have had to endure in Hong Kong enough of a burden.'

'Wow. A most generous gesture. Please thank him for us.'

Ken opened the door and two men in similar uniforms pushed the trolleys into the room and shut the door. They removed laundry bags from the trolleys and in one placed my golf clubs and our luggage. I watched as Sarah jumped into her trolley, lying down in the foetal position. I needed help, but within a few minutes the lightweight bags were placed over us and we were ready.

'Please do not speak or move until we are in the van and away from the hospital precinct. I'll give you the all-clear. It may be slightly bumpy moving from the lift to the van but we have to make it look as natural as possible. I don't know for sure Yang's men aren't snooping around.'

It was about five minutes before we were jolted into the van. I heard the rear doors slam shut and the front doors open and close. The engine started and I could feel the van moving. It was a few minutes before I heard Ken tell one of his men in the back with us to remove the laundry bags. Sarah and I sat up and smiled at each other.

'So far, so good,' said Ken. 'We aren't being followed so we'll head to a quiet alley where we'll do our swap. I know I said we'd change the decals on the van but we've been able to commandeer an authentic tourist maxi van, so you'll be able to travel to the wharf like legitimate tourists. We agreed it might look odd if someone saw you climbing out of a beat-up laundry van.'

'You're amazing, Ken,' said Sarah, reaching over to hold my hand. 'How's your head, big guy?'

'It feels good, considering I wasn't able to curl up like a cat. I used a bag as a pillow. That reduced the risk of me knocking my head on the framework.'

The swap to the new van was uneventful and we were soon heading towards the wharf. As we drew near, I was amazed at the ship's size. I'd never been interested in boats because my golf and poker commitments had necessitated quick travel between destinations. This was new to me.

I looked at Sarah. 'Have you seen anything this big before?'

'Not since I caught a glimpse of you climbing into the laundry trolley.' She couldn't hold back a giggle.

Ken cut short our banter. 'Sorry to interrupt but I'll be stopping soon. I want to get as close to the gangplank as possible so you can go straight onboard. Your friends will be arriving soon and they will do the same.'

But he stopped a short distance from the gangplank, and turned and faced us. 'I'll say my goodbyes now as I will be acting like a real tour driver when I get your luggage out and put it onto a trolley. They don't usually shake hands and get too friendly. Firstly though, once you arrive in Japan you can revert to your old passports when you make your arrangements to fly to Sydney. Your association with Hong Kong will be officially ended. I would appreciate you handing these ones to the Australian Embassy. They have been advised of your travel plans and will meet you when you disembark. Secondly, the Commissioner passes on his best wishes and is well aware of your involvement in bringing down a not-so-small-time criminal and his henchmen. Finally, I wish I had gotten to know you under different circumstances. You are fine people and don't deserve what happened to you. Unfortunately, our paths won't cross again, but I won't forget either of you. Oh, one last thing. Sarah, I think I might be in the running for a promotion.'

Sarah leaned forward, laughing, and hugged Ken, kissing him on the cheek. I shook his hand and thanked him again.

Ken drove to the gangplank, got out, walked around to the sliding side door, opened it for us and retrieved our luggage from the back. A porter loaded everything onto a trolley and proceeded to wheel it up the gangplank.

Ken gave us an ever-so-slight bow. Avoiding eye contact, he closed the doors and jumped back into the driver's seat. I caught a glimpse of a smile as he drove off.

We showed our tickets and were escorted onto the ship where a porter took us and our luggage to a penthouse suite mid-ship. We refused the offer to unpack our bags and requested privacy for the duration of the cruise.

I marvelled at our surroundings. 'This is like a luxury hotel except it's on water. I knew flash ships travelled the world but I never dreamed I'd be on one. I'm looking forward to exploring.'

'Perhaps when the others get here we can wander around,' said Sarah. She began unpacking her bags. 'I guess we've got the best part of six days, so don't go overdoing things. You're still recovering, albeit incredibly quickly.'

The phone on the desk rang. It was the ship's doctor. He asked if he could call on me and give me the once-over now I was under his care. He arrived promptly and removed the dressing. After checking me over he decided to leave the dressing off. The stitches were nearly ready to come out. He advised me to avoid too much excitement as my blood pressure was slightly elevated.

'Can I play poker?'

'If you stay calm.' He looked at Sarah. 'Do you think that's possible?'

'Oh yes. He won't dare misbehave if I'm around.'

Looking back at me, he told me he'd give me another check-up before we berthed in Tokyo and could remove the stitches before disembarking; but to let him know if I had any problems. He wished us a good trip and left.

'I'm pretty happy with that result, particularly if I can get a few games of poker in to while away the days. Although I was looking forward to the jogging track and the gym, I suppose I'll have to exercise some restraint.'

'You're a funny guy. You know what? I reckon walking wouldn't do you any harm.'

My phone rang. It was Keith. They were onboard, also in flash suites mid-ship, and were keen to see us. I gave them our suite number. Keith said they'd be along shortly.

We heard them before they even knocked. They sounded like misbehaving school kids. Sarah let them in. They were all over us.

'It's so good to see you both. Bloody hell, Tommy, you're looking a damn sight better than late last week.' said Harry.

'It's Neil. Neil Connolly. This is Jennifer Stokes.'

'Jesus. Who came up with those names?' asked George.

'Someone at the Australian Consulate, apparently,' said Sarah. 'We've been told to use them until we get to Tokyo. It will be interesting to see how we go.'

Keith piped up. 'The best thing to do if someone calls your name – your fake name – and you don't answer the first time, is to pretend you're hard of hearing.'

'How did you come up with that idea?' I asked.

'I read a lot,' he laughed. 'How about we have some champers to celebrate being safe and sound?' He looked at me and smiled. 'Well, as sound as we can be under the circumstances.'

He popped the cork and poured out the bubbly. We clinked glasses and toasted our good fortune.

'By the way, Tommy ... er, Neil,' said Keith, after quaffing half his glass, 'I took the liberty of ringing Mick to bring him up to date. I hope you don't mind.'

'Hell no. I appreciate you ringing him for me. As much as I want to talk to him, I haven't had a chance.'

'Apparently he's taken Angie to Sydney. They've booked into the Condor for a couple of weeks and Angie and Vicki – Angie's good friend who helped her out when she was in hospital – are showing him all the touristy things he should have already seen. Sounds as if they're having a good time. The big news is Angie is getting a passport. Things could be getting serious. They send their best wishes and reckon you should write a book about your time in Hong Kong.'

Harry joined in, 'Perhaps you could call it, *The Hong Kong Heroine – Low-Life – No Life.*'

Sarah laughed at him. 'I think you've had enough to drink.'

We went for a tour of the ship. It was huge; so many restaurants, casinos, theatres, shops – it was a floating city. After lunch the guys headed to the casino and Sarah and I decided to take it easy back in our suite. It would be a good opportunity to send Sylvia an e-mail and put together a list of phone numbers and e-mail addresses: Jack's sister Anne, Rachael in Vegas, Jack's lawyer and the car storage place. I'd give these to Keith so he could touch base with them once I'd contacted them and brought them up to date on what was happening.

My e-mail to Sylvia explained why we were going to Tokyo and that we'd be back in Sydney within a fortnight. I didn't go into explicit details regarding the attack and Sarah's fight, but told her there had been some trouble requiring our quick departure from Hong Kong.

We had agreed to have dinner together in the main restaurant but, as the dress code was slightly more formal than we had anticipated, we had to settle for a smaller restaurant on a different level. It didn't bother us because the food, wine and company were first class.

The next day was spent at sea. When the ship arrived at Taipei, we were keen to go ashore for a look around. The next stop was Okinawa, where we did the same, bearing in mind the next two days until we arrived in Tokyo would be spent at sea.

My days at sea were taken up with walking, yoga and lying in the sun. I was starting to feel as good as I did before the attack. My head was healing and, more importantly, my hair was growing back.

After lunch on the day before we were due in Tokyo, George asked Sarah if she wanted to try her hand at blackjack. She told him she was keen to give poker a try but I wanted to have a talk to Keith and Harry about LA before we reached Tokyo, so she agreed to blackjack. I told her we'd hit the poker tables after dinner.

I presented Keith and Harry with contact lists, together with copies of e-mails to and from Anne and the others. All my proposals were acceptable and I was particularly happy with Jack's lawyer's acceptance of the authority for Keith and Harry to act on my behalf. Armed with this information, including a detailed vehicle list supplied by the car storage manager, Keith and Harry would have time to research the cars online. Once in LA, they would be able to determine the best five. The manager had also provided a copy to the auction house, which dealt specifically with luxury cars. The guys would be able to compare the values they had with the reserves the auction house came up with. Knowing Keith and Harry and their business acumen I felt comfortable leaving them in charge. We would keep in touch through e-mails and I stressed they were to work at their own pace and not be pressured by anyone. The result was only a bag of money – but the fact I was donating it to charity made it worthwhile to make sure the bag was chock-a-block full.

The afternoon flew. As we were finishing up, Sarah and George reappeared with beaming smiles.

I looked at George. 'I hope you haven't been teaching this woman bad habits at the blackjack table.'

'No need. Take a look in her purse.'

Sarah sheepishly opened her handbag and revealed a wad of notes that would make any gambler envious.

'I think I got lucky.'

'I'd keep an eye on her if I was you, Tommy … er, Neil. I think she might have X-ray vision. She seemed to know when the right cards were coming out.'

'Would it have anything to do with your card counting, George?' I asked. 'Jennifer wouldn't happen to have been siting to your left, by any chance?'

He chuckled. 'I'm deeply offended, Neil.'

'Okay, you lot,' Harry ordered. 'Let's get cleaned up and head out for dinner and poker. Tomorrow, we hit Tokyo. Chop chop.'

Dinner was again superb. Harry reckoned it was because all our meals were compliments of the Hong Kong Police Department.

'This must be costing them a heap,' he marvelled. 'All our accommodation, meals and drinks. It's a shame they didn't cough up for our poker stakes.'

'Geez, you don't want much,' said George, giving Harry a friendly clip around the ear.

'Settle down, you blokes,' I said, 'or they'll put you in a lifeboat and set you adrift.'

We passed on dessert, keen to hit the tables. Sarah was excited about having her first real game of Texas hold 'em. Playing the guys in my hospital room while I was away with the fairies might have had something to do with it.

We arrived at a card room and noticed a game was about to start at a table where one seat was available, so I suggested Sarah grab it.

'I'd feel happier if you guys were playing.'

'Go on,' said George. 'You underestimate your ability. I think you're a natural. What can go wrong? So, you blow your dough; it doesn't matter. There's plenty more where that came from.'

'Okay. If you don't think I'll make a fool of myself, I'll give it a go.'

She got comfortable, acknowledged the other players and pushed her cash over to the dealer. He counted it, had it checked, and passed her an impressive pile of chips in various denominations. I sat at the rail directly opposite her. Why would I want to watch the sunset over an emerald sea when I could look at her across a poker table? She was gorgeous.

Eight players made up the table and after the blinds had been determined, Sarah was in position six for the first hand. The blinds were $25 and $50. The hole cards were dealt and Sarah checked hers like a professional, shielding them from prying eyes. She watched the others, seeing how they reacted. It was obvious they had played before as even I couldn't get a read off them.

The guy in position three was first to bet and he called the big blind. Player four raised to $100. Player five called – so did Sarah and player seven. The guy in eight on the button folded and so did the small blind. The big blind called, so six were left pre-flop, with $625 in the pot.

The dealer dealt the flop. It was the K♦, 3♦ and Q♣.

The action was now with the big blind, who checked. So did players three, four and five. Sarah didn't hesitate. She pushed a small bet of $250 over the line. Player seven called. The big blind and players three and four called, but player five folded. Another $1250 had been added to the pot. I was itching to know what Sarah had. She was a statue. She was giving no clues. For all I knew she could be bluffing.

It was interesting no-one raised, so I assumed no-one had a set. Maybe Sarah had paired one of the flop cards.

The turn card appeared. It was the 4♦. The big blind checked, along with players three and four. Sarah counted out $500 in chips and slid them over the line, announcing her bet to the table. Player seven folded and the big blind and player three called. It was too much for player four, who tossed his cards away.

The actions of the other two bemused me. What the hell were they doing? Surely they weren't waiting for the river card? I had a feeling Sarah might be holding diamonds, giving her either a king high flush or even an ace high. The pot was now over $3000.

The dealer flipped over the river card. It was the A♣. I noticed the big blind rushed a bet of $500 that was quickly matched by player three. Sarah watched them intently for a few moments. She raised another $500. I now felt confident she was holding a flush and I was also confident one of the other two had a set of aces.

The big blind called and player three re-raised $500. Sarah pushed $2000 in, which the big blind called. Player three wasted no time in re-raising. $4000 was casually pushed over the betting line.

I looked at the guys beside me. They were mesmerised and so was the growing crowd.

'Is she for real?' said Keith. 'This is her first poker game playing for real money and she's playing like a pro. I'd love to know what she's holding.'

'You're not the only one,' I said. 'I'd bet she's got a flush.'

'She could have a set of queens or a straight,' Keith added.

'All-in,' Sarah announced. She pushed $7500 over the line.

Excited 'oohs' and 'aahs' came from the crowd and the dealer had to raise his voice to the remaining players. He told the big blind he needed $7500 to call and player three, $5000.

They didn't need too much encouragement, although I reckoned they were mad. If they had taken any notice of Sarah when the turn card appeared, they should have had a fair idea she might have a flush, seeing as she made the bet. The pot must have had nearly $35,000 in it waiting, I hoped, for Sarah.

By my calculations, Sarah had bet a little over $11,000 so I now knew that's how much she'd won at blackjack earlier in the day. If she won this hand, she would win another $23,000, give or take. If she lost; well, it wouldn't matter as she'd been playing with other people's money, although it was a nice feeling to win with other people's money.

With all the bets in the pot a hush enveloped the crowd as Sarah was asked to turn her hole cards over. With a theatrical pause, looking up at me and smiling, she flipped over the J♦ and 10♦. Not only did she have a straight but also the flush. I knew immediately she couldn't be beaten.

The other players, although knowing they'd been beaten and didn't have to show their hands, elected to. The big blind showed Q-Q and player three

A-A. We clapped and cheered. I was convinced these players deserved to lose their money considering how poorly they'd played. The big blind in particular should have put up a decent bet after the flop. He had a set of queens; maybe he slow-played to keep more players in the game, thus building the pot.

Sarah was humble in victory, looking at both players and offering her commiserations. They were good sports and congratulated her in return.

Keith nudged me. 'There's another table opening. Let's head over. I think we can leave Sarah by herself. In fact, I'd prefer it if she stayed where she was. I want to hang onto my money for a while.'

I caught Sarah's eye and indicated what we were doing. She gave me a sexy thumbs-up and turned her attention to the next hand.

George headed over to blackjack and Keith, Harry and I got comfortable at the new table.

'How are you feeling, Neil?' asked Harry, talking louder than usual, with a cheeky smile across his face, emphasising my name.

'Real good, Alphonse,' I said. 'You should be on the stage.'

Keith chipped in. 'Shifting furniture or the first one out of town?'

We laughed, aware of the curious looks on the other player's faces who had taken their seats.

We played for the best part of an hour but I couldn't concentrate. I was thinking about Sarah and our impending arrival in Tokyo. I wasn't keen on hanging around. I wanted to get back to Sydney. I didn't feel I could relax until I was back in familiar surroundings. The threats from Yang still played on my mind although I was loath to let the others know, since they were having a pretty good time on the ship.

I'd lost about twenty thousand on wild bluffing and bad beats, so I called it a night. The other two were going gangbusters and were happy to kick on.

'How about we have breakfast together in the morning around eight and discuss our final arrangements?'

'Sounds good, Neil,' said Harry with a smile.

As I got up, I gave him a friendly shoulder punch and walked over to Sarah's table. She wasn't looking as upbeat as before. I noticed her chip stack had diminished so I assumed she'd lost a few hands.

She saw me and finished the hand she was playing. She folded as one player went all-in. The community cards made up a straight. Someone could easily have hole cards that would make a higher straight. She gathered her remaining chips and excused herself from the table.

'Fancy a coffee before we head back to our suite?' I asked.

'I'd love to. We can relate poker stories. Gee, I never thought I'd hear myself say that.'

We found a quiet coffee shop and Sarah recounted her unfortunate loss. 'My hole cards were the jack of diamonds and the five of clubs. The flop was the ten of diamonds, nine of hearts and the nine of diamonds. The betting went along as expected. The eight of diamonds came up on the turn so I was on a flush draw. Only three of us were playing. The other five had folded pre-flop.' She stopped to take a sip of her coffee, licking her foam moustache. 'The river card was the two of diamonds. I'd hit my flush so I kicked the betting along, only to be re-raised. In hindsight I should have folded; however, I called and got beaten by a bloody king high flush. I should have realised a queen, king or ace of diamonds was probably out there.'

'How much did you lose?'

'A tad over $13,000.'

'Not too bad. You've still got a tidy stash in your handbag.'

'I didn't think I'd let it get to me but, like you've said many times, it's an addictive game and it's not nice losing.'

I consoled her with a kiss. 'Better get used to it. You'll probably be like the rest of us – lose more times than you win. The trick is, when you win, make sure they're big ones to make up for the losses.'

'I'm not sure I'll ever be the player you are,' she said. 'I must admit, though, I did enjoy blackjack today. Perhaps when we're back in Sydney we can head down the coast for a few days and I can try my luck at Diamond Harbour.'

'I reckon when we get to Tassie we should give their casinos a touch-up. Who knows, Brian might even tag along. And Dianne too, maybe,' I said, my voice trailing off.

Sarah smiled brightly. 'Who knows?'

We finished our drinks and walked arm in arm to our suite. It wasn't until I'd walked through the door that I realised how tired I was. We got changed and went to bed.

'I arranged for us to meet the guys for breakfast so we can go over any last-minute things before the ship berths and we go our own ways. I've also got to see the doctor so he can take my stitches out and give me the once-over. I hope I'll be okay to fly.'

'Are you looking forward to getting home?'

'To be honest with you, I can't wait. If there's a plane available the day after we hit Tokyo, I'll be glad to be on it.'

'Me too,' she said. She kissed me and rolled onto her side.

DAY 36 – SUNDAY

Sarah's hair dryer woke me. I looked across the room to see her, in her underwear, finishing styling her hair.

Oh yeah. I'm feeling much better this morning.

'Are you getting up, sleepy head?' she said, looking my way. 'Why are you looking at me like that?'

'I'm allowed to look, aren't I? It's not my fault I'm sharing a room with a gorgeous woman who wants to jump back into bed with me right now.'

'In your dreams, big guy. We'll have plenty of time for hanky-panky when we're home. Right now, you need a cold shower so we can get along to breakfast with the guys.'

I smiled at her. 'I think I've worked out why they give old blokes Viagra.'

'Why?'

'To stop them falling out of bed.'

She laughed, came over and slid her hand under the sheets giving me a firm squeeze. 'That's all you're getting: now, hit the shower.'

'You've got to give a bloke points for trying.'

We got to breakfast and saw the others up at the bain-marie helping themselves to eggs and bacon, sausages, grilled tomatoes, mushrooms and toast.

As I got within earshot I said to Sarah, 'You'd better call the doctor. I can see three heart attacks in the making.'

George turned to us, laughing. 'We don't know when we'll get to eat again so we've got to make the most of it.'

Sarah dug him in the ribs. 'You haven't heard of yoghurt, cereal, wholegrain toast and poached eggs?'

Keith and Harry turned. 'Borrring.'

We sat at a table near a window on the sunny side of the ship and discussed what we were going to do once we berthed. The three guys were going to spend the week sightseeing in Tokyo. George would then fly to London and the other two would head to LA.

I looked at Harry across the table. 'Are you going to track down the talented nurse of yesteryear?'

'In hindsight I think that ship has sailed – so to speak.'

'What have you two got organised?' asked George.

'Well, once I've got these stitches out and the doc hopefully gives me the all-clear to fly, we'll hand in our false passports and try to catch a flight out tomorrow.'

'Make sure you keep an eye on Mick when you get back. It wouldn't surprise me if the bugger ups and marries Angie and settles into domestic bliss,' said Keith.

'I'll let you know what's happening when I hear from you about your progress with Jack's cars.'

'Don't you worry about a thing, Neil,' said Keith, smiling. 'Harry and I are looking forward to sorting them out. We'll contact you as soon as we hit LA and get into it.'

With breakfast done we agreed to meet dockside and say our farewells. The ship was berthing in two hours; enough time for me to see the doctor and get our bags packed.

The stitches were removed without fuss and after a check-up the doctor was happy for me to fly out anytime. He considered it unnecessary for me to visit the doctor in Tokyo. He would contact him and advise him accordingly. He suggested I take it easy for another week, meaning no golf, but swimming and yoga would be beneficial. He thanked Sarah for keeping me moving. I didn't share with him the actual moves she had me do.

Once we were back in our suite, we packed our bags and called the porter who loaded them onto a trolley. We followed him to the disembarking area. As luck would have it, the others were already there, so we stood at the rail and watched the captain masterfully bring the huge ship dockside.

When the gangplank was lowered, we gathered on the dock and waited for our luggage. I noticed a man in a suit holding a card that read 'Mr Connolly'. I ignored it until I realised it was my alias. I nudged Sarah and the guys. 'That's me.'

Sarah and I walked over to him and introduced ourselves. He showed us his identification and took us to an office in the terminal. After a chat, we handed him our false passports. He placed them in his briefcase, assuring us they would be shredded when he got back to his office. I mentioned that the ship's doctor had given me the all-clear and I was keen to get a flight out as soon as possible.

'If you want to fly to Sydney today, I'll see what I can arrange.'

I looked at Sarah who was nodding.

'Fantastic,' I said.

'Bear with me a few moments while I make a couple of phone calls.'

He disappeared into another room and after about a quarter of an hour returned with a smile on his face.

'If you're happy to fly within the next three hours, I can have you in business class on a Qantas flight, compliments of the Hong Kong Police Department.'

'Gosh. Didn't we cut our ties with them when we boarded the ship in Hong Kong? At least, that's what Senior Sergeant Ken Wong told us.'

'You'd be surprised what goes on behind closed doors. I'm not privy to everything that went on in Hong Kong but, as I understand it, you were instrumental in the dismantling of a serious crime syndicate. I think that entitles you to special treatment.'

Sarah slipped her arm around me and squeezed me.

I shook the official's hand. 'If you happen to be in contact with Hong Kong, please pass on our appreciation. We feel we've been spoilt.'

'I certainly will. If you don't mind waiting a while longer, I'll have a car drive you to the airport.'

'It's getting better by the minute,' I said.

'All part of the service. We always look after our own.'

'If you don't mind, we want to say goodbye to our friends who are waiting outside. Then we'll be ready to go.'

'Sure. The car will come into the terminal and park near this office. Come back in when you're ready. I need to get back to the embassy, so I'll say goodbye now and best of luck for the future.'

We walked out to where the guys were arranging transport to their hotel. This was the moment I was not looking forward to. I told them what we were going to do and it was another ten emotional minutes before Sarah and I walked back into the terminal after waving them off in a taxi.

'Shit, that was hard to do,' I said.

Sarah wiped tears from her eyes. 'I think we have to make a big effort to see them again soon. Not that we need an excuse to travel, but it would be nice, knowing what to expect at the other end. I'm sure they'd spoil us rotten in London.'

'At least we'll be keeping in touch via e-mails. You're right though, if these guys were waiting for us in London, it would be one hell of a holiday.'

As the taxi disappeared from the wharf an official-looking limousine drove slowly through the terminal and stopped outside the office. The driver got out and, after greeting us, checked his paperwork and passed us an envelope with instructions to present ourselves to the Qantas desk at the airport.

He loaded our luggage into the cavernous boot and opened the rear door. The trip to the airport was relaxing but solemn. It would take time to get over the fact the guys were going in the opposite direction. The good thing was Mick and Angie would be waiting for us in Sydney.

I looked at Sarah. 'I bet your mum will be excited to see you. Do you think you'll tell her everything?'

'I think it would be best to let her believe you got yourself into a couple of scrapes and now everything is okay. If she asks why we're home so soon we can tell her about Jack and you deciding to cancel your Vegas trip.'

'Good thinking. What happens in Hong Kong, stays in Hong Kong.'

She smiled. 'Something along those lines.'

We were treated like royalty when we arrived at the airport. Security staff ignored us as the limo pulled up in an exclusion zone. The driver loaded our luggage onto a trolley and wheeled it to the Qantas desk. He wished us a safe trip and left us with an attentive staff member. We were issued tickets, then ushered into the Qantas lounge. Our flight wasn't leaving for an hour so we were presented with champagne and a cheese platter. They must have done their homework as the champers was Bollinger and the cheeses true-blue Aussie favourites.

'I reckon now's a good a time to give Mick a ring and tell him we'll be home tonight. In fact, I'll also ring reception at the Marina. They might be able to spare someone to restock the fridge. Will you stay at my place tonight?'

'Try and stop me,' she said with a wicked smile.

DAY 37 – MONDAY

I woke to a glorious Sydney morning. I let Sarah sleep while I got breakfast ready, then gently woke her. We ate looking out across the marina, marvelling at the view. A scattering of yachts on blue that stretched to the horizon and continued into the sky. It was as if Mother Nature had run out of colours. It didn't matter.

Over a second coffee we talked about the day.

Sarah would go back to her place and catch up with her mum.

'Do you want to come around for dinner? I reckon Mum's looking forward to seeing you again.'

'You cook too?'

'I do a mean chicken cacciatore, if you're interested.'

'Oh yes. I don't need a second invitation, Wonder Woman.'

She gave me a friendly slap and disappeared into the shower. I cleaned up the breakfast things and when she reappeared, I had a quick shower.

Once we were organised, I grabbed my spare car keys and we headed to the basement car park. Lucky was in his office reading the form guide. I didn't think horses raced on Mondays. Goes to show how much I know. I left Sarah's case and my golf clubs at the door.

He almost fell off his chair when we walked in.

'Bloody hell, Tommy. What are you doing back?'

'It's a long story mate. Sarah, meet Lucky. Lucky, this is Sarah; the best thing to happen to me.'

Sarah blushed slightly as Lucky shook her hand.

'You're punching well above your weight, Tommy,' he said, looking at Sarah. 'And you're the best-looking thing, apart from me, that's walked into my office.'

'Calm down, Lucky. You're going to trip over your tongue.'

I looked at Sarah. 'See, I wasn't joking when I told you about this bloke. Can you imagine me letting him loose in LA?'

'What's all this about LA?' asked Lucky, pulling a rag from his back pocket and wiping down a couple of plastic chairs.

'Not now, mate. I'll have a chat to you later and tell you all the news. All I want at the moment is my car. I trust you've been looking after it for the last three weeks.'

'If the truth be known, I've only taken it out twice for a run. You'll be pleased to know I didn't even go to the races. If I'd turned up in it, I would have been arrested for car stealing, I reckon.'

We laughed as we left the office. After Lucky put Sarah's case in the boot, he handed me my keys and rushed to open the passenger's door. She smiled and thanked him.

I looked across the roof. 'I can see I'm going to have to keep an eye on you, Lucky.'

He closed the door and sighed theatrically. 'I can't help it if the ladies find me irresistibly charming.'

'I could say something but I don't want to spoil your day,' I laughed. I got in and rolled down the window. 'I'll see you later.'

We were going against the morning rush so it was a pleasant drive to Bondi. Sarah gave me directions and we arrived outside an expensive-looking block of six apartments.

I lifted her case from the boot. 'My place is on the top floor,' she said.

We walked through a small foyer that housed mail boxes and the lift entrance. Sarah checked her box. It was empty.

'How come no mail?'

'There's an elderly lady who lives in the other apartment on the top floor and she collects my mail whenever I'm away. I couldn't ask for a better neighbour. She's as quiet as a church mouse.'

'Does she complain about your wild parties?'

'She might now you're about, big guy,' she said as we got into the lift. 'Speaking of 'big guy', I'd be interested to see how much weight you've lost in the last three weeks. I've got scales you can try. You'd lost five kilos in the ten or so days between your first check-up and when you landed in hospital; I reckon you've lost at least another five since then.'

'I like your confidence. I think you might be right. After being laid up and not eating for a few days, and with my exercise routine and new diet, five kilos off would be a welcome result.'

The lift glided to a stop and we stepped out into a hallway. The sun was streaming in through the floor-to-ceiling windows that looked out over the suburb. The apartments were a short walk from the beach, pubs and restaurants, but far enough away to be private and quiet.

Sarah unlocked her door. Her living areas faced the same direction as the hallway so her apartment was flooded with sunlight.

I looked around. 'This is a fantastic place.'

'Come out to the balcony and check out the view.'

'It's amazing from here. How much better can it get?'

I considered my penthouse to be the duck's guts but Sarah's was beautiful. The walls were painted in antique white and she had added contrasting furniture and paintings to complement it perfectly. Small knick-knacks from her travels decorated well-placed shelves for maximum effect. The minimalist approach certainly worked.

She opened the sliding doors, letting warm morning air flow into the apartment. The balcony contained a variety of healthy-looking pot plants and a table separated two comfortable-looking sun loungers.

'Does your friend next door look after the plants?'

'She's marvellous. She might be in her late seventies but she loves looking after my place when I'm away. Do you know, the only time she uses the lift is when she goes shopping? Most days she's out walking the beach or catching up with her many friends. Several volunteer at the local library and they tend to feed off each other's energy.'

'I'm feeling tired thinking about it.'

I took Sarah in my arms and kissed her. She responded and we stood there, wrapped in each other's arms, until we heard a gentle knock on the door.

I waited on the balcony while Sarah went to the door. A lady I would have sworn wasn't a day over sixty followed Sarah into the lounge room.

'Louise, I want you to meet my husband-to-be, Tommy.'

I was momentarily dumbstruck, glanced at a beaming Sarah, and then reached out my hand towards Louise with an awkward smile. Instead of shaking my hand she pulled me towards her and kissed me on both cheeks.

She looked up at me with warm brown eyes, brushing her blonde hair off her forehead. 'You would have to be the luckiest man on the planet, and I'm so happy to meet you. It's about time someone grounded this beautiful woman.'

'I'm happy to meet you, too. Going by what Sarah has told me about you and how you look after her place while she's away, I half expect to see wings on your back.'

'If people can't help each other out every now and again something's wrong with the world, don't you think? Anyway, I'll get going. I only popped in to see how my favourite person was. It was lovely meeting you, Tommy. I hope to see you again soon.'

'It was nice to meet you, too, and I'm sure you will.'

Sarah walked her to the door where they hugged and said goodbye. She closed the door, ran across the room and jumped into my arms, wrapping her legs around my hips. After she kissed me hard, she pulled her head back and, with her face only inches from mine, said, 'I hope what I said wasn't too premature.'

'Not at all.'

I placed one hand behind her head and pulled her into a long kiss.

I put her down and we walked out to the balcony.

'How about we spend the day settling back in? I'll go and see Mum and you might see Sylvia and contact Mick. Speaking of Sylvia, I haven't met her yet. Make it happen, big guy. Dinner will be around seven.'

'Perfect. I'm interested to see how Sylvia's getting on at school and I reckon Mick's got himself a job as a tourist guide. I'm looking forward to seeing your mum tonight to see how well she's recovered. But what I'm looking forward to the most is us making plans for our big day.'

She smiled sweetly. 'I think we're in for wonderful times.'

She kissed me and took me into the bathroom where I hopped on the scales. The needle stopped at 98 kg. I was over the moon. Only eight more kilos to my goal weight.

Sarah looked at me admiringly. 'I'll have to think of a new name for you, big guy.' She raised her hand as I was about to speak. 'Not greyhound, okay.'

I lifted my shirt. 'Humour me. See if you can feel any ribs.'

'Nice try. I've got things to do. I can't spend all day rolling in the hay. Now, go.'

We kissed again at the door. I walked down the stairs and out into the fresh Bondi sea air. It felt good to be home although I had wondered on and off what it might have been like to get to LA, catch up with Jack, get fit and have a crack at the golf and poker double. As I got into the car, I had a brainwave. What if Keith was able to play in my place? It wouldn't take much to fine-tune his golf game and he's certainly no slouch at the poker tables. I realised he wasn't a celebrity as such but, under the circumstances, the organisers might make an exception. Jack would have told anyone who would listen about the casino heist last year and my big win, so Keith could use that to his advantage. I reckoned Jack would be pleased if someone associated with me could front up for the big event. Keith and I had grown close and, if he was happy to do it, it would be a fitting tribute to Jack.

I drove slowly to my penthouse with a hundred and one thoughts going through my brain. I decided I'd catch up with Sylvia, then jot down my ideas and send Rachael an e-mail in Vegas. I'd have to come up with a pretty plausible excuse for not playing. I couldn't mention the Hong Kong incidents.

Sylvia saw me as I walked in the front door after picking up a newspaper. Lionel assured me delivery would restart on Wednesday.

'Oh, Tommy,' she gushed, 'it is so nice to see you home. You have so much to tell me. Are you okay? We missed you so much.'

'Calm down, Sylvia. There'll be plenty of time to tell you everything. First of all, I want to know how school's going.'

She spoke slowly and deliberately. 'I am doing well. The teacher is pleased with my progress. My parents have noticed how my talking is different and they are happy.'

'Are your parents well?'

'Mum is so-so but they are going okay and are still grateful for your kind gift. I want for you to meet them one day.'

'I'd like to. I also want you to meet Sarah. I've told her all about you and she is impressed with your plans for the future.'

'She sounds like a lovely person.'

'What time do you finish work today?'

'I finish at four and school starts at six-thirty.'

'How about coming up to my place when you finish and we'll have a coffee and a good chat?'

'I would love to. I'd better get back to work, Tommy. See you later.'

I spent a while with Lionel, telling him about our Hong Kong adventures. I felt he should know. He's a good guy.

I took the lift to the fifteenth floor and walked the remaining six. I realised my fitness level had dropped and although I'd been swimming gently and doing yoga, my aerobic fitness needed work. No doubt Sarah would take care of that once we settled back into a routine. I was chuffed about my weight loss.

I made myself a coffee, sat at my desk and wrote down my thoughts from earlier on. I wasn't sure who to contact first – Keith or Rachael. I didn't want to get Keith's hopes up only to squash them if Rachael said no. On the other hand, I didn't want Rachael to say yes for Keith to then say he wasn't interested.

I decided to send Keith an e-mail. I outlined my proposal and, after editing the message a few times to make sure he understood that it was only a proposition at the moment, hit the send button. With the small time difference, I might get a reply before dinner. I'd be able to tell Sarah.

With time on my hands I decided to go and see Lucky. He sat, spellbound, for the best part of half an hour as I related what had happened. He inspected my head and pressed lightly on the area that was almost healed.

'Does that hurt?'

I couldn't help laughing. 'Piss off. What are you now, a fucking doctor?'

'I am today.' I'd never seen him look more serious. 'I'd better be careful around Sarah though. I reckon you need a permit to have her hanging off your arm. Shit, Tommy, you've scored yourself a winner. She's gorgeous. Look, mate, if you get tired of her, put in a good word for me.'

'The odds of that happening are about the same as you picking the Melbourne Cup winner for the next five years.'

He shook his head sadly. 'I had a feeling you'd say something like that. Anyway, if Keith and Harry get in over their heads and you need an expert in LA, let me know. I can leave immediately.'

'So, you can take time off from here and you've got a current passport?

'You're a fuckin' killjoy, Tommy,' he growled. 'Of course I haven't got a passport. I've never been out of New South bloody Wales.'

We kept chatting for a while but with my stomach rumbling, I left him to his racing guide and headed to Jacques for an early lunch. I was looking forward to the grilled ling.

A small glass of wine finished off an enjoyable lunch. I walked along the promenade, bought a coffee and wandered for an hour before heading back to my apartment.

I set up my snooker table and let my imaginary friend break. I was determined to win this time. He made a good break, running the white ball down the table, leaving it halfway between the baulk line and the bottom cushion. He'd left a red near the top pocket that I was able to sink before taking the black. I proceeded to make a break of fifty-three and was never headed. It was satisfying to get a win. I laughed. If people knew I played with myself they might think I was odd. I must teach Sarah. It would be fun playing with her. Be careful what you wish for, I thought. Knowing her, she's probably good at snooker too. It wouldn't matter. Having her near would placate the defeats I might endure. I replaced the table cover, and grabbed a coffee and my laptop.

I checked my e-mails but my in-box was empty. I heard a knock on the door. It was Sylvia. Her boss had given her an early half hour. She couldn't wait to see me. She threw her arms around me.

'I wanted to hug you before but people might think it strange,' she cried, as I showed her in.

'Never let location get in the way of affection,' I said.

'Did you make that up?'

I nodded, smiling awkwardly.

'You are a funny man and I like you more than any other.'

'I value friendship highly and to have a friend like you is important to me,' I said.

I made coffee and we sat in the big recliners near the window where I told her what I'd told Lucky. I saw tears run down her face as I described what I could remember of the attack and subsequent hospital stay. Her eyes widened as I related our escape from Hong Kong using laundry trolleys.

'From what you tell me, you need someone like Sarah to look after you. You not only attract a beautiful woman you also attract trouble.'

'The thing is, Sylvia, I did nothing wrong. I can't help it if I'm a good poker player and others aren't so good and take offence when they lose.'

She laughed. 'I guess you're right but still, good idea to have Sarah keep an eye on you.'

'I must say I'm impressed with the improvements in your grammar. I'm so pleased you're enjoying school. Are your parents happy with your progress?'

'They are so happy. They think I'm good enough to start teaching kids but I tell them I have so much to learn to become a teacher. I asked them if they would go back to Vietnam if I went there to teach but they say this is their home now.'

'Fair enough, I guess. They've been here a long time and no doubt would have made many friends in the Vietnamese community.'

'My father is the head of his local area and is well respected. He sometimes talks to politicians when they visit and tells them what the people need.'

'That's great. Things are going well.'

I glanced at the clock and hadn't realised how long we'd been talking. Sylvia needed to get going, so we finished up. As she walked out the door, she demanded she meet Sarah soon.

We laughed and hugged and as the lift doors closed, I walked back into my apartment, feeling happy.

I had time before I was due at Sarah's so I decided to ring Mick again. He answered after the second ring and after going crook at him for not replying to my previous call I had to apologise. He never received it. I told him I'd hang up, check my call log and ring him back. I could see no record of me making the call. I rang him back and, after dwelling on the mysteries of mobile communications, or, as he insisted, bangs on the head causing delusionary behaviour, we decided to catch up the next day at Jacques for lunch.

I got changed, packed a small overnight bag, and headed to the garage. Lucky had gone home but he'd given my car the once-over. It looked as good as ever. The traffic was heavier this time around but I felt relaxed. After picking up a bottle of Bollinger and a bunch of African marigolds – Sarah's favourites – I parked outside her apartment and, after buzzing her number to get in, walked up the stairs.

She placed the goodies on a small table inside the door and welcomed me with a soft mouth against mine. I never knew what to expect with Sarah's greetings but she never failed to disappoint. I held her for a moment or two in silent bliss, breathing in her scent. My peripheral vision caught sight of Rhonda approaching from the kitchen. I turned towards her and smiled. She was about the same height as Sylvia and looked as if she kept active. She was wearing stylish jeans, a pink T-shirt and a pair of open-toed sandals. Pretty trendy for sixtyish.

'Come on, you two, you can do that when I've gone,' she said.

I walked over to her and hugged her. She pushed me to arm's length and looked me up and down. 'With everything that's happened you're looking much better than I expected.'

'What's your daughter been telling you?'

'Enough to know you should take it easy and stay off strange golf courses.'

'Well, I don't think I'll be hitting the course for a while yet, but when I do it'll be on familiar territory. I must say, Rhonda, you're looking great. Have you recovered?'

'I'm as fit as a fiddle. In fact, if I was any fitter, I'd be a danger to men everywhere.'

Over the next three hours we enjoyed a fantastic meal, great wine and good conversation. When Sarah told her mother of our marriage plans, tears of happiness rolled down her cheeks.

'Does this mean you won't be going on any more overseas trips?'

'Only with this guy, Mum,' said Sarah, beaming at me across the table.

'You've made an old woman happy.'

Sarah smiled. 'I wouldn't call sixty-three old. What do you reckon, Tommy?'

'Well they reckon seventy is the new sixty and, with the way you look, I think you can take old out of your vocabulary for a while.'

'Oooh, he's a real charmer, this one,' Rhonda laughed, getting up from the table to make coffee. 'I wouldn't let him out of my sight if I were you, Sarah.'

'Don't you worry. I won't,' she said, sliding her bare foot between my thighs, lightly massaging my groin. I gave a gasp but didn't resist and enjoyed the attention.

From the kitchen Rhonda told Sarah to let her know if she needed help with any wedding arrangements.

'You'll be my first port of call,' Sarah assured her, removing her foot as Rhonda returned with the coffee.

My face was flushed and Sarah had a mischievous look on her face. We wouldn't be getting much sleep tonight.

Rhonda left soon after coffee and while we loaded the dishwasher, I asked Sarah about her other phone.

'Did you have any messages?'

'Not one, which made my life easier. I didn't have to return calls explaining my retirement. I've put another recorded message on it telling the caller I am no longer providing escort services.'

'Music to my ears. I can't believe only three weeks have passed since we first met, and here we are; you retiring and us planning to get married.'

She slid her arms around my neck. 'I wouldn't have it any other way.' She put her lips to my ear. 'Have you seen the double shower?'

DAY 38 – TUESDAY

Sarah hadn't closed the curtains so we woke to the sun warming our naked bodies. The bedding was on the floor and we made no attempt to cover up. We were comfortable with our bodies; me in particular, since losing twelve kilos.

'You know what?' I said, snuggling in behind her, 'I reckon when I've lost these remaining eight kilos people will be knocking my door down, pleading with me to pose for live art classes.'

Sarah turned her head smiling. 'I think I've found a new nickname for you. FOS.'

'What's FOS?'

'Full of shit.'

The tickling started and continued until she was a mess. She had tears of laughter running down her face and she was begging me to stop.

I looked down at her and gently prised her legs apart. I could feel the sun and her heels on my back. The only sound I could hear was her whispers. 'Please don't stop.'

'I think we've just had breakfast,' she said eventually, breathing heavily and gently pushing me off her.

'Have you tried dessert for breakfast?'

'What are you, a bloody robot?'

'It's your fault. How can I resist such beauty?'

She jumped out of bed and headed for the shower. I emptied the dishwasher and packed things away in the cupboards. I thought we could walk down to a beachside café. The plans we'd tossed around in Hong Kong about our immediate future would be good to revisit over a continental breakfast and coffee.

I waited until I could hear her hair dryer before I went into the bathroom. 'Is it safe to come in or am I at risk of being molested?'

Sarah laughed and directed a blast of hot air onto my bum. I felt it wise not to turn around.

I showered and got dressed and, with Sarah agreeing with my breakfast suggestion, we headed out. On the way I told her about lunch with Mick and Angie. She was keen to catch up with them and find out how they were getting on.

We found an outside table at a café where Sarah was obviously a regular. Staff and several customers greeted her. Approving smiles in my direction made me feel like the king of Bondi.

Over breakfast, we discussed going to Tassie in a few weeks and we agreed I would ring Brian closer to the time and explain to him my early return. If he was in a position to catch up with us, we would drive down to Melbourne, put the car on the Bass Strait ferry, the *Spirit of Tasmania,* to Devonport, then drive south to Hobart. It would be a relaxing overnight trip on the ferry.

Sarah would ring Dianne and when we hit Hobart, we could catch up with her as well. Whether there would be any matchmaking remained to be seen.

'Are we going to officially get engaged or simply work towards the big day?' I asked, as the waitress refilled our cups.

'I'm not into rings and stuff. I honestly think the engagement process is more for younger people. I would love for us to have a small civil ceremony somewhere outdoors like the Botanical Gardens.'

'What a great idea. Because we're not in a hurry we can take our time with the guest list. Let's enjoy being home and take thing easy for a while.'

Sarah gave me a cheeky look. 'I'd be keen for a trip down to Diamond Harbour for poker. I know we can play here but from what you've told me, the casino down there holds special memories.'

'It certainly does have an attraction. You'll have to be prepared for the attention I might get. The robbery last year is still a big talking point, as is my poker win.'

'How much did you win and how much did they get away with, again?'

'I won a million, less four thousand, and they got around ten million and a lovely collection of personal possessions from the patrons, including the watch I won as part of my golf win years ago. The ringleader slipped it off my wrist as smooth as a magician performing a disappearing trick.'

'And no-one's been caught for the robbery?'

'Not according to Trevor, the doorman who retired about a month ago and whose farewell the guys and I went to. The cops have bugger-all to go on.

The casino has put up a sizeable reward for information leading to the gang's capture and conviction. I have a feeling it might go unclaimed.'

We finished breakfast and took a long walk on the beach. I bought a paper on the way back to Sarah's apartment. I scanned the main stories and started on the cryptic crossword while she got changed for lunch. She looked gorgeous in a simple sun dress and sandals that accentuated her tanned legs. We drove back to my place and, as Lucky wasn't about, we were able to get to the lift without having him carrying on like an infatuated teenager. I changed into a fresh polo shirt and shorts and also put on a pair of sandals. My legs were no match for Sarah's but they kept my arse from scraping on the ground.

We took the lift to the foyer and walked to Jacques. We were shown to a table where we could see incoming diners. It wasn't long before Mick and Angie strolled in.

Sarah and I stood and greeted them both. Angie appeared tentative, being the outsider, but we quickly put her at ease with stupid jokes and easy talk.

'It's great to finally meet you,' I said to Angie. Mick was right about her green eyes. They glistened like emeralds. 'Have you recovered from your ordeal?'

She looked at me with concern. 'Yes, Tommy, I'm all fixed but, more's the point, how are you? The guys kept Mick up to date with your dramas. It sounded like you'd been in the wars.' She smiled at Sarah. 'Good job he had you looking out for him.'

'Everyone's been saying that,' I said, 'and it's true. Without Sarah I probably wouldn't be here now. I owe her heaps. I'm feeling pretty good now. I reckon another week should see me a hundred per cent.'

'Great news, mate,' said Mick. 'Let's have a toast to a happy future.'

We clinked our glasses and settled down to read the menu. Mick and Angie ordered a Caesar salad while Sarah and I ordered our favourite – ling with salad. We were given generous serves, which were delicious as usual.

Mick and Angie were keen to hear more details about our time away and by the time we'd finished our main courses, I needed to stop talking.

'How about filling us in on what you guys have been up to,' said Sarah, as the waiter passed us the dessert menus. 'A little birdie told us you've now got a passport, Angie. Anything we should know about?'

'Mick insisted I get one.'

Mick did a mock boy-scout salute towards Sarah and exaggerated his accent. 'One has to be prepared, old girl. One never knows when one might want to jump on a plane.'

Angie dug him in the ribs, then looked at Sarah and me. 'Well, you know about the events concerning Danny and the police; so, after we came up to Sydney a couple of weeks ago and visited all the touristy places Mick should have already seen, we headed to Ned Kelly country. We stayed at Wangaratta and toured around the area. Glenrowan was especially interesting. On the way back to Sydney we diverted to Canberra. We were keen to check out Parliament House, the War Museum and other interesting sites. I had to admit to Mick I hadn't been to Canberra so I copped a good ribbing.'

'Typical of Mick. Can't let an opportunity slip without having a dig at someone.'

'Now, now, let's not make it all about me,' said Mick in his modest overly-English accent. 'I should point out Angie dropped her phone into Lake Burley Griffin while she was talking to Vicki. I was certainly justified in ribbing her about that. Vicki didn't have a clue what had happened until Angie rang her on my phone. I must say, was she embarrassed or what?'

'What you've conveniently omitted is you were trying to get your hands under my T-shirt.'

Sarah was giggling. 'You men. You can't keep your hands to yourselves.'

'Well it's not our fault we're lumbered with gorgeous women who love us to death and can't bear to be away from us for more than a minute,' said Mick, giving me a wink. The girls noticed and looked proud.

We continued the back and forth banter until dessert arrived. Sarah and I told them about our plans to head down to Tassie in a few weeks and possibly catch up with Brian and Dianne. For Angie's benefit I explained who Brian was and told them about Sarah's friend Dianne. I also extended an offer for them to come with us.

Mick looked at Angie. 'Is that something you'd like to do?'

'I'd love to but unfortunately I can't be away from work much longer. I'll be running out of holidays and I can't afford to take leave without pay.'

'That's fair enough,' said Sarah.

Mick looked thoughtful for a few moments.

'Our booking at the Condor runs out on Thursday, so how about the four of us head down to Diamond Harbour.' He turned to Angie. 'Would you mind if we stayed at your place for a while? If your boss would give you time off without pay, I'd be over the moon if you'd let me pay your rent in advance and any other expenses so you could come to Tassie.'

Angie put her arm around him and sobbed. 'I can't believe I've met such a kind-hearted, caring man after being through so much. I don't know what I've done to deserve you.'

Mick drew her face to his and wiped her tears with a napkin, kissing her gently. 'I'll take that as a yes.'

She couldn't help but laugh. 'Yes, yes and yes.'

I looked at Sarah who was wiping a tear from her face. 'I guess you've got no objections to Mick's brilliant idea?'

'It's a great idea. It would be nice for the four of us to travel together. Once we've had a break at Angie's, Tommy and I can come back to Sydney and get ourselves organised for Tassie.

'By the way, Mick, how are you getting around? Have you been paying for a hire car since you came back from Hong Kong?'

'Yes, I have. I took a three-week lease that also expires on Thursday so I'll have to decide whether to extend it or hitch a lift with a mate.'

Angie reckoned she had the solution. 'If Tommy could drive us to my place, we can use my car to run around in. It's not as flash as the hire car but it'll keep the rain off us.'

'Getting better by the minute,' said Sarah.

The waiter started clearing our table and we left the restaurant. We'd spent the best part of three hours at Jacques and it was nice to get out into the sunshine again.

'Sarah and I'll pick you guys up at, say, ten-thirty on Thursday?'

'We'll be waiting at the door,' said Mick as we hugged and shook hands.

They hopped into the hire car, waving as they drove off. Sarah and I walked arm in arm back to my place.

'Do you mind running me home now? I'd like to spend the rest of today and tomorrow with Mum seeing as we'll be going to Angie's on Thursday. She wants to go shopping and wants my opinion on a few things. I suspect wedding talk might also be on her list.'

'Do you want to meet Sylvia before I run you home?'

'I'd love to.'

We walked into the foyer and through to the staff area. Sylvia was having a cuppa and she almost spilt it over herself in her hurry to get to us. She hugged Sarah like a long-lost friend. I thought Sylvia's enthusiasm might have surprised Sarah but she embraced the moment with equal fervour. She made us a coffee and we spent the next half hour trading conversation. When we left, I had the impression the girls knew everything about each other.

We managed to avoid Lucky again and enjoyed the slow drive back to her place. She talked about Sylvia non-stop. She refused my offer to walk her to her apartment.

'I know what'll happen if I let you in my door.'

'I've had no complaints so far.'

'I hate to admit it, but you've shagged me enough for a couple of days. I need a spell.'

I sighed. 'There's no pleasing some people.'

'Oh yes there is. That's why I need a break. Bye, darling. I'll ring you tomorrow night.'

She leant over and kissed me, then swung her legs out of the car in unison. She was all class.

I drove back to my place and on seeing Lucky parking a car he'd finished detailing, walked into his office and made us a coffee. We chatted more about Jack's cars and he said he'd be interested to know what values had been put on them.

'Why, are you thinking of putting in a bid?'

'Yeah. Why not? There's room here for half a dozen, you big knob.'

We traded friendly insults for a while then I took the lift to my apartment. I fired up my laptop and noticed Keith was yet to reply. No hurry. I logged out, closed it down and slumped into a recliner. I felt myself dozing off. I didn't fight it.

It was dark when I woke. I'd been asleep for nearly four hours. Bugger. I'd struggle to sleep when I was meant to. I decided to ring the casino. Poker was happening so I had a quick shower and drove over.

The place was busy for a Tuesday night. I asked a waiter why. Apparently two large cruise ships were in port with big-betting gamblers wanting to hit the local casinos.

I wandered to the poker area to find a spare seat. None. Not knowing how long I'd have to wait I decided to play blackjack. I was seated in fifth chair and was the only Australian among a horde of Yanks obviously off the ships. Their spotless white joggers were the giveaway. Unfortunately, three of them weren't experienced players, which may have had an impact on my game.

At one stage I leaned towards the player on my right who got to play before me and quietly advised him it's not the best strategy to ask for a card when you're sitting on twelve to sixteen and the dealer has a four, five or six. Likewise, when sitting on thirteen to sixteen when the dealer has a two or a three. He thanked me and apologised if he had taken cards that may have been handy to me.

'The thing is,' I said, 'no-one knows what the next card dealt might be; so, you might get a six, seven or eight when sitting on thirteen and end up with a strong hand.'

'Makes sense but upsetting other players is probably not a good thing. They might not be as understanding or helpful as you.'

We introduced ourselves and shook hands. He slowly began to win back his losses. When he got pairs, he was confused. While the dealer was re-shuffling the packs, I told him to always split aces and eights but never split tens, fives or fours. As far as the other pairs went it would depend on what card the dealer had and when it came to doubling down. I didn't want to confuse him any further at this stage. I told him I'd be happy to write down the options for him over a drink later. For the time being I told him I'd give him either a nod or a shake if he got a pair other than fours, fives, eights, tens or aces and didn't know what to do.

He smiled at me. 'You seem like a real nice bloke. Are all Aussies like you?'

'Only the nice ones,' I said with a laugh.

He slapped me on the back and we watched as the dealer restarted the game. My new American friend got a queen the first time around, then an ace. He was playing a hundred dollars a hand and was happy with a blackjack. The next hand he got a pair of sevens. The dealer had a five. The Yank looked at me and I nodded, so he told the dealer to split. He placed another one-hundred-dollar chip next to the second seven. The dealer gave him a ten on the first seven and a nine on the next. The Yank sat on both while the deal went around the table back to the dealer. He turned over a ten that gave him fifteen so he had to deal himself another card which was a jack. He broke and my friend picked up another two hundred dollars.

He was clearly chuffed with his progress but I was losing interest fast because I wasn't concentrating on my own hands. It probably didn't matter as I was getting shit cards anyway. You know things aren't going your way when you consistently sit on eighteens, nineteens and twenties and more often than not get beaten by one more. I stayed for a couple more shoes then told my friend I was heading over to the bar and either finding a seat at a poker table or going home.

He asked if he could join me so I could give him advice on splitting pairs and doubling down.

I smiled. 'It'll cost you a beer.'

'Lead the way.'

He bought a couple of beers and we sat at a table where I found a couple of clean coasters and proceeded to write down the preferred options for handling pairs and doubling down. I also included how to play soft totals where one card held is an ace and can be counted as one or eleven. After I'd finished, he looked at it and rolled his eyes.

'Goddammit. I never realised it was so complicated. If you hadn't come along, I could have lost a bundle. Thanks, Tommy. I wish I knew how to play poker because I'd love to sit beside you for a while. If you know as much about poker as you do about blackjack you must be doing alright.'

'Yeah, I'm doing alright,' I said with a wry smile. If only he knew.

We finished our drinks and after I'd refused another, I said goodbye to him. No spare seats at the poker tables, so home beckoned.

It was nearly midnight when I crawled into bed. It felt strange to be sleeping on my own. I could smell Sarah's natural scent around me and it almost made me take matters into my own hands. But tiredness overcame me and as the clock flicked onto triple zeros I slipped into dreamtime.

DAY 39 – WEDNESDAY

I woke to a cloudy morning, wondering if autumn was trying to bully its way into the end of summer. It probably wasn't as Sydney weather was usually good through March and April. May could be a calm month even though the days were short.

I slipped into my walking gear, drank a glass of milk and walked downstairs. I planned to walk for an hour, get back and have breakfast. If Keith hadn't replied to my e-mail, I'd give him a ring.

My head felt great and, as I walked, I could feel my lower back and leg muscles working well. It was the fastest I'd walked for a long time. When I got back to my apartment, via the lift, although I was buggered, I felt terrific. My pedometer told me I'd walked seven kilometres in a tad under an hour. Sarah would be pleased. I had a cool shower, a healthy breakfast, knocked over the crossword and made a start on the neuf-neuf. I doubted I'd call it a sudoku again. Thanks, George.

I gave up on the neuf-neuf after a frustrating hour, then threw my washing in the machine. I switched on the computer and opened my e-mail. Keith had finally replied.

Hi Tommy.

Hope you're mending well. I must admit I was surprised to get your e-mail. It would be pretty exciting to play golf and poker in Vegas. I'm pretty sure I could match them at poker but not sure about the golf. I do have a mate though who got me into golf years ago who now lives in London. He might be able to get me back on track. We've still got a while until the tournaments so things could work. Why don't you contact Rachael in Vegas and if she can convince the organising committee to let me play, then I'm in. If not, no harm done. I'll simply come back to Oz and whip your arse again and take your money. Ha, ha.

We've got a few days left in Tokyo. George is thinking about heading back to London tomorrow but Harry and I are having a ball. We met up with a pair of gorgeous identical twins at a bar and we've been shagging our arses off. Good job we've got separate rooms because I've got no idea who's who. According to Harry, his girl's got a small tattoo of an owl on her inner thigh. Fuck knows why an owl and fuck knows why on her inner thigh. Anyway, I said to Harry that doesn't help me when she's got clothes on. He told me she's more than happy to hoist up her skirt and show me if I'm in any doubt. I have a feeling we won't be taking them back to London. We could drop them off in LA but that'd be cruel. Anyway, it's harmless fun and they're good to have around. They've shown us places in Tokyo where tourists never get to go so it's been a real eye-opener ... and leg-opener.

Let me know what Rachael says and we'll go from there. We're looking forward to getting to LA and sorting out Jack's cars. We've been doing some research already and if the 1968 Ferrari 365 Daytona is in top condition it could possibly get around a million dollars. If that's the case I reckon it might be one of your five. Anyway, I'll let you know about the others in time.

Say hi to Sarah from us and when you run into Mick give him a clip around the ear.
Take care my friend, I mean it.

I sat back in my chair, smiling; contemplating not only their escapades with their oriental friends but also the good things my selected charities would be able to accomplish.

I decided to send Rachael an e-mail. I moved over to the desk where I could look through my paperwork. I was absent-mindedly fiddling with my letter opener while I read my notes. It eventually distracted me and my mind wandered to the day I'd received it, back in 1989 after my big golf win in Europe. I was pretty sure my mother had sent it to me as a way of apologising for the way she put her own life ahead of mine. Maybe after the way my father treated her, that was fair enough. I couldn't imagine what it would be like to also raise a child, even one as easy as me. Seeking the comfort of women was most likely her escape from reality. Shit. What would I know? I never did contact her. She died in 1991 of a stroke. She would have been fifty-two. A government department had written to me telling me she had died and I was her next of kin and all her belongings were now mine. I reluctantly went to Cooma after the formal paperwork was processed and, apart from the desk and some cash, I gave everything that wasn't crap to the Salvos. The crap became landfill. I had the desk brought to Sydney. I put it into storage in a mate's garage until I settled into my penthouse some years later. I never found out what happened to my father. According to the locals he'd sold his business and headed to Queensland. It wouldn't have surprised me to find out he became the chief taste-tester for the Bundaberg Distilling Company.

The low-battery beep from the computer snapped me back to reality. I plugged in the power supply and finished reading my notes. I was glad Keith wouldn't be too disappointed if things didn't work out. It took me a while to compose my message to Rachael but when I was done, I felt I'd given her pretty good reasons for Keith to play on my behalf and in memory of Jack. I couldn't be sure how long it would be before I'd get a reply but at least the wheels were turning.

I played online poker while my washing was going and, while I didn't have a big balance due to my scepticism of online gambling sites, I was pleased to see it growing. It meant I didn't have to constantly transfer funds from my other accounts that were attracting a generous interest rate. Should I feel bad having all this loot? Fuck no.

I looked at my phone, willing it to ring. I was loath to ring Sarah. It would be selfish of me to interrupt her time with her mother, seeing as we were heading off again tomorrow.

I wandered into the billiard room and looked along the bookcase. I noticed a book called *One of a Kind*. It was the story of Stuey 'The Kid' Unger; arguably the most remarkable and best poker player the world has seen. I'd bought it at a book fair for $5 a couple of years ago but had never made the time to read it. Now seemed like a good time to make time. I'd watched Stuey win the World Series of Poker Main Event in 1997 in Vegas and, although he had also won it in 1980 and 1981, he had still played like a man possessed. At the time I didn't think another player anywhere could match his fearlessness and aggressiveness. It was such a shame he died the next year. He was only forty-five.

I kicked back in my recliner with my phone handy and started reading. I became so absorbed that by the time the phone did ring, scaring the shit out of me, I'd read eighty-five pages. I never knew Stuey was also a champion gin rummy player. I'd heard someone say he was as shrewd as a shit-house rat.

We talked for the best part of an hour. She was in stitches when I told her about Keith and Harry's adventures, particularly the part about the owl tattoo.

I told her I'd pick her up at ten and we'd head over to the Condor and collect Mick and Angie. I wanted to keep talking but understood she needed to pack, as did I. I'd forgotten my washing. It was still in the machine. I'd give it another rinse to get rid of the wrinkles, hang it out, pack a case, and then hit the sack.

DAY 40 – THURSDAY

I was convinced my fitness program was having an effect because I now looked forward to going for my walks. The yoga was particularly helpful with my flexibility and mindfulness. Over the next few weeks, I would ask Sarah if she considered my post-traumatic stress was under control. I felt it was but my shrink reckoned it would take a while longer and recommended continued consultations. I smiled to myself. Yeah, her next overseas holiday had to be funded somehow.

I had a light breakfast and with time to kill, I headed to the pool where I swam laps for an hour. I was feeling great. My flab was disappearing and I could feel muscles where I knew they should be, but hadn't been able to find for the past ten years or so.

Showered, dressed and packed I headed to the basement where I saw Lucky in his office with his ear glued to the radio. As I got to the door, I noticed the racing guide open and scribble all over it.

'Interesting system for picking winners,' I said, walking in.

He obviously hadn't heard me walk in and he jumped in surprise.

'Bloody hell. You'll give a bloke a heart attack. You could at least cough or something.'

I laughed. 'You need to change your office around so you can see when people are coming. Imagine if I'd been your boss; your scam would have been busted and you'd be upstairs cleaning out the kitchen for the rest of your illustrious career.'

He looked sheepish. 'You're right, Tommy. I presume you're here for your car and not to spend an enjoyable morning with a guy who can give you guaranteed winners for today's races.'

'Spot on. Sarah and I are heading down the coast with friends for a while. We'll be back long enough to pack for Tassie. We're going over on the ferry so you won't have the privilege of cleaning my car for a while.'

'Make sure you stick your head in the door before you go.'

'Sure will, mate. See ya. Good luck with the nags.'

I put my bag in the boot and drove out into a bright morning. I arrived at Sarah's around ten. I walked up the stairs and knocked on her door. I didn't have to wait long to feel her in my arms and taste her mouth on mine. We shuffled through the door and only after she'd pulled away did she speak.

'Don't let me be away from you that long again, understand. I know it's only been a day but I've thought about you every minute. Even when I was out shopping with Mum, as nice as it was, I only wanted to be with you.'

'I'm sorry. I missed that. Could you repeat it?'

She gave me one of her playful slaps, another big kiss and hug, then walked to the bedroom where she was finishing packing.

I watched her walking. 'If I'd had my way, I would have taken you up to my place after lunch and not let you out until this morning.'

'Will I need swimwear?'

'Unless you're planning to swim naked, which I thoroughly recommend, then yes. The beaches down the coast are fantastic and the water should be balmy.'

She held up a skimpy bikini and a classy one-piece. I gave her two thumbs-up and she stuffed them into her case, leaning on it as she clicked it shut.

She wheeled it to the door, picked up her handbag and keys, and off we went. She was dressed in a pair of white shorts with a lemon polo shirt and white joggers. Her hair was tied back, revealing simple sleeper earrings. Even her ears were sexy.

She gave me a quick look up and down. 'Since when have hearing-aid-brown shorts and martian-green polo shirts made a comeback?'

'Well, it's your fault. Because you've had me on a get-fit regime, most of my clothes don't fit me anymore, so I had to resort to my old nineties clothing from the back of the wardrobe.'

'To be honest, my darling, I don't think they were in vogue even then. Never mind, we'll go shopping in Diamond Harbour.'

'I guess I can't argue with the queen of style. I must admit I thought the brown shorts weren't too bad.'

'Now I know you're joking.' She was laughing as we left the lift and walked to the car.

'We were meant to have a buy-up in Hong Kong,' she said, 'and although we got a few things, circumstances beyond our control prevented a shop-till-we-drop day.'

We pulled up outside the Condor. Mick and Angie were waiting, big smiles on their faces. I couldn't see Barry at his post. Mick told me it was his day off.

I helped them with their luggage. 'You guys look happy.'

'What's not to be happy about, old chap,' said Mick, slapping me on the back. 'The future's lookin' rosy. Here are us two blokes with two beautiful women by our sides, headin' down the coast. Who'd 'ave thought a month ago we'd be doin' this?'

'You seem to be putting on your Pommy accent more than usual this morning.'

'Sorry, mate. I get carried away when I'm in love.'

'Don't apologise. I love listening to you rabbiting-on in your native tongue.'

He laughed and slapped me again.

Sarah had hopped out and gotten in the back with Angie. Mick looked at her. 'Are you sure you don't want to sit up front?'

'I'm sure you and Tommy have got a lot to talk about and I'd like to get to know Angie better. I'm looking forward to hearing her waitressing stories.'

'And I'm looking forward to some escort stories,' said Angie, not missing a beat.

Sarah laughed. 'Those two had better block their ears. Things might get steamy.'

I pointed the car towards the coast road and engaged cruise control. We stopped after an hour for coffee, then continued on, arriving at Angie's place around one.

Mick and I unloaded the car and were carrying the luggage down the path when we heard a scream. We dropped the cases and ran through the door. Angie was screaming non-stop. Sarah was holding her to stop her from collapsing but she was struggling. She broke away and rushed from room to room, sobbing uncontrollably. The place had been trashed. Further inside we could see nothing had been left untouched. Every cupboard door had been ripped off its hinges; food containers spilled over the bench tops and floor. Violent hands had swept stacks of crockery, rows of glasses, and storage containers onto the floor. Also on the floor, the food from the fridge and freezer lay in a congealed mess. The dishwasher and oven doors were open, twisted out of shape by angry boots. In the bedrooms, the wardrobes were stripped; bedside drawers upended; bedding torn off the beds and the mattresses slashed. The bathroom was destroyed. The dining table had been dragged to below the ceiling access hole with scuff marks indicating someone had climbed into the roof cavity. The ceiling had holes in it from careless feet and some plaster walls had holes bashed in them.

We moved back to the kitchen where Sarah noticed a sheet of paper under a glass dish.

Angie was about to grab it when Sarah clasped her arm.

'Don't touch anything. We're calling the police. There might be finger prints they can use.'

'Can you read it without touching it?' I asked.

Hey Angie.

Tell Danny we want our five million. Just because he won't answer his phone doesn't mean we can't track him down. We know the people he knows. Maybe he's told you where he's hidden it. Tell him he's got until 16th March to call me. I'll be back in the country and I'll come visiting. His mate at the casino wasn't much help. Wasn't much of a swimmer either. Tell Danny I'm a reasonable man. I'll now take his share and he and you can live to tell your grandkids a lovely bedtime story about how a friendly monster saved you from dangerous sharks.

'The fucking prick is dead and he's still haunting me,' Angie sobbed in Sarah's arms.

Mick went outside and checked under the house and the garage. Angie's boxes of things she wasn't using had been ripped apart, strewn about and smashed. Her car was a wreck. The seats had been pulled out and the door panels prised off and slashed.

'The cops are on their way,' I said, hanging up.

I was gobsmacked. Danny was one of the guys involved in the casino heist. I could feel my head starting to throb. Where was the other five million?

'I know it's a small world but this doesn't make any sense. Did you suspect anything, Angie?'

She glared at me. 'I didn't even know he was *fucking married*, so how the hell would I know anything about this shit?'

'I'm sorry. I didn't mean to upset you. These guys obviously don't know Danny's dead. If he was hiding the money here, surely they would have found it. Look at the way they've gone through the place.'

Mick went over to Angie. 'You know Danny's gear I took to the Salvos? Well I didn't check in any of it. When you pointed out what was his I loaded it up to get it out of here. Is there a chance the money was hidden in it and now the Salvos have got it?'

She hooked her arms around him and looked at him with red eyes. 'It's possible, I suppose. He had a tonne of gear down there. I never looked at any of his shit but he never told me not to.'

'That was pretty smart of him,' said Sarah. 'By not drawing attention to his stuff you didn't become curious and go poking around.'

Angie came over to me and hugged me. I could feel her shaking. 'I'm sorry, Tommy. I didn't mean to jump down your throat. I don't need this crap. I thought all this was behind me. I'm trying not to imagine what might have happened if I'd been here when they called.'

We turned as we heard a light knock on the open door. Two plain-clothes detectives and a uniformed officer walked in. One detective said hello to Angie and Mick. Angie introduced him to Sarah and me. His name was Reg Harper and he had interviewed Angie after Danny's death. The other two introduced themselves and stood quietly by the door.

'Bloody hell, what a mess,' he said. 'I've seen heaps of burglaries in my time but nothing on this scale. These guys have been thorough. Have any of you touched anything?'

'We've walked through the house and Mick's been downstairs but that's all,' said Angie. 'They left a note.'

Harper read the note and a smile came across his face as he reached into his pocket and removed his note book. He flicked through a few pages.

'Ah. Here it is. Monday 25th. The Salvos received a big load of recreational gear in good condition. They recorded it and recall it sitting in the storeroom for around a week until they had time to sort it. On opening the bags they thought might have contained heavy ropes, wetsuits and the like, they discovered a huge amount of cash.'

He closed the book and looked at us, remembering what happened next. 'They immediately contacted us and we took all the gear to the station. We were able to lift fingerprints from the gear and ran them through the national database. The only ones we got a match for were Danny's. We knew he was dead so we tried to contact Angie but couldn't get through. When we called in here on the Tuesday, we got no answer and saw nothing untoward. The front door was locked. In hindsight we should have checked around the house but we had no reason to suspect anything. Was the front door locked when you arrived today?'

Mick looked at Angie who nodded, then at Harper. 'Angie and I were in Canberra when Angie lost her phone. That's why you couldn't contact her. She got another phone when we got back to Sydney but it's got a different number.'

'It's making sense now. In the meantime, we've been trying to track down any of Danny's associates. We've spoken with the Adelaide and Perth police. We even contacted the mine management in Western Australia. At least we know what happened to the guy at the casino. We've come to the conclusion these guys are pros but, as they now want their money, we're hoping they might get sloppy. I think the first thing to happen is you guys leave here. We don't want you getting caught up in any action. We'll put surveillance on the place and will be ready on the sixteenth and hopefully catch them.'

I turned to the cop. 'I'm confused with all this. The plane crash that killed Danny was reported in the main papers. Why wouldn't his associates know he's dead?'

'The names of those killed were never published, at the families' requests.'

I continued. 'It seems strange they would advertise the date they're coming back. Wouldn't they assume Angie would call you guys?'

'Not necessarily. Because they don't know Danny's dead, they would assume Angie would be too scared to call us, knowing what happened to the casino guy.'

'The haul from the casino was ten million. I wonder where the other five is.'

Harper humoured me. 'I'm presuming they split it up. Ten million takes up a fair bit of space. Danny's storage under the house was obviously good for half. Hopefully we'll catch the guys and they can answer all our questions. You seem to be taking an interest in this, Tommy.'

'Well, I was the bloke who won the big poker game the night the casino was robbed. The ringleader removed an expensive, sentimental watch from my arm in the process, so yes, I've got a personal interest in this.'

'I thought your face looked familiar. It was spread over nearly every newspaper in the state, if I recall.'

'Not to mention the London papers,' Mick chipped in.

He turned to Angie, apologising for his digression. 'Is your lease through a real estate or private?'

'Diamond Realty manages the property. I'll need to contact them.'

'No, we'll do that. We want the property left as it is until after Sunday. If they come back, we'll nab them and our forensic guys can go over the place. We might get fingerprints but I doubt it. I'm sorry this has happened, Angie, after what you've been through, and I know you want to sort out your things, but we do have procedures to follow. I hope you understand.'

Angie nodded again, tears welling up.

'I think we should book into the casino for a while until Angie can come back here and salvage what she can of her things,' said Mick, putting his arm around her and holding her tight. Her shaking slowed.

'I'd prefer it if you would get out of Diamond Harbour until this is over. The further away you are, the better,' said Harper.

I looked at the others. 'He's right. We should head back to Sydney. You can stay at my place for as long as you need to.'

Angie gave Harper her and Mick's phone numbers and a spare key from her purse and couldn't get to the car quick enough. We bundled the luggage back into the boot and headed back to Sydney.

Mick sat with Angie in the back. I barely heard a word from them until we stopped for a quick, late lunch at the café where we'd had coffee earlier. We settled for toasted sandwiches and coffee. I wanted cake but thought better of it. Angie barely touched hers. She looked pale and drawn. Mick tried to lighten the mood, with limited success.

'I know you're trying to cheer me up but I'm struggling. It wasn't meant to be like this. After we'd seen the cops a couple of weeks ago and given them statements, I thought it was all over. We had a great time in Sydney and out west and with plans for Tassie ...'

She put her head on Mick's shoulder and sobbed. Sarah suggested we keep moving. I paid the bill and followed them to the car. We reached Sydney late afternoon. I asked Sarah if she'd stay over and she agreed. Female company for Angie would be good, she told me.

Sarah and I made up the bed in the guest bedroom. Angie had a shower and went to bed. Mick looked in on her after a few minutes. She was asleep.

The three of us sat in the lounge room and, over a few drinks, recounted the events of the past six hours.

'I can't get my head around the fact Danny was involved in the heist,' I said.

'I guess him being involved with Angie, who is now involved with Mick, is purely coincidental; but it doesn't make it any easier to take in,' said Sarah. 'The old saying, dead men tell no tales, couldn't be truer. I only hope the cops know what they're doing. I can't imagine these guys waltzing back into the house looking for Danny or Angie or the money without making sure they aren't walking into a trap.'

Mick looked at us with sadness in his eyes. 'The thing that pisses me off the most about this business, is that Angie had to leave all her belongings back at the house even though she's had fuck-all to do with any of it. Why would they break all her nice things? We were only saying a while ago that, now that

Danny's gone, she won't have to put up with him throwing her favourite things around.'

'Who knows what goes on in the minds of guys like that,' I said. 'There's not much we can do about it at the moment. Rest assured, though, when Angie gets a new place, she'll get the best of everything. I can't imagine her wanting to move back into the house even after it's fixed up; too many bad memories.'

Sarah stood and walked to the fridge.

'We need comfort food. How about we ring out for Chinese takeaway? It would make our first night here nice and easy. Do you think Angie would be up for some? She didn't have much for lunch and she needs to eat.'

'She does like Chinese,' said Mick.

Angie surfaced after a couple of hours. I made us coffee and after she agreed to a meal, I rang the nearby Golden Panda with our wish list, and an offer of an extra fifty dollars if they delivered to the Marina reception and had them call me as soon as the food arrived. The service lift could be programmed to come straight up to the top floor. The meals would stay hot. Nothing was too much trouble for Tommy, they said.

Angie wasn't up for much talk and apologised. We told her not to worry. We'd take care of her. When the phone rang, it was Lionel at reception. The food was on the way up. I went out to the lift and waited. A kitchen-hand appeared as the lift doors opened and handed me a large plastic bag. I thanked her and took it inside. It smelt good. Sarah helped me spread the containers on the dining table where we could help ourselves. I opened a bottle of champagne and after a glass we started to feel chirpier.

Angie managed a smile. 'I need to drink this more often.'

She tucked into the food and after twenty minutes or so we'd stuffed ourselves. Mick said he'd have the leftovers for breakfast. I wasn't sure he was serious.

When we'd finished our coffee, Angie had got a few things off her chest. She was happy to stay with us until the cops contacted her.

I cleaned up the table and switched on the dishwasher while the others talked about what tomorrow might bring.

We said our goodnights and went to bed. Sarah slipped into my arms and I closed my eyes.

DAY 41 – FRIDAY

I woke to the sound of someone in the kitchen making a racket. I was about to get out of bed when Sarah's hand pulled me back in.

'This won't take long.'

After about a minute she reappeared from under the sheet, slid on top of me and, with her face using the pillow as a muffler, brought us to a happy ending.

We lay there giggling like teenagers. She got up and beckoned me to the shower. When we appeared in the kitchen Mick had finished off the leftovers and was putting the containers in the bin.

'Can I get you lovebirds breakfast? How about eggs, bacon, toast and coffee?'

I looked at Sarah. 'I've certainly got an appetite. How about you?'

She looked at Mick. 'Eggs sunny-side up, crispy bacon, well-browned toast and an espresso. Oh, and an orange juice. Thanks, chef.'

Our laughter brought Angie out. 'Having fun without me, I see.'

She'd had a shower and was looking much better than yesterday.

'Thanks, guys, for looking after me. I don't think I would have got through this without you. Do you think the cops will catch these guys?'

'Sunday can't come quick enough,' said Mick. 'When your phone rings let's hope it's good news.'

I knew Mick was trying to be optimistic for Angie's sake but I had a feeling these low-life scum would be hard to take down. I hoped my feelings were way offline.

Sarah asked Angie if she wanted to meet her mother and go clothes shopping. It might take her mind off things for a while. Angie willingly agreed so, after breakfast was done, we took the lift to the basement where Lucky was polishing a Porsche and chatting to its owner who lived in the apartment below mine. We gave Lucky a wave and he paused while he acknowledged us. I could see him giving Sarah and Angie the once-over.

'Fucking randy bastard,' I muttered.

Sarah dug me in the ribs. 'Did you say what I think I heard you say?'

'If it was, "bloody nice car," then yes.'

She gave me another rib poke, only harder.

Angie was cheering up and we drove out into another sunny Sydney morning and headed to Sarah's place. I asked Mick if he wanted to visit some antique shops on the North Shore. He was keen, so we agreed to meet up at Sarah's place for dinner. She would get her mum over as well. The more the merrier, she reckoned.

I dropped the girls off and we headed over the bridge. Our first stop was at a non-descript collectables shop at Mona Vale where Mick was amazed to find a cedar writing box. He didn't even haggle on the price. When we got back to the car, he was like a dog with two dicks.

'I never thought I'd pick up a gem like this in such a dump,' he marvelled, running his fingers over timber worn down by a century or more of hands opening and closing the lid.

'I'm happy for you, Mick,' I said.

We headed west to pick up the Pacific Highway to Gosford and decided to have lunch before checking out the three antique shops I had in mind. I had been intending to come here before now as I knew one shop had a supply of old billiard and snooker balls, along with early style cues. We could kill two birds with one stone as I had a feeling Mick would find a few more treasures.

As we entered the first shop, Mick's mouth dropped open. 'Fuck me dead, Tommy, I've never seen such a big collection of antique Villeroy and Boch in one place.'

The smell of old furniture and furnishings was strong on my nose but Mick was oblivious to any distractions. He selected half a dozen items and had them double wrapped. He wanted to make sure these didn't get broken.

The second shop revealed nothing except a pushy owner who was put out we didn't buy anything. I hit the jackpot with the third one. I found three boxes of early 1900s snooker balls and a set of billiard balls certified as being part of billiard-great Walter Lindrum's estate. I couldn't prove the provenance but I wasn't concerned. My knowledge of billiard and snooker memorabilia was good enough to know the balls were circa 1940s. I recalled reading that Lindrum performed thousands of exhibition games during the Second World War to raise money for the war effort. The cues, I was told, had been sold a while back. Mick found two brass carriage clocks in excellent condition and was still barking when we got back to the car. We packed our finds carefully in the boot and started our drive back to Sydney.

'This was a great idea, Tommy,' he said. 'I never thought we'd be doing this after yesterday.'

We arrived back at my place in plenty of time to get cleaned up, have a quick game of snooker, and drive over to Sarah's. I grabbed champagne and white wine from the fridge and a nice red from the cellar as we left. I'd find a spot for my purchases in the display cabinet tomorrow, along with Keith's fairway wood present I'd forgotten about and found in my golf bag. Mick asked if he could hide the Villeroy and Boch in my storage room in the basement for the time being.

It was a hug-fest when we arrived at Sarah's. Rhonda was over the moon to see me again and gave Mick a big, welcoming hug and kiss.

Angie looked at them and laughed. 'I'd better keep an eye on you, Rhonda, over dinner.'

'That's what I said when Mum first met Tommy. You know what, Mum? I think we better find you a man.'

'Why, when I've got two here to choose from?'

I opened the champagne and we raised our glasses to Angie, wishing her a good result on Sunday. She shivered and smiled and thanked us for caring so much. Over drinks the girls told us how successful their shopping trip was and said that, if we behaved, Mick and I might be in for a fashion parade later.

Mick told them about his writing box and clocks and I told them I found some balls.

'Tell me more, young man,' Rhonda implored.

'Mum,' Sarah scowled.

Because they were interested, I explained the difference between playing snooker and billiards. Angie suggested she and Mick take on Sarah and me the next day. The losers would buy dinner. We agreed and returned our attention to dinner.

Sarah, with help from Angie and Rhonda, had cooked up a storm. Although it was summer, Rhonda's minestrone soup went down a treat with garlic bread. Sarah's coq au vin was a winner and Angie's apricot sponge with sweet whipped cream had us pushing our bowls in for seconds. Mixing the food with champers and wine made us lethargic and it was Mick who had the stamina to clear the table, while the rest of us flopped into the lounge room.

It was a while before anyone wanted coffee. Rhonda had dozed off and I noticed Sarah looking at her lovingly. The moment took me back to another time I wished had been different.

We chatted well into the evening and it was getting close to midnight when we dragged ourselves out of the chairs. Sarah left the washing up in the dishwasher. She'd unpack it next time she was home. She packed her overnight bag and we headed off, dropping Rhonda back at her place.

She hugged Angie last. 'I hope everything works out for you. You're such a lovely lady and you've got a lovely man to look after you.'

'Stop. You're going to make me cry,' said Angie, holding Rhonda close.

We headed home to my place. In a matter of minutes, the only sound I could hear was Sarah's breath at my back.

DAY 42 – SATURDAY

After breakfast, Sarah and Angie were true to their word and treated Mick and me to a parade of their new gear. Angie credited Sarah's good taste with her stunning outfits and, in turn, Sarah blew us away with her selection of skirts and shoes.

Sarah was intrigued with Mick's writing box and listened intently while he told her about his antique collection back home in London, including the writing boxes he'd scored when he and Keith had headed inland last month. When she asked to see them, he told her he'd had them packed up and sent to London. He would probably do the same with his current purchases since he wasn't sure of his movements before heading home.

After I'd placed my acquisitions in my display cabinet and made coffee for everyone, I set the table up for snooker. The girls had played eight-ball before but never anything on a full-size table. Despite their best efforts, Mick and Angie couldn't beat Sarah and me and conceded dinner. I suggested we have dinner at the restaurant at the casino and maybe play poker afterwards.

Sarah's eyes lit up at the suggestion. 'I haven't had a game since we were on the ship heading to Japan. I've got fond memories of my big win and, if my memory serves me correctly, Tommy Dabrowski, you've got a stash of my money in your safe.'

'Damn. I thought you might have forgotten.'

'Never.'

Angie was familiar with gaming table atmosphere and, although having only played poker a few times, was keen to have a game with us that night.

I looked at Mick. 'I hope you don't get the grumps.'

'Not if this gorgeous lady is sitting next to me,' he said, giving Angie a hug and a kiss.

Even with Angie smiling I could tell she was preoccupied. I wished I could say something to take her mind off Sunday. Best say nothing.

I looked out the window at another superb Sydney morning and suggested we go to Manly for lunch. I knew a great fish and chip shop where we wouldn't get too full and spoil ourselves for dinner. A stroll along the beach wouldn't do us any harm either.

While the girls went to get ready, I fired up my laptop. It had been a few days since I'd sent Rachael the e-mail.

Above Keith's read e-mail was a reply from Rachael. Before I opened it, I called Mick over to read Keith's.

He spent a few minutes reading, making comments and chortling, particularly at Keith and Harry's forays with the twins.

'This car business in LA could turn out to be productive,' said Mick.

'It does sound promising. I think the guys will squeeze every last dollar they can out of the Yanks.'

I proceeded to open Rachael's e-mail.

Hi Tommy.

Thanks for your e-mail. I hope everything is going well. I understand your reluctance to come over and I don't think it's a strange request that your friend Keith represents you. I'll have to put your proposal to the organising committee. They've got a meeting planned for early next month so I should know something by the end of the second week. There'll be plenty of time to get Keith organised if we get a yes from the committee.

I must say, Tommy, it's been much quieter without Jack around. We miss his good humour and stories about you and him in your younger hell-raising days. I would have loved to have seen you guys play. Unfortunately, I was too young to be traipsing around the world watching golf – no offence. Anyway, we've got fond memories of him. If you decide to change your mind at any stage soon about coming over let me know. It would be nice to meet you and hear more of your experiences with Jack.

If the committee does, however, give the okay for Keith to compete, you wouldn't have long to let us know if circumstances change because they would be getting the programs printed and distributed well before the event starts.

Take care and I'll let you know their decision as soon as possible.

Cheers. Rachael.

'Well. All is not lost. Let's hope the committee is sympathetic to your request,' said Mick, after reading over my shoulder.

'It would be a good result. Although part of me wants to compete, a bigger part of me wants to stay here. Sarah and I've got big plans and at this stage going to America is not part of them.'

He raised his eyebrows. 'Anything you want to share?'

'All in good time, my friend. You'll be the first to know. Let's help Angie get sorted and go from there.

'As usual, the voice of reason,' said Mick. The girls reappeared, looking far too good for the likes of Mick and me.

'Let's get out of here,' Sarah urged. 'It's too nice a day to be hanging around indoors. We could do with a dose of vitamin D.'

'And a feed of fish and chips washed down with a good Aussie beer,' added Mick.

We took the lift to the basement. It was Saturday – no Lucky.

Mick and Angie sat in the back and we indulged in small talk. Sarah leaned around and told them she wouldn't be sitting at the same poker table as me tonight.

'I want a chance of winning but with this Einstein at the same table I reckon my odds would be longer than his old-fella.'

'So, odds-on you'd be a winner,' said Mick.

Mick's comment made Angie laugh but when I looked in the rear-view mirror I could still see sadness in her eyes. I wasn't sure what we could do to cheer her up, except be with her and have a few laughs.

'Enough unkind inferences, Jamieson,' I growled.

'That's the first time I've heard Tommy call you by your last name,' said Sarah. 'The only other time I've heard it was with the other guys at the airport when Qantas gave you all a hurry-up to get to check-in.'

'I bet you can't remember their surnames,' said Mick.

'I wouldn't be betting anything if I was you,' I said. 'Sarah's memory is like George's.'

'Shit, you don't mean pornographic.'

'No, you dickhead; photographic. And thank the gods she hasn't got a picture of you in front of her. She'd have a headache for days.'

Angie broke into laughter. 'Thanks, guys. You know how to cheer a girl up.'

It didn't take us long to get to Manly. We went straight to the fish and chip shop, which was licensed. We ordered takeaways and beer and grabbed a table with bench seats on the grassed area overlooking the beach. Blue grenadier, lightly battered, with thick-cut chips, double fried, couldn't be faulted and the beer was the perfect accompaniment.

Not so overfed as to spoil dinner we were able to kick off our footwear and walk for a good hour in the soft sand. Angie was looking forward to a lie down before dinner so we headed back to my place. Sarah decided to have a swim and a light workout in the gym and Mick and I played snooker.

We arrived at the casino around eight and Clive greeted us enthusiastically. Another generous tip would ensure the safe-keeping of my car. We were shown to our table and, as was our custom, champagne was the drink of choice.

Angie raised her glass. 'Thank you for trying to take my mind off things. I promise I'm not going to be a sad-sack forever. Hopefully there'll be a result one way or the other tomorrow and we can move on. Mick and I have been talking about things and he's left it up to me to decide what I want to do. While I was resting this afternoon, I made up my mind. I'm going to quit my job at Diamond Harbour and come to Tassie with you lot. Then I'm going back to London with Mick where we'll get married. What happens after that, who knows.'

Sarah gave a squeal of delight and rushed around to where Angie was sitting and hugged her. I looked at Mick and saw glistening eyes above a huge smile. He leaned over and gave Angie a tender kiss and a knowing look that couldn't be misconstrued for anything but love. I kissed Angie and shook Mick's hand. I was looking at a happy man.

We enjoyed a three-course meal that left us stuffed. We decided to have coffee later. Sarah was keen to hit the tables but Angie was too excited to play. She would watch from the rail. The place was busy and only one table had enough seats. Seven players were now ready to play. We emptied our plastic chip trays, sorted our chips and waited for the dealer to start.

Other players separated us so we weren't able to have much small talk. I glanced at my watch. It was a tad after ten. The next time I looked it was eleven-thirty and none of us had made inroads into each other's chips. We'd had some wins but nothing to write home about.

Mick leaned behind the player next to him and tapped my arm. 'I'm ready for coffee and cake, old boy.'

Sarah heard him as well and nodded her willingness.

'How about we play till midnight?' I said.

They nodded. Mick was in seat three to the left of the big blind, then player four, me, player six, and Sarah on the button.

We were dealt our hole cards. I had a pair of sixes. The blinds were $25 and $50. Mick raised $50 and everyone called. The pot was now $700. The flop was K♦, 10♣ and 6♣. The small blind bet $500. The big blind and Mick called. Player four folded and I only called. A set of sixes would be no match for three kings or tens. Player six called, as did Sarah. No-one's concentration was slipping so it was difficult to get a read from them. The pot was starting to grow and was now $3700.

The turn card was a 3♣. No use to me at that point. The small blind opened with a bet of $500. The big blind folded and Mick raised $500. I had a good look at him and not even a hair moved. He was good. I got nothing off him to indicate what he was up to. Against my better judgement I decided to call. Did Mick have a pair of kings or tens and was simply playing the hand out? Only time and money would tell.

When I'd been showing Sarah the finer points of poker, this was one aspect I'd had trouble with. A set – any set – is always a good hand in poker; but when the flop contains two cards higher than the one that made your set there's always the risk other players are holding pairs to those higher cards.

Sarah didn't hesitate. She pushed her $1000 across the line. The small blind stayed in with a $500 call. We now had a tidy $8700 in the pot.

I watched the faces of the players as the river card was dealt. I needed to get a read on them – nothing. It was like Christmas Eve – not even a fucking mouse was stirring.

It was the J♥.

The small blind leapt out of the blocks with a $1000 bet. Mick casually raised a $1000. It was up to me. I knew they had better than a set of sixes, so I folded. I also folded my arms and sat back to watch the battle. Player six called Mick's bet and Sarah raised. 'Dead-pan Leibenstein' is what I'd call her from now on. Without as much as a blink she counted out $4000 and moved the chips deftly over the line.

The small blind stared at Sarah out of the corner of his eye and I was starting to feel uncomfortable. It looked to me as if he wasn't thinking about cards. Couldn't blame him. She looked amazing. Stacking, unstacking and restacking her chips with slender, flawless fingers, she was distracting everyone.

The dealer asked the small blind to call, raise or fold so the game could continue. He decided to call and pushed $3000 over the line to match player six's raise of $1000 and Sarah's raise of $2000.

Player six was straight in with a $1000 raise, moving in $3000. The guy had hardly withdrawn his hands when Sarah pushed another $3000 out. She was raising another $1000.

Player one needed $3000 to call and was starting to look edgy. Sets of kings, jacks or tens were all I could, in reality, expect to be out there. Anyone holding ace-queen or queen-nine hoping to get a straight on the river would have to be crazy to bet against certain sets.

Player one was about to throw in his hand when he muttered, 'Fuck it,' and counted out $3000.

Player six sighed and slid $2000 over the line, calling Sarah's bet. The pot was $31,700.

I glanced up at Angie. She looked as if she needed to go to the ladies'. She was jiggling up and down but beaming from ear to ear, flapping her hands around. I motioned to Mick who turned around and cracked up.

'Come on, Sarah, show 'em what a girl can do,' she shouted.

Sarah looked up. 'Don't get too excited. The fat lady hasn't sung yet.'

I had noticed the two guys and their body language and had a feeling they might not have hands as strong as I thought. Maybe Sarah was holding kings.

The dealer asked Sarah to show her hole cards. She turned over an ace-queen that gave her an ace high straight. The two players either side mucked their cards. They looked like they'd been kicked in the balls.

'You sat on a gutshot straight right from the flop. Bold play,' said player one, extending his hand in appreciation.

Sarah shook it and thanked him while player six congratulated her.

I was speechless. I don't think I've ever waited for the river card to see if I could complete a straight when early strong hands were possible.

After Mick had hugged her, she almost jumped into my arms.

'That was amazing. I'm looking forward to you telling me what you were thinking. Like player one said, bold play. I'm proud of you, Crazy Dead-pan Leibenstein.'

Sarah threw her head back and laughed. 'What do you mean?'

'I'll tell you later. Are you done here?'

'I sure am. Supper's on me.'

The dealer pushed the pot to Sarah. Taking out her bets she ended up with $23,100. I helped her load up her tray and the four of us walked to the teller's cage. Sarah must have had a feeling about tonight. She had brought her handbag with her instead of her purse. It looked comfortably fat as we headed for coffee.

In the coffee shop, Sarah sat beside Angie. They were giggling like schoolgirls.

I looked at Mick. 'I threw away a set of sixes after the river card came out.'

'Stop your grizzling. I threw away a set of kings. When Sarah raised me two thousand, I knew it was time to bail out. She's got nerves of steel.'

'Are you guys singing my praises over there?' asked Sarah.

I looked at her with admiration. 'We most certainly are. What made you decide to keep betting?'

'Sometimes you have to go with your gut. Tonight, I did, and it paid off. I could come back tomorrow and in the same situation get cleaned out.'

'Exactly right. I've heard and seen it all before,' said Mick as our coffee and chocolate cake arrived.

Mick looked at Angie who was quietly watching the conversation.

'You know what?' she said, tearing open her sugar tubes, 'that's the most fun I've had sitting on my arse doing nothing; apart from drinking three glasses of champers.'

We laughed, and after a second coffee we decided to head home. Sarah was still on a high after her win. At one stage I thought we might all go home none the richer. Poker is a funny game. With all the skill in the world, if the cards don't fall right winning can be difficult.

I put Sarah's stash of around $30,000, along with my nearly-all starting money of $20,000, in my safe. No-one wanted another drink so we said our goodnights.

As we were getting undressed Sarah scruffed the front of my shirt.

'What's this Crazy Dead-pan Leibenstein business all about?'

'I thought you'd forgotten about that. Well, I thought anyone would be crazy to hold out until the river card to try to fill a straight, and you were.'

'What about Dead-pan Leibenstein, then?'

'Your betting after the turn card was made without the slightest expression. I was watching your face. It was as if you'd had a bucket-load of Botox pumped into it and couldn't move a muscle.'

'I'll accept those explanations without taking offence but, as I said at supper, I had a gut feeling I was doing the right thing.'

She unbuttoned my shirt, grabbed me lower down and led me to bed.

DAY 43 – SUNDAY

Angie was the first one up. She'd gone down to the nearby deli and stocked up on typical English breakfast food, consisting of eggs, gourmet sausages, bacon, mushrooms, and baked beans. She apologised she couldn't get black pudding. Mick laughed and let us in on the joke.

She presented us with a top-notch full English breakfast. I suspected she was doing it to keep her mind off what might happen during the day and also for the not-too-distant future when she might be spending time at Mick's London mansion. It was a leisurely breakfast, with Mick keen to know when we might head to Tassie.

Sarah and I had spoken about our wedding plans in bed after we'd finished celebrating her poker win again and decided we'd tell them over breakfast, even though I'd originally thought it better to wait until Diamond Harbour was sorted.

'Tommy and I are planning to get married in the Botanical Gardens, then head to Tassie for a honeymoon of sorts. We'd love it if you two would be witnesses. Mum will be there, of course, and Tommy wants to invite Lucky, Sylvia and Lionel from here. We're sad George, Keith and Harry can't be here but they'll understand.'

Another hug-fest ensued. It confirmed what I suspected; that we were making the right decisions. Over breakfast, I'd noticed Mick and Angie exchanging glances bordering on infatuation. It was great to see. I hoped my other three mates would also find love. Life appeared more fragile after the events in Hong Kong and Diamond Harbour.

As Angie stood to clear the breakfast things, she paused. 'Irrespective of what happens today, it probably won't be worth my while going back to my place. You saw most of my things smashed up and ruined and I've got by without it while I've been here, even though it's only been a few days. When I think about it, I can replace it if I want to. I can't let it get to me.' She walked around the table to Mick and hugged him from behind. 'This is the only possession I need.'

I looked at Angie through misty eyes. 'Wow. I never saw that coming. You're an amazing woman and Mick is one lucky guy.'

We spent the morning giving the washing machine a good workout, as well as the snooker table. Try as they might, Mick and Angie couldn't get close to beating Sarah and me. After four games we left them to try billiards. Mick reckoned he could teach me a thing or two but, as I wanted to sort out our lunch, I humoured him, conceding he was probably as good as Lindrum.

I looked in the freezer and saw pizza bases, so I put the pizza stones in the oven to preheat while I nicked down to the deli and picked up chicken pieces and a selection of spicy sausages and shredded cheese. I had tinned pineapple, leftover mushrooms and a couple of different sauces, so I prepared Hawaiian and meat-lover's pizzas.

The aromas brought the others to the kitchen and I told them Bollinger and pizza was the perfect combination. Mick couldn't get to the fridge quick enough. We'd drunk a bottle before the pizzas were ready. No-one complained when I opened a second bottle as we settled down to lunch.

With the pizzas gone we moved to the recliners with the remaining champers. Angie's phone rang.

She took a deep breath.

'Hello, Angie Kingston speaking.'

Angie listened for a few seconds, then spoke. 'Just a minute, Inspector. If you don't mind, I'll put you on loudspeaker. I have my nearest and dearest with me and I want them to hear what you have to say.'

She pressed a button on her phone and placed it on the coffee table.

'Okay, Inspector. We're listening.'

'Hello everyone, my name is Inspector Peter Collins. I'm the officer in charge of this investigation and am able to pass on some information. After your talks with Detective Harper, I authorised round-the-clock surveillance on the house. During last night, Detective Harper headed a team of armed police which was deployed in readiness for today. At eleven-forty-five this morning, three men were observed entering the house. It appeared they had a key. They didn't suspect anything. Once they had entered the house, my officers took up positions at the front and back. When the men were told to walk out with their arms above their heads they refused. Smoke grenades were lobbed through windows and, shortly after, two men appeared at the front door firing their weapons. The third man went out the back door, firing as he went. He was shot and killed, as were the two at the front. During the exchange of gunfire both Detective Harper and the negotiator were hit and died at the scene. We are extremely distressed that two of our finest officers are no longer with us. The house is still a crime scene and will remain so until our forensic team have completed their investigation. I would appreciate you remaining in Sydney until I contact you, which could be as early as tomorrow. The three men were carrying identification. From our database we have already found that one is, indeed, the ringleader. He has an extensive record in Victoria and Queensland. We have reason to believe he has been active in South-East Asia. We will confirm that over the next few days. We will be searching their last-known addresses for any evidence we can use to wrap up our investigations. We would, of course, like this to be kept from the media until we can catch others but I'm not holding my breath. Reporters were at the house not long after the shootings. I'm sorry, Angie, but the media might pursue you as more information comes out. Details of your relationship with Danny; the money hidden under your house; how you didn't know about his double life and so on.'

'We're sorry to hear about Detective Harper and his associate,' Angie said, wiping her eyes. 'He was extremely professional in his dealings with me right from the start and had such a caring manner. Did either of them have any family?'

'Reg Harper was single and his negotiator was divorced with no children, so it could have been worse. However, to lose officers who have been with the force for many years … to us it's like losing family members.'

'Would you please pass on our condolences to their workmates, and also accept our deepest thanks for resolving this horrible business. Will you need me to come to the station?'

'I'll let you know when we next speak. I should be able to bring you up to date with our progress.'

'Thank you for calling. We appreciate your time. Bye.'

'Goodbye.'

The phone went dead and we sat in silence.

Mick made the first move, helping Angie out of her chair and holding her close. I reached over and Sarah slipped her hand into mine.

'Are you okay, Angie?' asked Sarah. 'It's a lot to take in. I guess the best thing we can do is talk about it. The fact you're here will help with keeping you out of circulation. The papers don't know what you look like and you're only contactable through your phone, so you can screen any calls you might get.'

I got up and made coffee and found a box of chocolates in the cupboard. When I took them into the lounge room, Angie's eyes lit up. 'Good old Tommy. You know how to cheer a girl up.'

'Not so much of the old, thank you.'

We had a laugh and spent the rest of the afternoon going over what the Inspector had said. Sadness shrouded us again when talk turned to Reg and his mate.

'Do you think it would be improper for us to attend their funerals?' asked Mick.

'Perhaps I can ask the Inspector when I talk to him tomorrow. It would be a nice thing to do and maybe bring us closure,' suggested Angie.

None of us felt like going out so we each got ourselves something to eat in the kitchen and spent the evening watching TV and chatting. Angie ate the last chocolate. When I told her that was it, she pouted unconvincingly and suggested I stick the empty box where the sun didn't shine. She smiled as she pulled Mick from his chair, gave Sarah and me a kiss, thanked us for being around and headed to bed.

Sarah and I didn't stay up much longer. A good night's sleep wouldn't do us any harm.

DAY 44 – MONDAY

I was aware of Sarah getting out of bed. I opened my eyes to see her heading for the shower. When she reappeared, she jumped on the bed.

'Wake up, you lazy love-machine. We've got twenty laps and yoga before you even get the scent of a healthy breakfast.'

Try as I might to grab her and pull her back into bed, I failed. She was lightning fast. A pillow smacked onto my head made sure I was well and truly awake. She pulled the covers back, revealing morning wood.

'It's a shame to waste it,' she said, her gaze lingering, 'but I'll make it up to you, I promise.'

'In the deep end of the pool, maybe?'

'You're all class. Hurry up and shower. We've got work to do.'

An hour and a half later, we were back in the kitchen.

'Before we eat,' she said, 'hop on those scales I noticed in the bathroom. Not that I've been perving on you but I reckon you've lost more weight. In saying so, you've also gained muscle and, as muscle is denser than fat, you might not have lost as much as I think.'

'I don't reckon those scales work. I haven't used them in a long time. The spare batteries are in the pantry.'

Sure enough, the batteries were flat but after replacing them I was ecstatic. I had lost two kilos in the week since we returned from Japan. I was now ninety-six kilos and within six of my target weight. The yoga had certainly made me more flexible and, in turn, made swimming and jogging easier and more enjoyable.

As I stepped off the scales, I assumed a body-builder's pose. Before I knew it, Sarah had given me a jab to the stomach.

'Not bad. I have a feeling I'll be looking at a 90-kilo hunk by the end of the month.'

'If I haven't lost the remaining six kilos within a fortnight you can have your way with me any way you like.'

'A fortnight is the end of the month, numb-nuts, and I don't have to wait any time to have my way with you. You're so weak when it comes to a tug on your old-fella.'

'What's all this sex talk before breakfast?' said Angie, as she and Mick walked into the kitchen.

'Tommy's talking tough about playing hard to get.'

'That's a classic oxymoron if ever I heard one,' said Mick, manoeuvring his way to the fridge.

'Who's calling who a moron?' I asked.

'Oooh, someone's sensitive this morning,' teased Angie. She giggled and gave me a dig in the ribs as she grabbed a glass for a fresh juice.

'Must be pick-on-Tommy day,' I said. 'But don't worry, I'll have the last laugh.' I looked at Sarah. 'Remember those live art classes I told you about last week?'

'And remember the nickname I gave you?'

'What are you talking about now?' asked Mick.

Sarah beat me to the punch. 'Tommy reckons that when he gets down to ninety kilos people will be knocking his door down wanting him to pose in live art classes. It was then that I came up with his new nickname: FOS.'

'Full of shit,' Mick yelled out, and a startled Angie dropped the cereal box and spread Rice Bubbles over the kitchen floor.

We laughed and cleaned up the mess, then settled down to a civilised breakfast of Corn Flakes, toast and coffee.

Angie buttered her toast, spread on a light coating of jam, and hesitated before she took a bite. 'When do you reckon we'll hear from the Inspector? I'd love for us to be discussing your wedding plans. It would certainly take our minds off yesterday.'

'I couldn't agree more,' said Sarah, pouring more coffee. 'If we're welcome at the funeral it would be good to put that behind us, along with anything else the police need from you. Then we can nail down a date with a celebrant.'

'Because we don't know when he's going to ring, I'm thinking of heading to the golf course,' I said. 'A walk in the fresh air and smashing the shit out of a little white ball could be just what the doctor ordered. If you lot come too, we'll have Angie's phone with us so we won't miss him if he calls.'

The others couldn't come up with a better idea so we got organised. I rang Maurice at the golf club and arranged two ride-on buggies and three sets of clubs. I booked a tee off time for noon. Sarah wondered what we'd do for lunch and I told her the club bar sold a great variety of sandwiches and salad rolls, together with homemade pies and pasties.

When we were ready, we took the lift to the basement. On the way down I reminded everyone that today was the day Keith and Harry were flying to LA.

'I hope to hear from them once they've had a chance to give Jack's cars the once-over,' I said.

Mick was chuckling. 'I'll be interested to hear how they said their goodbyes to their recent acquaintances.'

'Whooo do you mean?' I asked.

'Cut it out, you two,' Sarah interjected. 'Just be happy they found …' She hesitated. 'I was going to say love, but I think it was lust, so carry on,' she laughed. 'Pretend I never spoke.'

Lucky's head appeared from the far side of my car. 'What's all this laughter in my basement?' he said, once again displaying a perfect set of teeth. 'Maybe this time, Tommy, you'll introduce me to your friends.'

'Mick and Angie, this is Lucky Phil. It pains me to say it at the risk of him getting a swollen head, but what this guy can't do with a car isn't worth doing. And, he knows how to pick a winner at the nags which might interest you, Mick.'

While they shook hands, I told Lucky that Mick was an ex-jockey and a poker mate from London, and that Angie was going to be his wife. I didn't think it necessary at this stage to divulge any further information.

They chatted about Mick's jockey days and Angie's casino work until I interrupted. 'We have a booking for twelve o'clock on the course, Lucky, so as much as I can see you enjoying your chat, we have to get going.'

'Bear with me, boss, and I'll get your clubs.'

'He calls you boss?' asked Mick quietly as Lucky unlocked my storage room and carried my clubs to the car.

I laughed. 'Shhh. Don't say anything. It keeps him in his place.'

'What are you guys nattering about?' asked Lucky, cupping a hand to his ear.

'We're talkin' about ya, not to ya,' I said, still laughing as we got in the car and drove out. The car smelt clean. Sandalwood.

Angie sniffed appreciatively. 'Is that Lucky's aftershave or car deodoriser?'

'Whatever it is, I like it,' said Sarah as we met the bright, late-morning sunshine at the top of the ramp.

Angie's phone rang. She glanced at the screen, turned it onto loudspeaker and said hello.

'I assume you've got me on loudspeaker?'

'Yes, I have, Inspector, if you don't mind.'

'That's fine. I hope you've managed to get some rest in spite of what's happened.'

Angie glanced at us. 'Yes, we're coping okay, thanks.'

'We've worked non-stop on this case and raided the crims' last-known addresses. At the ringleader's place, apart from finger prints, which we will process through our database, we found about three million dollars we assume came from the casino heist. It was carefully hidden in wall cavities behind timber dado panelling that could be unscrewed and reattached. To the untrained eye the room would appear normal. We also found a key-cutting machine and a heap of blank keys, which explains how they got into your house. The remaining two million has most likely been spent. Two current-model Porsches and three near-new Harley Davidson motorbikes were found in a locked garage behind the house. They probably account for some of it. We also found a large quantity of drugs; mainly marijuana and cocaine. It was hidden under a pretend dog kennel that had hinges on one end so it could be lifted up. The cavity was waist deep and near-on full, and also held two sets of scales and hundreds of ziplock bags. Whether the drugs were purchased with the heist money or are part of an ongoing drug ring remains to be seen. Over the next few weeks, we will try to track down other associates. I've been ordered from above to throw all our resources into this investigation. I can't predict an end date but, as far as I'm concerned, you can come back to the house and salvage what you can before you hand the property back to the real estate people. There won't be a need for you to make a statement. We have enough details. Call into the station and let the desk sergeant know when you're finished with the house.'

'That's great news because, like I told my friends, I have no wish to move back into the house. In fact, I'm leaving Diamond Harbour for greener pastures.'

'The sooner you can move on with your life, the better. It might pay to give the real estate an address where they can send any prepaid rent and bond.'

'Good idea. My friends and I were discussing the possibility of attending the funerals of your two officers, as a mark of respect.'

'I'm not privy to any details at this stage; however, I assume the relevant notices will be placed in the Diamond Harbour Gazette. I don't believe I gave you the negotiator's name. He was Patrick Spencer.'

'Thanks for that, Inspector, and thanks for calling back. We're impressed with how quickly you've made so much progress. Good luck with the rest of your investigations.'

'Oh, by the way, Angie. The casino offered a reward for information that would lead to the crims' apprehension and conviction. I've spoken to management and recommended you receive the reward. It may help you get over this drama. I did notice your car looking worse for wear. If you contact the casino's Public Relations Officer when you come down, she will discuss it with you. I will instruct the casino to deny media requests for interviews and also to withhold all information that might relate to you. If at some stage you wish to talk to them, that's up to you.'

'Firstly, I appreciate you having my back; and secondly, I never knew about a reward. That's amazing. Thank you so much.'

'It's the least I could do after what you've been through over the last few years. Take care. If you do come to the funerals, please make yourselves known. I would like to meet you. Good bye for now.'

'Good bye, Inspector, and thanks.'

Angie ended the call. I pulled up on the road shoulder. Once again, silence wrapped itself around us like a warm blanket. Angie was the first to speak.

'Well, come on, Tommy. We've got a golf tournament in half an hour. Stop dreaming and get the lead out. There'll be plenty of time to talk about this later.'

'Okay, money bags. Just because you're getting what you deserve there's no need to start bossing me around. I get enough of that from this gorgeous piece of work sitting next to me.'

A dig in the ribs was enough for me to start the car and rejoin the traffic flow.

We arrived at the course. Maurice was in the pro shop and selected clubs for the others, which they loaded onto the buggies. We grabbed a few eats from the bar and headed to the first tee. I suddenly remembered these guys would need golf balls. I had a dozen top-quality balls in my bag, which I was jealously guarding, so I raced back to the pro shop and bought two boxes of average-grade balls.

'How's your lady friend?'

'She's moved on. She took a liking to the greens manager and neither has been seen since they were caught in the rough beside the sixteenth green.'

'Sorry to hear that. I hope you can move on too. Things are not always as they seem.'

'You're not wrong. I thought we had a good thing going. Perhaps it was all about club selection.' A smile creased his face when he realised he'd made a good golf joke.

I headed to the door. 'Keep smiling, mate. It's the best medicine. There are still plenty of birdies out there.'

'I can't believe you get enjoyment out of this golfing caper,' said Mick as we drove our buggies up the hill to the ninth green.

Mick and Angie had more hits than Elvis and the Beatles combined, but Sarah was loving it. With her flexibility, strength and focus, she was only ten shots over par for the eight holes we'd played already. Near enough to bogey golf, which is what every high handicap golfer strives for before taking the next step and having lessons.

I was one under par and, with my tee shot a metre from the hole, I expected a birdie on this par-3, which would give me a two-under thirty-three for nine holes. Sarah and Mick were in the green-side bunker with their tee shots. Angie had picked her ball up and thrown it good-naturedly into the irrigation dam near the opposite bunker. She walked onto the green and stood beside me while the others attempted their bunker shots.

Sarah hit her shot thin and it ended up keeping Angie's ball company while Mick's shot made it onto the green, leaving him a five-metre putt. Angie held the flag. Putting was the better part of his game and he drilled it, ending up with a par. I tapped in for a birdie.

I could tell another nine holes would strain the bonds of friendship, so I suggested we hit the bar for a few drinks to celebrate a new start for Angie and Mick, and her good fortune with the reward.

The bar didn't stock champagne so we had premium beer that went down a treat.

'I reckon with a few lessons, Mick, you'd play pretty decent golf. You've got a good temperament and style.'

'Thanks for your encouragement, old boy, but I think I'll stick to poker. It's certainly less frustrating.'

'Well, if you change your mind, I'd be happy to give you some lessons.'

'The way you played today after your enforced lay-off you *should* be going to Vegas.'

'Yeah, it felt good out there today. But for some reason, the thought of going to Vegas doesn't appeal to me anymore. The fact Keith might be able to play makes it easier to say no. But if they tell me Keith can't play, for whatever reason, that will be the end of that. Jack's cars will get sorted, a couple of charities will get a kick-along and the lads can get home.'

'You're a good man, Tommy Dabrowski,' Sarah said. 'I reckon we'll be golfed out by the time we finish our visit to Tassie. Apparently, a mainlander can drive around the state in two days. If we took a couple of weeks, we could probably knock over every golf course.'

I beamed at the other two. 'How can I not love this woman?'

She took a sip of her drink as she leaned over and I kissed her beer moustache.

We weren't in a hurry to get home and, as we were sitting at a table overlooking the eighteenth green, we could relax and watch other golfers hit their tee shots to the green.

'Did anyone look in the paper this morning?' asked Mick.

'God, I never thought about it with slave-driver here getting me up at sparrow fart for a workout,' I said. 'With five shootings and the fact the press was hanging around, it's a fair bet there would be something reported.'

'As long as they don't mention me, they can write what they like,' said Angie. 'I guess it'll only be a matter of time though before they connect the dots. I can't believe the trouble those gutter snipes took to hide the money and their drugs. They seemed like real professionals but I can't get my head around the fact they got caught going back to the house.'

'Like the police said, the guys didn't know Danny was dead so they wouldn't suspect anything untoward at the house,' said Mick. 'When you boil it down, I think this is the best result. The crooks are dead, most of the money has been recovered and, best of all, Angie is safe and sound and doesn't have to worry about some arsehole trying to track her down for the five mil.'

'We can only hope they keep your name out of it,' said Sarah, leaning across the table to squeeze Angie's hand. 'It's unlikely, but if you keep a low profile and stick with us, hopefully the whole thing will blow over and some other drama will grab their interest. They have a short attention span.'

I had a feeling they would miss each other when Angie headed off to London with Mick. All the more reason for Sarah and I to do some world touring. It would be good to hit some London casinos with the lads and head to Scotland to give Keith a golfing lesson or two at the Royal and Ancient Golf Club of St Andrews.

'Let's have one more for the road. My shout,' said Angie. She pushed her chair back, stacked the empty glasses on a tray and walked to the bar.

She returned, balancing four large beers on the tray on one hand. Years of working at the casino carrying trays of drinks and dodging pissed patrons and wandering hands had made her an expert. I could barely carry a mug of coffee from my kitchen to the lounge without the risk of spilling it. If I weren't such a dickhead and didn't fill it up so far, I might be okay.

'Would tomorrow be a good day to go to Diamond Harbour?' asked Angie. 'It would be a good chance to sort out the house, head into work, and hand in my notice. The sooner I'm out of the place the less chance of getting hassled by the papers. Once the funerals are over you guys could start getting serious about your wedding.'

'There'd be nothing stopping us from talking to a celebrant before the funerals,' suggested Sarah. 'It will be a few weeks before we can organise everything and I'm sure the funerals will be over by then.'

'Do you think your mum would like to come with us tomorrow?' I asked. 'It would be a good opportunity to chat about the wedding. She was excited when we told her about our plans and was keen to help out.'

'If no-one minds, I'll ask her. The only condition will be that she sits in the back with Angie and me. I can't trust you two around her.'

Mick jumped in. 'I think it's your mother who can't be trusted around two hunky guys.'

'Yeah, that's it,' I said. Sarah looked at Angie, raising her eyebrows.

We finished our beers and headed to the car. We got back to my place around four. I picked up the paper as I opened my door. Sure enough, the headline said it all: FIVE DIE IN DIAMOND HARBOUR SHOOTOUT.

'You'd better grab a chair while I read this to you,' I said.

'Three gunmen and two police officers were killed yesterday during a siege at a house in Diamond Harbour, south of Sydney. Police are reluctant to release any details at this stage as they believe the gunmen are part of a larger gang. Reliable sources have told us the gunmen were caught in the house looking for money stolen from the Harbour Casino last year. Apparently one gang member was living in the house but had disappeared some time ago. When police ordered the men to surrender, a gun battle ensued and the gunmen and police officers were killed.'

Angela shook her head. 'How did the paper find out about the connection with the heist?'

'Let me read on.

'It is believed millions of dollars are still missing. This paper has contacted the casino for comment but there has been nothing forthcoming. Police have advised that people should go about their business as usual as they believe the apprehension of other gang members will not incur a risk to the public.'

'Well, so far, so good. No mention of you, honey,' said Mick.

'Isn't it amazing how the papers say that reliable sources have told them certain things. How can they know it's legitimate?' said Sarah.

'Anything to sell papers,' I said.

Mick and Angie wanted some time out, so Sarah and I headed to the pool again. We swam, canoodled, swam, canoodled some more and, after showering, did some yoga. I would have been happy to sit and watch Sarah but she wouldn't have a bar of it. When we finished, I had to admit I felt pretty good. The day had turned out to be a physical one and if it meant me getting a few more kilos off my magnificent frame over the next few weeks, so be it. I was ready for coffee and a generous portion of the chocolate cake we picked up on the way home. Sarah would protest but I would argue reward for effort.

We got back to find Mick and Angie sitting by the window, each with a glass of champers. Two glasses sat on the breakfast bar waiting to be filled.

'If you guys don't mind, I'll have coffee and cake.'

Angie's face lit up. 'I can eat cake with champers, Tommy. Bring it on.'

I cut four slices while the coffee brewed. Sarah took the cake and the plates to the coffee table.

'Is that Huon pine?' asked Mick. 'It looks like the same timber those Tassie animals are made of. What was the name of the restaurant, Holy Trail or something?'

'Hollow Tree, you idiot,' I said, raising my voice. 'Fuckin' Holy Trail. What drugs are you on?'

Mick laughed. Sarah and Angie looked at each other. Once again, they were none the wiser about our conversation.

I noticed bewilderment in the girls' eyes. 'Hollow Tree is a nice restaurant not far from the casino. I took the guys there, what seems like a lifetime ago. There's this sculpture made from Tasmanian oak and inside are carved figures of some of Tassie's unique animals, made from Huon pine. It's amazing. And yes, Mick, the table is Huon pine.'

'Why don't we go there tonight after a flutter at the casino? We could have dinner at Jacques first, then head over with our cash.'

I looked at Sarah who looked at Angie who looked at me. We looked at Mick.

'You know what, folks?' I said. 'I'm now convinced Mick does have a brain between his ears and not his legs.'

Angie giggled. 'He doesn't have room for a brain between his legs.'

Mick looked at her lustfully. 'You say the nicest things.'

'Okay, you guys,' said Sarah, 'let's enjoy our coffee and cake.'

I gave Jacques a quick call and reserved a table.

'While we're sitting here chatting,' said Mick, 'Angie and I have been talking about moving back to the Condor when we get back from Diamond Harbour. It's going to be a while, I suppose, until the funerals and we won't be going to Tassie until after your wedding. We don't want to be cramping each other's style.'

Sarah put down her plate and licked chocolate icing from her fingers. 'There's no way you're cramping our style. We love having you here but if you feel the need for some space, that's fine. It won't stop us getting together. We'll need your input for the wedding and the trip.'

Angie smiled at her. 'I can't wait until we get down to the nitty-gritty.'

'We can drop you off on the way back tomorrow, if you like,' I said.

'I'll give the Condor a ring now and see if they've got any vacancies,' said Mick. He went to the bedroom and returned not long after. 'They've got a deluxe suite available until the end of the month, which should do at this stage. We'll have a fortnight to see how things go. I'll try and remember to get a paper at Diamond Harbour. It might have some details on the funerals.'

While Mick had been ringing the Condor, Sarah had rung her mother. 'She can't wait to have a day out with us. I told her we'd pick her up at ten.'

We sat around for a while, then got ready for dinner. I'd built up an appetite and was looking forward to a big steak at Jacques. It was a pleasant stroll to the restaurant and Claude greeted us in his customary fashion. My favourite table was available even though the place was nearly full.

Our meal was first rate and when Mick was handed the dessert menu, a gentle kick from me under the table was enough of a reminder we were having supper at the Hollow Tree. We'd spent nearly two hours enjoying our meal before walking back to the basement where we piled into my car and drove to the casino. Clive wasn't on duty but he'd obviously worded up his fellow valets. The guy working tonight was so over the top with niceness it was a real struggle to give him a tip. 'Yes, sir; no, sir; kiss your arse, sir.'

We walked into the gaming area and noticed a large area roped off. The carpet had been pulled up and I counted six poker tables stacked at the far end of the room. The rest were occupied. A waiter came over and told us a burst water pipe upstairs had caused water to leak through the ceiling.

'Doesn't look as if we're going to get a seat for poker,' I said. 'How about we head over to blackjack?'

Sarah smiled. 'After my nice win on the cruise ship with George I'm up for it.'

'I haven't played much but if we could sit at the same table it might be fun,' said Angie.

Mick gave her a hug and we found a table being set up. The dealer showed deft hands opening four new packs of cards, mixing and shuffling them. Once they were in the shoe, he took our cash and supplied us with chips. Three more players joined us at the table and after exchanging pleasantries, the game began.

Sarah's game face appeared and she was a power of concentration. I could tell she was card counting. It's hard to count when four decks are used. In some games, when only one or maybe two decks are used, counting is much easier. Sarah was sitting in position one, with me in two and Angie, Mick and the others following on.

Mick and Angie were getting good cards and although Mick preferred poker, he was playing well and giving Angie good advice. I kept getting cards that let me double my bet but, unfortunately, the third card wasn't enough to beat the arsey dealer who was getting seventeens and eighteens – beaten by the others but not by me. Anyway, it was fun, which was what Angie was wanting.

'I've never seen Sarah so serious,' she whispered, leaning into me. 'Is there anything she can't do?'

'Well …'

'It was a rhetorical question, you big goof. You were probably going to tell me she can do handstands in the shower.'

'I wasn't, but now you've mentioned it …'

'What are you two whispering and giggling about?' asked Sarah, as the dealer removed the remaining cards from the shoe and began shuffling for a new round.

When I told her, she leaned forward so she could eyeball Angie.

'Have you been spying on me?'

Their laughter was cut short as the next hand was dealt.

Mick was chatting to the players on his left and was oblivious to our banter.

We played for another hour, then decided coffee and pancakes were calling. Sarah had won a tad over three thousand while the rest of us were left licking our wounds.

It was a short drive to the Hollow Tree restaurant. The girls were in awe of the sculptures as well as the pancakes. We left with full bellies.

'An early workout for you before we go to Diamond Harbour,' said Sarah. 'One hour of laps, half an hour of yoga, and a continental breakfast.'

I gave her a mock salute. 'Yes, Ma'am.'

'Don't you laugh,' said Angie, giving Mick the eye. 'I saw you shovelling pancakes like they weren't making them anymore. You might have to line up with Tommy tomorrow morning.'

'I thought I might need the energy for later,' pleaded Mick.

'In your dreams.'

Sarah was true to her word. I was up at six and after a quick shower was in the pool, trying hard to keep up with her. After half an hour I had to have a breather but I didn't get much of a break. She stopped, swam back to me, got up close and slid her hand into my shorts. She knew when to stop and moved away, beckoning me with her finger. If that wasn't a bribe to chase after her it was damn close. It took half a lap for me to settle down and no matter how fast I swam, Sarah stayed frustratingly out of my reach.

I flopped onto the edge of the pool feeling buggered. I'd never swum so fast for so long. I watched as Sarah walked slowly to the shower. I couldn't have done anything even if I'd caught her. She knew how to tease a man.

The yoga session was relaxing and, despite my big workout, the continental breakfast was all I needed.

Mick and Angie had declined our swim invitation, preferring a leisurely walk with breakfast at a nearby café.

Mick had grabbed the paper and left it open on page four for us to read the names of the two police officers who'd been killed, and details about them that we already knew. Angie had been relieved to not see anything more.

By nine-thirty we were ready. Sarah had rung her mother to make sure she was still okay to come. She was and would be waiting out the front at ten. Mick and Angie had packed their stuff and took it with them to my storage room. We'd pick it up on the way back from Diamond Harbour to the Condor. Lucky looked up and out his window as we approached. I noticed he'd changed his office around. He now had an uninterrupted view of anyone heading in his direction.

'You're a genius, boss,' he said, as we walked in. 'No-one can catch me reading the form guide now.'

'You goose. The problem is we can see it on your table. If we can see it, then your real boss will, too.'

A bashful look came over him. 'It'll take me a while to iron out the finer details but, as you know, my real boss doesn't venture this far underground.'

Mick, keen to jump in on the conversation, gave Lucky an upper-class look. 'Be that as it may, young man, one can't be too careful.'

We laughed at his posh Pommy accent as he continued, 'I say, Lucky. Are there races on this week?'

'Randwick had races yesterday, your Majesty, and again tomorrow and Saturday. If you're interested, I'm going Saturday. I know people who know other people who can get us a nice spot with easy access to the betting, drinking and food.'

'Did you have a bet yesterday, old boy?'

'As a matter of fact, I did. I backed five winners and two seconds. My cash reserves have received a welcome boost so I'm looking forward to Saturday. I think the Golden Slipper's on the nineteenth of April. If you're still around it should be a good day out. At this stage, I like Portillo, but that could change getting closer to the time, depending on the barrier draw.'

'Give me your phone number and I'll ring you Thursday or Friday and let you know. At this stage, Saturday could be a goer. I'll have to grab myself a form guide.'

Angie scowled. 'Come on, you lot. God, they reckon women can talk.'

'Women gossip, men discuss,' said Lucky. He barely made it out of Sarah's reach. He immediately raised his hands in submission, laughed and retreated behind his table.

'Lucky is an appropriate name for you. Not many people avoid the Sarah viper strike.'

Sarah nudged me towards the car and only after we were in did Lucky emerge from his office and wave. We got to Rhonda's right on ten and Sarah hopped out to let her in the back between her and Angie.

'Hello, boys,' she chirped. 'My word, there's room back here for another one.'

'Mum. I warned you. Don't encourage them. We've got a big day ahead of us and Angie and I don't want to spend it watching your every move.'

'Don't worry, I'm harmless,' she said. Mick and I laughed.

'I'm keen to get to the café down the coast for a coffee. I can't remember what it's called but you know the one I mean, don't you, Tommy?' asked Angie, once we were free of the morning rush.

'To be honest I've never taken any notice,' I said, 'but you can't miss it. It stands out like dogs' balls.'

The back-seaters giggled. Mick put an Eagles CD into the player. He didn't have it up too loud, so the women could talk tactics about the wedding.

'*Their Greatest Hits 1971–1975*,' he read. 'Do you know this is the world's biggest-selling album?'

'I would have thought it was Michael Jackson's *Thriller*, but what would I know?'

'You were close. *Thriller* comes in second. A great album too.'

'There it is,' said Angie, as we neared the café. 'The Owl and The Pussy Cat Café. I can't read what it says underneath.'

Mick squinted. 'Try our cakes with runcible spoons. That's from the poem where the owl and the pussy cat dined on mince and slices of quince, which they ate with a runcible spoon. Apparently Edward Lear made up that word.'

'What, mince?' I said, winking at Sarah.

'Yeah, mince, you dickhead,' said Mick, as we pulled up outside.

'I love that poem,' said Sarah. 'I know all three verses. I'll recite it to you while we have coffee.'

Mick and Angie shared a slice of apricot teacake and Sarah and I a slice of traditional chocolate mud cake. Rhonda chose a blueberry muffin. We used the runcible spoons. They were simply forks shaped like spoons, with one of the three tines having a sharp edge for cutting.

Sarah was true to her word and gave us a moving rendition of *The Owl and the Pussy Cat*, much to the delight of two small children sitting at a table next to us with their parents. As we were leaving, the café owner said she usually only heard the first five lines.

'Like our national anthem,' I said. 'Most people only know the first verse.'

'I know it all,' bragged Mick. 'I'll sing it to you when we get into the car.'

'Great; me and my big mouth,' I mumbled, as we walked across the car park.

It was nearing midday when we pulled up outside Angie's place. Things looked normal from the car. We couldn't see anyone loitering so we tentatively walked to the front door. Angie gave her key to Mick and took Sarah's hand as he opened the door. We walked over the threshold and were speechless. The place had been tidied up, presumably by the police. Angie's kitchen, dining and lounge belongings that weren't smashed were stacked neatly on the breakfast bar and dining table. The rest had been pushed into piles. Faint remnants of fingerprint powder were everywhere. Angie led the way to her bedroom. Her clothes had been hung back in the wardrobe and bedside cupboards up-righted with the drawers returned. It had the look of a female's touch. The same in the bathroom.

'Never let me bad-mouth the cops, after seeing what they've done here,' said Mick. 'I'm impressed. Back home they wouldn't lift a finger to put anything right.'

Angie, Sarah and Rhonda spent some time in the bedroom sorting out Angie's clothes and personal things. Mick and I went downstairs. Even though the car was a mess, it started. Unless Angie protested, he'd arrange for it to be collected and taken to a wrecker's yard. It wasn't worth fixing. With her reward money she'd be able to set herself up with a new one.

When we'd sorted out Angie's things under the house, the three of them had finished upstairs and came down. Angie spent a few minutes looking through it.

'There's a self-storage place down the road. It would be ideal for the time being. Would you guys mind helping me organise a lock-up and getting this stuff down there?'

We walked upstairs. Sarah grabbed the phonebook and rang Coastal Self Storage who told her they had a five-by-three-metre container Angie could hire on a monthly basis. Sarah told them we'd be down with a load within the hour.

We worked hard and by three-thirty Angie's belongings were safely locked away. She had signed a contract and prepaid for two months. She had given them Sarah's details, and authority for Sarah to act on her behalf if she wasn't about and the contract needed extending. An extra key was supplied for Sarah.

Mick and I had bagged up the remains of smashed crockery, vases and glassware and swept the floors. A quick once-over with a mop made the place presentable for when the real estate people came over.

Angie took one last look through the place and with a quiver in her voice said, 'Let's get out of here.'

By the time we'd dropped the keys off to Diamond Realty, called into the police station and taken Angie to the casino for her meeting with the public relations lady, we were jiggered.

It was five-thirty and we were starving, not having had lunch, but were in no state to enter any respectable eatery. I suggested we get Maccas and head down to the beach.

'I'll grab a bottle of champers and a pack of plastic flutes and we can toast the new start,' said Mick.

We found a bench seat under a sun that, although reasonably high in the sky, had lost its punch but was pleasant enough on our weary bodies. Mick shot the champers cork into the air and filled our glasses. We toasted our good work and tucked into the food. I had a feeling Sarah would be doubling my workload in the gym tomorrow.

While Rhonda and Angie finished off the champers, Angie told us about her meeting with the casino people.

'Well, I handed in my resignation that I wrote last night. The personnel guys said they were sad to see me go but understood. I went and saw Penny in PR. Do you realise the reward is a quarter of a million dollars?'

'Bloody hell,' I blurted. 'Sorry, Angie, go on.'

'She wanted my bank details as they will put the money straight into my account in a couple of weeks when the paperwork is done. They'll get a report from the police, which will seal the deal, so to speak. I hope you don't mind, Tommy, but I gave them your address for any correspondence.'

'I understand and I'm more than happy.'

'Oh, and one more thing. Penny had today's Gazette in her office and I had a quick flick through but didn't see any death notices for the two cops. When she asked why I wanted to know I explained that we want to go to their funerals. She said she'll keep an eye out and ring me when they're in. Trying to find a copy of the Gazette in Sydney's newsagencies could be hard. I've put her number in my phone so I'll know it's her and not some reporter ringing.'

Rhonda was listening intently and Sarah noticed. 'Sorry, Mum, I'd forgotten you weren't across the goings-on from the last few days. The casino put up a reward last year after the casino heist and the police recommended Angie get it due to her connection to one of the bad guys. As a result of what happened to Angie, the others were stopped in their tracks and most of the money recovered, as well as the busting of a drug gang.'

Rhonda shivered. 'It sounds scary to me. I'm so glad you've come out of it unscathed, Angie. Make sure that lovable rogue next to you takes good care of you.'

'Don't you worry, Rhonda,' said Mick, putting his arm around Angie. 'I won't be letting her out of my sight unless she's accompanied by another responsible adult.'

'Don't look at me,' I said. 'Hanging around with me can only get you into trouble. Isn't that right, Ms Leibenstein?'

'That's true, but I'm more than happy to hang around with you, Mr Dabrowski.'

I looked at my watch. It was nearing seven. I suggested we head back to Sydney.

We'd been on the road only ten minutes when I looked in the mirror and saw three sleeping beauties. I could see where Sarah got her beauty from. Rhonda was an attractive woman and she obviously took good care of herself.

She had been more than capable of keeping up with the rest of us while we were packing Angie's things.

'What?' said Mick.

'What?' I replied.

'You keep looking in the mirror. Surely you're not looking at yourself.'

'Of course not. Turn around and take a look.'

Mick turned around, held his look for a moment or two, then sat back facing the front. He gave me a thumbs-up and with a smile on his face, closed his eyes.

I slid Vivaldi into the CD player and drove us home.

It was non-stop back to Sydney where I dropped Rhonda off, then took Mick and Angie to the Condor after picking their bags up from my store room. It was nearing ten-thirty when Sarah and I got back to my place. We'd agreed to have tomorrow apart as Angie felt she needed a rest day and Mick was keen to catch up with Barry if he wasn't working the door at the Condor. Sarah and I were going to contact the marriage celebrant and lock in a date.

It had been a big day and after we'd showered to rid ourselves of the dust and grime, we hit the sack.

DAY 46 – WEDNESDAY

I rolled over and looked at the clock. It was eight-thirty. I rolled back and looked at Sarah. I moved my hand to her hip. It was enough to wake her. She smiled and rolled over, snuggling herself into me. I loved unspoken invitations.

Lying on our backs, shoulders touching with the sun streaming in, we discussed our day ahead. Once we'd nailed down the wedding date my jobs were to invite Sylvia, Lucky and Lionel, and book a big table at Jacques for a slap-up dinner. Sarah would ask her mother and we would ask Mick and Angie. Sarah would no doubt go shopping with the girls for some flashy clothes, as well as coming with me to a classy menswear shop for a new suit. I wanted to lose a few more kilos but that job could wait until after the big day.

I grabbed the paper and quickly flipped through it. A daily ritual until Angie was out of the state. Nothing. I reckoned the press were itching to get more information but hopefully the casino and Diamond Realty would clam up. If they found out Angie held the lease, there would be a feeding frenzy.

While I got breakfast, Sarah rang a celebrant she had short-listed and arranged for us to meet her at eleven-thirty. The address was in Neutral Bay on the North Shore. The late-morning traffic should be flowing well, so we could leave at eleven. Plenty of time for a leisurely brekky.

'The weather's settled, so do you reckon the Botanical Gardens is a goer?' I asked, pouring us another coffee.

'I'd love to be married there, Tommy. I know of a few venues but the Pavilion would be great seeing as there will only be a handful of us. Even if the weather turns, we'll be under cover. I'll contact the Gardens people for a booking and all we'll need is an esky with champers and glasses. A quick drink, then back to Jacques.'

'Are you happy for me to arrange the menu with head chef Erik?'

'Of course. You're most familiar with the place and you do know good food.'

'Even so, I'll get them to print out a menu with the various options and we can go through it just to be on the safe side. I'd hate for Lucky to have to eat fish if he's predisposed to beef. We'd never hear the end of it.'

'Good point,' she said.

'While I think of it, remember when we talked about whether we'd get engaged and decided not to and you weren't big on jewellery? Well, what are your thoughts on wedding rings?'

'If the truth be known, big guy, I don't need a ring on my finger to remind myself or anyone else I'm married. It's only symbolic and isn't going to make a scrap of difference as to how I feel about you.'

'Lovely answer,' I said, whipping her into an embrace. 'Do you reckon Lucky would drive us to the Gardens in my car?'

'I don't think you could stop him. I can imagine him going over it with spit and polish to make sure it's perfect for the day.'

'Would you like the Pavilion decorated with flowers for the ceremony?' I asked.

'I'll find out when I talk to the Gardens people and see whether they do it or if it's up to us. I'm not too fussed. The drinking of champers will take longer than the ceremony so it might be a waste. I think you've worked out I'm a fairly practical, no-nonsense type of girl.'

'I have noticed, even though a bit of nonsense every now and again doesn't hurt.'

We completed our to-do lists, had showers, got dressed, and headed to the basement. We could see Lucky in his office talking to someone who had their back to us. He wasn't his usual smiling self and, although he saw us, he didn't acknowledge us.

'That's strange,' I said to Sarah as we got in the car. 'He doesn't usually miss an opportunity to say hello and give you the once-over.'

'I miss the hello but more so the once-over.'

I watched her face break into a cheeky grin.

'We can interrogate him when we get back,' I said.

'You can, because I need to get back to my place to sort a few things out. I've got a mountain of washing and ironing to do, and the vacuum cleaner needs a workout. I know I want to be with you as much as possible but we have to be strong. Why don't you come over for dinner tonight? We can get a couple of pizzas and wash them down with a few beers. And if you behave yourself, I'll even let you stay the night.'

'I'll be on my best behaviour.'

The traffic was, as I suspected, flowing easily over the bridge. We arrived at the celebrant's house a few minutes before eleven-thirty. Sarah told me her name was Evelyn McCambridge. A late-model Toyota Tarago with stylish signwriting along the sides was parked in the first of four spaces. I took the third.

I looked up as I pressed an ornate brass button. We heard it ring deep in the house. Carved in stone above the door was 'McCambridge House'. The house was Georgian design with symmetry I loved. It appeared to have been extensively and expensively restored. The garden reflected the Georgian look. Carefully manicured hedges and mature trees had observed our walk along the crushed rock path to the door.

A tall, slim woman opened the heavy oak door. She appeared to be around our age with her blonde hair tied back, revealing a plain but strong face. Her blue eyes, however, provided a pleasant contrast and when she greeted us with a smile, her plainness turned into warmth. She was dressed in a floral blouse, black knee-length skirt and medium-heeled shoes. I noticed the ribbon in her hair was the same colour as her skirt. She looked classy, like the house.

We introduced ourselves and when she confirmed she was Evelyn and not the butler, the ice was broken. Once over the threshold our looks of awe didn't go unnoticed.

'Old money,' she confided. We gawked at the large entrance hall festooned with paintings, Egyptian vases, Venetian glass and antique side tables covered with old wares.

'It all belonged to Mummy and Daddy,' she continued. 'They've been dead for some years and now it's mine. Nothing has been removed or added since they died. I live in the back section. It seems such a waste with only me rattling around. Unfortunately, I spend my days arranging weddings for others but not my own. I suppose it might help if I got out more. Anyway, enough about me. Come through to the sitting room and I'll get us some coffee. You both drink coffee?'

'Yes, please,' said Sarah.

While Evelyn was making the coffee in what resembled a makeshift kitchenette across the hall, I took the opportunity to look around the room. It, like the entrance hall, was huge. I could fit my lounge room, kitchen and billiard room in this one room. One side and end were taken up with floor-to-ceiling bookcases with ladders on rollers attached to a rail to allow access to the top shelves. Reading tables with upright chairs, large leather lounge suites, and heavy coffee tables occupied the centre of the room. At the window end was a large, antique timber desk. Evelyn's paperwork, although neatly stacked, covered most of the leather-inlayed surface. Two matching timber filing cabinets that looked as if they'd been rescued from a 1920s office bookended a modern adjustable computer desk crowded with a late-model computer, printer and fax machine. They sat against the wall near the door. An out-of-character modern two-seater couch faced the old desk, giving visitors a view of the mature trees outside.

I wandered over to the far-end bookcase and noticed the books were covered in a fine layer of dust. I assumed Evelyn didn't have any domestic help or, if she did, they were occupied with more important tasks. I sensed Sarah standing beside me as if she was reading my mind, confirming what I was thinking.

'I get the feeling Evelyn lives in the house because she can't bear to give it up. She probably doesn't want to pay for hired help. She either doesn't have time or can't be bothered with housework herself.'

'Ah. There you are. Inspecting books, most of which have never been read. My father was a prolific reader and would buy books at every opportunity but he bought more than he could live long enough to read. My mother would nag him to stop but, like her cocaine addiction, he couldn't help himself.'

She spoke in such a matter-of-fact manner I laughed, then immediately apologised. She smiled. 'No need to apologise. When they were alive, I could count on one hand the number of people they mixed with who weren't doing coke. They considered coke much more civilised than marijuana. Passive smoking and all that.'

Sarah and I laughed as Evelyn poured percolated coffee into cups. They looked as if they should be in a display cabinet, not in general use. I picked mine up clumsily, fearing its fineness might shatter with my beefy finger trying to access the handle.

Evelyn noticed my actions. 'I'm sorry, Tommy, I should have offered you a mug. Don't worry; these cups have been around for years. They're tougher than they look and can't be compared to all the cheap shit coming out of China.'

We laughed again while she passed us a plate with slices of fruit cake. 'I made this myself. Two things I'm good at; weddings and fruit cake.'

The cake was the best I'd tasted. If it was any indication as to how our wedding was going to run, then I had no worries. No short cuts.

Evelyn slid behind her desk and with slender hands moved a pile of papers and opened her appointments diary. When we told her the twenty-ninth of March was our preferred date, she smiled.

'I'm free all day so whatever time suits you.'

I suggested six in the evening so we could go straight to Jacques after our drinks. She was happy.

When Sarah told her we were having the ceremony at the Pavilion in the Botanical Gardens with half a dozen guests, she smiled again.

'It's one of my favourite spots for a wedding. Ideal for small gatherings with minimal fuss.'

She proceeded to show us various ceremony formats and after we narrowed it down to two, I was happy for Sarah to make the final decision. She chose the shorter format and advised Evelyn we weren't having rings. Evelyn wasn't fazed and reminded us to write our wedding vows.

She told us she'd put everything together and contact us in a couple of days so we could confirm the arrangements.

'I'll give you a call tomorrow,' said Sarah, 'after I've spoken to the Gardens people and verified the Pavilion will be available on the twenty-ninth.'

We stood and shook hands. As Evelyn walked us to the door, I asked her how she looked after such a big place.

'Well, I have gardeners come in on a regular basis and a cleaner spends one day a week doing the basics. Most of upstairs is closed off, with all the furniture sheeted and, as I said, I mainly use the back section so there's not much that needs doing. I have some friends who are trying to get me to sell the place but I think I'd have trouble sorting everything out. I did donate my parents' clothes to Vinnies but there's so much more. I suppose I'll have to do something at some stage. The thing is, I grew up in this house, so there's the emotional attachment too.'

'One option you could consider if you do decide to sell,' I suggested, 'is when a contract has been signed, you have an in-house auction of the contents you don't want. That way you won't have the hassle of having to pack everything up. The successful bidders would have that task. You'll only have your things to move to your new place. The auctioneers will number the items and produce a catalogue. You would have to open the house up for a viewing day before the auction.'

Evelyn smiled at me. 'Thanks, Tommy, I'll keep it in mind.'

'Feel free to call me if or when you decide. I can put you in touch with a reputable auction house.'

She thanked me again. We shook hands once more at the door and said goodbye. Evelyn waved as we walked along the path to the car.

I nosed the car onto the main road. 'That went well,' said Sarah.

'Yes, it did. She comes across as efficient but I feel sorry for her.'

'In what way?'

'Well, since I met you, I feel everyone should be in love and happy. Her house could be made into a home again if she had someone to share it with.'

'You're a sweet, caring man,' she said. 'How come you know so much about auctions?'

'Over the years I've been to house auctions so I'm familiar with the process. I've acquired some bits and pieces in my display case from going to house auctions instead of auction rooms.'

'I have a feeling she might be in touch,' said Sarah. 'It does sound like an easy solution.'

It was one-thirty when I dropped Sarah back to her place.

'I'll bring your bag with me when I come for dinner. We still right for pizza and beer?' I asked.

'We sure are.' We leaned in and kissed before she hopped out. 'See you about seven.'

'Okay. Happy vacuuming.'

She gave me the sweetest smile and headed inside. I drove back to my place, keen to find out why Lucky had a face longer than the horses he follows. He was washing a pale blue Datsun 240Z that, even though covered in suds, looked as if it belonged in a showroom. I hadn't seen it in the car park before.

'Nice car,' I said to him as I got out.

'G'day, boss. She's a beauty. Done twenty-six thousand miles since new back in 1970. One of the first 240Z models. Belongs to a new tenant on the eighteenth floor. She's about sixty and has had it since new. To be honest, Tommy, they're both in good nick. She loves to flirt, too.'

'That's interesting, because I have a feeling I know the answer to my question. Was your boss giving you a dressing down this morning?'

'Yes, he was. Firstly, he caught me reading the form guide which, in my defence, I was doing during my coffee break. Secondly, an older tenant caught me with my pants down having it off with Mrs Fielding from 1105. Once again, in my defence, I was vacuuming her car when she surprised me and pulled me into the back of her Mercedes. I had no choice but to give her what she wanted. The unfortunate thing was the old duck who caught us complained to my boss saying she was suffering shock and embarrassment. I reckon she was jealous because I know for a fact they've had a feud going for years and she wanted revenge. It would have been round the building within the day. I didn't think it was fair I was dragged into it.'

'Isn't Mrs Fielding twice your age?'

'Possibly, but she's got the energy and the passion of someone half her age and, unfortunately, I've got no willpower when it comes to matters of love.'

'It's not fuckin' love, you moron, it's pure lust. No wonder your boss came to see you. He obviously hasn't sacked you, so what did he say?'

'Officially – keep my pants done up while at work. Unofficially – if I can keep Mrs Fielding satisfied, but after hours, go for it. If it stops her pestering him to look at non-existent problems in her apartment, he'll let me keep my job.'

'You're one fortunate son of a bitch. I suppose you'll try it on with the Datsun lady seeing as she's already shown some interest in you.'

'What can I say, Tommy. It would be bad manners to say no.'

'Good luck to ya. Anyway, let's get serious for a minute. Sarah and I are getting married on Saturday the twenty-ninth and we want you to come.'

'Geez, Tommy, that's great! Yes, I'd love to come, thanks.'

'It's at the Pavilion at the Botanical Gardens at six. After a quick ceremony we'll head to Jacques for dinner. There'll only be a handful of guests. I haven't asked Sylvia or Lionel yet, so keep it to yourself. Mick and Angie and Sarah's mother, Rhonda, will complete the guest list. And no, you can't bring Mrs Fielding or Datsun lady. Does she have a name?'

'I only know her first name at this stage; Jean. But I reckon it won't be long before I know everything about her.'

'Sounds like you've gone off the young women, Lucky.'

'I wouldn't say gone off; but what I would say is variety is the spice of life and if it's hot chilli they want, I'm the man to deliver.'

'Sarah gave me the nickname FOS a while back but I think the time has come to pass the baton.'

'What's FOS?'

'Full of shit.'

'I thought Sarah was nicer than that. I'll have a word with her the next time I see her.'

'You do that, Lucky, and I wish you well.'

'What's that supposed to mean?'

I slapped him on the back. 'You'll find out.'

'Thanks again for the invitation. I'm looking forward to it.'

'Would you be happy to drive Sarah and me to the Gardens?'

'What do you reckon?' he smiled.

I took the lift all the way then made myself a toasted sandwich and coffee. I decided to fire up my laptop on the off-chance Keith had made contact with the car storage people. A big part of me wanted Jack's cars sorted out soon so

I could devote my time to Sarah and me getting married and heading to Tassie with Mick and Angie.

You beauty. An e-mail from Keith:

Hi Tommy, how the hell are you?

We've arrived safe and sound and settled in to our hotel. You'll be pleased to know I've spoken to the manager at Prestige Car Storage and we're meeting him on Thursday. He tells me there's an auction at Partridge Classic Cars on 2nd April. If Harry and I get cracking with our value estimates we can compare them with Partridge's reserves and if we can agree, they can have the cars catalogued and ready in time. We're looking forward to checking out the Ferraris.

It's nice relaxing in LA after our hectic time in Japan. We're worn out. It was sad to leave the twins but we'll get over it. Lots of stories to tell you when we next catch up. Anyway, I'll send you another e-mail on Friday. Hopefully we'll have a better idea of what we're dealing with. We were talking to a couple of guys in Tokyo about the Porsches and they were interested. They reckoned they might even fly over for the auction. I'll let them know when everything's organised.

Hope you and the gorgeous Sarah are going well. I'll get in touch with Mick in a day or two and see how he and Angie are getting on. I haven't heard anything from George so I might touch base with him also.

I plan to keep up the golf on the off-chance Rachael comes back with some positive news. Let me know as soon as you hear anything.

Take care big guy.

It was going to be another three weeks before I heard from Rachael, so in my reply to Keith I told him to be patient. The car disposals would keep his mind off the tournaments for the next week or two. I brought him up to date with the goings-on at Diamond Harbour and the wedding news. I knew he'd be happy now Mick and Angie could get on with their lives and I hoped he'd be happy for Sarah and me.

I closed the computer, got changed into my walking gear and went down to reception where I found Lionel. We chatted for a while and as I was about to invite him to the wedding Sylvia appeared behind her trolley, heading to the kitchen.

'Have you got a minute, Sylvia?'

She was all smiles. 'Sure have, Tommy.'

I couldn't help myself giving her a big hug.

'Sarah and I are getting married on the twenty-ninth of March in the Botanical Gardens and, as it's an informal affair, we're not sending out invitations so I'm inviting you now. I've asked Lucky as well so it's the three of you and a few others. We're having dinner at Jacques after a short ceremony. What d'ya reckon, guys? Should be fun.'

Sylvia jumped into my arms. 'Yes, yes, yes, I'd love to come.'

Lionel looked at me from behind the desk. 'If I was ten years younger, I'd jump the counter and hug you too. Thanks, Tommy, I couldn't think of a better place to be on the twenty-ninth of March.'

I spent a few minutes with Sylvia while she brought me up to date with her study. She was happy with her progress. I chatted some more with Lionel until a couple arrived to check in.

'I'll catch up with you later, Lionel,' I said. He smiled as he nodded and turned his attention to the new arrivals.

It was a short walk to the nearby café and, with a coffee and blueberry muffin in hand, I found an unoccupied bench where I could people-watch while I enjoyed my reward for a productive day. I reflected on this morning's meeting with Evelyn and hoped she would take me up on my offer to help her arrange an in-house auction. I would love to wander through her home. Who knew what hidden treasures might lurk in the recesses of a Georgian house? Evelyn herself might not even know.

I finished my goodies, then took off for a brisk walk. I figured if I walked for an hour and did seven kilometres, I might put a reasonable dent in the muffin calories and have room for pizza and beer at Sarah's. No doubt I would burn them off later tonight. The thought of it made me walk faster. A cold shower might be in order when I got home.

Indeed, it was. I climbed the stairs and after some stretching and yoga jumped into the shower. It curbed my carnal desires – temporarily.

It was nearly seven when I buzzed Sarah's apartment from the foyer. It was only a minute before I knocked on her door. She flung it open and grabbed me into a loving embrace. I dropped my overnight bag. She deserved two arms.

'Mmm, you smell good,' she said, burying her face in my neck.

She walked backwards as I walked forwards, kicking my bag until we could close the door. She broke free, still holding my hand, and led me to the balcony where she had two beers waiting on a table between the outdoor chairs. We clinked our glasses, finding it difficult to wipe the happy smiles from our faces while trying to take a drink.

'This beer tastes different, but good,' I said.

'It's Tassie beer. I thought it would be a good idea to get in some practise before we go.'

I leaned over and kissed her. 'You're a legend.'

'Tell me what you got up to today,' she said.

I spent the next beer telling her about Lucky's escapades, which earned laughter and head shaking.

'No wonder he's called Lucky and no wonder he loves his job in the basement.'

We clinked glasses again, laughing and toasting Lucky.

Sarah went inside and rang the pizza shop. We had half an hour until our order would be ready, so while we were waiting I told Sarah about what was in Keith's e-mail and my reply. She smiled contentedly when I told her I'd invited Lucky, Lionel and Sylvia to our wedding.

'I rang the Gardens today and the Pavilion is available, so it's locked in. You can sort Jacques out and I'll ring Evelyn in the morning. Mum's beside herself with happiness and can't wait for the big day. I reckon Mick and Angie will be happy too, when we tell them. I wonder when Angie will hear from what's-her-name from the casino about the funerals.'

'I think her name was Penny. It is Wednesday; I'm surprised we haven't heard.'

She stood and came over to my chair and lowered herself into my lap. She snuggled in. She was a perfect fit. We sat in silence until the buzzer sounded. She got to the door and the well-mannered lad handed over the food. Sarah gave him a generous tip that extended his smile.

The pizzas were first class, as was the beer. We moved inside for coffee and relaxed on the lounge.

'You know what we haven't done yet?' I said.

'I feel you're about to tell me.'

'We haven't been for a ride in your car. I'd love to go cruising on a sunny day with the top down. We could grab a bottle of champers and drive down to Coogee Beach and look out at Wedding Cake Island. A quick drive down to Maroubra Beach for a meal to top things off.'

'What a great idea. Why don't we go tomorrow? The sunset's telling me it's going to be another perfect day.'

We spent the rest of the evening revisiting previous conversations about our lives together over the past five weeks.

'All the things we've done and experienced most couples would take months or even longer to do, if ever,' Sarah reflected. 'Do you think we've moved too fast?'

'I remember you telling me what your mother said way back about not missing an opportunity. Well, I wouldn't have wanted the past five weeks to be any different, apart from the bad shit in Hong Kong; but I do feel even that strengthened our relationship. When I think about Jack's death, I get emotional. He drove me nuts at times but although we went our separate ways, we had a bond I felt couldn't be broken. And as far as Mick and Angie are concerned, her ordeals, harrowing though they were, gave her Mick, who I reckon is the missing piece in her jigsaw puzzle.'

'They do make a pretty picture,' said Sarah.

'Pretty's not the word I'd use to describe Mick but I can't think of another, so it'll have to do.'

It had been a busy day. We cleaned up our meal things and headed to bed. The cold shower had worn off.

DAY 47 – THURSDAY

We got up early and got into our walking gear and headed to the beach. It was a working day but the beach was busy.

'You look surprised,' said Sarah. 'This is possibly the most popular beach in the Sydney area. Heaps of people get down here for a workout before they head into the city. Give it a couple of hours and the demographic will change; people on holidays, mothers with kids, dole bludgers and, if the surf's right, plenty of board riders.'

An hours' brisk walking, obligatory stretching, and yoga gave us an appetite. We had breakfast at Sarah's regular café where I checked the communal paper and didn't see anything more reported. Feeling relieved again, we walked back to her apartment hand in hand, enjoying a glorious morning.

While Sarah had a shower, I rang Mick to see if they'd be free for dinner at Jacques tonight. We could kill two birds with one stone; invite Mick and Angie to our wedding and book the tables for the wedding dinner.

*

Angie's phone woke her. Mick didn't stir. It was Penny from Diamond Harbour Casino. The death and funeral notices were in the paper. Patrick Spencer's funeral would be held at the Eastern Suburbs Memorial Park in Matraville next Tuesday at ten-thirty. Reg Harper's would be a graveside service next Wednesday at two o'clock at the Diamond Harbour Lawn Cemetery.

'I'll give Tommy a call after breakfast,' said Mick, after Angie told him the details. 'Hopefully they'll still come with us.'

'They'll come for sure. That's what good friends do,' said Angie as she prepared breakfast. They'd decided to spend an easy morning in their suite. They had plans to discuss.

Sarah emerged from the bedroom wearing a short dressing gown, with a towel wrapped around her head. She looked as natural as the day she was born, only taller. They talk about natural beauties. I was staring at one right then.

'Close your mouth, you might catch a fly.'

I stood and walked towards her. She side-stepped me.

'Keep walking, randy man. The shower's that-a-way.'

'You'll keep,' I said, pausing at the bedroom door. 'Oh, I've spoken to Mick and they'd love to come to Jacques tonight. Penny rang them this morning about the funerals. I've written the details on the notepad.'

By the time I'd showered, Sarah was dressed and had the esky ready with the bubbly and two glasses, carefully wrapped in paper towel. Two ice packs surrounded the bottle ensuring it stayed chilled. A picnic rug completed the picture.

'I thought we might call at Mum's on the way. We can tell her about the funerals. I'm not sure whether she'll want to come, although she is fond of Mick and Angie so she might want to support them.'

Sarah's BMW was a beauty. It was low to the ground. The low-profile tyres, wider than standard, gave the car the appearance of a black panther ready to pounce. It was only a short drive to Rhonda's but already I could see why Sarah loved it. It had everything a car enthusiast would want, although my gut feeling was that its power was the main attraction for her. The passenger-side leather arm rest was slightly puckered. Maybe Rhonda was a nervous passenger. Maybe Sarah's rapid departure from Jacques after our first lunch date wasn't due to excitement but the fact she always drove fast. Maybe today's trip would confirm what I felt; maybe I'd need to say something. But, time and place, I reckoned.

'You're quiet. I bet you're up to no good,' said Sarah, nosing the car into Rhonda's driveway.

'Well, I was thinking if you got tired or overindulged in the champers at any stage, I could drive this beast home.'

'You only have to ask, my darling.'

'Do you think I could have a drive of your car today?'

'Fat chance.'

She dug me in the ribs and jumped out before I could grab her.

Rhonda greeted us, then put the kettle on. A plate of Tim Tams appeared, which we followed into the sunroom. Rhonda was a minimalist even though she'd lived in the house for many years. I now knew where Sarah got her style from. It was a little run-down but in a clean, comfortable way. Years of handling had worn the paint down to bare timber on drawer knobs, door edges and table tops. The distressed style was happening naturally; perhaps without Rhonda noticing. Or, if she did, it didn't bother her. I think her busy lifestyle gave her more to think about than contemplating interior decorating. Through the glass window, looking back into the dim sitting room, I glimpsed framed photographs of a handsome man in various stages of life. Some of them showed him with a tape measure draped around his neck. It had to be Sarah's father, Reuben. No wonder Sarah was so attractive, with such handsome parents.

'Yes, that's my darling Reuben,' said Rhonda, carrying our coffee into the room and seeing me looking at the photos. 'One day I'll get the albums out. I've got heaps of Sarah when she was growing up.'

'No hurry, Mum.'

'I think it would be a good idea for Tommy to see some family history, seeing as he's about to steal you away from me.'

'Nothing's going to change except you're going to see a lot more of this man around the place,' said Sarah. She stood and placed a loving kiss on Rhonda's forehead.

We spent the next half hour or so chatting and talking about the funerals. Rhonda said she wanted to attend. She also agreed to come to Jacques that night.

'We'll pick you up at seven,' said Sarah.

Rhonda gave us a hug on the way out. 'I'll be waiting.'

Sarah reversed out the driveway with the engine growling. The tyres squealed as we moved forward.

As we headed down the coast with the warm breeze on our faces, I told Sarah the story about my MGB.

'It's a shame I didn't keep it. I reckon I could fit into it now. You would've looked pretty damn good in it, too.'

'Never mind, that's in the past. Your current car will be great to take to Tassie. I've only seen a bigger boot in one other car. Dad had a Leyland P76 monstrosity back in the seventies and one day, for a laugh, Mum and I hopped in the boot. Dad could have almost fitted in as well but he was having too much fun shutting the lid and pretending to walk away. Mum started to freak out, banging on the lid, yelling profanities at him and warning him he'd be sleeping in the spare room. The boot was opened in a flash.'

After I stopped laughing, I suggested we could fit Mick and Angie in the boot.

'They wouldn't take up much room.'

'I know Angie is well on the way to getting back to a hundred per cent but a stint in the boot would probably set her right off,' said Sarah. 'I wouldn't even mention it if I were you, even in jest.'

It didn't take long to get to Coogee Beach. We found a nice spot at Grant Reserve that gave us an uninterrupted view of Wedding Cake Island.

'We should have brought our swimwear. Wylie's Baths would be a nice spot for a swim,' I said, retrieving the esky from the boot.

The grass was soft under the rug and we spent a peaceful hour sipping champers and enjoying each other's company. The wine had made me peckish so we packed up and, after a couple of minutes, arrived at Maroubra, where we fed our faces with fish and chips and a couple of beers.

My scheme to get Sarah unfit to drive didn't work and she made a point of keeping the keys hidden in her handbag. I wasn't too worried. I was going to grow old with this woman. She couldn't watch her keys forever.

The afternoon flew and when we got back to Sarah's she had barely enough time to get ready before we picked Rhonda up. We took my car back to my place where I made myself more respectable. Then we walked to Jacques.

We were all pleased to see each other and it was great to see the happiness on Mick and Angie's faces when we invited them to the wedding. We talked about the funerals and Angie appreciated that we were coming along. I arranged to take everyone in my car. Angie was extra pleased when I told her nothing else had been reported in the paper.

Before we ordered desserts, I went and spoke with Claude, the manager, and booked seating for nine for the wedding dinner. He provided me with some menu options, which looked great. He suggested getting back to him with our choices by Monday. Head chef Erik would have plenty of time to buy in anything special.

Desserts, port and coffee went down a treat and by ten-thirty we were ready to head home. The basement was deserted and our louder-than-usual banter echoed off the concrete walls. Lucky's office was in darkness. I wondered what had gone on in there since we'd last spoken.

I drove out into the night. It was good to see laughing faces when I related my uncensored conversation with Lucky.

'Saturday's races should be interesting,' said Mick. 'I'll have to keep an eye on him. Don't want him disappearing on me behind the grandstand for a quickie.'

Angie laughed. 'Perhaps I'd better come along to keep an eye on you.'

'Perhaps we should all go and keep an eye on each other,' said Sarah.

'You know, that's not a bad idea,' I said. 'Even though I'm not a huge horse racing fan it might be fun if we had a day out.'

Everything went quiet. I could almost hear brain gears meshing.

'I'm in,' said Rhonda.

'Yeah, me too,' said Angie.

'Count me in, I don't want to be home alone while you lot are having fun,' said Sarah.

I looked at Mick. 'You don't mind some classy company, do you?'

'Not at all. Now I'll be able to concentrate on the nags and not have to worry about Lucky horsing around.'

'Very funny,' I said. 'He'll have his uses though. He reckons he can get a good spot close to the facilities.'

'You know what?' said Angie. 'I think Rhonda, Sarah and I should go shopping tomorrow for some classy racing clothes.'

'Sorry to rain on your parade but tomorrow is Good Friday. Won't the shops be shut?' I said.

'Good point,' said Angie. 'Perhaps we can still have a day together. I'm sure we'll find something to do.'

Seeing as I would have a free day, I would be able to go over the menus for the wedding dinner, check in with Keith, and maybe head down to the golf club. Now I was back into golf a four-hour walk would do me the world of good.

Mick decided he'd go antique hunting. He'd put together a list of good antique shops and, although they were spread throughout Sydney, it didn't matter. His love of train travel would make his day enjoyable. Being a public holiday, he might have to be patient with public transport. I suggested he ring the antique shops to see if they were going to be open.

I dropped Rhonda back at her place and Sarah to hers. We spent a few minutes eating each other's faces, then she headed upstairs.

I got back to my place and was ready to hit the sack.

DAY 48 – FRIDAY

I got up after nine. I felt good. I got my paper from outside my door. I looked on my desk as I walked back to the kitchen and noticed several letters. Sylvia most likely brought them up yesterday when she came to clean. I'd look at them over coffee. I was hopeful I'd hear from Keith. It would have been around mid-afternoon the day before for him, so he might have met up with the car storage people. Knowing Keith and Harry, they were probably enjoying a big lunch with plenty of booze after their meeting if things went well. I might be pushing my luck to hear anything at all today. The longer those two drank, the more stupid they got. I laughed to myself. I wasn't too worried. I knew Jack's cars were in good hands.

I knocked up poached eggs on toast. They went down a treat. I took a big coffee to the table near the window. I had a quick look through the paper. I found nothing more on the Diamond Harbour shootings. Perhaps the Inspector could tell us why on Tuesday.

I grabbed the letters and my opener. A buff-coloured legal-looking envelope stood out from the rest. Queensland Public Trustee was printed on the top left corner and CONFIDENTIAL printed in red below my name and address. My name was shown as Tomasz Dabrowski.

I slit it open, unfolded the pages and started to read. It wasn't until I'd finished the first page that I had a sip of coffee and looked out the window.

So, the old man was dead, aged seventy-two. I'm surprised he lasted that long. Died in October last year after spending the last six years in the Alzheimer's wing of a nursing home on the Sunshine Coast. I bet the old bastard gave them a hard time.

The Trustee, as executor of his estate, was now informing me that I was the sole beneficiary. What the fuck would he have that I'd want? Reluctantly I looked at the next page. It was a computer-generated spreadsheet with gridlines. Only two entries were on the entire page. Under the heading ASSETS

I read he had a term deposit and an on-call bank account with the Bank of Queensland. The balances were $1,620,437.26 and $6784.15.

There must be a mistake. How the fuck would he have had that much money? When I went back to Cooma after my mother died, I'd been told he'd sold his business and gone to Queensland. I couldn't imagine him making much from the sale. I turned back to the first page where, on the last line, was the name Gerald Knox, and his number. I could call him with any queries. I certainly would. I hadn't been angry since Yang in Hong Kong but right at that moment, I was seething. I could feel my head starting to ache. The old man had been a pain in the arse when he'd been alive and nothing had changed now he was dead, except the location of the pain. I needed to do some deep breathing.

I stood tall. Four seconds in, four seconds hold, four seconds out. I did ten repetitions then grabbed my coffee.

I flicked over to the third page. It was similar to the second but had the heading LIABILITIES. Half a dozen entries including his care costs, funeral expenses and Trustee fees. A total of $9458. The net value of his estate was $1,617,763.41. The final page was a release form I needed to sign.

I threw the letter onto the table and opened the other mail. Fucking power bill, fucking car rego and fucking driver's licence renewal. Could it get any better?

My head was still aching so I decided to lie down.

*

I could vaguely hear someone calling my name. I opened my eyes to see Sarah filling my vision. As she moved back Lionel came into view.

'What's going on?'

'We might ask you the same question,' said Sarah. 'I've been trying to get a hold of you for three hours. In the end I came over and got Lionel to let me in.'

'Hi, Tommy,' said Lionel. 'Are you okay?'

'I think so, mate.'

'I'll leave you two alone. I'll catch up with you later.'

'Thanks so much, Lionel,' said Sarah. He turned and walked out.

I rubbed my eyes and looked out the window, it was nearly dark.

I looked at my watch. It was creeping up to eight o'clock.

'I'm sorry, darling. I was reading my mail this morning after breakfast and had to lie down. My head was aching. I'd gotten upset so I did some slow breathing but it obviously didn't work. I must have been out of it for the best part of ten hours.'

'Tell me what happened.'

'Go and grab the letter off the coffee table and have a read.'

Sarah returned and sat on the edge of the bed. After she'd read the last page, she looked at me.

'Bloody hell, that's out of left field. What were you thinking when you read it?'

'I got angry because I don't want anything to do with the old man. This sort of thing drags up the past, which I don't need.'

She lay beside me, sliding her arm under my neck pulling my head towards her chest. She felt warm and comforting.

'It might pay to ring the Trustee and ask some questions. I'm sure you've got plenty.'

'I sure have. I was thinking to myself this morning how the hell could the old prick have so much money, and why leave it to me? We've had nothing to do with each other for over twenty years. As far as I was concerned, he didn't exist.'

'How are you feeling now? Do you need to go to the hospital for a check-up?'

'I think the sleep did me the world of good. I'd kill for a coffee.'

Sarah withdrew her arm, got up, and went to the kitchen. I came out a few minutes later and sat by the window, watching as the night lights of Sydney slowly took over from Mother Nature.

'I should give you a key to this place. I'm sorry you had to get Lionel to let you in. I'm also sorry to drag you away from your place.'

Sarah put two mugs of coffee on the table, kissed me and sat in the recliner opposite.

'He didn't mind. He's got a lot of time for you, based on our conversation in the lift. When I rang, before Mum and I had dinner around five, and you didn't answer, I wasn't too worried. But when I rang another half a dozen times and you still didn't answer, I did get worried. I didn't hesitate to come over. Lionel checked the basement and saw your car there so we assumed you were here.'

I reached over and covered her hand with mine. 'I don't know what I've done to deserve you but whatever it is, I'm glad it happened.'

'Shut up and drink your coffee.'

'That reminds me, I was going to look at the menus today. That ship has sailed. Maybe tomorrow before we go to the races.'

'Do you think you'll be up for it? How about waiting until the morning and see how you are. I think you should pack an overnight bag and come back to my place. I'd hate for something to happen to you while you're here alone.'

'That's not a bad idea. I can't ring the Trustee until Tuesday, Monday being Easter Monday and a public holiday. We've got Patrick's funeral at ten-thirty so I might call them when we get back.'

We took our time drinking our coffee, marvelling at the Sydney lights. Better views than ours would be hard to find.

With a bag packed and my laptop bag over my shoulder, we headed down to Sarah's car. I decided to leave checking my e-mail until tomorrow. I'd brought the Trustee's letter and the menus with me. I could look over them tomorrow as well.

It was not long after ten when we got to Sarah's and we decided to go straight to bed. As we lay there, I got around to telling her about my childhood and adolescent years. At one stage I looked at her and she had tears in her eyes.

'I'm sorry. I didn't mean to upset you with my stories.'

'I feel sad for you. I had a charmed childhood with the most attentive and encouraging parents anyone could wish for. I assumed other kids would have had much the same.'

We snuggled together. 'There'd be heaps of kids who had a worse time than me, I reckon. Anyway, I haven't turned out too damaged.'

'You're a loving, caring, well-adjusted man, Tommy and I couldn't think of my life taking any other direction.'

She kissed me as she turned out the light.

DAY 49 – SATURDAY

'I think I'll give the races a miss, if you don't mind. I've got a few things to sort out today.'

Sarah sat at the table, bowl of cereal in her hand. 'I think it's a good idea after what happened yesterday. Are you sure you don't need to see the doctor?'

'No. I had a good sleep and I feel much better, but as a precaution I think avoiding too much excitement with the others is a good idea. I'm sure they'll understand. I'll ring Lucky after breakfast, then Mick. Lucky can use my car. I'm sure he won't say no. He'll probably have Rhonda sitting in the front seat.'

'He's a try-hard after all.'

'Me not going to the races doesn't mean you can't go,' I said.

'I know but I want to spend the day with you. I'm not convinced you're a hundred per cent yet.'

'You're marvellous.'

With phone calls done and everyone happy, I opened my laptop. Nothing from Keith. Maybe later today.

I drafted some questions for the Trustee. I'd go through them later. No doubt there'd be more. We walked down to the beach for morning tea. Once again, the sand felt good under my feet as we took the long way home. By lunchtime we had agreed on the menu for next Saturday. A choice of two entrees, four main courses, two desserts and the obligatory cheese platter, all washed down with champers, wine, beer, spirits and coffee. I'd drop our requests back to Jacques on Tuesday.

'Would now be a good time to book our tickets on the ferry to Tassie? We could leave Sydney on Sunday, hopefully not too hung-over, and drive down to Melbourne to catch the evening sailing on Monday. I know of a motel in Bega where we could stay Sunday night. No sense rushing. It's not five-star like we're used to but for one night I reckon it'll do. Once we hit Tassie we can drive to Launceston, perhaps stay at the casino for a few days, take in the sites and slowly head south. We can give Brian plenty of notice.'

Sarah smiled brightly. 'I couldn't plan it any better. I can't wait. Hopefully Mick and Angie can fit in. Perhaps ring them now. They always get excited when we mention Tassie. I know they're booked in at the Condor until the Monday but they could give them early notice. They've been good customers so I wouldn't think it would be a problem.'

'If Brian's got other things on,' she continued, 'we can hit a few golf courses and wineries and take our time. There must be heaps to see and do.'

I rang Mick. They were so easy to get on with. Their only condition was a flash cabin on the ferry. Shouldn't be too hard to arrange.

While Sarah made lunch, I went online and let my fingers do the talking. By the time lunch was on the table we were booked in at Bega, and had deluxe rooms on the ferry and two nights at the Launceston Country Club Casino that included complimentary breakfasts. I had booked during a special offer period – stay two or more nights and get free breakfasts.

'Do you think Mick and Angie will be happy to tag along with us the whole time?' she asked.

'Well if they want time to themselves, I guess they could hire a car and do their own thing. We'd only be a phone call away to arrange to meet up. You did say it's a small place.'

We ate in happy silence, sharing a bottle of last year's Wolf Blass Eaglehawk Chardonnay leftover from a previous get-together.

We plonked ourselves onto the lounge with our coffee and after a while Sarah asked if I wanted to go over my questions for the Trustee.

'Now's as good a time as ever. How about you read what I've written. Then, with your shrink cap on, you might be able to look at things from a different angle?'

Sarah spent considerable time reading and thinking. I loved sitting there watching her expressions. If I died and had to come back as part of her it would have to be her brain. Bloody incredible.

An hour later and I had a revised list that would keep the bloke at the Trustee's office away from other cases for a while.

'Have you given any thought to what you might do with your inheritance? I know it's a sore point so feel free to tell me to mind my own business.'

'As far as I'm concerned, my business is your business and nothing you could ask could make me think otherwise.'

She slid across and eased herself onto my lap. I closed my eyes and lost track of time. She felt so calming and natural. We were doing each other a big favour, I thought.

Eventually cramp in my lower leg caused me to tickle her so she'd get off me. She moved to the end, facing me with her legs tucked under her.

'I have been giving my inheritance some thought. You know how Sylvia wants to go to Vietnam and start up a school for disadvantaged kids once she graduates; well, I'm going to ask her to find out how much it will cost. I'll pay for it with the old bastard's money. I realise it'll be a few years before she's in a position to go but the money will grow in that time. Whatever's left I'll put with the money I get from Jack's cars and invest it. Each year I'll distribute half the interest to various charities. The principal will increase and there will always be money to hand out. If I do it through my Swiss accounts it'll earn a much higher rate. Simple, eh?'

'You know yesterday when I called you loving, caring and well-adjusted? Well, I missed something – a fucking philanthropic genius.'

'Well it seems like the right thing to do. I don't deserve, or want, the money, so why not? The old man will be spinning in his grave and Jack will have a smile on his dial.'

Without hesitating, she said, 'I wouldn't say you don't deserve the money. Based on what you've told me about your childhood it's probably right you get it but I can see how strongly you feel about your relationship with your father.'

'Hopefully the answers I get on Tuesday will go a long way to putting everything right.'

'Are you happy to stay here again tonight?'

I couldn't help but smile at her. 'What do you reckon?'

<h1 style="text-align:center">DAY 50 – SUNDAY</h1>

'With all my shit going on yesterday and Friday I forgot to ask how you and the girls got on without us men on Friday.'

Sarah pushed bread into the toaster and walked to the table with steaming coffee.

'I picked Angie up and took her over to Mum's. We spent some time there, then went out for lunch. A few shops were open so we did some spending and I went into Clarence Williams, one of Sydney's better menswear stores. I asked the guy why they were open and he said he wasn't a great believer in Easter. I made the most of it and picked out three suits you might like to try on. I've got my favourite but I won't let on until you choose. Perhaps we could go there on Wednesday morning. Reg's funeral isn't until two in the afternoon. If the suit needs any alterations they could be done before Saturday.'

'That's a good idea. I reckon I'll scrub up alright in a new bag of fruit. I bet the girls are disappointed they couldn't get more involved in the wedding arrangements. It's all they can talk about lately.'

'They understand we only want a simple wedding and I think Angie might be more excited about going to Tassie. The further away from Diamond Harbour, the better.'

'You can't blame her,' I said. 'Although I must admit, as each day goes by, she seems to be putting it further behind her. The fact she doesn't have to go back to work is a good thing. The reward money will set her up for life. If George was here, he'd be able to give her some good investment advice.'

'Well he's only an e-mail away,' said Sarah. 'It wouldn't hurt to discuss it with her and if she's agreeable, chat to George. Knowing George, he'd use it as an excuse to fly over.'

'Bloody George doesn't need an excuse. I reckon a rainy day in London would be enough to get him on a plane to sunshine.'

We finished breakfast and while Sarah showered, I fired up my laptop. I glanced at my watch. It would be Saturday afternoon in LA. God knows what the boys would be up to. I opened my e-mail and finally saw a message from Keith:

Great news about you and Sarah tying the knot. Harry and I are rapt. Pity we can't be there but someone has to be working ☺. We met with the Prestige Cars people on Thursday and checked out Jack's cars. They are fantastic. He sure knew a good car when he saw it. We've looked at all fifteen cars and we reckon the five below should bring the best price for you.

1968 Ferrari – 365 Daytona

1973 Ferrari – 365 BB

1975 Ferrari – 512 BB

1974 Porsche – 911 Turbo

1979 Porsche – 911 Turbo 3.3

I won't bore you with all the reserves, suffice to say that Partridge Auctions are happy with what we've put up and they are optimistic about the auction. They are impressed with the quality of the cars. They're not sure yet whether they'll put them all up on the same day or hold some back for the next auction in May. Anyway, they're the experts but I've told them I want the five listed above to be in Wednesday week. We could be looking at over 1.5 million.

We're having a ball in LA and are heading to Vegas for a few days because we can. We miss you both. We could all be having fun if you were here. I suppose there's no word from Rachael yet. No doubt she'll contact you when she knows something.

Good luck on Saturday, have a great time.

Cheers mate.

I was over the moon. With that sort of money, I could achieve a lot of good things. I grabbed another coffee and fired off a reply. It was a good opportunity, once again, to bring them up to date with the Diamond Harbour saga and the upcoming police funerals. I mentioned our honeymoon to Tassie that I was sure would make them jealous. I cc'd George because I knew he was keen to sample the Tassie seafood; plus, I hadn't been in contact with him since he went back to London.

By the time I'd typed a full page and sent it off, Sarah was showered. I showed her the e-mails. She was amazed the cars were worth so much and agreed with me that there would be some very appreciative charities.

I rang Mick and told him we'd pick them up at nine-thirty on Tuesday morning. He spent ten minutes filling me in on their day at the races. Lucky had been on his best behaviour and, apart from Rhonda, they left with more money than they arrived with.

Sarah rang her mum and passed on my commiserations for her poor horse tipping ability. Apparently, I'd be getting a slap the next time she saw me. Worse things have happened, I thought.

We spent a quiet morning together then decided that tomorrow, being a public holiday, we would do what a lot of people do on a public holiday. Head to the national parks. A day out in the fresh air would do us no harm. Sarah packed a bag including walking gear and drove us to my place.

After a light lunch we spent a couple of hours in the pool and gym, followed by spaghetti bolognaise, garlic bread and a 1999 Penfolds St Henri Shiraz for dinner. It had aged well. We had an early night but it was late when we got to sleep.

DAY 51 – MONDAY

Ku-ring-gai National Park was buzzing. People everywhere. Another three national parks were close by and we reckoned they would be popular too. We got to West Head Road, keen to see Aboriginal engravings and handprints. From the Resolute picnic area, where we decided we'd have lunch, it was a minute's walk to Red Hands Cave to see some ancient ochre handprints. It was only 500 metres along Resolute Track to an engraving site. We easily managed the short, steep section along the way. I couldn't have done it six weeks earlier. We checked out three other sites, then headed back to the picnic area. We'd worked up an appetite.

The day was still young so I pointed the car towards Bilgola. We spent the best part of an hour in the saltwater pool, then had showers and settled back into the car for a drive down the coast road to Manly for coffee. The cafés were fairly ordinary, but the one we chose had good coffee.

As the day drew to a close, we headed home and decided on an easy dinner and an evening watching TV.

DAY 52 – TUESDAY

Patrick Spencer's coffin was lowered level with the ground so mourners could sprinkle sand from the chrome bucket or rose petals from the cane basket. The Minister moved among the crowd, accepting thanks for a service befitting a police officer killed in the line of duty.

Inspector Collins had delivered the eulogy in the chapel and once we saw him on his own, we approached and introduced ourselves. He was a tall, thin man with a strong but kind face that commanded respect. He smiled and graciously accepted our condolences. He appeared genuine in his concern for Angie and when she told him she was fine he smiled again. Natural, not forced. I liked him immediately.

'If you casually look over my shoulder, you'll see reporters hovering like vultures. I guess they are going to try and ask questions when the time is right. I would suggest you make a subtle exit from the other side of the crowd. I reckon they're interested in those in uniform with shoulder decorations like mine. I can keep them occupied while you make good your escape.'

'A quick question before we go,' I said. 'We've noticed there's not much being reported in the paper. Is that because no-one is talking?'

He leaned in to our group. 'The casino and real estate people are saying nothing so all they've got is hearsay or whatever your neighbours have told them, Angie.'

'I've had bugger-all to do with my neighbours. I don't even know their names. Everyone keeps to themselves. Plus, I wasn't there much and Danny was only there on his week off. Anything they said would be rumour, I reckon.'

'Are you coming down to Diamond Harbour tomorrow?' he asked.

'Yes,' said Angie. 'We think it only right to see Mr Harper off.'

'Well, I'll see you then.' He glanced over his shoulder. 'I think you'd better go now. The vultures look hungry.'

We shook hands and casually walked to my car. I saw Angie relax as we drove out the cemetery gates.

I drove back to Rhonda's place where she had earlier prepared sandwiches, pastries and cakes for lunch. The mood was subdued but we were appreciative of her hospitality. I arranged to pick everyone up at eleven o'clock tomorrow for Reg's funeral at Diamond Harbour.

After stopping at Jacques to drop off the menu for Saturday, it was mid-afternoon when Sarah and I got back to my place. It was time to ring the Trustee and get some answers.

Gerald Knox had a polite and calming voice. 'Ah, young Tommy,' after I'd introduced myself, 'nice to finally talk to you.'

'Do you know me?'

'Not personally but I was a good friend of your father. He called you Tomasz, you know.'

'Yeah, I know.'

'I met your father in 1993. He was working for a big cleaning company that specialised in high-rise office complexes. It was pure chance we met. I was working late this particular night when he came into my small office and asked when he could clean it. I told him he could work around me and he laughed – I'm a 5XL in shirts. Anyway, we had a cuppa and got talking about what I did and he happened to mention he didn't have a will.

'He came back the next morning and, among other things, asked me if I knew of any good investments. He wasn't a big fan of bank deposit rates and thought there must be something else, apart from the share and property markets. When I told him I'd recently bought a part share in a couple of race horses he asked how much he'd need to buy in. Naturally I thought he was kidding. He didn't look the horse type. He told me he'd sold his upholstery business back in Cooma in 1991 and had a tidy amount in the bank that wasn't doing much. I suggested we get his will sorted first, then we could look at some other options. I made it clear I wasn't a financial planner but he told me I looked honest and he felt he could trust me.

'I won't bore you with too many more details,' he continued. 'Suffice to say, he did buy into the syndicate and over the next seven years we won two Doomben Cups, heaps of Group One races and plenty of minor placings. When the horses, both stallions, retired to stud, so did your father. Not to stud, just retired,' he said, laughing.

I liked this guy but not his choice of friends.

'I lost touch with your father for a couple of years until I'd heard he'd been admitted to a nursing home with early-onset dementia. The Trustee took over the day-to-day running of his accounts, paying his nursing home expenses and whatever he needed to ensure he was comfortable. We rekindled our friendship and I'd visit him most weeks where we'd play crib and reminisce on our great wins. He'd talk about you and how proud he'd been when he heard you'd won a major golfing tournament in Europe. I did ask him if he wanted to get in touch with you but he thought you didn't want anything to do with him, so he didn't want to create an awkward situation. Making you sole beneficiary was his way of trying to make amends. Sadly, during the last year of his life, bloody Alzheimer's knocked the shit out of his brain and he didn't recognise me anymore. I can tell you this much, Tommy; he died peacefully, blissfully unaware of anything going on around him. He was a favourite at the nursing home.'

'All I can say, Gerald, is he must have become a changed man. It's as if you're telling me about someone else.'

'I was aware of his earlier history. When he got on the grog, he would tell me about his time in Cooma and say things that, when sober, probably wouldn't have entered his mind. I can understand where you're coming from. He had given up the grog before he got crook but the damage had already been done.'

'What happens now?'

All I had to do was sign the release form, provide a certified copy of my birth certificate and driver's licence and post them, together with my bank details, to the Trustee. When probate issued, the money would be transferred to my account.

'Do you have any more questions?' he asked.

'No. I don't think so. I've got enough to digest at the moment. Do you mind if I ring you again if I think of anything else?'

'Not at all, Tommy. Take your time returning the forms. There's no deadline. Obviously the sooner the better, as far as you're concerned, I suppose.'

'Yes. I'm getting married on Saturday then heading to Tassie for a while so I'll get the paperwork in the mail by Friday.'

'Congratulations. I wish you and your wife a long and happy life together.'

'Thanks, Gerald, and thanks for everything you've told me. It certainly fills in the blank spaces from the last seventeen years.'

I hung up and looked at Sarah. She was mesmerised. 'I've got a feeling you've got an amazing story to tell me.'

'I certainly have. But first, how about a glass of champers.'

'It's that good?'

'Oh yeah.'

We kicked back into our recliners and I relayed what Gerald had told me, pausing only to sip my drink.

'Wow. That was a good story,' she said. 'A changed man alright. If he had contacted you, would you have reciprocated?'

'That's a tough one. I don't know how I would have reacted. But I'm certainly not going to dwell on it. It's in the past and I'm looking to the future.'

Knowing tomorrow would be busy I set about reading through the paperwork again. I wrote my bank details where applicable and signed the relevant forms. I dug out my birth certificate and driver's licence and went down to Lionel and used his photocopier. All I needed to do tomorrow was go to the post office, get them to certify the forms, and post the lot to Gerald.

DAY 53 – WEDNESDAY

We were up at sparrow fart so we could get to my suit fitting before picking the others up at eleven. I looked through the paper before we left. Patrick's funeral was mentioned but nothing about Angie.

I tried the suits and looked good in all three. I let Sarah make the final choice. A few alterations were needed but it would be ready to pick up on Friday. The guy at the post office helped us out and Sarah and I had time for a coffee.

On the way to Diamond Harbour I told them about my father and my inheritance. It was only natural they wanted to know what I was going to do with the money. When I told them, I had to look in the rear-view mirror to see if they'd been struck dumb. They were speechless and I could detect six moist eyes.

'Come on, you guys. Don't get too sentimental on me. It feels like the right thing to do. What sort of life would I have lived if I hadn't helped others when I could? I would hope after I leave my mortal coil my legacy can live on.'

Mick wiped his eyes. 'You never cease to amaze me, you big, lovable bastard.'

That broke the solemnity and it wasn't long before we arrived at The Owl and The Pussy Cat Café for a quick bite and coffee.

We reached Diamond Harbour Lawn Cemetery fifteen minutes before the service was due to start. We saw Inspector Collins and had a chance to say hello. He was proud to tell us they were making good progress on their extended investigations. Four more arrests had been made, and another big drug bust. At this stage he wasn't in a position to elaborate. Once again, he recommended we don't hang around too long after the service. Angie nodded in agreement.

The funeral home had set up speakers around the perimeter so everyone could hear the Minister. We signed the Attendance Register as we had done at

Patrick's funeral and received an Order of Service so we could follow the proceedings. I could sense Angie's nervousness and suggested we try and blend in with the mourners.

The police formed a guard of honour again as the coffin was carried to the grave and placed on the lowering mechanism. It hovered above the ground on two green straps during the service until it was lowered so the top was level with the ground. Grieving colleagues and friends dropped sand and rose petals onto the lid. Angie paused as she placed a small bouquet of flowers she'd brought with her. I heard her whisper, 'Rest in peace, brave man.' Then she moved on.

It was a while until the gathering started to move off but we saw it as an opportunity to move with them. I could see the vultures on the perimeter, scanning the crowd, trying to pinpoint a likely meal. Their cameras and recorders were ready to roll. I'd be interested to see if they reported anything in tomorrow's paper.

We made it to the car and within ten minutes were back on the highway heading home. I drove non-stop to the Condor as we'd decided to have dinner there and maybe a flutter afterwards. Rhonda wasn't au fait with the goings-on of casinos so I told her I'd take her home after we'd eaten.

Dinner was subdued until Mick, stating the bloody obvious that it had been a big week so far, raised his glass and proposed a toast to the soon-to-be Mr and Mrs Dabrowski. We clinked glasses and had a good laugh.

'Sounds strange,' I said, looking at Sarah, who was beaming. 'I guess you have no objections to the name-change?'

'None whatsoever.'

Dinner turned out great and after coffee and port I took Rhonda home. It gave us a good chance to have a chat about the future. She got all misty-eyed when I told her I couldn't believe it was possible to love someone like I loved her daughter.

'It's about compatibility,' she said. 'You're an easygoing, gentle giant who I've noticed is honest, well-mannered, kind, generous and loving. It's those sorts of values Sarah looks for in people. She's found them in you and I've never seen her happier. I know you'll take care of her.'

'Goes without saying, Rhonda; but if the truth be known, I reckon she'll take care of me.'

I walked her to her door. I had to stoop so she could hug me. We laughed and said goodnight. She waited at the door and waved as I drove off.

I got back to the casino and noticed Sarah with a huge pile of chips in front of her. Mick and Angie were at the rail watching.

'She almost ran to the table after you two had gone. One seat was available and she wanted it. She must have had a wad of notes with her all day because she slapped them on the table as she pulled the chair out,' said Mick. 'After she'd got settled, we wandered around for a while, grabbed a drink and came back to see how she was doing.'

'Ah. That's my Sarah. The modern-day girl scout; always prepared. I'll have to keep an eye on her in Tassie. She'll want to spend all her time at both casinos. It's only a couple of hours between Hobart and Launceston.'

Sarah looked across at us and smiled.

'What did she do to win so much so early?' I asked.

'I asked a couple of guys if they'd been watching and they said within a dozen hands she'd cleaned up a big pot with four nines. She beat a set of aces, a flush and a full house.'

'Those guys won't be happy but Sarah's charm will calm them down. Look at 'em. She's got 'em eating out of her hand; smiling graciously, commiserating; using her psych skills to make them drop their guard.'

'To say nothing of her gorgeous looks and blouse unbuttoned to the top of her boobs,' said Angie.

I laughed. 'I did notice an extra button undone that wasn't when we were having dinner.'

Mick and Angie headed back to the blackjack table while I stayed at the rail waiting for an empty seat, hopefully next to my wife-to-be.

I watched the cards being dealt. Sarah had the big blind which was $100. It wasn't a huge game in terms of blinds but with betting, the sky was the limit in cash games. Some guys would beg, steal or borrow so they could keep playing. Some big gamblers even had a line of credit with certain casinos.

Eight players occupied the table and everyone called Sarah. The flop dealt up the Q♣, 4♦ and 9♣. The small blind folded and Sarah checked. The guy next to her, who must have had neck problems because he kept glancing to his right, bet the pot, which was $800. Bad neck my arse. He couldn't keep his eyes off Sarah's cleavage. He was looking straight down her blouse. I couldn't blame him, I suppose. The next four players called the bet and the guy on the button – Button Man – raised another $800. The pot was now $6400. Sarah needed to call with $1600 or raise. She called. Rubber Neck called, as did the guy on his left. The other three folded. The turn card was the 5♥. Pretty shitty community cards, I thought. It was too early to wonder what the players' hole cards might be. That's the beauty of watching poker on TV where the lipstick cameras show each player's hole cards for the home viewer. You can shout abuse or encouragement at your screen. Unfortunately, it doesn't help the players in their decision making.

A pot of $9600 was building. Sarah checked and so did Rubber Neck. The guy to his left also checked and Button Man bet $5000. It didn't look like a confident bet to me. I hoped Sarah picked up on it. With the reading she'd been doing on poker strategy, I reckon she could smell a rat. She didn't miss a beat. She pushed $10,000 across the line while watching Button Man's face. She's good. Even from where I was sitting, I could see a flicker of annoyance cross his face. A certain indication he was hoping to steal the pot with a bluff. I didn't think he was expecting Sarah to raise, seeing as she had only been checking and calling from the start.

Rubber Neck folded, as did the guy on his left. Rubber Neck remained sitting forward. He could now focus all his attention on Sarah's cleavage. Button Man was in a quandary. He could fold, call the $5000 raise or re-raise. The river card was still to come. I was dying to know what Sarah had. Could she be bluffing? We'd soon find out. The dealer asked Button Man to make his play. He meekly pushed $5000 over the line.

Sarah was watching Button Man when the river card was dealt. She had no idea what it was until after she'd observed his look of despair. The 6♣. It was Sarah's bet. She, too, got a hurry-up from the dealer, then tapped the table, signifying she was checking. Button Man was not happy and I could understand why. He looked confused as well. The river card looked like it didn't suit Sarah, otherwise she would have probably laid down a big bet. Or maybe it did and she wanted him to think she hadn't improved her hand.

He looked at Sarah. Face, cleavage, face, cleavage. He fumbled with his chips and placed $10,000 over the line. Without hesitating she pushed her remaining chips out in front of her and said, 'All-in.'

Button Man didn't move. The dealer counted Sarah's chips. Button Man would have to front up with another $12,000. He had lost the advantage and now the pressure was on him. I didn't have a clue what either might have in their hole cards. The five community cards were among the shittiest I'd seen in a long while. If someone had a seven and eight, they would have a straight but you'd have to be crazy to keep them until the river card. If someone had two clubs, they'd have a flush but it's risky waiting until the river card. Pairs of queens, fours or nines would have sparked more betting early. I was pretty confident Button Man didn't have any of those pairs based on his body language unless he was an excellent bluffer – all part of poker.

It was painful watching him. I could almost hear his brain jumping around inside his head.

'Ah what the hell. If I have to lose, I'd prefer to lose to someone like you than the bloke next to you who can't keep his eyes off you,' said Button Man. 'I'll have to call because I can't go to my grave without knowing what you've got. I know you won't show me your cards if I fold. I do think you're bluffing.'

Sarah didn't flinch. She knew he was trying to get under her guard and make her react to her hand. Fat chance.

He fiddled with his chips, watching for a chink in Sarah's armour. It was bullet proof. He sighed and counted out $12,000, which the dealer re-counted. Sarah was asked to turn over her hole cards. She looked up at me and smiled as she turned over the jack and two of clubs. A flush. Button Man leaned forward. He couldn't believe, it along with everyone else who had congregated along the rail.

My heart was beating out of my chest. It was swollen with pride and admiration for a gutsy poker player who was soon to be Mrs Dabrowski.

Button Man slid his cards, facedown, to the dealer, stood, and walked around to Sarah, his hand extended.

He smiled at her as he shook her hand. 'Well done, you're a good player. I had two pairs at the flop,' he said quietly. He walked off, gently shaking his head.

It took a few moments for the applause to die down. The other players complimented her and she was once again gracious in victory.

The dealer pushed the pot towards Sarah and she asked for a tray. She was obviously not playing any more. I couldn't wait to hug her.

The cashier told Sarah she had $73,600. She asked for a receipt. She would have a tidy credit for the next time she played. She could redeem all or part whenever she wanted. It was nice being known.

'Nearly forty grand profit,' she announced proudly. 'Not a bad evening's work. Let's find Mick and Angie and have supper on me.'

We found them sitting at the bar drinking champers and laughing.

'Come on. Share the joke,' I said. We pulled up a couple of stools and ordered drinks.

Mick put his arm around Angie's shoulder and pulled her close. 'This arsey one was walking past the roulette table and pulled out a fifty-dollar chip I'd given her earlier, and whacked it on five red as the croupier said, "No more bets." Thirty seconds later she's stuffing all thirty-six of the bloody things in her bag.'

'We're in classy company,' I said. 'Sarah won another big hand. Cleared forty grand.'

'Fucking hell!' exclaimed Angie.

Mick laughed. 'Yeah. We're in classy company alright.'

Sarah nearly choked on her champers. 'I think coffee and cake might be in order before we head off.'

We walked contentedly towards the main door after enjoying our usual chocolate cake and strong coffee. 'I've arranged for a taxi to pick you up at five-fifteen on Saturday,' I said. 'Lucky is driving me to Sarah's where we'll collect her and Rhonda. I've also got taxis for Lionel and Sylvia. They live out in the western suburbs so I reckon it would be nice to have them driven to the Gardens.'

'Everything planned to perfection as usual, old boy,' said Mick, as we said our goodnights. Sarah and I walked out into a warm night. I'd left my car along the road. A walk wouldn't do us any harm.

DAY 54 – THURSDAY

I got up early so I could catch Sylvia before she started her shift. I threw on my tracksuit and joggers, left Sarah a note on my pillow, and light-footed it down the stairs to the staff room. Sylvia was loading up her cart ready for another morning of cleaning rooms. I wished I could fast-track her studies so she could realise her dreams sooner but it doesn't work like that. She ran over to me and hugged me hard. She was always happy, which should have made me feel happy; but I felt pangs of sadness. Such a divide between our lifestyles, yet we were both happy with our lot. I guess Sylvia had never experienced the way I live; never having to worry about a job or having enough money for life's basics, being able to gamble, travel and afford expensive accommodation and cars. It would be so foreign to her. Conversely, I don't know what it would be like to work for a boss five days a week and have to watch every dollar I earned and help support a family.

'Would you like a coffee, Tommy?'

'I'd love one, thanks. I must say, that was pretty fancy talking.'

'I am trying hard to speak properly,' she said. 'I have a good teacher who encourage me. I have started teaching my parents more English. They are bad students. Don't want to learn.' She laughed as she placed a coffee mug in front of me. I looked at the pattern. Women in bikinis in various seductive poses.

'Would this be Lucky's mug?'

She giggled with her hand over her mouth. 'How did you guess? He sometime comes up for a drink when the boss is away.'

'I don't know what we're going to do with that boy. Have you heard about his fooling around in the basement?'

'The whole building know about him jiggy-jiggy with Mrs Fielding. He always look proud.'

'That was the impression I got, too. As long as no-one is getting hurt then live and let live.'

'You wise man, Tommy.'

'You *are* a wise man, Tommy,' I said.

'That what I said,' she joked.

'On a more serious note. When you're getting closer to deciding about going to Vietnam to set up your school, can you let me know? I know it's a while away yet. You've got to get through uni first and these things take a lot of planning. Government approvals, building approvals, construction and so on. I'm able to pay for it and to cover the running costs, including your salary. I'm also prepared to pay for you to study full-time at uni. You can't hold down a day job and do uni at the same time. All you need to do when the time comes is tell me what you're being paid here and I'll match it. As far as you're concerned, you'll only have to concentrate on your studies. I've been fortunate to inherit a lot of money and I'm keen to help out various charities as well as your project. Each year there will be a good dividend from my investments, which will mean I'll have ongoing funds.'

She had tears running down her face. 'Oh, Tommy, I do not understand everything you tell me but I know enough that you are not only wise man but most kind in whole world. What have I done to deserve this?'

'Our paths have crossed at the right time. You are a hardworking, loyal person – not only to your parents but to everyone here. You've had a hard life so you deserve good things to happen.'

I took a sip of my coffee, looking at Sylvia over the rim of the mug. The look on her face was more than enough to convince me I was doing the right thing.

'Sarah and I are going to Tasmania for our honeymoon and we hope to catch up with some people while we're there, so I'm not sure when we'll be back. Would you keep an eye on my place? There will be food in the fridge that needs using. Please take it home.'

'I will look after your place like it is my own. You want me to tell Lionel to cancel your paper?'

'No, that's okay. I'll be seeing him after I leave you. Thanks anyway.'

We chatted a while and I told her the taxi would pick her up at five o'clock on Saturday. She looked at the clock and told me she had better get to work. She hugged me again and scurried out, wiping her eyes with one hand and trying to steer her trolley with the other. My pangs of sadness were fading.

As I sat there finishing my coffee, Lionel walked in to rinse his mug and spent a few minutes with me while I filled him in on my movements for the immediate future. I'd checked my diary and saw no incoming bills for at least the next three months and, with my paper cancelled, I didn't have any domestic issues to worry about. I asked him to send me an e-mail if any letters arrived addressed to Angela Kingston. If we were staying somewhere in Tassie for a while I could have him redirect them. Angie might be looking forward to getting confirmation of her reward. It would be due in her bank account tomorrow.

'I know you well enough to know what mail I should notify you about,' said Lionel. 'You don't have to worry about a thing. If you think of it, bring me back a Tasmanian tiger. They reckon there's still a few running around.'

'Sure thing, Lionel,' I said suppressing a smile. 'And perhaps a fox as well.'

'Don't be silly, Tommy. Everyone knows Tassie doesn't have foxes.'

'Goes to show I don't know everything,' I said, washing Lucky's mug before setting it back on the shelf. It certainly stood out from the birds and floral motifs.

'Don't forget your taxi will pick you up at a quarter to five on Saturday.'

'Thanks, Tommy. I'm looking forward to the get-together.'

'So am I. See you then.'

I climbed the stairs and was puffing when I opened my door. Sarah was sitting by the window, holding a bowl of cereal. An orange juice sat on the coffee table. I kissed her, grabbed some cereal and plonked down next to her. I scanned the paper. A small article on page four mentioned Reg's funeral and a possible link between the dead crims and a mine worker killed in a plane crash in Western Australia back in mid-February.

'Bugger it,' I fumed. 'The bastards have got a sniff of Danny. I think it's only a matter of time before they link him to Angie. The sooner we're on the ferry the better. If Angie hasn't seen the paper, perhaps we shouldn't say anything. She's made huge progress the last couple of weeks. It would be a real shame for this to set her back.'

'You're right, of course. I wonder how they found out about Danny.'

'There's always some scumbag willing to sell a story for a few bucks,' I said. 'Could be a cop. Who knows?'

'How did you get on downstairs?'

'Sylvia is over the moon with my proposals. I think I'm as excited about her future as she is. She told me she's trying to teach her parents more English but not having much luck. I hope it doesn't dampen her enthusiasm for teaching children.'

'Many older people are set in their ways. Sylvia's parents probably don't see the need to learn. They've obviously got by all these years. And, living within a Vietnamese community, English is most likely their second language. The way you talk about Sylvia I'd be surprised if she took a backward step.

She's determined to achieve her goals and with your help – you wonderful man – she should smash it.'

The over-cooked toast set off the smoke alarm and Sarah looked sexy in her silk mini-dressing gown, standing on a chair waving a tea towel under the alarm. I told her to stand still for a moment and ran my hands up her flawless legs. I got as far as her knees when she flicked me with the tea towel, instantly killing my lustful intentions.

'Time and place, big fella.'

She laughed as she jumped down off the chair into my arms.

We enjoyed toast and coffee with the sun streaming in. It was a good time to be talking about Saturday and the next month or so. We didn't want to plan too far into the future.

'I've been thinking about our living arrangements for when we get back and settle into domestic bliss,' she said, between bites of toast slathered with raspberry jam.

'I would love to live here, if you didn't mind,' she continued. 'Louise, the lady who looks after my place when I'm away, has a friend who wants to rent in Bondi. If she's as fastidious as Louise, I'd be more than happy to rent my place to her. I don't want to sell it because Mum might one day decide her place is too big and want to downsize. She could move into my place for as long as she wanted.'

'I'd love for you to live here. I can arrange another car spot in the basement so your beast will be safe. Lucky can look after it while we're away. A gentle run once a week should keep it in good order.'

'How come everything is so easy for us to work out?' she said.

'We don't sweat the small stuff and I think we're compatible, considerate and respectful of each other. When I took your Mum home last night, we had a chat and she reckons we were meant to be.'

'How sweet.'

We washed up the breakfast things and had a leisurely shower. Time and place had arrived.

Lunch at Jacques, a movie – *Death at a Funeral* – and a ham and asparagus omelette for tea. An evening of snooker won me more than bragging rights.

I received my snooker prize not long before we drifted off to sleep in each other's arms.

Two hours of swimming, gym and yoga set us up for a good day. A quick check of the paper revealed nothing. We decided to have breakfast at a trendy inner-city café before heading to Clarence Williams for a final fitting of my suit. I had to admit I looked pretty sharp. They'd done a good job on the alterations.

I looked at my side profile in the full-length mirror. 'Does this suit make my arse look big?'

Sarah took a look. 'No, darling, it's all that fucking ice-cream you've been eating.'

The guy serving us looked like he was going to faint.

We couldn't wait to get out of the place. Our laughter was so loud we attracted many sideways glances as we sauntered arm in arm back to the café for a coffee.

The rest of the day consisted of long walks, an easy lunch and silly jokes. We were excited about the next day. The adrenaline was pumping.

Sarah rang Evelyn to make sure everything was okay for Saturday, then rang the Gardens. We were set. I rang Jacques. They had everything under control.

We decided to wind down and watch TV and have an early night. It had been a fun day.

*

Mick took breakfast into the bedroom. Angie was sitting up in bed. He placed the tray on the bedside table, sat on the bed-edge and passed her a glass of freshly squeezed orange juice. She took a few sips and handed it back. She pulled him to her, undoing his dressing gown. He was naked. Just how she liked him …

They lay there without speaking for some time until Angie perched herself on one elbow and reached for the orange juice. The pith from the oranges had settled on the top. She didn't care. She needed a drink. Her mouth was parched. She sipped and passed it to Mick. He gulped a mouthful and fell back on the bed. Angie finished it off then swung onto her other elbow looking straight at him.

'How fucking good was that? You can bring me breakfast in bed any time you like.'

Mick stroked her face. 'Let me know if you want lunch or dinner in bed.'

They laughed together and lay in silence. It was an hour later when Mick woke. Angie had been in the shower and was looking down on him.

'Come on, lazy bones. We've got an appointment with the bank. I got a call from Penny to say the reward money was transferred overnight. We should get an account balance. It'll be fun to see a six-figure balance instead of a three.'

Mick had a quick shower while Angie ate her belated breakfast. They'd grab celebratory coffees later.

Balance - $250,872.53. Available Balance - $250,872.53.

Angie looked at the ATM docket and passed it to Mick. He took her in his arms and kissed her hard. As he released her, they broke out laughing.

'No-one deserves this more than you,' he said. 'For what you've been through and to be where you are now is remarkable.'

'I couldn't have done it without you. Your love, kindness, consideration and huge cock have made it all possible.'

People passing by were thrown out of their rhythm and some almost tripped over each other.

'I didn't think I spoke too loud, did I?'

'You could say the word *cock* underwater and people's ears would prick up,' said Mick.

She giggled. 'You said prick.'

They linked arms and walked contentedly half a block to a café. They shared a muffin with their coffees.

'I can't wait for the wedding,' said Angie. 'I think those two are a perfect match. When I look at you and Tommy, apart from the size difference, you are so much alike. You've got all the qualities a woman wants. Like Sarah said, you make us feel appreciated, safe and feminine. You're caring and funny and if I might talk out of school, hot in the sack. Don't you tell Tommy I told you. Sarah will kill me.'

'Mmm, I think I've finally got something I can hold against you.'

'That's two things then.'

'If the truth be known, I reckon Tommy and I must be two of the luckiest guys around. You and Sarah are so easy to be with. You don't want for much and are happy. You must tell me, though, if I do anything you don't like. I don't want you putting up with things simply to keep the peace. It's not a perfect world and there probably will be times when we're out of sorts. We just have to talk it through.'

'Same goes for you. I'm still getting used to having a man around who respects me so if I sometimes seem overwhelmed with your kindness, don't get upset. It's not personal. After years of wondering what was going to happen next and not being able to see clearly, I've got some adjusting to do.'

Mick held her hand. 'I know enough of what you've been through, based on what you've told me, so take all the time you need. We've got the rest of our lives if I've got any say in it.'

Angie stood and moved around to his chair and sat on his lap. She put her arms around his neck and nestled her face next to his.

'I love you, Mick.'

DAY 56 – SATURDAY

I took Sarah home after breakfast. Lucky wanted me to have my car back with him before noon. He wanted to have it sparkling for tonight. I picked up a roll of white ribbon from a small Bondi haberdashery and left it on the front seat with a note for him. I'd drop in and see him mid-afternoon.

I went to the pool where I had no trouble swimming for an hour. I skipped the gym but did some yoga. I couldn't get my head around how something so simple could make me feel so good.

I jumped on my scales for the hell of it. The digital reading was flashing 93.5 then 94.0. I settled for 94 kg. Two kilos in a tad over two weeks – four to go.

I wasn't overly hungry so I made a banana smoothie and read the paper by the window. Nothing about the heist. Fair chance there'd be nothing in Sunday's paper and, as we were heading out of Sydney tomorrow, we would be off the grid.

I spent an hour reading the paper from cover to cover. I killed the crossword and made a start on the neuf-neuf. If I didn't finish it, it would still be here when I got back. It was another toughie so I left it and got my clothes ready for the wedding. I also packed what I could into my suitcase. It wouldn't take long to finish off in the morning. I could feel the excitement building. To think it was a tad over a month ago that I met Sarah and now we were getting married. How crazy; but how normal it felt. We had been through a hell of a lot in such a short time, as had the others. Mick and Angie were joined at the lips and hips. She had been through the wringer and Mick had dragged her out with love and caring. I would put big money on them being together for ever. The trip to Tassie would be icing on the cake for Angie. No more worries.

My phone rang. It was Mick.

'Guess what, old boy?'

'You've had a face-lift for the wedding?'

He laughed. 'Don't be a smart arse. Angie's reward money has hit her account. How good's that?'

'Fantastic news, Mick. Give her a big hug from me. She deserves every bloody cent.'

'You're not wrong. We're getting our bags packed for tomorrow. What time will you be picking us up?'

'Hopefully we won't be too hung-over. How does eleven sound?'

'Great. I can let reception know today we'll be checking out a day earlier. I don't think they'll mind.'

'They shouldn't. You've been good customers.'

'Good point. We'll see you at the Gardens. We're excited for you guys and also looking forward to the next stage of our relationship.'

'Where do you see it heading?' I asked.

'The way things are going, I reckon wedding bells might not be too far away.'

'That's fantastic, Mick. I was thinking about you two before you rang. You've got an extremely strong physical bond as well as an emotional one. Both are important in a relationship.'

'What are you now? A fucking psychiatrist?'

'I am today. See you tonight, old mate.'

I hung up and gazed out the window. Life was good.

I knocked up a ham toastie for lunch, washed it down with a coffee, then headed to the hairdresser. After she made me even more irresistible, I called in on Lucky.

'She scrubs up well, boss,' he said, as I approached a gleaming vehicle.

'Wow. You've excelled yourself today.'

It looked better than when I drove it out of the showroom. He was soft-clothing the rear bumper to a shine. He had blacked the tyres and polished the mag wheels; they looked new.

'The white ribbon will look classy against the silver paintwork,' he said as he stood, stretching his back. 'What time should we leave here to pick up Sarah and Rhonda?'

'If we head off at four-thirty that should give us enough time to collect them. Being a Saturday, the traffic shouldn't be too bad. I guess you've brought your good gear with you?'

'I have, boss. All I need to do once I've finished here is have a shower and get dressed.'

'Do you want a shower at my place?'

'No, I'm good. Remember Jean? The lady with the Datsun. Well, she's taken a shine to me and yeah, well, that's where I'm having my shower. Apartment 1808.'

'You're incorrigible, Lucky.'

'What's that mean?'

'It means you're a naughty boy. See you back here at four-thirty.'

'Will do, boss.'

'I presume the six bottles of champers are in your fridge?'

'You presume right, boss. I'll put them in the esky with the glasses when we're ready to go. If I remind you and you remind me to put them in the boot, we shouldn't have any problems.'

I walked along to the nearby florist where my order was waiting, then took the stairs back to my apartment. Even though the lactic acid was ripping through my legs, I was enjoying it. The fact I couldn't have conquered the stairs a fortnight ago made it all the more enjoyable. I was getting fit for the first time in over a decade. I needed to live a long life. I had plenty to live for.

I had a leisurely spa and a shower. By the time I'd dressed it was show-time. I took the lift to the basement. I needed to stay cool. There would be plenty of time later for exercise.

Lucky looked a treat. I'd never seen him in anything other than work gear. His suit was shiny silvery-grey – the latest fashion, I reckoned. His pink shirt, white tie and what looked like new white shoes made me wonder why Jean in 1808 had let him out.

'Where are you staying tonight?' I asked, knowing full well the answer.

'1808, boss, as if you didn't know.'

'I must say, you're looking good, Lucky.'

'You don't look so bad yourself. I've noticed you've lost some weight but you still scare me with your bulk. Is that a new suit?'

'Sure is. Picked it up yesterday. It feels good. Do you think the tie goes okay?'

'You're the master of style, boss.'

'I thought you'd say that. Let's get going. When we get to Sarah's place, I'll get in the back with her. Rhonda can sit up front with you. You won't be distracted, will you?'

'It'll be hard to concentrate but I'll try my best.'

Lucky parked outside Sarah's place and waited while I went up. When she opened the door, I was blown away. She looked stunning. She was wearing an off-white sleeveless dress that fitted her curves down to her waist. From there it fell loosely, reaching midway down her calves. Her high heels automatically gave her goddess status. Her hair rested gently on her shoulders and the thin gold chain she had worn to our first lunch was around her neck. Her lipstick made me want to mess up her lips with my mouth.

'Cat got your tongue?' She grabbed my lapels and pulled me towards her, kissing me lightly.

'If you could read my mind, we wouldn't be going to no wedding. I'm lost for words. You look gorgeous.'

'Oh, stop it. You're embarrassing me. You look pretty amazing yourself.'

'You should never feel embarrassed. I don't know of another woman who could hold a candle to you.'

She laughed. 'You should get out more.'

'Only with you.'

'We'd better get going. Lucky's waiting for us.'

I picked up her overnight bag and pulled the door shut behind us. We met Louise on the stairs.

'You two look like you've just stepped out of a movie,' she said.

'Beauty and the beast,' I said with a laugh.

'If I was twenty years younger you could put your slippers under my bed.'

'Mrs Davis,' Sarah scolded, 'I've never heard you talk like that before.'

'I've never seen a more handsome man close up before.'

'You dodged a bullet there, Louise,' I said.

She gave us a warm hug and wished us a happy wedding. As we continued down the stairs, I glanced around to see her opening her door. She was looking down at us, smiling.

Lucky was waiting at the rear passenger's door and opened it as we appeared.

'Always the gentleman and looking sharp,' said Sarah, sitting in backwards and swinging her legs into the car. Always the classy lady.

'How could I be anything else in this sort of company,' he said, giving her a dazzling smile.

'I must say, Lucky, you've done a great job with the car. I love the ribbon.'

'It was the boss's idea.'

I put Sarah's bag in the boot and jumped in the other side as Lucky got back in the driver's seat. Sarah looked at the bouquet of African marigolds on the seat between us, then up at me. She didn't have to say a word. She loved life's simple things.

Rhonda walked out of her front door as we pulled up. Lucky was out in a flash and had the door open before she had reached the footpath.

'You look extra handsome today,' she said, giving him a hug.

'And you look sensational, Mrs L.'

'Thank you. You can keep that talk up all evening.'

'Get in, Mum, we've got a wedding to go to,' said Sarah, giving her mother a smile only a loving daughter could give.

We arrived at the Gardens where I saw Evelyn's Toyota. I told Lucky to park next to it. We walked to the Pavilion. Sarah held her bouquet in one hand and my hand in the other. She was holding on tight. It was the first time I'd sensed her nervousness. Rhonda had her arm through Lucky's. His free hand carried the all-important esky. As we neared, we could see the Pavilion had been decked out with beautiful flowers and ribbons. Surely the Gardens people wouldn't have done it. Evelyn was waiting with Sylvia and Lionel. They had introduced each other and once I introduced Rhonda and Lucky, I asked Evelyn whether she had arranged the adornments.

'I wish I could take the credit. It looks lovely. I presumed you lot must have.'

'We certainly haven't,' said Sarah. 'We were playing it low-key but I love it anyway.'

'Bloody Mick and Angie, I reckon,' I chuckled. 'Here they come now. Time for interrogation.'

They were dressed as if they were the ones getting married. They made a great-looking couple.

'You've got some explaining to do,' I said, after I'd done the introductions.

'What do you mean?' said Mick innocently.

I turned him purposefully towards the Pavilion.

'What?'

'The flowers and ribbons. This is your doing isn't it?'

'Nothing to do with us, old boy.'

'Then who? Someone is responsible.'

Sarah looked at Sylvia, Lionel and Rhonda. They were shaking their heads.

'Well, bugger me. It had to be you, Lucky,' I exclaimed, as everyone looked at the beaming Lucky. His teeth were dazzling.

'It's the least I could do for such a fantastic couple.'

'You can tell us how you managed it over champers,' I said, giving him a man-hug. Sarah kissed him on the cheek, leaving an imprint of her lipstick and causing him to blush.

The Pavilion had waist-high rails around three sides, allowing entry from the front. Evelyn stood near the back rail with Sarah and me facing each other but turned a little towards her. The others were able to form a semi-circle behind us. It was an intimate setting. Evelyn didn't need a PA system. She could have whispered and we would have heard her reading the marriage rites.

We traded our vows. Nothing we hadn't already said over the past six weeks, but it was nice to say it again, particularly in front of our friends. Well most of it. Some of it would have made them blush.

'By the authority invested in me by the State of New South Wales, I hereby pronounce you husband and wife. Please kiss her, Tommy, we're dying of thirst.'

I didn't need a second invitation. I took Sarah in my arms and we kissed until Lucky told us to get a room. After happy tears, laughter, hugs and handshakes, the champagne was flowing. Sarah and I took a moment to sign our papers with Mick and Angie as witnesses. I looked around me wishing Keith, Harry, George, and Jack could have been here. It wasn't to be. I felt confident though that Keith would get the nod to take my place in Vegas. A sense of calm and completeness hung happily over my shoulders.

Lionel had brought his camera and was busy taking some formal snaps along with candid shots which would no doubt get some laughs down the track.

'Well come on, Lucky. Spill the beans on your clandestine activities,' I said. We moved in on him. We had him against the rail. He had nowhere to run.

His perfect teeth couldn't disguise his guilty looking grin. 'It wasn't difficult, to be honest. I rang the Gardens and found out they leave it up to the people hiring the Pavilion to decorate it if they want to. After I heard you two talking about a no-fuss wedding, I took a punt and went to the florist near the Marina earlier in the week and arranged for them to decorate it this morning.'

'I take back all those things I've said about you,' I said as Sarah gave him another kiss.

'What things?' he said, blushing again.

'Probably better if I don't tell you. I don't want you driving off without us.'

Lionel filled Lucky's glass and, while they were chatting, Sarah put her arms around my neck and her lips on my ear. 'I love you so much.'

I didn't want the moment to end. It couldn't get any better. I was aching with love for this woman.

We spent another half an hour filling the air with laughter and good cheer until it was time to head back to Jacques. I asked Evelyn whether she had room for four passengers. She did. She told me her van was mainly used for carting her PA system, folding chairs and tables but, seeing as she was travelling light today, she had room for passengers. I helped Lionel pack up the empty bottles, corks and wrappers into the esky. We walked happily to the exit.

Lucky drove us back to the car park where he removed the ribbon before we walked to the restaurant. The weather could not have been better.

Our table at Jacques was a round one in a small room off the main dining area. It looked great. I noticed Sylvia and Lionel were looking somewhat out of their depth, but hoped that once we were seated and had started eating, they would be fine.

And start eating we did. The food was exceptional. After the entree I stood and thanked Evelyn for marrying us and told everyone there'd be no other speeches. This was an informal gathering and what we were doing now was eating, drinking and enjoying each other's company.

By the time the main course had arrived Sylvia and Lionel had indeed loosened up. I think the champers might have helped. I caught Sylvia's eye. She smiled. 'Thank you for inviting me. I could get used to this. How is that for good English, Tommy?'

'Pretty good. You should drink more often,' I joked.

Evelyn raised an eyebrow, so I spent a few minutes telling everyone about Sylvia's study and her ambitions. Without prompting everyone clapped. Sylvia lowered her head. She would never lose her humility.

'Please stop, everyone. You are making me cry. But they are happy tears.'

Lionel raised his glass. 'Here's to Sylvia. May she achieve her dreams.'

'To Sylvia.' We clinked our glasses.

The conversation quietened while we tucked into our food. Lucky was raving about the steak. He reckoned it was the best he'd had. Rhonda, who was sitting next to him, had ordered potato gnocchi, pumpkin, pepitas and spinach. She looked relaxed, enjoying Lucky's attention.

'If Lucky wasn't staying in 1808 tonight, I reckon those two would be getting up to no good,' I whispered to Sarah.

'You do realise that's my mother you're talking about,' she said. 'And what's 1808 all about?'

I took a few minutes to tell her about Lucky and his recent liaisons. She laughed and told her mother to behave. Rhonda gave her a thumbs-up as she took another long sip of her wine.

'I have a feeling there might be a few sore heads tomorrow,' said Mick, who had been listening to our conversation.

'Well I hope they won't be ours,' I said. 'We've got a big day ahead. Tassie, here we come.'

'Yay,' said Angie. 'It's been a while coming. So much has happened. But we're good to go.'

I looked around the table. All the choices for main course were on the table. I was happy I'd catered for everyone's tastes.

Evelyn was enjoying talking to Lionel and Sylvia. They traded stories. Their life paths were so different, yet they provided the same type of service – dealing with people.

After the main course was finished the waiters cleared the table and took orders for dessert. At this point Evelyn got up and told us she had an early appointment in the morning. She thanked us for having her at our celebration and said goodnight. I walked her to the door and gave her an envelope.

'I hope you don't mind cash.'

'Cash is king,' she said with a smile. She didn't count it. She slipped it into her handbag.

She would get a nice surprise when she opened it.

The desserts were on the table when I got back. Once again no-one was disappointed. The coconut panna cotta with wild berries and the chocolate parfait were popular.

'Can we share chocolate cake for old time's sake?' said Sarah. Her lips brushed my ear, sending electric pulses through me.

'I love it when you talk dirty.'

Lucky leaned closer. 'Who's talking dirty?'

'Talk about big ears,' I said.

'Sorry, boss. Old habits die hard.'

It was a double chocolate mud cake. The slice was enough for four. Mick looked over. 'If you can't eat it all, slide it this way. Angie's still hungry.'

Angie slapped him playfully on the arm. 'Don't listen to him, Tommy. You know what? I think he's inherited your nickname.'

'I think you're right. The same one as Lucky.'

The others were listening. 'FOS,' I laughed. 'Full of Shit.'

Everyone laughed.

Sarah looked at Lionel. 'It seems to me you're the only one who doesn't talk rubbish.'

'Wait till he have a few more drinks, then you won't say that. You should hear him when we have happy hour at work. You would think he was Kerry Packer. Big important business man.'

'This is interesting, Sylvia. Please tell us more,' probed Sarah.

'Yes, Sylvia, tell us more,' was the chorus.

Lionel was blushing and laughing at the same time. 'And I didn't think she was paying any attention to me. I'll be more careful next time.'

They looked at each other and smiled. I detected a slight connection. How nice.

Sarah fed me chocolate cake, which I washed down with a great grandfather port. I glanced at my watch. It was ticking over ten-thirty. Time to head off if we were going to get a clear-headed start tomorrow.

I noticed the others were starting to slow down. They'd finished their desserts and coffee. I tapped my glass.

'I know I said there'd be no speeches but I want to say thank you for making our wedding such a memorable occasion. We're fortunate to have friends such as you and I'm especially proud to have Rhonda as my mother-in-law. You have raised the most beautiful, smart, funny, caring person I've ever met and I can't believe how lucky I am to have her beside me.'

'You deserve each other,' said Rhonda, wiping her eyes. 'I never thought the day would come when I would be happy to let her go. But I know she's in good hands and you'll take good care of her.'

I was about to suggest we call it a night when Lucky tapped his glass, pushed his chair out and stood tall.

'Go crook at me if you have to, boss, but I want to say a few words. I want to thank you for counting us as your friends and, from what I've seen, I've no doubt you'll live happily ever after. Don't stay away too long. You're our favourites at the Marina.'

Acknowledgements

I would like to thank:

My family for your support and encouragement.

Forty South Publishing in Tasmania for being so generous with your time and advice.

Alix Kwan at Moxie Editing for your editing mastery and reassurance.

Luke Buxton, Graphic Designer, for bringing my book cover ideas to fruition.

Ian Andrew and the team at The Book Reality Experience for your guidance and expertise in coordinating the whole process and making it painless.

About the author

Marcel Legosz was born in the 1950s in Tasmania, the beautiful island state to the south of mainland Australia. He grew up in Hydro-Electric villages throughout the state and it was in one of these villages that he commenced his working life. He later moved to the capital city, Hobart, where he continued his public service career spanning a total of thirty-eight years. He then spent time in the funeral and taxation industries (the two certainties of life).

Marcel dabbled in short-story writing, which led to his first published novel, *Suited*. His interests include poker and golf hence their strong presence in the story.

Marcel has two wonderful sons, two lovely daughters-in-law and four cheeky grandchildren.

Thanks to the idyllic lifestyle that Tasmania offers, Marcel and his partner have no desire to move further afield.